Moira Turned and in the Dark, Beside Her Bed, Loomed a Large Figure, Towering Over Her.

His hand went to her mouth to stifle the scream that had begun to form on her lips. Her eyes stared up in terror at a face that had Michael's eyes. She twisted away, frightened, and he let her move, his hand falling to her shoulder, and pulling the front of her gown loose.

She sat perfectly still, watching the eyes that devoured the sight of her nakedness. She was acting like a wanton, she told herself, she should cover herself. But she wanted him to touch her again.

"Michael," she said, her voice sounding husky and deep in her throat. She looked away. "I trust you. I have always trusted you." Moira reached to pull him close.

He was gone.

Dear Reader,

We, the editors of Tapestry Romances, are committed to bringing you two outstanding original romantic historical novels each and every month.

From Kentucky in the 1850s to the court of Louis XIII, from the deck of a pirate ship within sight of Gibraltar to a mining camp high in the Sierra Nevadas, our heroines experience life and love, romance and adventure.

Our aim is to give you the kind of historical romances that you want to read. We would enjoy hearing your thoughts about this book and all future Tapestry Romances. Please write to us at the address below.

The Editors
Tapestry Romances
POCKET BOOKS
1230 Avenue of the Americas
Box TAP
New York, N.Y. 10020

Fire and Innocence

Sheila O'Hallion

A TAPESTRY BOOK
PUBLISHED BY POCKET BOOKS NEW YORK

This novel is a work of historical fiction. Names, characters, places and incidents relating to non-historical figures are either the product of the author's imagination or are used fictitiously. Any resemblance of such non-historical incidents, places or figures to actual events or locales or persons, living or dead, is entirely coincidental.

An *Original* publication of TAPESTRY BOOKS

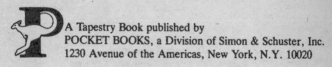

A Tapestry Book published by
POCKET BOOKS, a Division of Simon & Schuster, Inc.
1230 Avenue of the Americas, New York, N.Y. 10020

ISBN: 0-671-50683-8

First Tapestry Books printing March, 1984

10 9 8 7 6 5 4 3 2 1

POCKET and colophon are registered trademarks
of Simon & Schuster, Inc.

TAPESTRY is a trademark of Simon & Schuster, Inc.

Printed in the U.S.A.

Fire and
Innocence

Chapter One

In the Year of Our Lord, A.D. 1825

SOMETIME AFTER MIDNIGHT THE RAIN DIED DOWN TO A SOFT DRIZ-
zle, the sound of the sea rising in the sudden silence. The shock
of the tides, building to almost forty feet, pounded up against
the gray granite cliffs of western Brittany, sending tremors
through the cliffs and inlets and river valleys that fed down to
the Atlantic.

Dark, misshapen specters resolved themselves into an oak
tree's heavy branches, hanging with the weight of the water that
still dripped from them. They no longer tossed in the wind,
beating up against the roof of the lone cottage that clung
halfway up the leeward side of the nearest cliff.

Perched high above a small Breton fishing village, the cottage
looked down toward a narrow inlet filled with small boats, their
blue and hennaed sails furled tight against the night. The
cottage stood apart, the village below to the south, the sea
encroaching to the south and to the west, where the crest of the
cliff stood bare.

Only the dull, monotonous roar of the sea now filled the late
September night, the water slapping far below against the
western wall of the somber cliffs, the smells of sea salt and

1

bracken coming inland from the head of the cliff, rolling down past the cottage, permeating everything they touched.

Inside the cottage the fires were banked, the old wooden beams that supported the structure creaking now and again with small familiar night noises.

When the pounding began, heavy thumps of weathered fists against the thick cottage door, Moira sat straight up in bed, her heart pounding along with the staccato beat of the fists.

Coming awake quickly, she threw aside her soft, down-filled comforter and stood up. Her bare feet hit the cold wooden floor as she heard the sounds of her father's movements in the next room; the creaking of his bed, the door to the tiny upper hallway opening. She opened her own door just as he started down the narrow stairs, his pipe in his hand.

"Papa, what's wrong?" Her young voice rose higher than she could control.

"Hush!" He was at the front door already, opening it as old Solange appeared from the kitchen, sleepy-eyed and irritable, her lumpy body enshrouded in a shapeless blue robe.

"Wake the dead . . ." Solange muttered darkly as two men stomped into the oak-panelled hall, the first speaking quietly as the other glanced over at the fat woman near the kitchen door. Then he looked up toward the head of the stairs where a young woman stood, her auburn hair sleep-tossed, falling free to the shoulders of her thin white nightgown.

"Edmund, we must—" the other visitor was saying, Edmund cutting him short with a gesture.

"In here," her father said as Moira took one more step down, watching him lead the men toward the back parlour.

"Papa, what is it?" she asked.

Edmund looked up at his daughter. "It's all right. Go back to bed."

"Is there trouble?" she inquired anxiously. "It's been so long since there's been any trouble—"

The first man turned around to stare at her father. "You said none knew—"

"Enough," Edmund cut him off. "Inside my study, please. Moira, go back to bed." He looked back at Solange who still stood watching them. "Since you are already up, put some water on to boil. I'll make the tea myself."

"Since I'm up!" She turned away, her broad back disappearing into the kitchen. "As if civilized people could sleep with all that pounding in the middle of the night!"

2

The door to the study closed, the men closeted inside, and then the kitchen door banged shut behind Solange. Moira, still on the stairs, stared at the closed study door, as if to see through it. No one brought good news in the middle of the night. Unless—

Her heart skipped a beat. Unless they were the Duke's men, unless he had come back. Unless his ship was out there, offshore . . . finally and at last coming back.

Slowly she came all the way down the steps, smelling the wet water-soaked wool of their cloaks now, the heavy tobacco scent of her father's pipe. He must have been awake, waiting for them. She shivered, the drafts from outside still chilling the narrow hallway.

Her cloak was of dark brown wool, hooded and warm. She reached for it and slipped out the front door before any could stop her, throwing the cloak over her thin cotton nightdress, pulling the hood up to cover her head as rain still dripped from the tree branches.

She glanced down the narrow track, familiar track, toward the village below and then turned, hurrying up it; following it as it wound through the gorse, climbing higher. She bent forward against the fierce winds that whipped across the promontory, her bare feet muddied and cold as she reached the crest. Heavy salt-laden mists blew low through the few stunted trees that dared to grow this near the cliff's edge, swirling around her knees as she reached the edge herself.

The salty tang of the sea filled her nose and mouth, rising high in her throat along with the lump of expectation that had quickened her senses, that had sent her running out here in the wet night to strain for a sight of his ship. His ship.

The Atlantic Ocean washed up against the rocks far below her, sea winds whipping around her cloaked figure, eddying masses of sullen white water drowning the rocks below and then falling back out to sea, leaving only algae and seaweed clinging to the shore.

Far out to the west the moon came out from behind a low-scudding cloud, the moonlight shimmering low across the water, visible for brief moments and then swallowed up again behind low clouds in the crachin, the wet, gray, swirling mist that permeated everything it touched.

Through the mist and fog she strained to catch a glimpse of the outline of his ship. Her breath caught, staring out toward something, trying to make out whether the misting light was

3

playing tricks or whether a ship did lay drifting in the heavy fog, far out from shore, its sails furled. She tore her eyes away, looking down toward the base of the sheer cliff, following the edges of the narrow cove, looking for a rowboat along the shelly sand, a rowboat the men could have used if they were from the Duke. None was there.

She looked back toward the horizon, the fog dancing before the moon, touching the choppy waters and eddying upward again. Now something was visible, almost visible, and then it was swallowed up again and again as she stood on the cliff, her bare feet muddy, her cloak drooping wet and salty around her.

Out across the western waters, on board ship, the bow rolled and plunged into the water, great bursts of white spray crashing across the decks as the ship pitched and tossed with the wind and the waves. The masts swept forth and back, creaking as the wind flew through the loose rigging, the men above-decks lashed to their posts, the crew below dodging the stores that slid back and forth, banging into the cabin walls. The crew's hammocks swung wild as the ship heaved with the swells.

A husky, dark-faced man beat his way up the ladder toward the large man lashed to the poop deck, his spyglass to his eye.

"Your Grace!" he shouted against the wind, straining to make the other man hear him. "We can't go in any farther, the sea's running too high! She'll broach!"

Michael Daniel Henri Sutton de Bourbon, Fifth Duke of St. Maur, caught the last of Talbot's words. "Aye, she's heeling too far over." His words, mixed with the sea salt and the wind, carried only inches. He unlashed himself, making his way down the ladder and holding onto the railing, forcing himself toward the companionway hatch inch by inch through the freezing wind. The ship pulled out from beneath his feet and then slapped back against them as the swells receded.

Once below-decks, Talbot close behind, the sounds carried more of the creaking hull, but the roar of the wind whistling against their ears softened, letting them speak. They braced themselves against the pitch and toss, heading for the door to the captain's cabin.

"We've got to make it in before daylight!" The Duke spoke loudly still, over the roar of the elements.

Talbot was just behind him as he opened the cabin door. "You'd best be telling the Almighty and not me, Your Grace. Try and we'll dash up against the rocks if this wind doesn't change."

4

The Duke's face, wet with sea spray, turned harder as he spoke again. "I know how to handle my ship. And if I have to kedge her in, we'll get in before daybreak!" Seeing the hurt in Talbot's eyes, the Duke sank into his wide leather armchair, nailed into position near the specially designed fireplace. "No offense, Mr. Talbot." He sighed. "Do what you can. . . . Do what you can."

"Aye." Talbot's voice held strain. "I'll do all anyone can."

The Duke's eyes closed, Talbot leaving him there alone, as sensations of turbulence, of nausea, of helplessness beset the large man in the oversized leather chair.

The next thing he knew Talbot was pounding on the door, his voice jubilant. "Your Grace! The wind's changed, you can smell land!"

Standing quickly, the Duke reached for the door, wresting it open and following Talbot out, up onto deck. He took the brass spyglass from the other man and swept the length of the narrow ledge of sand that edged the bottom of the towering granite cliff. "We're in closer than we thought. Lower away anchor."

"Lower away anchor!" Talbot shouted, his words repeated by old Tom, the second mate, ringing out over the moonlit waters as the ship's bells proclaimed two o'clock in the morning.

"Lower away anchor, laddies!" As the words died away, the anchor cable rumbled through the hawsehole, plunging downward toward the ocean's green and briny depths.

The Duke closed the spyglass, handing it back. "Ready my boat. I'm going ashore."

He went below, pulling off his oilskin while he moved. When he came back out on deck the boatswain's shrill call sounded in the night, piping him off the ship. He climbed into the mizzen chains, pulling them taut with his six-foot frame, towering over his men when he stepped off into the waiting rowboat, Talbot watching from above.

Standing in the small boat, the Duke called back up toward Talbot. "Take her off the point and tell Andre to stand ready!"

"Aye, she'll be snug and waiting, Your Grace." Part of Talbot's words were carried off by the wind, but the Duke nodded, hearing enough. Then he turned his gaze toward the shore as the men rowed him in, the moonlight shimmering on the water around them, the fog now low along the shoreline.

On shore a tiny speck of darkness moved down the narrow stretch of sand, running toward where they were landing. The

5

Duke's eyes narrowed, his expression ominous. He watched it near, relaxing slightly when he made out the outlines of Moira's cloak and then her face as she ran forward toward where he was now stepping off onto the sand, the surf rolling up toward his shiny black Wellington boots.

Her hood fell back across her shoulders, her arms waving wide as she came toward him. She was shouting, he could see, but the wind took her words and scattered them back behind her. She ran forward, this child of Edmund's, as she had for the ten years they had been exiled here, rushing headlong at him as if he were a long-awaited present.

His eyes softened, an emotion he would have been hard put to identify welling up within him. She had almost reached them, her cloak falling wide, her thin nightdress clinging to her body. He felt his features hardening, something almost like jealousy angering him as he saw his men turn to stare at her.

She stopped, ten feet away, the nightdress almost transparent as the wind and the dampness plastered it back against her body. Moonlight fell on her, clouds parting to let it burnish the auburn hair that was tousled wide around her head, pulled by the wind into strands that curled out away from her face. Two large green-blue eyes stared up into his dark face, his dark eyes; his tall, angular frame outlined by the black cloak that billowed out with the breeze. Almost a foot taller, he stared back at the eyes that seemed to hold all colors at once, from green to turquoise to hazel. He was acutely aware of his sailor's eyes on her; on her creamy, translucent skin and the huge, trusting eyes of the child who no longer existed. She had matured in this last year. A young woman hesitated before him and then, slowly, came forward.

"I hoped it was you," she said.

"And what if it hadn't been?" he said more harshly than he intended, the sailors behind him averting their eyes, turning the small boat back out into the surf. "Pull that cloak around you, Moira, you're sopping wet!"

She reached to comply, hurt by the tone of his voice. He spoke as if to a wayward child. "When those men came so late, I—"

"What men? Came where?" he demanded, cutting off her words.

She stared at him, suddenly frightened. "To, to the cottage," she faltered. "Aren't they with you?"

"What do they look like?" he asked, his voice grim.

6

She stared at him through the gloom, the fog swallowing up the moon again and again. His dark cloak billowed out with the wind, and his eyes were unreadable. In the misting dark, with his dark hair and darker eyes, he looked fierce. Dangerous.

"What's wrong?" she asked, his tension palpable. Her fear chilled her, making her pull her cloak even tighter, holding it closed with her hands. "French," she answered finally. "They spoke French. Not Breton. I didn't see more than a glimpse of them, but father seemed to know them. Are they trouble?" She hesitated, her eyes trying to search his. "Is my father in danger?" She whispered the word "danger" and he realized he was frightening her. "Is it beginning again?" she asked faintly.

"Is what beginning?" His patience was short. He began to walk toward the path that led back up the cliff, precipitous and direct, to the summit.

"You and Papa . . . disappearing . . . people coming in the night . . . What is it all about? I'm not a child any longer, I should *know*." She was hard put to keep up with him as he strode easily up the sharp incline, just ahead of her.

"Nothing's beginning." His tone was calm, quiet, matter-of-fact. He stopped once, partway up, reaching back to take her hand, helping her up the incline, his concentration sobering her thoughts. An edge of danger had crept to the surface, an edge he kept carefully concealed, layered away under the polish and gloss of his title, his position.

And yet still, with all the fear and worry that were beginning to encroach, still the touch of his hand warmed her, calmed her. She felt his strength as he pulled her with him, making her keep pace, climbing fast toward the top of the granite headlands. This was the man of her childhood dreams, the hero of all her childhood stories.

In every one, as Solange or her father lulled her to sleep, the Duke's figure became the prince of the fairy-tale, rescuing the fair damsel in distress, righting all wrongs.

"Moira—" His voice cut across her thoughts, frightening in its calmness as they reached the top. "We will go in quietly, by the back door. The kitchen door. Do you understand?"

"No." Her voice was small and miserable as she kept pace beside him, her hand still in his.

He realized that he still held her hand, and now that they were on flat ground he dropped it. "I do not want to be . . . bothered . . . by unknown visitors. See if they are still there, still with your father. Will you do that for me?"

He stopped in the narrow track, staring down at her. She swallowed hard. She would do anything for him. She almost told him that and then stopped, her voice small. "And if they are?" was all she said.

He began walking again. "If they are," they reached the rear of the cottage, and his words became soft, "Ask your father to help you a moment and bring him to the kitchen. Is Solange there?"

"She was."

"And where are the—visitors?"

She hesitated. "They were in the study when I left. They came pounding on the door—"

He nodded, walking silently now that they were beside the back walls of the cottage. No study windows looked out toward the back. He hesitated. "Were they in uniform?"

"No. Why?"

He shrugged. "It means nothing. Either way. Go in and tell Solange that I will be behind you. And pull that cloak tight!"

Moira obeyed, opening the kitchen door and slipping inside as the Duke moved silently to the far side of the white-washed cottage, angling toward the nearest edge of a small, diamond-paned window. Drapes covered any view of the room, the wind rattling the open shutters, obliterating the sounds from within.

By the time the Duke opened the kitchen door, Edmund Walsh was already there, coming out to get him, Moira banished upstairs to dry herself and get to bed.

"Michael, I knew you'd come!" Edmund grasped the Duke's arms, his smile genuine. "Thank God you made it in time!"

The Duke relaxed slightly, shrugging out of his cloak. "Who are your friends?"

"From Paris." Edmund's smile left. "With rather bad news."

"Already?"

"There's been trouble. Come along. Solange!" he called out to the closed door off the kitchen. "Bring some hot negus, we have royalty soaked straight through!" Edmund held the door to the hall open, smiling again. "How the bloody hell *did* you make it in on a night such as this?"

They walked down the hall, leaving Solange to grumble to herself as she moved toward the kitchen and the cups and wine, berating visitors who got civilized people out of bed at all hours of the night. "Devil's work in the Devil's hours," she muttered darkly. "Not good Christian people about on a night such as this!"

8

In the hallway, before they reached the study, the Duke stopped Edmund, his hand on Edmund's arm. "Moira was out on the cliffs—alone. At this hour of the night."

Edmund Walsh smiled at Michael. "Searching for you, no doubt. She has a sixth sense about when you're near. You know how she's always been, wanting to be the first to see you when you come."

"Edmund, she's no longer a child. In any sense of the word."

"No?" Her father's eyes were amused. "Are you quite sure? You don't have to live with her."

"My sailors' eyes were very sure. She had only a nightdress under that cloak—a thin nightdress which was plastered against what is no longer, by any stretch of even a father's imagination, a child's body."

Edmund hesitated before opening the door to the back parlour, to his study. "You're suggesting?"

"I'm not suggesting. I'm telling you. You should, you *must*, explain the facts of life to that girl. She can no longer run pell mell through the countryside, without thought of safety, unless you both are beyond common sense."

Moira's father looked at his old comrade. "Common sense. I've never professed to having much of that, have I?" He hesitated. "And the facts of life . . . A woman should tell her those."

The Duke stared at him. "You mean she knows nothing? At—what? Seventeen?"

"Just turned this last March."

"Just! She'd be out in London! Edmund, someone *must* talk to her. And Solange is hardly the choice."

"No." Edmund's mouth twisted into a wry grin. "Even I can concede that. I don't suppose you'd volunteer. No. I suppose it becomes you even less than it does me."

"You must see to it."

"Yes. You are right." Edmund opened the door to the study. "I will. You *are* right." The men within looked up as they entered.

Upstairs in her room, Moira could pick out her father's voice in the rumble of different tones that filtered up through the floorboards. Her father's voice and then a harsh, French-accented one, rising agitated and loud.

And then the Duke's voice, quieter, firmer, stopping the others.

She threw her wet cloak over a narrow wooden chair, catching a glimpse of herself in the looking glass as she started to lift off the damp and clinging nightdress. She let it fall back, staring at herself and then stepping closer to the glass, facing directly into it.

The moonlight from her small casement window threw very little light into her room, clouds covering the moon and then floating away, tree branches cutting shadowy patterns in the half-light. And yet she could clearly see the outlines of her body beneath the thin, wet cotton. Her cheeks began to burn with color as she stared at herself, seeing the swell of her bosom, the curve of her hips. . . . Pull that cloak tight! he had said. She had thought he had meant against the cold.

She turned away from the looking glass, ashamed, unsure why she felt humiliation growing within her, but sure that he thought the less of her, sure that he thought she was growing up to be a great cow of a female, like Solange. Like the village women, obvious, and earthy, and unappealing.

Unappealing. She pulled her wet nightdress off, shivering as she changed in the cold room. Unappealing. How could she appeal to him? He knew Parisian women, London ladies. Her father had told her of them . . . elegant, refined, dressed in the latest fashions, a world apart from the only world she knew.

She climbed into her bed, pulling the comforter up close around herself, wondering at the tears that began to fill her eyes. She knew so little, understood so much less, that the tears were a surprise, spending themselves and then letting her fall asleep to the rumble of the words below.

"Moira. . . . Moira. . . ."

She opened her eyes, her mind fuzzy with sleep.

"Moira." Her father stood over her bed. "Don't be frightened. I have to leave for a little—"

"Leave!" Blinking back sleep, she started to sit up, her bare arms hugging the comforter close. As she moved the comforter slipped down across her lap, her father staring at the young woman before him, thinking of Michael's words.

"Shhh. Someone is in danger and we must help. Do you understand?"

"No. Please."

"Listen to me." He sat on the edge of the bed, reaching for her hand and then finding himself suddenly awkward with her. Michael was right. He must talk to her. "Moira, there is no time

10

to explain. I did not want you waking and looking for me. Or the Duke. We will be gone for part of the day. Do you understand?"

"Yes," she said quietly, other nights from her childhood coming back to haunt her. She stared across the moonlit gloom at her father. "I'm awake now."

"Good. If anyone asks, in the morning, I am not feeling well and I am staying in bed. And you have not seen the Duke. He has not been here. Is that clear?"

Her eyes filled with worry. "What's happening? Those men—"

"Shhh. Those men were just friends come a little late; there is no reason to be concerned. None. And don't be alarmed if we're back a little late. Tell Solange that we may bring back some visitors."

"Visitors?" Another thought occurred to her. "Solange will ask what—"

"Don't concern yourself about Solange, she can keep her tongue in her mouth; she knows what to do. And say. Now, can I trust you, too?"

"Of course!" Hurt stung her words and her expression.

He reached down, brushing hair back from her eyes. "I thought so. It won't be long, I promise. And when I come back, you and I are going to have a long talk."

"Talk?"

"Yes. About—life, and—everything. All right?"

"Yes. Please." She looked up at him, her worry so apparent that he reached down to kiss her forehead.

"It won't be long," he said again.

She watched him go, watched him close the door, heard him move back down the stairs. Her eyes closed again as the house became quiet, the voices gone.

Dreams came slowly to her, troubling her with their mixture of present and past . . . of bleak granite cliffs and soft, long-gone Cornish springs that never ended. A young boy played high on a moor in her dreams, racing ponies with her and laughing at her fears. Tristan. His name was Tristan, and she knew he was the Duke's son without quite remembering it . . .

He smiled up at her, this Tristan, the Duke's son, smiling up out of her dreams and then saying something awful, something she could not catch. Something mean about her mother. Tears, her tears, the taste of their salt deep within her throat as the

11

Duke suddenly loomed above them, overhearing his son's words, slapping Tristan and mixing the dream with the salt of her own tears and the sea mist rising across the moor. . . . The feeling of running free, running hard, toward him on the beach. His big black ship laying out from shore, its sails furled. His black cloak whipping back away from his body. He loomed dark and distant in her dreams . . . cold. The Devil wore black. But so did her childhood idol . . . the Duke of St. Maur. Idols became devils in her dreams, fear and trust mixing together, her feelings confused by the power of his grasp when he pulled her along the pathway, up toward the summit of the cliff. She felt again the warmth of her hand safely within his.

Then bits and pieces of other nights intruded, stretching back into the past, back through her childhood. Her father and the Duke disappearing for a night, for nights on end, filling her dreams and turning her back and forth in her sleep.

The troubled dreams continued until dawn, visions of children, and of terror, of curse words and great deeds, of her father and the Duke, all mixing together, giving her no rest.

Chapter Two

PALE EARLY AUTUMN SUNLIGHT FILLED MOIRA'S ROOM, HER EYES opening to the sound of Solange banging pots and pans in the kitchen.

Throwing back the covers in the cold morning air, she reached quickly for her robe. Drawing it tight she went downstairs, walking into the kitchen. Solange looked up truculently.

"I suppose you want your breakfast."

"No, no. I'm not hungry."

"Good. There's hot tea there, if you've a mind. Staying up all hours like the Devil himself! Keeps a civilized person from getting any rest at all."

Moira listened as she went for a cup, pouring tea from the pot and reaching for milk and sugar. "Isn't Papa up yet?"

Solange's silence stopped Moira. Looking up she saw the old woman's expression. "He's not feeling well this morning," Solange said.

"Oh." Memory flooded back over Moira. "Oh! Yes, he did say he—didn't feel well." Moira looked down, stirring her tea, worry enveloping her now. Part of all those strange dreams was true then. But how much? She had no one to ask.

Moira turned toward the aging housekeeper who had raised her since time past remembering, since they had moved here when she was small. "Did you know my father's visitors?"

"And how would I know any visitors, slaving away out here?"

Moira bit back hasty words, thinking of all the prying at doors and peeking through windows she'd caught Solange at over the years. "I'd never seen them before," Moira said.

"Well, and where have I been that you have not, young miss? And speaking of where you've been, when did you slip out to the cliff last night? And why, as if I didn't know?"

Moira looked down, tracing patterns on the edge of the rough kitchen table. "No reason."

"No? I thought you'd stopped mooning away over the sea."

"I do not!"

"You tell your father what you want. I see what I see."

"And what do you see?" Moira asked, more upset than she wished to show.

"I see a young chit mooning away over things that'll never be, that's what I see, don't think I don't know."

"What will never be?" Moira demanded.

"I know what I know," Solange said complacently, looking up from the peas she was shelling.

"And what is it you think you know?" Moira asked. "Don't talk in circles so! If you have something to say, say it!"

"I know that men like that black Duke mean trouble for any that go mooning after him. Trouble for everybody." Her scowl worsened. "He always has and he always will."

"That's absurd."

"Absurd, is it? Well, I don't know the fancy words your father's been teaching you, but what passes in a man's mind, *that* I do know. Full well, if the truth be told. And I know what goes on in the mind of a chit that would like to throw herself at him, too."

Moira ignored the last of Solange's words, harking back to the beginning. "And what do you think passes in the mind of the Duke of St. Maur? As if you'd know." Moira's back was to the old housekeeper, reaching for more tea. Rain began to beat remorselessly against the small-paned kitchen windows.

13

Solange sniffed. "Weightier things than thoughts of you, my pretty one."

Moira turned to face Solange then, putting the kettle down on the table between them. "Am I pretty?" Her serious face, her worried eyes, stopped Solange's quick retort. "Solange, truly, am I pretty?"

"Of course you're pretty, you have eyes."

Moira stared at her. "You're not just saying that because you work for us."

Solange watched the young girl who was growing into womanhood. "Do you think I'd compliment you for naught? For money?"

"No," Moira said hastily, not wanting Solange's anger. She had grown up with this woman. Solange was the nearest thing to a mother that Moira could remember. "No. But from kindness, out of caring for us, then, yes. I think you'd stretch the truth rather far."

Solange shrugged, her massive shoulders and arms straining full against her workdress and apron. "I would, I'm sure, if need be. But you have a looking glass, you see the girls in the village. Go look yourself, if you disbelieve me."

"I can't see how others see me."

"Others like the Duke?" Solange asked slyly.

"Or how others look," Moira went on, ignoring Solange's words, her knowing smile. "Far away from here, Parisian ladies, or London ones—what do they look like?"

Solange sniffed. "That's no concern of ours."

"Papa said I'll have to go to London soon. Or Paris."

"Your papa's a fool if he intends to take you anywhere such as that."

"Why?"

"Because you know nothing of the world, of how people such as that live. Great cities and the way people live in them."

"Is it so different? The way people live there?"

"Yes. For some. For you it would be."

"Why me?"

Solange shrugged again. "Don't ask silly questions. Just accept what I tell you. You belong to a different class."

"What does that mean?"

"That means," Solange spoke slowly, emphasizing her words, "that you can never be the simple country girl your father has tried to make you. Not in a city. Mark my words."

"He says with my coming of age and all that we can't stay

14

here much longer. Why is that, Solange? What has my age have to do with anything? I hardly remember anything else, any place else. Except for the Duke and ourselves, everyone I know has lived here always . . . their whole lives long. I'll feel so out of place in those cities, I know I will. What will happen to me?"

Solange sniffed. "A protector will come to your rescue. Of one stripe or another."

Moira stared at her old nursemaid. "What does that mean?"

"It means, young lady, that you had best learn to keep your own counsel. And to stop daydreaming about handsome dukes who have more on their minds than some chit of a girl. And you'd better pray he never does think overmuch about you."

Moira looked down. "He likes me. I know he does."

"Of course. And he likes warm milk, furry kittens, pink babies, and oatmeal. You remind him of his youth. Just don't ever remind him too much. And don't ever think the likes of him would take the likes of you seriously."

"Why not?"

"Why not?" Solange laughed outright. "The little chit does have her cap set for nobility, doesn't she? Well, first my young miss, he's got ladies aplenty—who'll do anything he wishes, I'll warrant. He has no need for the likes of you. And more importantly, he's a bad 'un. Not so bad as to take advantage of his best friend's child tho', even I don't say that about him. Leastways as long as she doesn't throw herself too hard at him." Solange gave Moira a sharp look. "But at bottom he's a black devil, and none can trust him far. As he's proven before."

"What do you mean, proven? And what do you mean, take advantage of me?"

"What was that?" Solange looked toward the front hall, alert.

Moira glanced toward the doorway. "I heard nothing——" And then she did. "The rain?" Moira turned toward the hall, putting her cup down, listening. She told herself that the rain was knocking oak branches against the front of the cottage.

The light knock persisted. Moira walked toward the front door, unlatching it slowly, afraid of what she might find behind it in spite of the gentle sound of the rapping.

She opened it to find a beautiful woman staring back at her. The woman's hair was golden, her bonnet softest peach. A dark rust cloak covered a peach-colored gown above which soft blue eyes were fixed appealingly on Moira.

"Please, may I speak with the Monsieur Walsh?" The woman's French-accented English was halting. Beside her,

15

huddled against the folds of the russet cloak, was a dark-haired boy of seven. He stared up at Moira, his eyes wide and watchful.

Moira stared at the woman. Then she stepped back. "Please, come inside." As the woman led the small boy forward Moira shut the door behind them. "Forgive me, I wasn't expecting—I mean we receive so few—visitors."

The woman smiled, her perfect oval face warmed by the soft light in her eyes. "Ah, then please forgive our intrusion—is it Madame—Walsh?"

Moira smiled back at the woman shyly. "No. I am Miss Walsh."

"Ah." The woman's smile was tinged with weariness. "But of course. How stupid of me. And this is my child, my son, Jean-Marc."

Moira looked down at the boy as his mother continued to speak: "You will, I hope, forgive our unheralded approach but I am, we are, to meet His Grace here."

Moira stared at the woman then, caution tinging her words. "I beg your pardon?"

The woman stared back at Moira. "Is he not here?" Fear fled across her features. "We were to come here if—I mean, he was to be here if—" She stopped. The boy reached to cling closer to his mother, and her hand found his shoulder, caressing it gently as she looked back at Moira's unsure expression.

Moira hesitated. "Please, come into the parlor." She led the way for them, giving herself time to think.

"If he is not here, then do you expect him?" the woman was asking as they entered the small front room.

"I—I have no way of knowing," Moira said finally.

"He was to be here. Please, I am sorry, but—" She stopped, her fear plain across her face. Then in a very low tone she spoke again. "May I sit down?"

"Of course." Moira watched the beautiful blonde woman throw her cloak aside and sink gracefully down onto a chair, pulling her son close.

"Don't worry, my pet." She looked up at Moira. "All will be well. He will come, I am sure."

"And you are?" Moira asked finally, when the woman said no more.

"I am Genevieve." She said her name as if this would explain all. "I'm sure he will come. He promised. You do not mind if

16

we," her voice became frightened, "if we wait a little, for him. Do you?"

Moira stared at the woman. Was this a trap, or was this the visitor her father had mentioned? If so, then where were they, where were her father and the Duke?

"No, of course not." Moira looked down at the boy, smiling a little. "You may wait. Have you come far?"

"Very far indeed." Genevieve watched Moira. "You don't know about me? He didn't tell you?"

"No." Moira spoke stiffly. "No one has mentioned you."

"Ah." Genevieve sighed. "I see." She lapsed into silence.

The little boy snuggled against his mother, as if to gain warmth as well as safety.

"Would you like to—to change? To rest?" Moira asked.

"Oh, yes. But I'm afraid we brought little with us, that is to say, nothing. To rest for a little . . . yes. Thank you."

Moira still stood, irresolute, in the middle of the room. "I'm sure something of mine should fit you. And my room is at your disposal." She opened the door to the hall, glimpsing Solange's back as the old woman disappeared back into the kitchen. "If you'll follow me, I'll see that some food is readied for you. My father—is not feeling well, but I'm sure he will be able to see you—later."

"Thank you, you are most kind." Genevieve's eyes were soft with gratitude. "Come along, Jean; we shall rest a little and then Monsieur le Duc will be here to take care of us."

"Monsieur!" His eyes lit up. "Will he truly be here?"

Moira walked ahead of them up the stairs. As she listened to Genevieve reassuring her son that the Duke would soon be there, would soon take care of them, a small knot twisted within her stomach.

Jealousy was a new experience. She didn't recognize it, did not understand why Genevieve's words to her son, why even Genevieve's beauty, saddened her, turning the day bleak.

"It is not very big." Moira spoke as she opened the door.

"It is quite lovely." Genevieve turned to smile at Moira. "Truly. You can't know how grateful we are."

Moira tried to smile back, reaching for her dress and slippers as Genevieve continued: "My thanks are not sufficient, I know, but I am sure Monsieur le Duc will know what to do, to say; for your courtesy in letting us wait."

Moira swallowed, feeling ashamed. She nodded a little,

17

uncertain what to say, and then closed the door between them. The small upstairs hall was silent; empty. She glanced toward her father's door and then, on impulse, opened it.

Only the cold bare room lay before her. She closed the door, looking back toward her own room, and then walked down the stairs, carrying her dress and slippers.

"Well?" Hands on her hips, Solange stared up at Moira from the kitchen doorway below.

"I don't know." Moira followed Solange back into the kitchen, neither of them speaking until the door closed behind them.

"Did she ask questions?"

"A few. I told her nothing."

"One question is too many." Solange said darkly. "She has a Parisian accent. I have never seen the like of it in any Christian home. Can you credit her nerve, her with one name."

"What are you talking about?" Moira asked her.

"Bringing his by-blows here of course. Anyone with eyes in their head can see he looks just like that black devil."

"Stop calling him a black devil! He's not black and he's not a devil!"

"His skin may be white, but his eyes and his hair and his soul are as black as they come."

Moira stared at the old woman. "What you said, about by-blows—"

"Hush! You should not speak so, it isn't proper!"

"Well, you said it! What do you mean?"

Solange turned back to the food she was preparing. "Bless me, but you are an ignorant one. I told your father book learning was no proper training for a lady."

"Solange—" Moira's voice rose, her impatience growing.

"A by-blow is a child born without benefit of marriage."

Moira started to speak and then stopped. "You mean," she began finally, "children can be born when people aren't married? Don't be—"

"Absurd?" Solange smiled, a small, dark smile. "I told you I knew the way of men's minds. I know that your father had best be spending some time learning you the facts of nature along with all those foreign languages you prattle on with."

"I'll change in your room," Moira interrupted. She did not want to hear Solange, did not want to feel the tiny pinpricks of jealousy and envy that were assaulting her this morning.

Solange was busy with her cooking, not even looking up

18

when Moira opened the door and came back out into the kitchen. "I'd best go down to the village early," Moira said. It was Tuesday, shopping day. "May I take your cloak, Solange? Mine's in my room, with them."

Solange shrugged. Moira picked up the old gray cloak, starting out the door as Solange finally spoke. "Don't be leaving me here too long, with strangers in the house. I can't be responsible."

Moira shut the door firmly between them.

Chapter Three

IN THE SMALL BRETON VILLAGE A SINGLE NARROW STREET WOUND along the northern edge of the inlet. It started near the base of the cliff where white-washed cottages topped by steep thatched roofs stood here and there. The cottages began to crowd closer together and then stone houses led the way past the church, two-storey houses whose upper storeys were built out over the narrow lane, almost meeting in the middle.

The ground floors housed the shops of tradesmen; sheet-metal signs hung outside, creaking on their hinges in the winds, proclaiming the specialties of their occupants. The front rooms of the houses were dark, all the air and the light coming into the back rooms, where windows looked out on gardens filled with flowers and cauliflower, beans and potatoes on one side of the narrow cobbled lane. On the other side smaller gardens grew right up to the sea-wall, the fresh morning winds making the air sparkle.

Moira walked past the village church, the stone bench along the wall of the gothic porch filled with old men smoking and talking, the squared-off belfrey quiet on this mid-week morning.

Village women in black dresses with white scarves and white net coifs over their hair passed from shops to home, shopping bags full, the street market filled with Tuesday marketmen, their wagons loaded with their wares.

In the distance across the inlet rosy granite headlands blended into gray and mauve cliffs, scarred, rent, and crumbling under the constant pressure of the restless sea. But here in the

19

village, safe along the leeward side of the northern cliff, shoppers bought Nantes biscuits and Rennes pralines, gray partridges and Morlaix ham, fresh legs of mutton and flat scones. Drinking cider, they passed the time gossiping about their neighbors.

As Moira passed among the crowds, she was nodded to occasionally but not stopped, not spoken to with the easy familiarity they gave their own. She had lived here with her father for almost ten years, but they were still the "Cornish people" to the villagers, still temporary visitors who lived alone in their large cottage far up the cliffside track, unvisited and unknown. They were gentry and not to be trusted.

Even Solange was not accepted by the villagers although her own village was not that far away. She might be Breton but she was not from the village, not one of their own. They gave her a wide berth, as much for being a stranger as for her acid tongue, and she herself, widowed and wary, was glad to be left alone.

Moira finished her shopping, her thoughts filled with the strangeness of being among so very many people and yet still being so very much alone, so completely left out of their lives. She pulled her shopping sack closed and started back up the narrow track, listening to the mournful call of the seabirds as they swept up around the shoreline and then back out to sea. The wind whistled over the brush and gorse, the sky overcast and as changeable as the sea beyond.

A feeling of dread began to assail her as she neared the cottage, afraid of what she would find. But when she walked in the kitchen door, putting the sack of potatoes and the milk and the meat down on the old wooden table, Solange was as she had left her, stirring the contents of the big iron pot.

"Have they—has anyone—come?"

Solange shook her head.

"Nothing?"

Solange shrugged.

"And the woman and the boy?"

"She hasn't stirred since you left." Solange nodded toward the front of the house. "The boy's in the parlor."

Moira hung Solange's cloak up, hesitating for a moment. "I'd best see to him then." She started for the door.

The parlor was filled with pieces from their estate in Cornwall, all of the furniture too big for the small room it now filled.

When Moira opened the door the young boy jumped, turning to stare at her, terrified. "It's just me, Jean."

20

"Jean-Marc," he said after a moment, relaxing only a little.

"Jean-Marc. That's a beautiful name." She walked on in. "I didn't mean to startle you."

"I thought—" He stopped.

"Yes?" she prompted. "You thought?"

He stared at her. "Nothing," he said finally.

"You speak English very well." When he did not reply, she looked around the room. "There's not much here for you to do, to play with, I'm afraid."

He looked up at her solemnly. "I can't play. I have to take care of my mother. My father said I have to until he can."

"Who is your father?" Moira asked.

"I—" He stopped. "It's—I'm not supposed to say."

She stared at the boy. Genevieve had not given a family name. Now the boy would not say his father's name. "Why not?" she asked finally, a small catch to her voice.

He looked up at her. "It's a secret."

"Oh." She tried to sound calm. "I see. That's unusual." She looked down at him. "Jean-Marc, do you know any card games?"

"No." His trusting young eyes fastened on her face.

"Would you like to learn one?"

He smiled shyly then. "Yes."

"Good. Come along, the cards are in my father's study."

"Do you live here with your father?" Jean-Marc asked as they walked out into the hall.

"Yes." She found herself swallowing hard. "We live here together."

He looked around wistfully. "That must be nice."

She opened the study door, letting him go in first. "Don't you live with your father?"

"No. Something happened and he couldn't, Mama says. But she says we will now. Soon."

Moira reached for the playing cards, sitting down at a narrow table. Jean sat down across from her, watching her carefully. "First you must learn to shuffle the cards," Moira said, speaking quietly, watching the young boy's attention keep reverting to the closed door. "What is it, Jean?"

"I thought I heard my mother." He looked over at her, his dark eyes solemn. "She wouldn't leave me here."

"Of course not!" Moira stared at him in shock. "Why would you think that?"

And then she heard something too. It sounded like a muffled

21

exclamation from the kitchen. She stood up, laying the cards down. "You practice trying to do that for a moment, I'll see what Solange is carrying on about. I'll be right back."

Before he could argue, she opened the door to the hall and then closed it behind herself, staring toward the kitchen door as it began to open. Solange, white-faced, held the door open a moment and then the Duke came through it, supporting her father who half-walked, who was being half-dragged, by the taller man.

Moira's fist went to her mouth, stifling the scream she felt building in her throat. The Duke looked up to see her. There was blood on her father's shirt, blood spattering down onto the clean wooden floor as the Duke spoke. "Help me get him up the stairs."

She pulled her fist from her mouth, walking toward them. Her father's eyes were dulled with pain, his words slurred as he tried to reassure her. "I'm all right . . . Moira . . . don't . . . worry."

She lifted her father's arm gently, holding it around her thin shoulders as the three of them started up the narrow steps. She pressed close against her father, moving one step at a time.

"Good girl," the Duke said. "Don't fall apart on me."

As they reached the top step, Moira thought of the visitor, her words coming slowly, her breathing ragged. "Someone's in my room, she'll hear us . . . Genevieve."

"She's here," Edmund said. "Thank God for that . . . they're safe."

"So far," the Duke replied, looking over at Moira. "And the boy?"

"He's in the study." Her voice was as low as his as they walked on.

The Duke held Edmund's door open with his shoulder, slowly leading him inside. Moira stayed in the doorway, watching as the tall man laid her father carefully back onto his high, narrow bed.

"Do you know anything about medicines?" The Duke's voice was calm, only the grayed-over pallor of his sun-bronzed face bespoke his concern.

Moira stared at him, her thoughts disconnected. He looked like a farmer, his skin so bronzed; not like a duke at all. He must have spent long months aboard his ship to look so dark.

"No," she spoke finally, her thoughts coming back to the words he was saying to her. Her voice was faint, the shock beginning to wear off. "Solange always takes care of us if we're sick." Moira walked forward, unsure how to help.

"She's bringing water and cloth," he interrupted. "Don't fall apart on me, we must bind this before he loses more blood."

"Michael—" A quiet voice spoke from the doorway. Moira saw the softness that came to the Duke's eyes when he looked up to see Genevieve standing there.

Moira bent to unbutton her father's shirt, pulling it gently away from the wounded flesh, poor pale flesh, of her father's chest. The Duke was striding across the room, folding Genevieve into his arms. "Thank God you weren't hurt," he said.

"I heard you ask about medicines. I may be able to help. Growing up in the midst of revolution has its compensations." Genevieve spoke softly, and after a moment he brought her nearer to the bed.

The Duke looked down at Moira's trembling hands, reaching for them, pulling her back. "Come, child, let Genevieve do this. She knows how."

Solange appeared at the door, bringing a basin of hot water and cloths, more cloths across her arm. Moira stepped back from the Duke, out of the way. Slowly she took another step backward, and then another, watching her father bleed across the bed as Solange and Genevieve bent over him. The Duke stood beside Genevieve, and stared down at Edmund, listening to his faint groans.

Genevieve said something in French and the Duke turned to see Moira, pressed hard against the wall, staring at them with huge eyes. "Moira—could you see to Jean-Marc? Stay with him, keep him downstairs?"

She stared at him and then nodded, mute, slowly turning to go. Her brain was numb. They wanted her out of the room. They were banishing her to where the other child was. They thought her still a child . . . he thought her still a child.

The Duke caught up with her at the head of the stairs, turning her around to search her eyes, holding her shoulders in his large, bronzed hands. "Are you all right?"

She stared up at his coal-black eyes. "I don't know."

"I've sent for the ship's doctor. He'll be here soon."

Moira heard the words float past her, felt her knees begin to buckle.

She heard the sharp slap before she felt it, before she felt the sting of blood rushing to her cheek. Her hand reached up to her cheek as her eyes filled with hot tears. "Do you think that was

23

necessary?" she asked, both her cheeks now stained with red, burning with anger and hurt.

"Yes."

Moira turned away. "I'll see to the boy," she said.

He watched her walk down the stairs, watched for signs of more fainting, half-following her until she reached bottom and walked slowly toward the study, her fists clenched at her sides.

Then he turned back toward the small bedroom and Edmund. Moira walked into the study, looking over at the boy who sat huddled in a chair, his eyes wide, listening to the strange noises from above.

Chapter Four

THE DAY HAD GONE DARK BY THE TIME THE SHIP'S DOCTOR ARRIVED. Accompanied by a short Frenchman who talked circles around the silent doctor, their arrival brought the Duke to the top of the stairs, motioning them up.

The doctor nodded to Moira and the boy beside her, and then headed up the stairs, leaving the Frenchman to stare, now silent, at the young woman before him.

After a moment Genevieve appeared above, seeing the man and coming down toward him, greeting him warmly in French.

Jean-Marc ran to his mother's side, grabbing hold of her wide skirts and not letting go. Moira watched the three of them walk toward the parlor, chattering happily away in French.

At the door Genevieve turned, calling back to Moira to join them. Moira stared at her and then shook her head, turning toward the kitchen. She went through the kitchen door to where a grim-faced Solange was back stirring the contents of the large stew pot. The smell of onions drifted over the kitchen, the view bleak and dark out beyond the windows.

"You haven't eaten all day," Solange accused her.

"I'm not hungry."

Solange looked over at Moira. "You'll be no good to him if you're as weak as he is."

"Have you—" Moira stopped, then began again. "Have you seen other wounds such as his?"

"Worse. You don't credit it?" Solange said when she saw Moira's expression. "Why, I was a girl when the Revolution began in '89 and such things we saw before Boney took over in '99 you'd never believe. And then all the fighting he caused afterward. Boney didn't leave many without one wound or another, not even in these parts. Why I remember back in the last of 1814—"

Moira interrupted her. "It is a gun wound, is it not?"

Solange didn't answer.

"Solange, what's happening? What do you know that I do not?"

Her back to Moira, Solange still stirred the stew, patiently keeping the bottom from sticking and burning. "I know there are stories. About pirates. And I know there are some things best not asked. Or answered."

"Pirates?" Moira's questions became fears. "What do pirates have to do with this? Why did we leave Cornwall? Do you know? Why do we have no friends except the Duke?" She went on slowly, "And why does an English Duke visit us here?" Moira's questions tumbled over each other.

"Ask your father when he's better."

Moira stared at Solange's broad back. "Will he be better?"

"I'm not a witch. Nor a fortuneteller." Solange turned then, turned to look toward the young girl finally, seeing the door to the hallway fall shut, the girl gone.

"Miss Walsh—Moira . . ." Genevieve spoke from the parlor doorway as Moira started up the stairs. "Would you like to—to talk?"

Moira shook her head no, her hand on the oak bannister.

"I don't think you should go up there now." Genevieve spoke again. "I mean, the doctor is still working and—"

"I won't disturb them." Moira stared back at the woman. "This is my home. And I am not a child, Madame—?" She let the question trail off, looking toward the boy who stood farther inside the room, beside the man the Duke called Andre. "Solange," Moira added finally, "will make you and your son comfortable in the parlor for the night. Have you eaten?"

"Yes. Thank you."

Moira turned away, hearing Genevieve's soft words of apology behind her as she walked up the steps and into her own room. She stopped, staring over at the wall which separated her room from her father's for long moments before she finally sat down on the bed. Ages seemed to pass, and still

25

she waited, curled up on her bed now, worry and thought and pain and fear and hope and dread all mixed together within her.

"Not now!" the Duke's voice barked out, carried through the wall by the force of his feeling. "Edmund, stop this. You're not helping yourself. Or anyone. We'll talk about all that later."

"And if there is no later?" Her father's voice rose. "We must talk *now!* She's totally unprepared, you were right." His voice came out with surprising force, an urgency behind his words forcing strength into them. "You must, Michael, you *must* do it! For Moira's sake—"

His words fell away to a murmur, Moira sitting up at the sound of her own name. The sound of raw fear, of desperation, was in her father's voice, riveting her attention to their words. The door to his room opened, the sound carrying through the quiet house. Moira stood up, walking to her door and opening it slowly, looking out at the deserted hallway.

The doctor was walking down the stairs, his back to her. The slump of his shoulders bespoke weariness. Or despair. She couldn't tell which. It had been hours since he had come, hours since he'd entered her father's room. And now they had let him go. Had sent him away. To argue amongst themselves.

She stepped out into the dark hallway, looking toward her father's door. Then she walked toward it, stopping just outside.

"No!" The Duke's voice carried out into the hall and then fell away, the partially open door behind him. "It's preposterous!"

"Michael . . . Michael. . . ." Edmund was pleading. Moira had never heard her father plead before. With anyone. For anything. The sound made her cringe. "Michael, you owe this debt," he was saying. "You owe this . . . there's no other solution."

"For God's sake, there must be another way!"

"She'll lose all. . . . *all!* Do you want that on your conscience?" There was bitter anguish in Edmund's words, his voice weakening. "Do you think I don't know how you feel? That I would have allowed—sanctioned—" Her father's voice broke off, pain stopping his words until, "There's no time." His voice was even weaker. "There's no time. . . . You are the only one."

"Lie still," the Duke spoke quietly. "And think. What of Genevieve? What of the boy?"

"Moira. . . . What of Moira? I've never asked a thing of you."

"No," the Duke's voice faltered. Moira stared at the partially

26

closed door, amazed at the sound of hesitation now in the Duke's voice. He was the strong one, the positive one. About everything. Always. "No," he said again slowly. "You haven't."

"You owe this debt. You could be in gaol . . . in *jail*—or worse—"

"Do you think one day goes by that I do not remember? Do you think I could ever forget what I owe you?"

Moira stood transfixed, listening to their words, trying to sort them out into some kind of sense. Why did he owe her father so much? What was this talk of jail, and worse?

"So terrible . . ." her father's words slipped away and then came back stronger. "The only thing I care about, the only thing I've lived for, is Moira." His voice rose. "I won't have her destitute! I won't! I still have Lucy's letter, Michael." Edmund's voice faltered over his words. "I have Lucy's letter."

"Don't threaten me!" The Duke's voice turned hard and cold. "You know me better than that. *Don't* threaten me!"

"Promise me. Promise me you'll do as I ask. Let me die in peace. Say it!"

The Duke hesitated. "You shall not die! But, if need be, if *need* be, then yes. As you demand, as I owe, I shall."

"Swear to me you'll do it now, while I can see. *Now*, Michael, swear it."

There was a long pause, and then the Duke spoke in a flat, tired voice. "I swear it. I swear I shall do as I owe."

"You'll marry Moira. Now."

The Duke hesitated. "I'll marry Moira. Now," he repeated slowly.

Moira's gasp turned the Duke to stare at the door. Striding toward it, yanking it open, he saw her white face, her eyes large and filled with pain.

"How much did you hear?" he demanded, his voice harsh, his eyes cold. "How much!?"

"Michael . . ." Edmund called weakly from his bed and the Duke unwillingly turned back to stare at him.

"Stay here," the Duke told Moira and then walked back inside the room, walking close to the bed, speaking quietly.

"I'm here," he said. When he looked up toward the doorway Moira was gone. "Edmund, does she know any of it?"

"No." Edmund shivered. "No. . . . Oh God, she knows nothing."

"I have to speak to Genevieve. I'll have to explain what's happening . . . why. . . ."

27

"Yes." The word was almost a sigh. Edmund lay still now, drained of all energy. "Yes . . . you must tell Genevieve. . . ."

Downstairs a little later, the Duke sent Andre up to sit with Edmund, to call out for help if need be.

"Where's Goreston?" the Duke asked.

"The doctor's eating," Genevieve replied.

The Duke reached out for Jean-Marc, taking him in his arms, hugging him close. "How are you doing my boy?" The boy did not answer, just hugging close to the big man as the Duke looked over the boy's tousled dark hair toward his mother. "Genevieve, I must explain—" He stopped. "Edmund is dying," he added finally.

"*Mon Dieu,*" her eyes filled with tears, "it is our fault. If he hadn't tried to help us—"

He shook his head. "No. If we'd reached you earlier, before you left, before word was out—" He stopped. "None of which is important now. I—before we leave here—before Edmund—" He stopped again, trying to find the right words. "I have promised him I will marry Moira."

"Marry?" Her eyes rounded with surprise. "What are you talking about?"

"Marry. Now," he added.

"But you cannot! We—" She stopped. "But *why,* Michael?"

Jean-Marc tugged on the Duke's arm, pulling Michael's eyes down to the boy's. "Are we leaving, sir?"

"Soon, Jean-Marc," the Duke replied absently. "Soon."

"Are we going to go on horses, too?"

"Yes, yes we will all be going soon, darling." Genevieve spoke quietly, her eyes never leaving the Duke's face. "*Chérie—*"

"Too?" The Duke leaned down to the boy. "What do you mean, Jean-Marc, too?"

"I want to ride a great dark horse like the lady's."

Before Jean was through speaking, the Duke had pulled away, sending the boy toward his mother, racing up the stairs to Moira's room, to Edmund's room, to the small spare room. Only Andre looked up to question him as he opened and closed doors.

Downstairs the Duke threw open the door to the study and then reached for his cloak as he raced toward the kitchen. Solange looked up at him, startled, as he burst into the room.

"Where is she?" he demanded.

"I—" Solange stared at him. "What?"

28

He pushed past her, opening the back door, heading toward the small stable across the damp grounds behind the cottage. Only the chestnut mare remained tethered inside. Cursing to himself he saddled it, leading it out and then looking at the two tracks that led from the cottage, one to the village, one toward the cliffs.

Heaving himself into the saddle he headed up toward the edge of the cliffs, through the hilly forest. The night mists swirled low to the ground as he rode through them, covering the brush and gorse with a salty wetness, making the mare step carefully.

He pushed the chestnut as fast as she would go, straining to see ahead, through the mist and shadows. He came out of a stand of oak trees finally, onto the flat, wind-whipped promontory. Reining in, he stared into the distance and then rode north, along the edge.

It was completely barren along the summit, the somber cliffs sheering off into the roiling waters far below, salt permeating everything, darkness everywhere. She could have had no more than a few minutes head start. It had only been minutes since he'd seen her in the doorway. The vision of her in that doorway filled his mind, her eyes large and haunted, her eyes frightened at what she was hearing.

He rode on for the better part of an hour, unwilling to give up, determined to find her, to bring her back. But finally, finding nothing, he turned the horse back, riding along the cliff's edge, riding back toward the cottage where Edmund lay dying. Where the boy and Genevieve waited with Andre, waiting for him.

The high cold wind stung his cheeks, blowing through his dark hair as he rode more slowly now, his eyes turning toward the sea. He pulled the mare off the track, picking his way through the gorse until he neared the edge of the high granite cliffs, the wind roaring at his ears, biting at the uncovered flesh of his face.

Far below the narrow beach stretched empty and silent, growing wider as the ebbing tide left the sea to lap more gently up toward the shore. He kept his eyes on the sand, heading down the coast, the salty winds pushing back at him.

And then he saw her. She was walking along the edge of the foam, the great black horse pacing behind. She was hunched forward, as if in pain, the mist of the sea spray matting her hair back. Heavy with the salty dampness her cloak hung bedraggled around her.

He found a path down, the chestnut testing daintily until she reached level ground again, and then he ran her forward, loping near the black before Moira heard him over the roar of the wind and the sea.

He reached her side as she looked up and then away, her tear-stained face turning back toward the Atlantic. "Go away."

"I can't." He reached for the black's reins, and, holding them loosely, he stepped down, to pace beside her, the horses walking behind. Surf lapped up over their feet. "Moira, your father is dying."

"Don't you think I know that?" Her words rose and fell with the wind, blowing out to sea. She could taste the salt of the air mixing with the salt of her own tears. And then his hand took hold of hers, his leather glove soft against her cold skin.

"I know you heard some part of what was said. I agree with your reticence. I share it, in fact. But, there are reasons, compelling reasons. . . ." He trailed off.

Her voice was hard. "There can be no reason on earth for what my father was asking. Nothing could make me force myself upon—upon anyone." She stopped walking, turning away from him again. "How could he ask that? What was he thinking?" She spoke the words out to sea, her eyes fastening upon the distant moon.

"There are considerations—many considerations and reasons that you do not as yet know about." He could see the look of defiance in her eyes. "He should be the one to tell you." He stared at her across the gloom, his own frustration turning his voice hard. "Do you think I would agree simply on a whim? Even the whim of a dying man?"

"I cannot imagine why you would agree to marry me." Her voice faltered over the word marry. Her eyes were hurting, her voice shaking with emotion as she stared up at the man whom she had built so many fantasies around. "I heard the revulsion in your voice. If you think I would force myself on—on *any* who did not want me near—" Her voice trailed away until it was only a whisper. Reality was tearing her daydreams apart.

He reached to turn her, holding her shoulders in his hands, forcing her to face him. "You obviously did not hear enough." His voice was clipped. "Now you will hear it out. You are not safe here anymore. You would have been leaving soon in any event."

"Then I will leave!"

30

"It's not that simple! Your grandfather's will makes it impossible for you to inherit your estate while you are under age unless you are married."

The horse's breath was warm on her back. Moira did not speak.

"Did you hear me?"

"Yes."

"If this had not happened, your father would have been leaving. As it is," he stumbled over the words, "as it is, you will have nothing. Absolutely nothing if your father dies before you are married."

"That's—" Her voice was faint. "That's not possible."

"It is not only possible, it is unfortunately legal and it is the truth."

"But—how could he do that? *Why—?*"

"Do you think your father would create such terms!?" The Duke stared at her, angry. "How little you know him! Your father has no say in the matter. The estate was entailed. He can do nothing but abide by the provisions of the will."

"He cannot die." Moira's words were spoken so softly he had to lean in to hear them over the winds and the surf. She looked up at him with those same large eyes that had always adored him. But in place of trust he saw fear.

"Moira." He spoke more quietly. "You are being forced to grow up overnight. There are so many things that you should know, should have been told. You are not prepared for any of this."

She heard the gentleness, saw the sadness in his eyes. He looked as if he too had lost something this night. "What are the terms, exactly?" she asked quietly.

His eyes hooded over at unwelcome memories as he answered her. "If your father dies before you reach your majority, which in your grandfather's will is eighteen years of age, you must either be married or forfeit the entire Walsh estate. And you must be married before you inherit in that circumstance. In other words, before your father dies—or you forfeit all."

"He never mentioned any of this. Never."

"There was no need. You would have been taken to London for the season this coming year . . . and, well, nature would have taken its course," he finished uncomfortably.

"What does that mean?"

He didn't know how to answer her. "I'm not the one to

31

answer that. The season is in reality a marriage mart as far as I can see. Distastefully direct."

She did not speak. Walking along the edge of the sea, watching the patterns the foam made as it came lapping up toward them, she stared at the dark water that kept trying to engulf their feet. "Why?" she asked finally.

"Because it is no different than a cattle mart."

"What? No, I meant why did my grandfather write something such as that into his will?"

"I suppose to ward off fortune hunters. I assume he felt if you married with your father's approval that the choice might be a wiser one."

"I see. Well, I need no husband. I need nothing. I can work."

The Duke paced beside her. "That's all well and good, and easy to say, when you have a roof over your head and food in your belly. What do you suppose you would do to earn your keep?"

Her chin quivered, but her voice was firm. "I have an education."

"In what? Farming? Or governessing, perchance? Or mayhap you'd fancy learning to be a barmaid. And what credentials would you bring to any of them? Where have you worked? Who will recommend you?"

"I shan't be forced to marry!"

"I agree this is not suitable," he said stiffly. "That would be obvious to anyone. But we are not talking about a—true—marriage. Beyond that, beyond that there are other reasons why this—obligation—cannot—could not last." He picked his words carefully. "Believe me, as you heard, if there were another way I would insist upon taking it." He paused, his words coming more slowly, "I would never forgive myself if I were the cause, even inadvertently, of your losing your position in the world. You have no idea of what that would mean . . . alone, destitute . . . at the mercy of all. That cannot be allowed."

"You do not wish to be married to me." Moira spoke the words directly, her breath caught in her throat as she waited for him to speak.

"My proposal is simple," he said. "We will marry, we will wait until either you are legally of age or until my solicitors can find a way of breaking the codicil and then have the marriage annulled."

"Can they do that?"

"Break the codicil? It's possible. I don't know."

"And—annulment?"

"You will live as my wife. As the Duchess. In name only of course."

"In name only?" She looked up at him, uncomprehending.

"Of course! Surely you do not think—" He stared at her. "Do you know what that means?"

"No."

He hesitated again. "Do you, I mean, have you any knowledge of, of normal—normal marital—arrangements?"

She looked up at him, her face innocent of all understanding. "What do you mean?"

He groaned, looking down at her confusion. "Lord help us, this should never have happened." He saw the quick tears come to her eyes. "You will be free to do as you wish when you are free of these entailments, when the marriage is annulled. You need not worry. I do not think you are making any more of a sacrifice than I am," he finished stiffly.

"Sacrifice?"

"There are certain duties—marital obligations—that I will forgo—obviously—so that the annulment can take place."

"What are you saying?" She stared up at him, her eyes trying to search out the black depths of his.

"I am saying that, as a gentleman, no—advantage—will be taken of your situation." His voice became ever more stiff, even more formal.

She turned away. "I've never heard you sound like this." A forlorn note crept into her voice. "I don't want your charity."

He stopped walking, turning her around to face him. "You will have none, I assure you. You are being thrust into a situation, a social situation, you are totally unprepared for, that you know nothing of. And I do not intend to endure censure for your acts or be taken for a laughing-stock who has succumbed to the attractions of a youthful—" he stopped, taking a deep breath before he continued. "We will be forced to seem, to all outward intents, man and wife. If it can be proved something is amiss the entire estate will be forfeit. And you would be truly forced upon the charity of others. The charity of strangers."

Her chin quivered. "And if my father survives this?"

"God willing he will—and then there will be a quiet annullment and none need know. Moira, we must give him what peace we can. Or do you not care about him; about his grief, his worry?"

Her voice was strained and tight. "I care. . . . We'd best get back," she added finally.

"Yes. I hope we're in time."

"Do you?"

He looked down at her. "Of course." His voice was almost as strained as hers. He turned back, helping her onto her horse.

As he himself mounted Moira spoke. "Why would my grandfather write such a will?"

The Duke's voice hardened. "He did not think overmuch of women's judgment."

They rode in silence for a moment, Moira's thoughts far away. When she spoke he had to lean closer to hear her. "And I dreamt of sailing the South Seas and living on bananas and coconuts."

"What? What are you talking about?"

"Nothing. Nothing at all."

He watched her. "Sailing?"

"You knew my grandfather—did you like him?" She changed the subject, unwilling to have this stranger know of her dreams of him.

He hesitated. "I pitied him. I thought him a very unfortunate man."

"Why?"

They were riding toward the trail that led up the cliff, the surf lapping at the horses hoofs as it came in and then fell back away, the mist swirling about them.

"He had the misfortune of seeing people as they are, rather than as they seem. Or as you wish them to be." His voice was as cold as the wind that blew across the heights now that they crested the hill.

"You mean women, don't you?" When the Duke said nothing, she spoke again. "You agree with him." When he still did not speak, she continued, "What happened tonight? If he dies, I have a right to know how he was killed."

There was a long pause before the Duke replied. "We attempted to rescue some—people—from the new French king's 'mercy'—from Charles X's guillotine."

"Why? How did you come to be here?"

"Your father wrote to me. You must speak of none of this Moira. You must speak to no one."

34

"I am not the child you seem to think. Or, if I am, I will not be by the time this night is over." As they rode on she spoke again. "And the woman, Genevieve? And the boy?"

He stiffened. "What about them?"

"They must be gotten away?"

"They will leave, too."

"Too?" She looked over at him as they rode the heights.

"Obviously you will have to come with me if—you will not be able to stay here alone. Especially after all this."

Her heart almost stopped. Not stay here. Marry this man. Her adolescent dreams were coming true, but they had become so distorted by reality, so overgrown with fear, that unknown feelings were welling up and spilling over the gentle emotions of her nighttime dreams. To have her father gone, to go herself to unknown places with this man she barely knew, this was not what she had imagined. This was too real, too frightening.

"Why are they in danger?" She asked the question of Genevieve and the boy, afraid to ask the other one, afraid of what he'd tell her of himself and her father.

"They are related, the boy is related, to the Bourbons. To the new King Charles."

"As you yourself are," she said, her words quiet, her heart heavy.

"I am English. The boy is a French citizen. And since Charles himself wrested his crown from his own brother, Louis XVIII, he does not overmuch trust the rest of his family not to attempt to undo him. Any close relations are in danger."

"I see." She paused. "And so Jean-Marc must flee. And the boy's father? What about Jean's father? Isn't he in danger, too?"

He stared at her across the dark of the cliffs. "It is not necessary for you to know of the boy's father."

She let a long moment pass. "You and my father, you've done this before."

He helped her horse over a rough spot. "Ever since the Revolution the guillotine has been thirsty. Any who did not agree with the political party of the moment were in danger. And since the party in power changed so drastically so often, most were under suspicion. These are not things you need know, Moira. It's dangerous. Especially now. Charles X is no better than the Jacobins. It's simply different beliefs that are killed now. Then it was pro-Royalists, now it's anti-Royalists.

Bloody death for abstract ideas. And it doesn't end. It just doesn't end."

She watched him. "Your friends can't be anti-Royalists. You are a duke—and a Bourbon."

He spoke slowly. "I have friends who escaped to England. And elsewhere, when the Jacobins wanted their crowns. I have other friends who fought cheek by jowl with the revolutionaries, who are now called regicides when all they wanted was a little freedom. Since the monarch's been reinstated, none are safe."

They rode in silence for a bit. "I see," she said finally. "You rescue them. And now you rescue another friend's daughter. Whether she wants it or not."

The wind whistled shrilly around them, easing a little as they reached the forest's edge, the wild peat cold and damp under the horse's feet. "What would you prefer, Moira?"

She took her time replying. "I would prefer to marry someone who wanted me."

"Mayhap someday you will."

He did not look toward her. He did not see the tears that welled up again at his careless words. Moira felt her heart breaking within her, too many losses for one solitary day to hold. Her father lay dying, her life was being torn from around her, even her dreams of this romantic stranger were being torn from her by his own careless words. He had no idea of her feelings.

She shivered, the wind cold, the whole world gone cold and forbidding around her as she stared ahead into the gloom.

The track was slippery, the horses stepping carefully. They were a long time getting back to the cottage, each of them unwilling to face what lay ahead.

Chapter Five

THE WEDDING WAS QUIET, THE PARISH PRIEST CALLED TO THE DYING man's room. It was witnessed by Genevieve and Jean-Marc, by Solange and Andre, the doctor gone back to the ship, the Duke stiff and proper beside Moira.

It was all a dream, she kept telling herself, a bad dream. She would wake and it would be gone. Her father would be well, the woman and child would not be here. The Duke would not be her husband, standing as if a stranger beside her, but would once more be the hero of her daydreams.

"Moira." Her father's voice cut through the fog. "Say yes."

"Yes." Her voice was so low it could barely be heard in the quiet room.

The Duke's voice was firmer, his yes short and hard.

And then the priest, speaking over her father, blessing them, blessing him, walking outside with Andre. Moira stood near her father's bed in the plain brown merino dress she wore to church every Sunday. The Duke turned away, toward Genevieve and they walked out, into the hall, Jean-Marc's little hand in Michael's.

Moira sank down onto the narrow chair beside her father's bed. "Papa, are you happy now?"

His eyes opened, the dullness that overlay them lifted for a moment. "Happy," he said.

"Papa, have you and the Duke been—rescuing—people all along?"

He stared at her blankly. "Rescuing?"

She watched him. "Last night—"

"Last night—" he shuddered, "last night never should have gone. . . . He said . . ."

"He said what, Papa? Who said? Do you mean the Duke? Papa . . . Papa?"

His breathing erratic, his eyes closed, she half-stood, ready to call for help. His eyes opened suddenly, his hand reaching for hers, clawing at her.

"Moira! It has to be this way. I'm sorry . . . so sorry. I should have told you long ago."

"Tell me now, Papa."

"Bad . . . bad things happened. . . . Hold on to the letter. He'll never hurt you. . . ."

She stared at her father. "Why would he want to hurt me? What letter? I don't understand."

"I—" His words died away and then he roused himself. "You'll have Lucy's letter. Michael . . . Michael . . ."

"I'll get him, Papa," Moira stood up, and ran to the doorway. "Michael!" His name sounded strange on her lips. "Come quickly!"

37

Her voice carried down the stairs to where the Duke stood with Genevieve and the priest. He turned, coming up quickly, the priest hesitating and then following.

The Duke brushed past Moira at the top of the stairs, the priest waiting to walk with her back into the bedroom. "He wanted . . . Michael," Moira said. The Duke turned back toward them from beside the bed.

She stared at the man who was now her husband, at the strange expression on his face. "He's dead isn't he?" The priest went forward as the Duke came back to stop her, to turn her away, toward the door.

"I want to see him," she said. "I—have to." She looked down at her left hand, at her mother's ring, which now banded her own finger. "Married. We are truly married, aren't we? How strange."

The Duke saw the old priest look up, puzzled. "She is not herself. Too much has happened."

"Of course." The priest's English was heavily accented and so Michael began to speak to him in French and then in Breton, until finally the priest spoke back warmly, voluble in his native tongue. Moira walked slowly to her father's side.

The Duke looked over at her as she knelt, holding Edmund's cold hand. "Moira." He reached for her, forcing her to her feet. "Come along."

"He's so cold. . . ." Her voice was distant, sounding to her as if it came from someone else, someplace else. "You speak Breton. I didn't know."

"Come sit down. You need food." He walked her out and to her own room, calling to Solange to send up soup. "You must eat."

"No."

He sat her down on her own bed, staring at her. "I told the priest we will bury Edmund now, before we leave." He watched her startled expression. "He will give us special dispensation. We cannot take him with us. We cannot leave him here—like this."

"But—so soon?"

"It's better this way. We must leave today." He saw Solange coming near. "It's too dangerous to stay. Now eat, it will be a long day ahead for you."

She saw him step back, watching Solange approach. "I can't."

"Yes, you can." The Duke stood back, motioning to Solange

to come near. "Solange will sit with you. Here, one spoon at a time." He reached for the spoon himself, filling it with the chicken broth, putting it to her lips. Slowly she opened her mouth, watching his eyes, accepting the food as a small child does. He handed the spoon back to Solange. "See that she eats."

Solange raised a spoonful to Moira's mouth as he walked out. "Child, child, what have you done?" Solange's voice was a heavy whisper. "Why would your father let you marry that devil?"

Moira tried to swallow the hot broth. It burned. "Please. Don't."

"He says you are sailing today, you must eat now, before you go."

"Please—stop!" Moira stood up and then, dizzy, sat back down. She took the spoon. "I'll eat it. But leave me to do it alone. Please."

Solange straightened and then stood up slowly, her broad hips straining at the seams of her dress. "Child, listen to me. You must watch yourself. You must be very careful."

Moira stared at Solange's worried eyes. "Why?"

"He's a bad one, girl, truly."

A chill swept through Moira, the simple words so stark and cold. "You've never liked him!"

"And you've always liked him too much . . . I know what I know. About that man I know too much . . . too much."

"What is it that you know?"

"More than I'll tell. You're better off not knowing now. Safer. The Black Saint's best left alone."

The old woman left. Moira's hand trembled and she laid the spoon down, shivering in the chilly room. Then she reached for a shawl, and wrapped it around her shoulders. The floor creaked in her father's room. She looked toward the wall and then stood up, walking slowly toward the small upper hallway.

No one was outside her door, the sounds of conversation coming up the stairs. Genevieve talking with Andre, the boy Jean-Marc calling out something, their words muffled by the floors and walls between.

She walked the few steps to her father's door, stopping when she realized that the Duke stood within. His back to the door he was searching through the drawers of the dresser, pulling clothing aside, shoving the drawers closed again, one after another. Moira stood still, watching as he finally straightened

39

up. He started to turn and she shrank back against the wall. She waited but he did not come forward, did not walk out. Slowly she moved a little forward. He stood over her father now. For one horrible moment she thought he was searching her father's pockets and then she realized he was sinking to a chair beside the bed, holding her father's hand and staring at him.

He was too far away for her to tell if what she saw were really tears. But then he reached up with his other hand to brush at his cheek, to wipe it dry, and her own began to fall.

She turned back toward her room, blinded by her tears, groping for the door. Collapsing in a chair by the bed she sobbed until she could sob no more.

The small chapel was empty that afternoon, only Moira still inside. The few villagers Edmund had known stood off a little outside, watching the Duke and the village priest as Edmund Walsh was laid to his final rest.

The autumn sun was far above the small cemetery, the cold salt air luminescent with mist outside the thick stone walls and narrow stained-glass windows. She smoothed the old brown cloak over her lap, over the dark brown pelisse and her brown merino dress. He'd said to pack nothing, that she had nothing suitable, that they'd buy new in London. He'd said . . . tiredly she looked up toward the carved ivory crucifix . . . he'd said so much. So quickly. To everyone. But she kept remembering him sitting by her father, unaccustomed tears following the creases of his cheeks. The memory of that moment warmed her and then she chilled over with the vision of his search. Did he want the letter her father spoke of, first to him, then to her. What could be in a letter that was so important, so threatening—

The sound of light steps behind her on the stone floor brought Jean-Marc to her side.

"Jean-Marc—the Duke said you were to stay at the cottage, with your mother—"

"Shhh." His finger went to his mouth. "Mama is still resting; I wanted to see."

"There's nothing to see."

The boy sat down beside her, his dark eyes solemn. "Mama said your papa's gone away."

"Yes." Tears began to fill her eyes again. She clasped her hands tightly together, willing them to stop as the boy watched.

"Will he ever come back? Your papa?"

"No."

40

"Oh." He looked down. "Is Monsieur going to be your papa now?"

Moira swallowed. "No, he's not my—papa." She looked down at the little boy's hand as he laid it on hers. "I won't have any more papas now. I'm all grown up."

"Mama says you're just a child. Why is she so angry about you and Monsieur?"

"I don't know."

"Do you know any stories?" He sat closer, looking up at her wistfully. "Do you?"

"No. I don't." She saw his disappointment plain in his eyes. "Well, I know one my father told me a long time ago but I don't know if I can remember all of it."

He looked up at her expectantly. "You'll remember it. Try. What's it about?"

"It's about the Bay of Douarnenez. Do you know where that is?"

"No."

"Well, it's very close to here. And a long, long time ago there was a city in the bay."

"In the water?" he interrupted, his eyes large.

"No, it was a very long time ago, and there was no water in the bay, for the people had built walls to keep the ocean out and doors to let a little water in when they wanted it. And there was a princess who lived in the city and who was entrusted with the keys that unlocked the doors—"

"Was she beautiful, like my mama?"

"Yes. She was very, very beautiful. Just like your mama. And they were silver keys that she held, the silver keys to the ocean doors. And she wore them on a long silken cord around her neck. Like a necklace."

"My mama has necklaces."

"Yes. I'm sure she does." Moira spoke a little wistfully. "At any rate, a stranger came to the city, and he was very— handsome and very masterful and he had—dark eyes. Dark, dark eyes."

"Go on," Jean-Marc told her when she sat staring at her hands.

"What? Yes. He had dark, dark hair and dark, dark eyes and he had been all over the world, searching. Searching for someone he could trust, someone he could love. And soon the Princess fell in love with this stranger because he was—so handsome, and so—sad. And one night he asked her to prove

41

her love for him. She said she would, she would do anything. And he said if she really, truly loved him she would give him the keys to the ocean doors. For, you see, he didn't believe she trusted him at all, because he trusted no one."

"Did she trust him?"

"Oh yes." Moira's voice was almost a whisper. She caught herself, speaking in a normal tone now. "She loved him very, very much. And trusted him even more. And so she gave him the keys."

"And did they live happily ever after?"

Moira hesitated. "No. No they didn't. When she was sound asleep he got up and he went out and unlocked the doors, to see if they really were the right keys."

"Why would he do that?"

"Because he did not really believe she trusted him for he did not trust her or anyone else in the whole world. And so he went out to prove that she was like all the others. Only she wasn't."

"And then what happened?"

"Then the sea flooded in and covered all the lanes and all the cottages and even the palace and the church steeple itself while they all slept. And that city is still down there, under all the water in the bay."

"Were they all killed?"

"No one knows. No one ever found out. For no one can go down far enough to tell. But every year, to this very day, the priests go out on fishing boats and say Mass over the drowned city on the day it disappeared. And when they do, do you know what happens?"

"What?" His eyes were round with wonder.

"The ringing of the bells far below the water can be heard in answer."

"Have you ever been there?" he asked. "Have you seen the Bay of—of—"

"Douarnenez. Yes I have. My father told me the story when we were there. He said if it is very still and very calm you can see the tops of the buildings of the city still, far away down below."

"And did you?"

"No," she said softly. "No. It was very windy when we were there."

"Well, one day I will go there and I—"

"You will not be going there soon." The Duke's voice came

42

from directly behind them. "You should not even be here now, Jean-Marc. I am very cross with you. I told you to stay with your mother."

Moira turned quickly seeing him sitting directly behind. He did not look cross when he looked at the boy. He looked at him with affection. With love. As he used to look at her she thought, before the wariness, the unreadable strangeness that now met her eyes when she looked into his. "How long have you been sitting there?" she asked finally.

"We have to leave," he said. "Come along, Jean-Marc." Jean-Marc stood up, reaching for the Duke's hand and then reaching back shyly for Moira's. The Duke watched her take the boy's hand in her own.

"Have you been on a ship before?" Jean-Marc asked her.

"Yes. A long time ago when I was about your age. It was the same ship you will be on now."

The three of them walked out of the church together, walking up the narrow track that led to the cottage. Halfway up the hilly incline Moira stopped once, looking back down at the small stone church and the little plot of cemetery ground beside it. The thatched-roofs of the cottages stretched away in the distance, the single lane of stone houses clinging close to the waterfront.

When she turned back she saw the Duke of St. Maur's eyes watching her. "Your Grace?" she asked him, as if he wanted something of her. She saw his eyes hood over.

"Moira, I think you would be better advised to call me by my name." He paced beside her now, Jean-Marc skipping ahead, unaware of the heavy hearts around him.

She hesitated. "What will happen to Solange?"

"I thought you might want her to come with you—"

"No!"

He was startled by the vehemence of her response.

"Then I think she will stay on here until the estate is settled and all can be sold—taken care of."

"That will please her."

There was a pause and then: "By the by, do you happen to have your father's correspondence?"

A cold chill swept through her. She drew her cloak around her, holding it with her hand at her throat now. "No. Why?"

"He kept it in his study, did he not?"

"I believe so. Yes."

43

"All of it?"

"Yes."

"I see." He turned his attention back to the path ahead then, walking on in silence. As she kept pace beside him, Moira watched his profile, more disturbed than she should be, she kept telling herself. They neared the lone cottage on the cliff, the Duke walking inside first.

Chapter Six

THE SHIP LAY A LITTLE WAY FROM SHORE, JUST INTO THE DEEP waters. Her sleek black lines rode the calm sea elegantly, from the high stern to amidships, where the well deck swept on up into the neat low forecastle.

His sailors rowed them closer, the St. Maur flag of black and gold flying at the mizzen. A golden rampant lion of England was surrounded by golden fleur de lis on the black ground of the cloth.

The bos'n's shrill pipe saluted them as the Duke stepped on deck, the men lifting the boy and the two women, Andre climbing behind, directly after the few cases Moira had brought with her.

The Duke turned toward old Tom. "All's ready?"

"Aye, Your Grace, Mr. Talbot's seeing to the last of the gear."

The Duke nodded. "Take Andre and see our passengers to their cabins. We'll make sail as soon as they're settled."

"Aye." The wind-burned old man motioned to a mate, and they picked up the small cases. "Andre," Tom called out. "You see to the missus and the boy, I'll see to the young-un here."

The Duke turned back toward them, his voice carrying across the deck. "Thomas, this is my wife, Moira, Duchess of St. Maur. Please inform the crew."

Thomas's mouth almost dropped open. Staring first at the Duke and then at the young scrap of a girl before him he nodded, dumbly, and then started past her.

"Ah, your ladyship, if you'll follow me. . . ."

Her cheeks burning, Moira followed meekly behind him. As

they moved she could hear Andre saying something low to Genevieve, her silvery peal of laughter following Moira as she walked down the companionway behind Tom.

The oak-panelled cabin he showed her to was large and light, windows to the side and back, the wood dark and warm as old wine. A silver spirit lamp hung over a burnished mahogany table, gleaming down onto a silver coffee service on the piecrust-edged table.

"Why—it's beautiful," Moira said, looking from the oil paintings to the marble fireplace to the brass bed across the room.

"Aye, the Duke likes his comforts, begging your pardon, Miss . . . Your Ladyship, I—"

"Please," Moira interrupted him. "I'm not used to all this. Is there something else you could call me besides Your Ladyship?"

His curiosity was bursting from his eyes, but he held his tongue, nodding as he set her case down onto the floor near a chest of drawers. "Yes, Milady, anything that suits you."

"I don't remember this cabin. Are all the cabins like this?"

He stared at her. "Remember, Your, ah, Milady?"

"We sailed from Cornwall ten years ago aboard the Duke's— I mean, aboard this ship."

He still stared at her. "You be Edmund's little tyke?"

She smiled. "I was."

"Oh! By the blessed saints, Your Ladyship, we were all that sorry to hear about your father. Why, I remember you playing in the galley when we came across in '15, seems like yesterday. I didn't recognize you." He stopped. "Course, whatever it seems, it's been that long." He watched her now, seeing the sadness in her eyes. "Well, all the cabins—no," he answered her question finally. "Not all like the captain's here. Not quite anyway." Tom's words were interrupted by the Duke shouting his name, striding into the cabin before Tom did more than turn around. "Your—"

"Not here!" The Duke's voice was harsh. "The main cabin for my wife and the fore cabin for Madame and the boy!"

"But Andre's taken them already—"

"Curse him for a fool!" The Duke turned on his heel. "He should have known better!" The Duke strode down the narrow hallway, wrenching open the next door, his boots thudding hard on the smooth planking, leaving a dead silence behind.

Slowly, Moira walked out of the captain's cabin and toward the door the Duke had opened, listening as he blistered Andre in French. Moira hung back as Genevieve said something softly and then called to Jean-Marc, Michael quiet now as Genevieve and the boy walked with him out into the narrow hall and then across to another cabin door.

"Je suis désolé . . ." Michael's voice faded as they walked into the smaller cabin. Andre, coming behind, stared at Moira before following them.

She walked inside the smaller main cabin, seeing much the same things as in the captain's cabin. He was sorry. *Je suis désolé.*

"I'm terrible sorry, Your Ladyship." Tom was beside her again, setting the boxes down. "I didn't think about him having to run the ship and all . . . us in and out of the cabin at all hours."

Moira smiled at the kind old man. "Thank you, Tom. Thank you very much."

"Anything you be needing, you just ask for old Tom."

She nodded, standing in the middle of the small cabin, watching him close the door behind himself. Then, slowly, she sank into a large chair nailed to the flooring. He had not apologized to his wife. Only to Genevieve. She looked down at the band of gold on her finger, twisting it back and forth. It did not fit very well.

Up on deck, the Duke climbed to the poop deck, walking along the taffrail and then striding back to the break of the poop. "Mr. Talbot, man the windlass!"

"Aye, aye, Your Grace. *Man the windlass!!*" The words carried down the chain of command.

"All hands make sail!"

"All hands make sail!"

Down the length of the ship, repeated by the mates, the words carried, sailors going aloft, hanging out over the yards as the windlass pulled the anchors up to the cathead, the pawl catching into place.

The men were running up the rigging, voices carrying out: "Spread her wings, boys!" "Give her the muslin!!"

The topgallants and royals were spreading wide, catching the breeze as they set foresails and staysails and jibs.

"Mr. Talbot, take a bearing." The Duke stood, his legs spread apart, his hands in his pockets as Talbot went to the binnacle,

46

reading the bearing carefully before stowing it and coming back alongside the Duke.

"Due north, Your Grace."

"Due north it is. We'll head north till morning and then north, north-east till we round the point." He watched her sails bellying out with the wind, the spray sheering up over the bow as she cut through the Atlantic's choppy waters, heading for home. He felt the wind around him and the pulse of the ship beneath him, a huge surge of joy filling him, smoothing his brow as he stared across the ship that was his, toward the distant horizon.

He knew these waters as well as he knew his own name, had sailed them forever. For the first time since he'd left England he felt good, he felt in control again.

Moira walked onto the deck below, feeling the quickened pulse of the ship itself as it cut through the water. One lone cloud scudded low on the water at the western edge of the sea as they headed north. A roller breaking over the bow dazzled rainbows out of the afternoon sunlight.

Four bells rang out. Two o'clock and they were under way. Married at daylight, her father buried at noon, on her way to England by two. He had been right. It would be a very long day, this tenth of October, 1825. She looked up to where he stood, a tall, dark-haired figure, still in the doeskin riding trousers and black morning coat he had worn on shore, black knee-high Wellington boots outlining his calves.

As he stood there, staring ahead, the sharp linear shadow of the main mast cut across his body, throwing his face into the shadows.

Moira shivered, pulling her cloak close. This man she did not know or understand held her life in his hands. She had no one else, no place else, except where he directed.

Unnamed fears clutched at her, chilling her body as they did her heart. She turned and went below.

The routine of the ship settled down into its own accustomed lines as the days passed by, passengers or no; the bells rang out the hours, and the halves, each watch succeeding the one before, scrubbing, coiling loose rigging, tightening and replacing and repairing shrouds and stays; halyards, lifts, and braces replacing others, rove to in place of any that seemed unfit. The chafing gear was taken off, mended, replaced along the countless yards and ropes that touched the standing rigging. Painting,

47

varnishing, polishing, scraping, rubbing, greasing, oiling, holy-stoning, the work went on from morning till nightfall.

As they set, reefed, and furled the sails, she flew across the water, the decks scrubbed, the brasswork blinding when the autumn sun shone down upon it.

"Eight bells! Rise and shine! Show a leg there! Show a leg, me laddies!!" The bells rang out from forecastle and poop, the sound filtering into the main cabin where Moira lay abed, feeling the roll of the sea, getting used to the pitch and toss.

She'd been a good little sailor they'd said when she was eight years old. She closed her eyes, wishing herself back to eight, to her father and Michael laughing on deck, to being able to hang around the crew and listen to the stories of the China Seas, of the Barbary pirates, of the doldrums and the white monkeys with yellow eyes, of fan palms and banana trees and blue-bellied tarantulas that crawled leisurely away from you in South American jungles.

A knock at the cabin door startled her. "Yes?"

The Duke opened the door, starting in and then stopping. "Oh, I'm sorry. I thought you were up."

"Wait!" She sat up, pulling her robe close around her. He stopped in the doorway, his back to her. "Your—" She stopped, then began again. "Michael—we'll be seeing more of each other than this in the time to come. And you've seen more of me already."

He turned slowly then, looking toward her, his eyes unreadable.

"Thanks to the rain," Moira continued. "And my foolhardy dash down the cliffs." She was standing now, next to the bed. "Would you care to sit?"

"No. Thank you. How are you feeling? With the sea, I mean?"

"I'm fine. It doesn't bother me. Don't you remember?"

A slight smile crossed his face and was gone. "I seem to remember you had to be hauled off forcibly. You wanted to stow away to the southern seas."

"I believed the tales they told me. I wanted to see the white monkeys and blue spiders."

He hesitated. "Genevieve is quite ill, she's never been on board ship before."

"Oh?"

His eyes raked across her face, trying to read her expression. "Yes, well, that leaves the boy."

"Who does not suffer from *mal de mer*."

"Precisely."

She watched the man she had known so long and not known at all. "What do you require, Your Grace?" Her words were said quietly.

He looked for mockery and found none that he could see. He spoke stiffly. "As I've said, it's obviously not necessary, or even correct, for you to call me that. And I require nothing. I assure you I intend at all times to remain aware of the—delicacy —of our—of the situation we have been thrust into. In fact, as soon as we reach London I am employing solicitors to endeavor to find a way to break the provisions of your grandfather's will so that we will be freed of this—difficult—situation, as soon as possible."

"Freed," she repeated softly.

"Yes." He lapsed into silence.

"You wanted something for the boy?" she asked after a moment.

"I—" he stared at her calm eyes, "merely wondered if, since you seem to like the boy, you might be kind enough to spend some time with him."

"Of course."

He still stared at her, and then, slowly, he nodded. "Thank you." He reached for the door and started out, stopping as she spoke.

"Michael, what is the boy to you?"

He did not answer immediately. And when he did his voice was low, his composure slipping a little and then firmly pulled back into place. "He is my flesh and blood."

"Oh God." Before she could stop them, the words slipped out and she sank to a chair, her eyes closing. When she opened them he was gone. "Oh, Papa, what have you done to us?" she whispered the words aloud, unable to think, pain filling her heart. She did not want to know more. She did not want to know anything. She simply wanted the months to pass and the solicitors to find a way to free her, to get away from this man who made her dreams beautiful and her life a nightmare.

As she sat there, trying to sort it all out, another thought began encroaching. What had happened to Genevieve's husband? Who had actually shot her father? And why? What was really the truth of it and what would happen now?

Moira stood up, dressing, and then walking out of the cabin, up on deck, the sunlight hurting her eyes at first, after the dark of the interior.

"Moira!" Jean-Marc came skipping up to her. "Monsieur said you are going to keep me company."

Moira stared at the dark-haired boy who looked so like Michael. "What would you like to do?" Moira asked.

"Do you think we could climb the masts?"

"No. I don't think quite that. How about hide and seek?"

"But I don't know where to go."

"Neither do I, so we'll be even."

"All right." He smiled, his little face lighting up. "But I'm to hide first!"

She smiled. "I'll close my eyes and count to fifty."

He was off, running abaft as she began to count out loud.

Later that day, as the sunset warmed the western sky, Moira and Jean-Marc watched the dogwatch take the sounding, the leadsman well aft, the hands along the rail between the heaver and the leadsman. The thirty pound dipsey was straining up, each man in turn hollering, "Watch there, watch," as he dropped it; until the ship's forward motion brought it opposite the leadsman.

"What are they doing?" Jean-Marc asked.

"Finding out how deep it is," Moira replied. "If it was very, very deep we'd have to stop the ship to check—"

"And if it's shallow," the Duke came near them, leaning against the rail, "or risky waters, we'd have a man in the mizzen chains all the time. Or a boy. Would you like to do that, Jean?"

"Oh, yes, Monsieur!" The boy looked up at the Duke. Moira could see the reflection of softness in the man's gaze. She glanced off, across the beam, wondering if he found that look of pure hero worship in all children's eyes. She could remember staring up at him like that herself.

"Monsieur," Jean asked after a moment, "what would I do?"

"Well, you'd have to swing the seven-pound hand lead and keep checking the depth so we'd not run aground."

"And if we did?"

"If we did!" The Duke straightened up, looking down with mock sternness. "Why we'd be wrecked and have to make the boy who wrecked us walk the plank!"

Jean-Marc's eyes were wide and round. "Have you ever had to have anyone walk the plank, Monsieur?"

"Not on my ship! But you ask old Bill Toomy about the Straits of Bally-Bang-Jang."

"Bally-Bang-Jang?" Jean-Marc asked.

"Aye. In the old days, before he sailed aboard the *Black Saint,* he used to sail the Orient—"

Moira's smile died away. "The *Black Saint?*" she asked faintly.

The Duke glanced at her. "That's what she's called." He rubbed the smooth ebony railing with one hand.

"Why?" Her voice was almost a whisper, and she had to repeat it before he heard her over the wind.

He shrugged when he did hear. "An old legend; an ancestor of mine, was called that, it's said."

"The Black Saint?"

"Yes."

Solange had said . . . had said . . . what? She tried to remember.

"Moira," Jean-Marc was tugging at her sleeve. "Come find him with me, come find old Bill Toomy."

"You go on," she said. The wind was whipping up, the sun near to setting now as she stood beside the man who was her husband under the law if not in truth. "Do you think it possible," she began, "that we might someday be able to talk again? You were my only friend." She tried to read the expression in his eyes. "And now I have none."

He was quiet. "This was thrust upon both of us, Moira. I, it is not that I blame you.' There is no blame—" He looked out across the bronzed sky, the sun veiled beneath western copper-colored clouds. "No blame," he repeated softly.

"You blame my father and so do I." Her eyes filled with tears, surprising her; she had thought they were all spent. "God forgive me, but I do. And you hate yourself for the feeling, as I do, and so you shun me in an attempt to forget it, forget all of it. But, Michael, we can't shun each other forever! For however long it takes to end this. I don't think I can live like that."

"If we can find a way to break the provision—"

"And if we can't, what then? Couldn't we at least try to be a little—friendly?"

He stared at her. "Friendly."

"Weren't we—I mean, I thought we used to be—"

He looked past her, at the men hauling in the lines below and saw her as she had come flying down the beach toward him night before last. Her auburn hair streaming back from her face, her eyes alight, as alive as the sea. He turned back to stare at them now, amazed he'd never seen them before. They were green and blue and mixtures in between. As alive as the sea. As grown-up as the body that had come racing toward him. He shook his head a little.

"Weren't we?" She looked up at him with sad eyes as he shook his head.

"What? Oh." He turned toward her then. "You are so young, Moira. You are still a child in many ways—" He saw the sadness in her eyes. "And you don't understand any of this, do you?" He watched her for a long silent moment. "Would you care to join me for dinner?" He stared into those clear green-blue eyes. Someday a man would drown in those eyes as surely as one would drown in the sea. Tricked too far from any shore. And drown.

She was smiling now, smiling for the first time since he'd arrived, the sight warming him. "Oh yes. Please."

Andre came toward them, stopping a few feet away, ending the moment. "Excuse me, Your Grace."

"Yes?" The Duke was a trifle short with him, as if annoyed at the interruption.

"Mr. Talbot is waiting, Your Grace."

The Duke nodded then. "I'll be there." He held out his arm, and Moira took it, putting her hand on his sleeve. "And Andre, prepare dinner for two tonight in my cabin."

Devoid of expression, Andre nodded. "Yes, Your Grace."

The Duke of St. Maur lead Moira to the steps and then helped her down them, walking her to her cabin.

Chapter Seven

THE KNOCK ON MOIRA'S DOOR CAME AT EIGHT THIRTY, THE BELL ringing, the nightwatch at their posts. She smoothed her hair, touching the ivory lace at her collar one last time, fingering the lace at her cuffs as she walked to the door.

When she opened it Andre stood before her. "Your Lady-ship."

52

She followed him, ill at ease with the man. He rapped once on the captain's door and then opened it, stepping back.

In the candlelight the burnished oak panelling glowed, a fire set low in the fireplace, a table spread with food nearby.

Michael stood up from his desk, a little awkward, watching her walk toward him. She wore the same brown merino dress she'd been wed in, threadbare and patched. But the firelight caught at the red lights in her hair, haloing it about her shoulders.

"Good evening," he said, at a loss for conversation.

"Good evening," she replied softly, a little hesitant herself as she stepped forward, Andre moving past her toward the table, busying himself with the food. The Duke walked around his desk, reaching to hold a chair for her, and she sank gratefully into it.

"We can serve ourselves, Andre," the Duke said. Andre bowed slightly and left the room. As he left the Duke indicated the dishes set before them. "Cold chicken, Scotch broth, cheesecake, and preserved apricots—"

Moira smiled a little in acknowledgment, and watched him pour sherry for them both.

"You set a king's table aboard ship. Or a duke's."

He looked up into her smiling gaze and smiled back. "Or a duke's."

"Thank you for inviting me," she said.

He handed her a cut crystal goblet of pale cream sherry. "Thank you for accepting my invitation."

His eyes took on depth from the fire's glow, the intensity of his gaze mesmerizing her until he looked down, helping himself to the platters of food.

"Unfortunately, it will be the middle of the season in London when we arrive, and though I'll try to avoid it, we may be forced into some few social engagements before we can leave for St. Maur. It depends upon how long I must spend with the solicitors."

"You sound as if it is to be regretted."

"It is." He looked up at her. "You are not prepared yet. And there are always old tabbies who mind everyone's business but their own, trying to ferret out any gossip they can trade at tea."

"Why?"

"Why?" He stared at Moira. "Because their lives are barren of aught else I suppose."

"What is a 'season'?"

53

"My dear Moira, has your father told you *nothing* of the world? His world? Your world now?"

"It hurt him to talk overmuch of home—"

"And of life?" Michael's tone was almost sarcastic. "You are as fit to be presented in London as a convent-raised nun would be."

"Why?"

"Why, why, why. You sound like young Jean-Marc!"

"I'm sorry," she said when he stopped to take a bite of chicken. She looked down at the food she had put on her own plate. "How else does one learn?" When he didn't answer, she went on. "How soon will we be leaving London then?"

"As soon as humanly possible, I assure you. It will be next to impossible to keep up this charade in that setting even for me, let alone you. However, I must take care of some other— business—and inform your father's solicitors of all that's happened. And see my own solicitors as well." He stopped. "It would be prudent to say nothing of the terms of our—marriage —to any of the household staff once we arrive. Let them all think what they will for the time being." When she did not comment, after a moment he went on. "After having gone through all this, it would be senseless to do anything that might jeopardize your inheritance."

"I see."

The Duke scanned her expression. "You do not sound very interested in your estate. You have not even asked what you will inherit."

She shrugged. "I'm not much concerned with business matters. Or money."

"That will change. At least the last part." The hard edge that came into his voice made her question him.

"Why do you say that?"

"Luckily you have a very large estate. But I'll warrant even that will not be enough once you are introduced into society. It never is." His tone became embittered. "I've never met a woman who was not aware of the last farthing a suitor possessed."

"Why—forgive me, but—why?"

It was then who he shrugged. "Your life is going to be very different. In some ways." He looked so searchingly into her eyes that she could not take her eyes from his. "It's a pity that it has to happen. If one could stay as you are now—" his words

54

stopped, but he continued to stare at her, great waves of emotion visible under the intensity of his gaze.

"Why must I change then? If you like me as I am, I'll simply remain so." She was afraid to withdraw her eyes, afraid the spell would break.

He roused himself then, looking back toward his plate. "Pretty sentiments. But impossible, believe me. I know. You are unspoiled. That will quickly change. It is always a pity to see that. In anyone." His voice was matter-of-fact, his attention on his food.

Moira picked up an apricot from her plate, taking a bite and then reaching to taste the sherry. Her hand trembled a little; she felt something she did not understand, something a little frightening, very powerful and even dangerous; but yet something that drew her closer to this man. A strong current, something that willed you into its path and then ripped away your moorings, carrying you with it out to sea.

"What's wrong?" he asked.

"Nothing." She took a long sip of her sherry. "I was just thinking of what you said. Michael—"

He looked up from his food again. "Yes?"

She tried to see past the curtains that he had drawn over his eyes, back into the morass of emotions she'd caught a glimpse of. "If you don't want me to change, I won't. Ever."

He laughed, the sound sharp and harsh. "That's asking too much of friendship, my dear girl. Besides, you will not be able to resist the current. It runs in your family."

She stared at him, as if he'd read her mind. "Current?"

"Emmm. Society's call to folly and insincerity. Mark my words, in a year's time you will be able to flirt and coquette with the best of them."

"Why do you say that?" She was hurt.

"Because you have the equipment for it. And you are bright besides, a lethal combination to loose upon those London fops. You'll want to live there, I'm sure, when this is all over. The country will be much too tame for you. And you'll want to try out your new-found wiles on them all. It might be interesting to see. Besides . . ."

When he didn't continue she finished it for him. "Besides, as you said before, it runs in my family." She saw his eyes harden, and she wondered what her mother had done to him to make him dislike her so. Then she turned her attention to her food, dutifully eating her meal, finally speaking again about other things. "What will they all think—your friends—when you turn up suddenly—married?"

"I'm not sure I have any friends. In any event, I turn up suddenly all the time and I imagine they'll take it in stride. London thinks me eccentric, at best. We shall be the topic of conversation for a fortnight, until something better comes along."

Andre's knock at the door was answered by the Duke, and then the door opened to show Andre bowing slightly. "Your Grace, Madame Genevieve asked if it was possible to see you."

"Tell her I'm—wait." The Duke stopped. "Tell her I'll be there directly."

"You're not through eating," Moira said.

"I've had enough. If you will excuse me." He stood up, his voice formal, correct.

"And if I won't?" Moira asked lightly.

"I shall go in any event. She's been through enough, Moira, these past days. Truly. The shock of it all has not been easy for her."

Moira looked down, feeling the intruder again, the interloper who had wandered in and disrupted their lives. And yet, and yet, she hadn't asked to. She'd been forced into this situation, and in the process of whatever had happened, because of Genevieve, her father had been killed. How much more had Genevieve been through than Moira herself? How much more sympathy was Genevieve deserving of simply because she could not stomach the sea? And how could he care for someone so squeamish?

Moira said nothing as he left, putting her napkin down and staring at the fire for a long time afterward. When she left, she looked over at Genevieve's closed door before she went inside her own cabin, closing her door against them both.

Later the motion of the ship changed subtly, the pitch and toss rising and falling more rapidly. Moira heard steps outside and then Talbot's voice as he knocked at the captain's door. "Your Grace!"

After a moment the door across from Moira's opened, Michael's voice booming out. "Yes?"

"Oh!" Talbot sounded surprised and then recovered. "A squall brewing, Your Grace." Talbot's voice came back toward Moira.

56

"Get the royals in," the Duke said. "I'll be on deck at once."

The Duke moved past Moira's door. She could hear his boots and then she heard him go out and up as overhead, outside, the mate was yelling to the men to hasten, to raise the clews of the crossjack and mainsail. Michael's voice rang out soon after, "Let fly the topgallant halyards! Call all hands!"

Mr. Talbot repeated the orders. Moira reached for her cloak, unwilling to be below. Moving carefully, staying out of the way along the inside edge of the deck where the cabin walls met the companionway hatch, she held fast to the side of the hatch, watching the men.

"Bring her round! Bring her round!!"

"She won't make it, it's—"

The squall struck, the dense bank of clouds pouring at the ship from what had moments before been leeward, catching the ship flat aback.

The topgallant halyards had been let fly, volleying like great guns, the ship laying over, the crossjack afoul of the main topsails when she began to swing round, the men racing aloft, trying to straighten the rigging out before the sails were ripped wide.

The ship was diving heavily now, running hard to larboard. "Luff! Luff!! Let go those topsail halyards!"

"Keep your luff there! Starboard your helm!!"

Michael's voice rang out, and then he took the wheel himself, tying himself into place as he used brute force to keep her steady, to keep her from broaching to and capsizing, the ocean shoving the stern, shaking the keel furiously, as Michael swore at the sea and the winds and the gods that be, holding her steady by main force.

The sound of retching filled Moira's ears as she bent to go back inside, to stay out of the way. Then Jean-Marc's voice crying from outside somewhere could be heard.

The ship plunged and tossed through the sea, heavy sheets of water flying across the decks as Moira grabbed a lifeline and held on tight, gasping for air as a breaker crashed over her.

When she could see again, the water streaming from her face and eyes, she searched for the boy, praying he hadn't been washed overboard by the waves. And then a faint sound made her look up. She could see the boy clinging to the mizzen topsail yard, jerking violently, arcing out across the water and then back in over the deck, back and forth, over and over.

Another heavy wave from the weather-side knocked a sailor

into the lee scuppers, carrying him with the torrent of water as the ship rolled leeward. The water poured off in a torrent as he grabbed hard to a loose line and held on tight.

There would be no chance to loose lifeboats in the storm. Somewhere in the back of her mind Moira realized that as she carefully made her way to the bottom of the mizzen yard, grabbing it as it jerked by, cursing the skirts she wore that swirled and clung between her legs, soaked and heavy with salt water.

"Jean!" she called out as loudly as she could, closing her mouth before the next wave crashed over them. "Jean, hold on!" She climbed slowly, hampered by her skirts, thankful the boy had gotten no farther up. Inch by inch, she climbed closer.

Talbot, making his way hand over hand to the wheel, saw her skirts in the rigging and began to swear at her. Then he saw the boy, higher aloft, and held his breath as a heavy wave burst over them. When he could see again the yard had swung out, over the water, but they were still on it, swinging back with the ship's motion as Talbot forced his way back and up to the wheel.

"Cap'n!" he shouted into the blow, all protocol gone, and pointed with one hand toward the yard where Michael, when he looked up toward it, could only see Moira.

"God damned fool, what the—"

"The boy!!" The words faded away, but then, as they swung back, Michael could see the boy, pinned down between the rigging and Moira's spread-eagled body, a crumpled figure holding on for dear life, just barely visible as lightning lit up the sky for seconds at a time and then died back away. They flew back out over the roiling waters as he watched.

"Holy Mother of God!" Old Tom was beside the Duke now, staring at the apparition, his line tied tight around him.

Michael's attention was on the wheel, his full force keeping her to, his hands raw and blistered through the leather gloves.

"She's dying off!" Talbot called out finally, ages later.

The howl of the wind was dying away slowly, the squall passing by. The ship was still heavy, pitching into the trough of the sea where she'd wallow, her decks awash, until she'd come bow up again, the breakers leveling off, the water calming as rain poured down in a steady torrent now, the worst over.

Michael handed the wheel to the mate, staring up with frightened eyes to what he might not see. But they were still there, two of the crew climbing toward them already, reaching them before the Duke did.

They brought them down slowly, the boy covered with vomit down his blouse, his little body shaking as they carried him toward Michael.

"Is he all right?" Michael stopped then, looking at the huddled mass of salt-soaked little boy.

Jean's eyes opened, and he looked woefully up at Michael. The Duke patted his head, turning back to the sailors who now had Moira almost to the deck.

The Duke reached to grab her by the waist and then they let her fall back against him as old Tom grinned at him, jumping down lightly onto the deck, beside the younger sailor who'd helped him. "Right gallant she is, your lady, Captain. But she'd not let go of the rigging. I was afraid I'd have to chop off her fingers."

Michael held her in his arms and then lifted her up, carrying her down and inside, kicking the door of her cabin open.

Her teeth were chattering as he laid her down upon the bed. "You crazy fool," Michael said. "Climbing in a rig such as you have on."

"Is he . . ." her teeth chattered more as she tried to speak. "Is he—"

"He's fine. Until he gets the spanking of his life." The Duke stared down at her. "Why did you do that?"

She stared up at him, gasping for breath still. "The crew was busy. No one else saw."

"You could have been killed." He looked down at her. "And you saved his life."

She watched him turn and leave, the cabin door still open. A moment later he returned with a decanter of whiskey and a glass. "Here." He poured a strong shot of the amber liquid into the glass and lifted it to her lips.

"I can't—"

"Just hold your nose and drink. It's medicine."

She swallowed, gagged, coughed and then he made her swallow again. He let her lay back as old Tom appeared at the door.

"Be she all right, Your Grace? The boys were that worried—"

"She'll be as good as new. But we'll have to find her some sailor's nankeens and put her on the duty roster if she's going to be climbing the rigging."

Old Tom laughed, his missing front teeth turning his grin into a grimace. "I'll leave you be then." He closed the door to the cabin as the Duke watched her shiver.

He reached to unfasten her cloak, raising her to pull it off the bed, letting it drop, heavy with water, to the floor.

He hesitated and then reached for the buttons of her dress, speaking in a calm, flat tone as his fingers began to unbutton them.

"I did not think to procure an abigail for you till we reached London. And it seems Genevieve will be in no condition during all this to leave her bed, much less help you out of this wet clothing, so we shall have to make do as we are."

Moira's hands went instinctively to her salty face, to her bedraggled hair, pushing it back, away from her face. "I, please, I—"

"You have hardly enough energy to lift an eyelid and you'll catch pneumonia if I don't get you out of this clothing. . . . I don't want people saying I let you die of—" His tone hardened, his thought cut off before the rest of his words were out.

"You're wet too."

"It's no matter—sailors never get sick. We're used to it."

As he spoke her hands reached up to stop his. He looked down at the smooth white hands, small hands, that grabbed his. Her fingers were long and well shaped, and palest cream against his own bronzed and weathered skin. "Please—" she said.

Her hands were still on his, and for a moment he stopped, feeling the warmth creeping slowly back into her hands, feeling their smoothness. Then he reached down unbuttoning the long line of buttons that lined the front of her brown merino dress, opening it to the chemise beneath. Her hands were still on his, the gentle pressure unnerving him. He pulled his hands from hers, abruptly, holding her up to a sitting position as he reached behind her shoulders, releasing the dress from her shoulders and arms. He let her lay back as he moved down, to pull the wet dress off.

Avoiding her body, he studied her wet slippers, taking them off and then, reaching for her stockings, he stopped. His hand on her calf, he stared up the length of her body, covered now only by the thin, wet chemise.

His eyes found hers, afraid to look elsewhere. She watched his face, his eyes, feelings she could not put a name to welling up. "Michael. . . . Michael—"

He straightened, his hands trembling. He looked down at them, astonished. "You're quite right. The rest is—here." He pulled the covers back, and she turned, his eyes unwillingly following the movement of her body, the curve of her hips, as she moved to slip underneath the covers. He pulled them up, reaching across her to tuck them close. His face was bare inches from hers, his cheek so near she could almost touch it without moving.

"Thank you." Her voice was breathy, her heart stuttering within her as she felt again that frightening current of emotion that had filled her at dinner.

For one brief moment he hesitated, turning to see her eyes, still reaching over her, his mouth near hers. And then he straightened, his face set into hard planes. "It's nothing, I assure you."

He turned and walked out, away, closing the door firmly. She knew he was angry. Very angry. But she did not know why.

Helpless, alone and shivering, she pulled the big down pillow into her arms. She buried her head in its softness, crying herself to sleep, aching for she knew not what.

Chapter Eight

DAYS LATER, NEARING LONDON, THE FIRST GRAY STREAKS OF DAY-light blurred out over the eastern waters, filling the vast breadth of the sea with a melancholy foreboding until the weak sun climbed higher in the October morning sky.

The Duke stood near the wheel, watching as they beat their way up channel toward London, a strong easterly hitting them as they reached the Straits of Dover and the chops.

They reefed the topsails, the wind moderating a little, and then finally they hit a patch of smoother waters, the wind turning, letting them carry topgallants, the royals still set down.

"Land! Land-ho!!"

The sounds rang out along the decks, each of them straining to see a patch of English soil.

And later the Duke stood by the wheel as Mr. Talbot turned them neatly up the Thames, heading toward London as the

Duke of St. Maur called out to old Tom. "Thomas, let 'em know below!"

"Aye, aye, Your Grace!"

But below Moira was ready, her cloak on, her hood up over her fresh-washed hair. Old Tom grinned at her, and she smiled back at him trying to mask her fears. "I'm ready, Tom."

"Aye, Your Ladyship, I'll just be seeing to the landlubbers, then."

Moira walked out, onto deck, watching the London river traffic as the boats and ships, barges and Geordies and tugs began to fill the waters all around.

They beat their way up the Thames until the river pilot came alongside, Genevieve and Jean-Marc coming out onto deck.

"Haul that mainsail up!" the river pilot was shouting. "Give us your rope!"

Jean-Marc walked toward Moira, staring up at her solemnly. "I am to say how very grateful I am to you for saving me and, and—" he stopped, trying to remember the words.

"I think that was perfectly sufficient," Moira said, smiling down at him. "How do you feel?"

"Better," he said. "A little."

Genevieve, her paleness making her if anything more appealing, walked slowly toward them. Her pale peach silk dress hung softly around her curves, a lacy shawl about her shoulders. Moira, seeing her, felt the salt-burned skin of her face and arms. She thrust her hands into the pockets of her brown cloak as Genevieve stopped in front of her.

"I shall never be able to thank you enough."

Moira shook her head, speaking stiffly. "There is no reason."

"No reason!"

"I mean, it is not necessary."

"But it is! Michael has told me of your great heroism, your bravery, and I must tell you I admire you more than you can know. For reasons you do not know."

Moira looked straight at the woman. "Possibly I do know."

An alarmed look crossed Genevieve's face. "But surely he would not have spoken of—" she stopped, unsure what to say. "Michael said—" she stopped again.

Moira's ears heard only the easy familiarity with which this woman spoke his name. "Genevieve, Mi—my husband—would do nothing to—compromise—your position."

62

The older woman stared at the younger one. "Then I must again owe you my thanks. Your Ladyship."

The bos'n's voice was ringing out now and again, other voices following in the orchestrated confusion of coming in to port, some of the words floating back to where the two women stood with the boy. "Man the clew lines! Brail up the driver! Make fast the vangs! All snug on the larboard tack, sir! All snug to starboard!" Voices rang out across the length of the ship.

Moira watched the Duke come down toward them, his tunic and pantaloons freshly ironed, his job done as they docked. Andre appeared as Michael stopped in front of them.

"The carriage is waiting, Your Grace," Andre said, handing Michael a calf-length greatcoat which he shrugged into. Looking up toward Talbot the Duke spoke. "Keep her in one piece, Mr. Talbot!"

Mr. Talbot saluted the Duke, grinning. "Aye, that I'll try, Your Grace!"

"Shall we?" The Duke motioned, and Moira waited for Genevieve and Jean-Marc to precede her before she moved forward beside the Duke. Andre led the way across the gangway that stretched over the steel-gray water to the shore beyond, the bos'n piping them off.

A liveried coachman bowed low to the Duke, glancing at Moira's drab appearance and then at Genevieve and the boy as the Duke handed them into the carriage. Andre climbed onto the coachman's bench and the coachman, turning up the steps, shut the shiny black door with the golden lion and the fleur de lis encrusted on it, and climbed up beside Andre. He took the reins of the two black stallions, leading the great, shiny black coach forward.

They drove through the muddy lane, a light drizzle beginning as they passed ragged street urchins who played in the mud barefoot. The children ran after the coach, laughing until the horses clip-clopped away.

Moira stared out the window, excitement and fear mixing together to bring a lump to her throat. Butterflies fought each other in her stomach now. She glanced over at Genevieve who reclined against the opposite cushions, Jean-Marc beside her. She looked bored and tired.

"Are you sure you're feeling well?" The Duke's voice showed his concern.

Genevieve managed a wan smile. "I shall survive it all. In

fact," she smiled over at Moira, "I intend to learn to rise to the occasion as Moira, forgive me, as Lady St. Maur does."

The Duke laughed. "Ah, Genevieve, you and I have lost the youthful verve that a child such as Moira has."

Moira turned back to the window, staring out at the drizzling October rain, trying to escape the easy camaraderie of those two. Other carriages rolled past them now, traffic thicker as they turned into Pall Mall. They angled up Regent Street then, heading for Berkeley Square.

Shiny barouches clip-clopped by them in the gentle rain, the shop windows along Regent Street filled with exotic wares. They turned into Picadilly, driving past great West End mansions. Finally, they reached Berkeley Square, travelling around it to a long brick wall with the heavy wooden gate at either end that took up half one side of the Square.

Moira watched as they went through the gate, staring at the huge house set back from the street. She sat back, not looking as they stopped under the plain pillared porch.

The coachman helped her out, waiting for her as she turned to stare back at the wide lawns, at the old elms that stretched back into the gardens.

"This way, Your Grace." Moira realized Andre was addressing her at the same time the coachman did. He stared openly at her for a moment before he regained his composure.

Moira walked inside, into a great entry hall with a domed ceiling, gilded and painted above the vast mirrors and chandeliers, above the marble and alabaster staircase leading up, circling round and round overhead, gilded ironwork balusters following the curve, a solid crystal handrail sweeping up along them.

Moira turned toward the Duke, who had followed her in. "I—"

"Yes?" He watched her.

"I had no idea," she said finally.

"No," he replied. "I thought not." He turned toward his valet. "Andre, please see that her ladyship is comfortable and introduce her to the housekeeper." The Duke turned back to Moira. "I may be quite late. I must see to lodgings for Genevieve and the boy and—and—other matters. Please eat and go on to bed if I am not back."

She stared at him. "I can't handle—I mean, the servants—"

"Andre will see to all." He looked back over at the smaller

64

man. "I'll ride in the morning, see that Cyclops or Royal Charles is ready."

Andre bowed, watching Moira's concern as the Duke strode out of the hall and into the waiting carriage. When she turned she saw Andre's expression.

"I should have said goodbye to Genevieve and Jean-Marc. I thought they were staying here. With us."

"Here!" Andre looked shocked. "That would never do!" He hesitated. "Would you care to see your room first?"

"Yes." She suddenly realized how tired she was. "Yes, I would. And—would it be possible to have a light dinner in my room?"

"Of course, Your Ladyship. Anything you require is available."

They started up the magnificent staircase, Andre pacing slowly beside Moira.

"And I think I'll wait until morning to deal with, to meet with, the housekeeper."

"Whatever you wish, Your Ladyship."

She looked over at him. "I'm sure you could use the rest yourself, Andre."

"Rest?" His face showed his surprise. "I will wait up for His Grace, of course. He might require something when he comes in."

"Is he usually out a great deal?" They had reached the second floor.

"Yes, Your Ladyship, a very great deal."

They walked down the wide upper hall, past Rembrandts and Tintorettos. Andre opened a door into a blue and silver boudoir. Moira stared at the rich, silvered, mirrored expanse, looking from crystal to porcelain to the sky-blue velvet of the chairs and drapes.

"This—is mine?"

"Yes, Your Ladyship. It is furnished just as the Duchess, as, ah, the late Duchess, left it."

Moira stared at the richness that surrounded her. "I do not remember her. She has been dead a long while?"

"Ten years, your ladyship."

"Ten years? Ten years ago we moved to Brittany."

Andre did not reply. After a moment he walked forward. "Your bedroom, Your Ladyship, and the main doors to the hall. And to the Duke's suite." He pointed as he spoke, but she was

65

lost looking at the opulent bedroom before her. It looked as if it had been transported from some Arabian Night's dream, Oriental, forbidden, exotic.

"And the bell pull, to summon your maids." He touched the silken cord.

"Are there—" she stopped. "Did she leave clothes? I've brought nothing except—"

"Yes, Your Ladyship," Andre said when Moira did not continue. "I believe there is some clothing in the closets. Here." He walked forward into another smaller room off the dressing room. "She kept only a few things in London. Of course, these are out of style, but they may suffice."

Moira felt censure in his words, but his expression was correct, subservient, if a bit smug.

"A robe is all I need. Something for morning possibly. My own is salt-laden at the moment."

He bowed and moved toward the door. "Unless you require something else, I will see to your dinner. And inform the cook and the housekeeper of your wishes."

"Thank you."

He stopped in the doorway. "What would you prefer for dinner, Your Ladyship?"

She looked over at him, past the expanse of silver and blue. "Whatever there is, is fine."

"I'm sure there is anything you may require."

"Whatever is easiest."

"But—" He stopped. "Possibly you'd allow me to—"

"Yes. Of course. Thank you." And then as he began to close the door to the hall: "But light, Andre, please."

"Light. Of course. I will send up one of the maids to see to your refreshment."

When he closed the door, when she stood alone in the dressing room, she began to realize the enormity of what had happened. Slowly, she walked to the doorway between the two rooms and stared at the room full of clothes, the few things. She thought of Genevieve and realized that Genevieve must hate her. Truly hate her. For Moira was standing here instead of Genevieve.

Moira walked back into the large bedroom, sinking down onto a gilt chair, staring at the opulence around her.

Finally, slowly, she stood up, removing her cloak, removing her pelisse, removing her dress.

She took a lamp from the boudoir, going into the closet room

66

and walking down the rows of clothes. She touched a silk here, a velvet there, finding a robe of rust-colored velvet finally and putting it on, setting the lamp on a small table, staring around her.

Feeling as if she were trespassing, she began, hesitantly, to open drawers, looking at linens and silks scattered still all through the drawers. Ten years later.

A knock at the boudoir door startled her. She stood up quickly, shutting the drawers. Feeling ill at ease, Moira walked back into the boudoir. "Yes, Andre?"

The door was opened by a plump young woman in uniform and cap. "It's not Andre, Your Grace. I'm Frances, Your Grace, and Master Andre told me to see that I helped you unpack or undress or—whatever you needed, Your Grace," she finished clumsily.

Moira looked into the girl's face. "How old are you?"

"Seventeen. And a half, Your Grace."

"And are you new here?"

Frances blushed to the roots of her thin, pale hair, her freckles standing out red in the pinkness. "Yes, Your Grace."

Moira sighed. "You have no idea how grateful I am about that."

"What, Your Grace?"

"Frances, I am seventeen—and a half—and I'm new here, too, so maybe we can bear together."

"Oh, Your Grace!" Frances stared at her, shocked. "I mean, yes, Your Grace."

"I'd like a bath, Frances. I'd like to get all this ocean salt washed away."

Frances curtseyed. "Master Andre said to show you the bath, Your Grace, and, and whatever you required."

Moira followed Frances through a small connecting door and found a silver, gold and pale gray bathroom. A gilded wash-stand, gilded tub, gilded basin and ewers, rosewood and tulipwood fittings, met her eyes. Moira turned to see a ther-mometer and a copper kettle and then looked toward the tall cupboard off to one side, surrounded by a ducal coronet.

Frances stepped toward it and opened the wooden door. "Here, Milady, Your Grace," she added belatedly.

Moira followed the girl, coming nearer to peer in the open door. "Milady is fine, Frances. What is this?"

Frances looked reverently at it. "A shower of water, hot and cold, Milady. I'd never even seen one before." She breathed the words, obviously enthralled with the mystery of its workings. "Can you imagine how anyone could think of such a thing?"

Moira looked at it suspiciously. "But how can it work? Is it new?"

"Oh no, your, ah, Milady. It was installed in '15, Mr. Moffat says, just before the tragedy."

"Tragedy?" Moira, disliking herself for it, tried to pump the girl for information.

"Her Ladyship's dying and all. And here," Frances opened another narrow door off the bathroom, "is the water closet. Mr. Moffatt says the Duke is the most modern master in all of England and has everything for everyone's convenience everywhere."

Moira heard the complacent assurance in Frances's words. "Obviously Mr. Moffatt would know."

"Oh yes, Your Grace, he's, I mean, Milady, he's the head steward in charge of all the Duke's estates. Would you like a bath or a water shower this evening, Milady?"

Moira turned back to look at the gilded tub. "I think a bath. I had showers enough aboard ship. Salt water ones."

"Yes, Milady." Frances curtseyed, and Moira walked back out into the dressing room, staring at herself in the pier glass that stood in a corner of the large room. The velvet robe fit well, its big sash wrapping around her narrow waist twice.

She caught a glimpse, through the looking glass, of the door across the large, Oriental-looking bedroom, the door that led to the Duke's room. Rooms, she corrected herself. She walked slowly across the room, touching the door handle to his suite.

It opened effortlessly onto a room which looked very much like his ship's cabin; all oak-panelled and dark, dull red carpet. A writing desk was piled high with papers, a brass four-poster bed dominating one whole end of the large room.

Mahogany wardrobes and tallboys were nearer where she stood, a dressing gown of emerald green brocaded silk thrown across a chair.

"Did you wish something, Your Ladyship?"

Andre stood across the room, in a doorway leading off to the other side.

"I—did they say when dinner would be up?"

"I assumed you wish to freshen first. I sent the maid—"

"Yes, that's why I asked. Thank you." She closed the door between her room and the Duke's, feeling her cheeks burn red.

She told herself she had every right, every right to go where she would, look where she wished.

But she knew she did not. And so did Andre, it seemed. Andre had been with the Duke for years. She remembered him vaguely, a shadow character in her childhood, always hovering near about.

She wondered what the Duke had told Andre about all this. How much he knew. And whether Michael had told him, or if Genevieve had.

Pride goeth before a fall. She thought of the words and of how little right to prideful feelings she had. She had been rescued by her father's friend, because he owed her father, rescued at great inconvenience, and, if truth be known, the sooner she was off his hands the better, in his opinion. Of that she was positive. A feeling of helpless anger welled up. She had not asked to be rescued. But then her father had not been forced to go with those men that night either. They had been there before the Duke arrived. She shivered at the thought of what might have happened if the Duke had not come. Had not been there.

Would her father have gotten back at all? Would days have gone by while she waited, not knowing what had happened? Would they have done anything for her, those mysterious men, or would they have vanished as carefully as they had come, leaving her to wait forever for news of her father?

There alone with Solange.

The evening dragged past, her bath taken, her dinner eaten, the house silent around her, Michael still gone. At least on board ship he had never been far away. She curled up on the huge, canopied bed, staring up at its Chinese hangings, her candle guttering down on the mahogany table beside the bed, her eyes slowly closing.

Rain began to fall again, gently. She thought of the storm and Jean-Marc caught on the sails. The Black Saint's sails.

Solange had warned of the Black Saint.

And her father had warned her to keep the letter. But he'd not said what letter, nor where it was. Why was the letter important? Why did Michael ask about correspondence, why did he search the drawers? Her thoughts trailed off in a muddle of fear and tiredness. Michael . . . she called him Michael now, out loud. For years she had called him that in her dreams . . . in her daydreams. . . .

"Moffatt!! Moffatt!!"

She woke to hear his voice booming out next door. Her candle out, her room was in darkness. Then she heard his steps on the stairs, his voice roaring out again, none too sober, from the staircase. He was outside, not next door, outside in the hall, yelling for the steward.

And then she heard his boots clomping down the hall toward her doorway. She sat up, holding her breath, willing him to open the door, to come in and—and . . . talk . . . or tuck her in as he had that night aboard ship, that one night.

"Your Grace?" Andre's voice came from outside. "Do you wish to see Moffatt? At this hour?" The question had just the right touch of incredulity softened by Andre's accent to the hint of a reproach.

Moira could hear Andre open the door to the Duke's bedroom.

"Is she—here? All right, I mean?"

"Yes, Your Grace."

And then their voices were softened. She could hear rumblings, hear them moving about in the room beyond the connecting door. But she knew he would not open the door. Would not look in this night. Andre would see to it.

Moira lay back on the large bed, wondering what Andre had to do with Genevieve. And why he didn't like her. She was sure he did not, had not, from the very first.

As Moira lay back, her eyes wide, Michael was staring at his valet in the next room. "Are you telling me to be quiet, Andre?"

"Of course not, Your Grace."

"Of course not." Michael tried to sound stern, but the wine coursing through his blood made him waver as he walked forward. His skin was the color of a gypsy's, his great dark eyes staring at the smaller man before him. He ran a hand through his thick dark hair. "I think I'd best sit down," he said as he fell back onto the large chair by the fireplace.

Andre came forward, helping him off with his boots as Michael's words slurred with the warmth of the fire and the lateness of the hour. "You're a good man, Andre. I don't know why I keep you on."

"Thank you, Your Grace," Andre replied smoothly, taking no notice of the last sentence. "Do you wish to bathe, Your Grace?"

"Don't be daft," Michael was mumbling now, tearing his shirt

70

open, staring into the shooting flames behind the grate. Sighing, Andre moved to wake the Duke from his thoughts, pulling him up and toward the bed, helping him fall forward across it.

Andre pulled the covers over his master, turning down the lamp and then leaving the muddied boots beside the door, to be polished in the morning.

The hallway was dark and silent, its broad expanse drafty in the small hours before dawn. Andre closed the door and then stared over at the door to Moira's room. After a moment he walked back toward his own bed in the room just beyond the Duke's.

Moira still stared up at the ceiling, listening to the silence for a very long time before she fell back to sleep.

And when she did it was to dream of black ships and blacker seas. And a tall, dark man astride the helm of a large black ship, unfriendly and distant, with her life in his hands.

Chapter Nine

THE RINGING OF A BELL WOKE MOIRA, AND FOR A FEW SLEEPY moments she thought she was back aboard ship. Then, sitting up, she saw the ornate room around her, the bell ringing again from outside somewhere.

She turned back the covers, pushing the Chinese silks into a pile. Slipping out of bed she padded barefoot to a window that looked down onto Berkeley Square.

An old man bundled into an ancient frock coat and a young boy dressed in rags with a cap upon his head stood at the side of the road, the bell now silent as uniformed maids clustered around them. On the old man's arm were large, flannel-swathed baskets full of muffins, the flannel thrown back to reveal his wares.

The light sound of laughter and conversation floated up toward Moira. She opened her window, leaning out to look down at the sunlit square and the hedges which lined it. On the other side of the square a creeper-covered lodge was across the way from Moira's window, plane trees rising behind wrought-iron gates, a tall Palladian house beyond the lodge. The trees rose toward the blue morning sky, framing the house.

Moira reached for the bell pull, the shock of all the recent events beginning to recede, leaving a feeling of desolation in its wake. For the first time in her life she felt the need of someone to talk to, to confide in. Someone who could reassure her. And she had none on whom she could call.

Tears sparkled in her eyes. She did not want to be alone.

A tap at the door brought her to face the day, calling out for Frances to come in as she swallowed back the tears.

"Good morning, Milady. His Grace asked that you be told he will meet you at three in the small study."

"At three?" Moira repeated faintly.

"Yes, Milady. And there are to be guests for tea."

"Guests!"

"Yes, Milady. And I am to accompany you to purchase whatever you require this morning. Mr. Moffatt has sent ahead to the shops to explain the Duke's wishes, and we are to be back in time to change by three." Frances finished her recitation a little breathless. "I don't think I've forgotten anything."

Moira took a deep breath and then nodded. "We'd best start out as soon as possible then. What time do the shops open?"

"Ten, Your, ah, Milady. Would you like your breakfast here or—?"

"I'll come down. I'll dress first and then be down."

"Yes, Milady." Frances stepped forward and Moira stared at her. Slowly she realized that the young maid expected to help her.

"I can dress myself this morning, Frances. There's so little to do."

"Your hair, Milady?" Frances looked alarmed.

Moira hesitated. "Ah, well, thank you."

When Moira came down to the great black and white tiled entrance hall, when she crossed it, led by Frances, to the Italian dining room, a servant stood by the mahogany sideboard, bowing low as he stepped forward to hold her chair.

Her heart sinking, Moira sat alone at the long burnished table, staring at the Adam fireplace to the far end of the room, taking a muffin, an egg, one sausage, from the myriad covered plates the footman proffered and then set back on the buffet. Porridge, kippers, ham, jellies, toast, rolls and biscuits, fruit and meat pies, and hot chocolate were all offered in silence and rejected with a shake of the head. Tea was poured, sugar

72

and clotted cream set before her, and then the footman stood, at attention again, beside the sideboard, awaiting her pleasure.

He stood a little behind her field of vision. She was grateful he did, grateful she did not have to see his eyes taking in her tired brown dress. What a lot it had been through these last weeks.

Weeks. A few weeks and her whole life was turned upside down. The only thing left from her childhood was the Duke himself, and he was nowhere to be seen. She found herself wishing she had asked Solange to come after all.

Solange would have been out of place here, too, miserable in the servants quarters no doubt, driving them to blasphemy with her waspish tongue. But at least she would have been someone familiar, someone to talk to, to ask questions of, to just be here, so that it wasn't so lonely.

A polite cough came from the doorway. Moira looked toward it and saw a tiny woman in a somber black uniform. "Your Ladyship, His Grace said to introduce myself. Rachel Taft, Mrs. Taft, Your Ladyship, the housekeeper."

"Oh." Moira watched the woman's impassive face. "Do we need to discuss anything?"

"I'm sure that's up to you, Your Ladyship."

"Yes. Well, I'm not used to such a—large—household. And I am to shop this morning for clothing. . . ." Moira trailed off, realizing from Mrs. Taft's uncomfortable expression that she was not used to having the family make conversation with her. "I'm sure you've handled everything, Mrs. Taft. If I need anything, I'll ring when I return."

Mrs. Taft nodded. "As you wish, Your Ladyship." And nodding again, she turned and left, leaving Moira to stare down at her plate.

After a few moments Moira laid her fork down. "Please tell Frances I am ready."

The footman bowed unseen and left, Moira standing slowly, walking toward the hall where Frances already waited, Moira's wilted pelisse in her hands.

The imperious knock at the front door startled them all. A footman moved to open it as the bell was pulled with fervor on the other side.

An elaborately dressed woman strode past the footman once the door was opened, trailing a maid and two lackeys.

"My *dear* Duchess, you must forgive this unheralded intrusion but I was afraid you would be gone before I arrived. I'm Sarah, Countess of Jersey," she added, stopping directly in front of Moira, taking in the whole of Moira's appearance in one long astute glance.

"Gone?" Moira spoke faintly, completely overwhelmed by the aura of authority that poured out of the fortyish woman now standing before her, watching her intently.

"Shopping! I can't imagine what Michael's thinking of, sending a young chit like you, forgive me, dear, out to obtain a London wardrobe on her own, without the least notion of what's what." Lady Jersey stopped for breath, looking Moira up and down. "Oh, my dear, you are from very far out in the country, are you not? Well, no matter, come along . . . come along."

Holding out her hand she placed it under Moira's elbow, walking toward the front door, the footman holding it wide as they walked through it, their maids and footmen following.

"What is your name, dear?"

"Moira Walsh—ah—Sutton."

Lady Jersey allowed herself to be escorted down the steps by her coachman. "I know the Sutton part; Moira is a very pretty name. Walsh. Walsh, not Edmund's girl?"

Moira stared at her. "Did you know my father?"

Lady Jersey grimaced. "I know the family. Is he here with you?"

Moira hesitated. "No," she said a little belatedly.

"Well, come along. I think we'll use your carriage. Harry!" She called out to her coachman who had walked on ahead. "Follow along, we'll need you for parcels."

"I'm sure I can't presume to ask you to—" Moira began but was cut short.

"You are not asking so do not bedevil yourself about it. Someone must take you in hand and help. And I am dying to hear how on earth you snared St. Maur. I daresay none of us thought there'd ever be a Lady Michael again. After Lucy."

"Lucy?" Moira's heart stopped. Lucy was the name her father had spoken, the name on the letter she was to keep.

"The first Duchess, or rather the Duke's first wife. Surely you remember? Or possibly you don't, you were too young to know her well." Lady Jersey continued as they settled into the elegant open barouche, its black lacquered sides sleek in the early morning sun. "How old are you, by the by, sixteen?"

74

"Seventeen! And a half."

"Emmm, better than I thought. Not that it signifies."

"I'll be eighteen in March," Moira spoke stiffly.

Lady Jersey smiled. "Don't rush it, my dear, you'll soon wish to forget all your birthdays, as the rest of us do, Black Saint or no."

"Black Saint! What do you mean, Black Saint?" She stared at the woman, finally finding someone to ask.

Lady Jersey regarded Moira quizzically. "Don't tell me some delicacy of principle kept your father from informing you of Michael's—reputation."

Moira looked down at the plain brown reticule that she carried, twisting its cord back and forth within her fingers. "My father died."

"Oh. Oh?" Lady Jersey assimilated this new information. "Well, well, so you are now Walsh Abbey's heir."

The barouche turned onto the broad expanse of Oxford Street, Moira's maid Frances staring at the tall glass windows of the shops behind which delicacies could be glimpsed as they passed by.

They stopped near a fruiterer's, a pyramid of pineapples, figs, grapes, and oranges behind its handsome wood-edged windows.

"Can you credit that?" Lady Jersey said, looking over. "All that fruit at this time of the year. I wonder who brought it to London. I'll warrant it's more than dear. Now, Hayward's Lace at number 73 is the best, and we must take you to the furriers, and then—" the coachman helped her down onto the inlaid flagstone pavement.

"I don't think—" Moira began as Robert helped her down behind Lady Jersey.

"Nonsense! First things first, however. Just come along, I won't have it any other way. After all, my dear," Lady Jersey indicated with a sweep of her bejeweled hand Moira's present costume. "You can't very well be seen anywhere in *that*! When did you arrive?"

Moira attempted to answer, attempted to keep up, Robert watching after them as they walked into a nearby shop, Moira swept along by the elegant London matron, from one shop to the next: linens, dressmakers, lace and shoes, hats and furs. All were paraded before Moira's eyes in a swirl of colors. Frances valiantly tried to stay close.

"Oh, that russet muslin trimmed with dark brown ribbons is

just the thing for that auburn hair of yours. Yes, the cherry red over the white with the cherry velvet bonnet, too. Don't let them tell you not to wear red, my dear. You've enough brown in your hair to absorb it and enough auburn to set it off. Let's see, the honey-colored satin with the gigot sleeves I think, and you'll need a riding outfit. The purple velvet I think for that, the braided jacket there, that's just the one. Let's see it on, please. Ah, it's close-fitting, perfect. You'll hardly need your seamstress to go over these, my dear."

Moira opened her mouth and then closed it again as Lady Jersey continued, "Over a full, long violet skirt I think. The veils should be lavender on the top hat, Mr. James. Can you make it up now?"

"Yes, Lady Jersey. Of course."

"Certainly, Lady Jersey."

They moved through velvet fur-lined boots and delicate satin shoes, Wellingtons for country-walking, tuckers of lace, tippets of lawn, gauzy silk scarfs and neck ruffs, bustles and panniers. Ladies of impeccable manner delicately showed Moira how they were to fit, which would become what, all decided upon by Lady Jersey. Sleeves short, sleeves puffed, cut on the cross, leg-of-mutton, bishops, imbecile, on and on. The sweet emerald velvet with the high frill at the neck and the low-cut satin with the stiff petticoats.

"Yes, thank you, that will be all."

"Of course, Lady Jersey, Lady St. Maur, so pleased, please come again. If there is anything, anything at all, don't hesitate."

The shopkeeper next door, in his morning suit, complete with tailcoat, nodded happily, rubbing his hands together. "Ah, you'll not be disappointed, Your Ladyship, I assure you. The fringed parasol, Arthur, with the ivory handle." He spoke to his assistant and then turned back to box up the black beaver riding hat, its high crown and tricorne brim wrapped in tissue and boxed while Frances stared at the fans, the purses, the scent containers on silken straps to hang about the waist.

Moira, on impulse, looked down at what Frances was fingering. The diamond-shaped reticule was softest blue velvet, embroidered with tiny seed pearls. "And Mr. Cross, this too, please." Lady Jersey, her maid, and Frances all looked up as Moira spoke for one of the few times in the whole shopping tour. "In a separate package, please." Moira smiled at Frances. "From me to you."

"Oh!" Frances's eyes widened with surprise and pleasure, her words tumbling out. "Oh, Milady!"

"How thoughtful," Lady Jersey said. "But Moira, my dear, a word of warning. Don't spoil them too much or they'll not respect you."

"Oh, *thank* you!" Frances grabbed the package from the shopkeeper's hands before anyone could change Moira's mind, clinging to it as they walked out into the sunlight.

"Lady Jersey, I'm extremely grateful, but I've shopped all I am able today." Moira spoke quietly and very firmly, looking up as the last of the packages was loaded by Robert and Harry into Lady Jersey's staid landaulet.

"Of course, my dear."

Lady Jersey started to walk forward, but Robert moved more quickly, opening the half-door, reaching for Moira's hand. "Your Ladyship." He handed Moira up first and then reached to help Lady Jersey, the maids following behind and settling in on the opposite seat as Robert climbed up behind the black mares.

"Through Hyde Park, please," Lady Jersey said and then to Moira, "It's such a lovely drive, it will quite revive you."

Moira, thinking of the remark about the Black Saint, nodded. "Yes, possibly."

"I'm sure I'm quite exhausted myself, it will do us a world of good."

"I can't thank you enough," Moira began, sincerely grateful for the help, if not the questions and the very obvious curiosity.

"Don't mention it." As they headed west, toward the park, Lady Jersey glanced back at her own carriage, following behind, and then turned her attention toward Moira. "But you haven't told me of how you came to marry."

"I think," Moira said quietly, "it would be best to ask—Michael—that." She hesitated, the sound of his name strange on her lips.

"Oh my, now you really shall have my curiosity aroused."

"What did you mean by the Black Saint?"

"Hmmm?"

"Earlier. You mentioned a Black Saint."

"Oh. People call him that, you know. Not to his face, of course. But gossips persist no matter what. And since the business with his brother and all, and then when Lucy died, well, the story was revived, and I'm afraid people do love to talk. It crops up now and then. Not that there's anything to it, of course, but, well, he is so above it all, and many would not mind seeing him taken down a peg or two."

"Lady Jersey," Moira said plainly, "what are you talking about? What story?"

They turned south onto Park Lane, Robert skillfully weaving through the gigs and curricles that paraded there, pulling up and stopping near a shady stand of plane trees. A high hedge surrounded a riot of flowers, stretching off into the distance before them, carefully nurtured through the early autumn frosts.

"There's a bench. Shall we stretch a moment?" Lady Jersey asked, her expression conveying she did not wish to speak more in front of the servants.

"Yes," Moira said, letting Robert help them down.

Lady Jersey turned toward her maid. "Florence, you may wait here. You, dear," she continued to Frances, "may accompany us, but we shall walk on ahead."

Moira allowed Lady Jersey once more to take charge and soon they were strolling onto the narrow path through the park. Lady Jersey began to speak after a bit. "The St. Maurs were French, originally, you know. Actually a Bourbon branch. Of course, who *wasn't* Bourbon over there before the little Corporal decimated the family. At any rate, two hundred years ago or so Michael's great, great whatever came to England with his wife and son, named Henry, by the by. Some dispute over the succession and all. At any rate, he distinguished himself admirably, built the St. Maur Castle in Cornwall, married an English girl, his first wife had died, and then they had a second son, called Michael."

They walked through the greenery, through the autumn flowers, stopping near a large stone bench and then sitting, Frances drifting off down the path ahead of them.

"Somehow," Lady Jersey continued, "the oldest son died, mysteriously, and the surviving son, Michael, was blamed. They began to call him the Black Saint, for he was St. Maur, always wore black, and then, of course, his reputation had been blackened, too. At any rate he was said to be a pirate and a very distant, disagreeable sort—"

"A pirate!" Moira interrupted. "But why would he become a pirate?"

"For sport, I suppose, my dear. Some men are like that." She saw the expression on Moira's face and misinterpreted it.

78

"There are pirates in all the best families, my dear, don't let it worry you. Back somewhere you'll always find a black sheep in the most civilized of families."

"But, what has any of this to do with Michael?"

"Well, his oldest brother, whose name was also Henry, as it happens, was killed one hundred years to the day, or very nearly, after the first Henry was. He and Michael were serving together at Trafalgar and Michael, it was said, had somehow stumbled or fallen and thrust his brother into the line of fire."

"But that was in battle! That was an accident—"

"Of course it was," Lady Jersey said. "I told you there was nothing to any of it. But when poor Lucy died so mysteriously—"

"Mysteriously?" Moira's voice was low.

Lady Jersey hesitated. "I'm sure that Michael will tell you all about that himself."

"How did it happen?"

"It seems that she—killed—herself."

"Then why bring Michael into it?"

Lady Jersey surveyed the young woman before her. "You really do not know any of this, do you? I can't imagine why someone hasn't told you, with your family so involved. At any rate, there was some question as to how Lucy could have done it, since she was—well, you'd best ask Michael about the rest of it, dear. . . . I am beginning to feel very like the gossips we were talking about earlier. But it never occurred to me that you would know none of it. After all—"

"After all what?" Moira insisted when the woman did not continue. "And what did you mean about my family being involved?" Her heart had gone cold, the fears that had crept up on her through these last days and weeks beginning to encroach on this sunny, London morning, in broad daylight now.

Lady Jersey spoke after a long pause. "Your father proved that Michael could not have been involved for he said Michael had been with him. And there was no reason to lie about his own sister's death—"

"His sister's?"

Lady Jersey did stare then, stared outright at Moira. "Well, surely you knew that Lucy Sutton was your aunt, didn't you? That Michael was your uncle by marriage?"

Moira stared at her. "No . . . no."

They sat beside each other; the older woman dressed in the height of fashion, the younger in a drab brown pelisse with the

79

battered merino dress peeking through underneath, both fallen into a silence that neither knew how to end.

A child's high-pitched laughter broke into their separate reveries, both of them glancing toward the sound. But when Moira saw the dark-haired boy racing after a small white dog she stiffened, staring intently. The boy was dressed in a schoolboy's Eton suit: black jacket, gray trousers, a crisp white shirt fast becoming dirty in his play.

"Child." Lady Jersey's voice was filled with concern. "With your father dead and now you his wife, too, Michael has control of the entire Walsh fortune. Your father knew you were to marry Michael, did he not?"

"He insisted upon it," Moira replied, watching the dog chase the sticks the boy threw.

In the quiet moments that followed, the boy and the dog ran further off. Lady Jersey hesitated over her words. "He was not still—upset—over your mother's death, was he?"

Moira turned toward her. "What do you mean? Why should he be? He never even mentioned her all these—he loved me!" She burst out suddenly, "He didn't blame me for her dying at my birth—you can't think—"

"Of course not! Dismiss the thought, child! Now that I know you knew none of it I am glad that I told you. Moira, you will hear things, but you will know that there is nothing to them. Michael's been alone for over ten years. He's made his share of enemies through his life—more than his share. And, if truth be known, many have set their caps for him and their jealous tongues may be heard too. Now they need not concern you with their innuendos. You know the whole of it."

"Do I?"

"You *must* come to St. Maur! There's no other way!" Michael's voice rang out suddenly, startling both Moira and Lady Jersey.

Moira froze, realizing he was on the other side of the tall hedges. A soft, languid voice answered him in French. "There would be much talk, how could you explain it? And what of Moira?"

"Confound Moira! You know why I've done all this! I promise you nothing has changed. Nothing. We *shall* go forward."

"She knows—" Genevieve began in English.

"She knows nothing! And it won't matter for long whether she did or did not. You must trust me on this. There was no other way!"

80

Genevieve's soft voice almost did not carry through the greenery when she spoke again: "Haven't I proven how much I trust you? I am here, am I not? Waiting."

Their voices were fading away, walking on. Moira started to stand up. Lady Jersey restrained her, her hand upon Moira's arm. "Wait!" She hissed the word. "Do you wish him to see you just now?"

Moira, blinking back tears, turned away, only to see Frances's mortified expression. The maid stood a few feet away, stock still, staring at her mistress.

Moira did stand up then. "Shall we go?" she asked, her voice a little unsteady but her bearing stiff, erect, as they walked back down the narrow, twisting path, toward the waiting carriages.

As Moira sat down in the barouche she saw Jean-Marc and the tiny white dog racing toward Michael's tall lean figure. Michael leaned down to pick the boy up as Genevieve tousled the little boy's curls.

Moira turned away, staring in the opposite direction as they pulled into the stream of horses and carriages, heading toward Berkeley Square.

"Lady Jersey, why did you come this morning?" Moira turned wide anxious eyes on the elegant woman beside her.

The older woman smiled. "You are almost as direct as your new husband, are you not?" And then at Moira's expression: "Do not credit all you hear, my child, men make many promises they have no intention of keeping." She patted Moira's arm. "I would like to tell you that I came this morning out of charitable impulses, but curiosity is more accurate probably since you insist upon being honest about it. My steward learned of your existence and the carte blanche given at the shops. I must confess I was stunned. I rather wondered as to how and to whom Michael had so mysteriously, and suddenly, been married. I was also told you were to leave immediately for the country. In the morning in fact, so I had little time to assuage my curiosity."

"Then you know more about it than I." Moira caught the look of discomfort and pity in Frances's eyes as she turned back, sitting quietly until they reached St. Maur House.

It was shortly after one when they arrived, Robert helping them down as Henry and Lady Jersey's two footmen handed packages and more packages to the St. Maur footmen.

81

"Would you care for some refreshment?" Moira asked politely.

"No thank you, dear. I will not impose further. But I am nearby, just across the square. Number 38. And you are most welcome," Lady Jersey said with deliberate emphasis. "At any time."

"Thank you."

Lady Jersey moved with her abigail toward her own carriage as the last of the packages was transferred. She turned back to look at the frail young woman standing in the dowdy brown costume in front of the huge St. Maur mansion. "Stand up to him," Lady Jersey told her, her face unsmiling. "Men must always be shown just how far they can go."

Moira did not answer. She watched Lady Jersey disappear inside her carriage and then turned to walk into the huge black and white entry hall, Frances behind her. "I shall rest until two."

"Very good, Your Ladyship," Frances said quietly.

Chapter Ten

FRANCES TAPPED ON THE DOOR PROMPTLY AT TWO. MOIRA TURNED toward her, willing Frances not to speak of what had happened earlier, her expression distant.

"Frances, you mentioned you were good with hair, did you not?"

"Yes, Milady. I've been told I am."

Moira stood up. "Very well. I think I shall wear the green velvet, and I'd like my hair more—more formal."

Frances turned away, to ready the dressing table, while Moira walked toward the bathing room and the water closet beyond.

Downstairs, Michael paced the dark-colored Turkey rug in the library, a pile of letters left unanswered on the desk in the study beyond.

A discreet knock preceded Andrew Moffatt into the library, his large plain face with its small trim mustache at once curious and subservient. "Your Grace?"

"Ah! Moffatt." Michael turned toward his steward.

"All is ready and awaiting your command. There is no other word yet."

Michael nodded. "We shall leave for St. Maur then in the morning as planned." And then, as an afterthought, "And as soon as my—my wife—has finished her London shopping."

"Yes, Your Grace."

Michael saw a slight smirk in Moffatt's eyes, in his tone. "Yes?" Michael demanded.

Moffatt, momentarily at a loss, stared at his employer. "Your Grace?"

"I assume there is some explanation for that impertinent tone."

Moffatt hesitated. "I assure you—"

Michael interrupted him. "You assure me? I assure you that I expect my wife to be treated with the respect that is due her dignity and her station. Is that clear?"

"Perfectly, Your Grace."

Michael stood stock still, in the middle of the room, watching the man who had been his chief steward for almost eleven years. Since his grandfather, old Duke Henry, had died at the ripe old age of seventy-seven. Duke by default many said—his father dead in the French Revolution helping relatives escape the bloody streets of Paris, long dead by 1815. And then his older brother Henry dead for almost ten years by then, too. Leaving only Michael to outlive the old Duke. To become Duke the same year Lucy died.

"Good." Michael roused himself, realizing Moffatt was still standing before him. "My wife deserves and shall have the respect due to her person, as well as her title."

"Of course, Your Grace." Moffatt bowed low, straightening up as a voice was heard from the doorway.

"Michael?"

Michael turned sharply, his eyes turning to hard coals as he stared at Moira. Moffatt bowed toward her and then left.

Michael still stared at the velvet-clad apparition before him.

Moira watched the man she had married, the man who all these years had been not her father's friend but his brother-in-law. "Are you well? You seem—is something wrong?"

He stiffened his body, coming to an erect stance and nodding regally. "No. I mean, of course. I'm well. I, that is, you look different."

83

"Do I?"

The vision of her aboard ship, wet, salty, unconscious of anything but rescuing the boy, superimposed itself over the velvet-clad vision before him. "The gown," he said finally. "It's too old for you." She was not the girl he knew. "And what did you do to your hair?"

Her hand rose to touch the curls piled high upon her head. "I thought—" She stopped, her hand falling back to her side. "You said you wished to speak at three," she added finally.

"Yes." He motioned toward an ornate leather chair. "I hope you've been comfortable."

She sat down, looking up at him intently.

"Did you find everything you needed?"

"More," she replied. "Even a shower of water."

He smiled. "Did you try it?"

"Not yet." She found herself smiling too, glad to see his eyes warm.

"Believe me, you will become addicted to it."

Her smile faded away. "Will I be here long enough to become addicted to—anything?" When he didn't reply she began again. "Did you find out from the solicitors? Or have you had time to see them?"

"Yes, I have." He sat down across from her. "First, I contacted your father's solicitors. They have some items of a personal nature that were to be held in trust for you. They are being forwarded to St. Maur."

"Did they say what they were?" she asked faintly, thinking of Lucy's letter.

"No." He watched her closely. "Is it important?"

"No."

"They are also ascertaining, as are my own solicitors, what can be done to break the marriage provision of your grandfather's will. It states that you must be over eighteen or be married to inherit, as you know. The solicitors assure me that this means that you must remain married until you are eighteen, according to the exact wording. After that there are no restrictions, no provisions. And," he hesitated, "I fear I must also inform you of what they have told me: namely, that there is little likelihood of changing the provision."

"Eighteen . . . that would only have been until March . . . five months. . . ." She looked up into his eyes. "Such a little time when you think of it."

84

"And rather longer in a situation such as this." His tone was formal, cold.

"Yes." She looked down then. "You have been inconvenienced terribly by this, I realize that . . . I am sure it seems dreadfully long to you. Do you plan to—continue—like this, until then? If need be?" she added quickly.

His reply was stiff: "I do not go back on my word."

"No." She looked down. "Of course not. Then I am to be your—wife—for five months."

"You still have not asked about your estate."

She looked over at him, a thousand questions she dared not ask standing between them. She thought of the ease of their conversations before this; suddenly she was unsure of how to even broach her thoughts to him, of how he would react. "Should I?" she asked finally, her thoughts full of Genevieve's voice and Michael's words: confound Moira!

He answered indirectly. "It is extensive. You are an exceedingly wealthy young woman. The sum total of the estate goes to you now, since you are, technically at least, married. There are no other surviving relatives on your father's side. There was only your father and—his sister."

"Aunt Lucy." She watched him.

"Yes. Lucy." He said it as if she of course already knew. And as if he did not want to even mention her name.

"What was her inheritance?" Moira asked, her heart in her mouth.

He stared at her. "Why? It's immaterial in any event. It reverted to your father, in trust for you."

"But she had children—"

"Yes." The word was clipped. "Your father and I, as co-executors, agreed that it should revert to you. Lucy's children did not need it. They have the St. Maur money."

Moira stared at him. Lucy's children. He distanced himself from them as if they were someone else's, not his own flesh and blood. Flesh and blood. She remembered asking about Jean-Marc and being told the truth.

"What is it?" he was asking her.

"I—nothing. Lady Jersey called this morning."

"Damn and blast!!" He sat straighter, watching Moira intently. "Why? When?"

"As I was leaving for the shops. She said she would accompany and advise me on what to buy."

85

"*And!?*"

"And what?"

"Did she? Did you let her!?"

"I couldn't very well not."

"What did you tell her?" His voice was cold now.

"I beg your pardon?"

"What—did—you—tell—her?"

"Nothing. Nothing at all." She came close to saying that he himself had told her more than he would have wished.

"What then, pray tell, did you talk about?" His tone was sardonic now, disbelieving.

"There are other subjects," Moira said quietly, earning a flash of amusement within his eyes. "We talked of clothes mainly. And—history." She faltered and then resolutely went on. "Our family history. She wanted to know what my father thought of our marriage."

"And you said?" He was standing now, towering over her, his voice deceptively soft.

"I said he wished it. She said she knew him and my—aunt—your wife, very well. Knew all my family."

"She did." His whole demeanor was distracted. "And did you speak of the circumstances?"

"What circumstances?"

"Your father's death, of course. What else?"

"No, other than to tell her that he had died, we did not speak of him. But she was curious as to why you decided so suddenly to marry your niece."

"Niece by marriage. What did you reply?"

"I told her if she wished to know that she would do better to ask you herself."

He laughed then, the sound surprising Moira. "She'd not dare. Not even the powerful Lady Jersey." He hesitated. "And what did you say of, of the boy. And Genevieve?"

She looked up at him steadily. "I did not mention them." She replied truthfully, then, after only a brief hesitation, "We drove home through Hyde Park."

His eyes narrowed as he watched her. "Yes?"

She looked away. "It was quite nice today. Warm."

His lips pursed. He stood over her still and then, deliberately, he relaxed his stance, turning toward the marble fireplace. "Yes. Well, I suppose no harm's done. And I should have known that you yourself would not have chosen what you are wearing."

The distant sound of bells over the massive front door came through the walls, their chimes deep and resonant.

Michael glanced at an ornate clock that stood near the door to the Adam sitting room.

"I'm afraid you'll have to bear with a visit from my sister Eunice and her husband. I could not seem to dissuade her when she sent her footman over to announce it this morning." His brow furrowed into impatient lines. "Let me handle her curiosity. I know how to get around her, generally." He stopped. "You do pour, don't you? If not, she can."

Moira looked at him sharply. "I am capable of pouring tea, Michael."

He surveyed her for an instant, humor glinting and quickly gone. "That's the first time you've said my name without making it sound like medicine that must be swallowed. Come." He strolled toward the doorway and stood aside for her to pass, walking beside her into the green damask of the sitting room.

"My dear Eunice." Michael sauntered toward his sister, his arm now around Moira's waist. Eunice glanced from Michael's easy smile to the surprised expression on Moira's face. "Hallo, Pomfret," Michael continued. "Sweetheart, this is my insatiably curious sister and her long-suffering husband, Pomfret. And this is Moira."

"Oh, I say!" Pomfret grinned at Moira as her head spun with the sound of the word "sweetheart." "Pleased I'm sure," he said.

"We've met." Eunice's tone was not unpleasant, but she knew her brother and human nature well enough to know something was not as it seemed. "The last time I saw you, my dear Moira, you were being chased around the grounds by Michael's son Tristan and one of the spaniels, as I recall."

Moira blushed to the roots of her hair, and Michael laughed. "I remember that. Eunice, just fancy, that was back when you were still trying to get Moira's father to marry you."

"Oh, I say." Pomfret stood up for his wife. "Don't go bamming the girl now." He peered kindly at Moira over his pince-nez glasses. "Can't listen to these two, you know. Always having at one another."

"Me and Edmund, what a mistake that would have been!" Eunice sat down, primping her beribboned skirt into more graceful folds as two footmen and the butler brought a great silver tea service in. "Can you imagine me rusticating all these years with Edmund in that godforsaken barrenness they call Brittany? And now I would have become my own brother's mother-in-law!"

"Gad!" Pomfret said into the silence.

"No, I can't," Michael added truthfully, his arm still around Moira. "Fortunately it would not have arisen. You would have been, at most, a step-mother-in-law, Eunice, my pet."

"Don't you 'my pet' me. Do you pour, dear?" Eunice asked, turning toward Moira.

"Yes." Moira moved away from Michael, feeling his eyes as she sat down at the tea service. She picked up a fragile gold-encrusted porcelain cup and saucer.

"Ah, Grannie's silver service." Eunice watched Moira for a moment as she carefully poured and then looked up at Michael. "I've always envied you that, you beast, and you know it."

"Would you like it? It's yours."

Eunice stared at him. "Are you serious?" A footman handed her a plate of gingerbread cakes. "I must say, Michael, marriage is agreeing with you if it makes you so generous."

"Cream?" Moira asked.

"Yes, I am serious," Michael said. "And yes, she loads it with mounds of cream and sugar, Moira, can't you tell?"

"Thank you," Eunice said as the footman handed her the cup, "Michael, for reminding me that you haven't changed all *that* much."

Pomfret sat down on a needleworked stool near his wife as Michael lowered himself into the chair beside Moira's.

"Pomfret?" Moira smiled at him.

"Just a touch, thanks awfully, and no sugar."

Moira poured, spooned, and handed the cup to the nearest footman.

"And I, my dear," Michael said casually, "will as usual have none. Wilkins," he glanced up at the butler, "rouse me up some brandy, will you?"

Wilkins bowed and motioned to the footmen, ushering them out. Michael yawned prodigiously into the sudden silence.

"Don't blame the company, we haven't gotten a lot of sleep," Michael said blandly.

Moira looked down at her own teacup.

"You are to be congratulated, Moira," Eunice said. "Half of London will be agog over your capturing this Corinthian brother of mine—"

"Only half?" Moira asked quietly, earning a true laugh from

Michael and then a brief smile from Eunice as Pomfret roared into peals of laughter beside his wife.

"Oh, I say, Michael, you've done yourself proud! Don't make a cake of yourself, dear," Pomfret added to his wife. "Take your claws in and admit you've been enacting a Cheltenham tragedy over nothing."

Eunice started to retort and then, as Wilkins walked back in with the brandy, she slowly smiled, really smiled. "As usual, Pomfret's right."

"Oh my," Michael said.

Eunice still smiled at Moira. "Don't mind me. Or your husband. The whole family has atrocious manners. Comes of having the blood of all the Howards and the Bourbons besides."

Moira relaxed at the sudden warmth in the older woman's eyes. "Is that true?"

"Which, the pedigree or the bad manners? In any event, both are true, as one and all will tell you. Surely you must remember that little beast Tristan and—"

"Eunice!" Michael's voice snapped and his sister backed off, sipping quietly at her tea.

"Well," Pomfret said into the silence, "how soon do you leave for the country, Michael?"

"Almost the moment you're out the door."

"Michael, be reasonable!" Eunice interjected. "It's almost winter! Surely you're not planning on driving all that distance now, in dreadful weather. And besides the season is in full swing!"

"And that, my dear sister, is precisely why we are leaving. I have had enough London seasons to last a lifetime, I assure you."

Eunice glanced shrewdly at Moira. "And what of your new wife's wishes?"

Moira spoke before Michael could reply. "I wish what Michael wishes. More tea, Eunice?"

Michael gazed at Moira, his expression softening.

"My, my, what a wicked spell he has put you under," Eunice replied. "No, thank you, I've had enough tea. And I can see he's already chafing at the length of our sociability. Fifteen minutes is all he can take of polite society, and then his foot begins to tap as you see him doing now."

Moira glanced at Michael's foot, which he now held still. "I'll watch for that. Thank you, Eunice."

Eunice stood up as Michael toasted her with his glass. He took a long swallow before standing too. Pomfret put out his hands to Moira, and she took them.

"Congratulations, Lady Michael." Pomfret grinned. "I hope you'll be exceedingly happy."

"And what of me?" Michael asked as he escorted them out, his arm around Moira again as they walked toward the great hall.

"You," Pomfret added, "obviously will be happy, with such a wife. Who wouldn't be?"

"Oh, Pommy!" Eunice touched his bearded cheek. "You should have been a poet." Eunice stopped and turned, reaching to hug Moira as Michael released her. "I hope you're happy. And that you always will be." She straightened up, turning her cheek so that Michael could lean down to kiss it. "And you too, my reckless brother, you too," Eunice added, earning his grin.

A footman opened the door to their waiting carriage. Eunice turned around, staring at her brother intently. "We've not even left yet and you've already given over holding your bride?"

Michael's arm went back around Moira's waist. "I did not realize you were such a suspicious wench, Eunice. When we think about it we do at least attempt propriety. However, if you're so skeptical you're welcome to stay the night."

"Michael!" Moira felt the sudden tension in his muscles. He pulled her so close that she was leaning in against him.

"Thank you, no," Eunice said. "It's not my business in any event." And so saying she stepped up into her carriage. Pomfret turned to wave back at them as he stepped inside and sat down.

Moira waved as the carriage moved slowly down the drive toward the wrought-iron gates.

As it pulled through the gates Eunice was turning back to wave. Michael leaned forward, covering Moira's lips with his own.

Shock stiffened her spine as their lips met. And then, when he did not let go she relaxed against him, a sudden warmth filling her. His touch became urgent, searching her lips, making her respond, bringing feelings welling up that she had never experienced before. Her arms found his neck, her body melting against his, willing him never to stop.

He straightened then, abruptly. She felt as if he had wrenched himself away from her. She stared up at the dark eyes which were searching her face as if he'd never seen it before. Then he turned away.

"It's quite cool, this evening," he said as they walked inside.

The doorman studiously avoided their eyes as he closed the great oak door behind them.

"My brandy," Michael said finally. "Would you care for some sherry, or—"

"Yes." The word was more breath than speech. "Something. Please."

She walked beside him through the huge salon, its high ceiling decorated with panels of flowers surrounded by gold leaf. They crossed into a small study to the rear of the house, its walls lined with India paper, its chairs large and comfortable.

A fire had been laid in the grate, the wooden mantelpiece above lined with bronzes. The room seemed cozy and warm to Moira. Michael shut the door and then walked to a small intricately carved cherrywood cabinet, reaching for crystal decanters of brandy and sherry.

"There are glasses, there, on the top shelf," he said as he took the decanters to a round table near the fireplace.

Moira looked for and found two thin-stemmed glasses of clear ruby glass, bringing them to him at the table, watching him for some sign of what he was thinking.

He motioned toward one of the chairs drawn up before the fire, and she came round to sit down slowly, her eyes on his hands as he filled the goblets.

"You must think me demented," he said, handing her a glass.

"I just don't understand," she said in a tremulous voice. "I don't understand any of this."

"I know." Michael stoppered the brandy decanter and sat down in the chair opposite the small round table between them. "My sister, bless her, is the worst gossip on two legs. If she has the slightest inkling of anything being amiss all within earshot will know it soon enough." He paused. "I did not want her to spread tales of anything other than a May–December romance." He observed Moira carefully. "For both our sakes, that's the safest explanation."

"I see," Moira replied.

"And—being that all will be talking of us and she will be regaling them with all she can think of, I wanted to give her something to say that would—lend credence—to the story."

"And so you kissed me." Moira began to blush fiercely,

looking into the fire now, watching the flames shoot upward as a log crackled and fell.

"And so I went through the motions of holding you and kissing you."

"Went through the motions!" She stared at him. He had felt something. If only for a moment she knew he had felt what she did.

His voice was cool and very proper. "I beg your pardon for my forwardness. It was not part of our agreement, and it will not happen again." She was silent. He watched her stare into the fire. "And I must thank you for your behavior all afternoon. You played your part well." He watched her closely. "In the coming years you will do very well indeed in London."

She did look over at him then. "That is not a compliment, coming from you, is it?"

"You think not?" His brow rose, a sardonic smile catching at the lips she now stared at.

"No. Not from your lips."

His gaze became intent. "From my lips?" he repeated softly.

She stared into an abyss. "Your lips." Her voice was soft, throaty.

Still he stared. "Don't attempt to know me too well, Moira. You will not like what you find."

"What is it?" she asked, in a tremulous voice. "What is it, that's so wrong?"

"Wrong?" He repeated the word, his eyes turning away to find the decanter and refill his glass. "Nothing is wrong." He glanced back at her and then put his feet up on a small stool, staring into the flames. "You have not touched your sherry."

"I—" She faltered, looking down at the glass. "I'm no longer thirsty."

"Drink up. Sherry's not for thirst. It's for courage."

She gazed at his profile as he stared into the fire.

"We leave," he said, "at first light."

"So soon . . ." When he did not reply she continued: "Is it a long trip?"

"A very long trip."

She sipped at her sherry, sitting across from the elegant man in the fashionable pale yellow breeches, his black topboots exquisitely polished, his black jacket braided and frogged. A pale yellow cravat topped his cream-colored shirt. And above it all the austere planes of his handsome face, his dark eyes large in the glow from the fire. A very long trip. . . . he could not be far away from her in a coach. . . . he could not disappear as he had here in London . . . it would be as it was aboard ship. Except it would be only the two of them. No Genevieve. The thought made her smile to herself.

A colza oil lamp burned on the table between them, burnishing the dark hair that lay tousled about his head as if he had repeatedly shoved his fingers through it.

Moira sat as quietly as he, staring at the fire as the minutes ticked by. The touch of his lips, the sound of the word "sweetheart" on his lips . . . the look in his eyes when he still held her for that one brief moment filled her with a disquiet she could not appease. She looked down at her hands feeling again the melting ache his lips brought to her heart.

She looked up to find him staring at her.

Chapter Eleven

THE WEATHER HAD TURNED DAMP AND COLD, THE COACH SWAYING in the high wind along the open spaces as the driver, muffled in a great dark coat and cloak whipped the horses into a faster pace, trying to make Salisbury before nightfall.

The Duke of St. Maur sat silent, Andre beside him, Moira and Frances across from them on the damp leather seats. Frances reached beneath her navy cloak now and again to finger the reticule Moira had bought her. And then her eyes would surreptitiously stare at the Duke. A sidelong glance. Until Andre would turn in his seat, whereupon Frances would drop her eyes to the floorboards, or look out the small window at the gray, dismal scene beyond.

A second coach, piled high with luggage, followed them through the chill day, racing to reach the Stag and Hound before the storm that was threatening could break across the nearby hills.

It was long past dark when the horses hoofs clattered sharply onto the stones of the inn yard, warm yellow candlelight escaping from between cracks in the night-shuttered windows.

The innkeeper threw open his doors, coming forward to greet them as they alighted from the carriage. They walked into the small white-washed inn, brass and copperware gleaming in the front rooms they passed through.

Bowing low, calling out to his wife and sons, the innkeeper motioned to his sons to help the coachmen as he ushered the Duke and Duchess in, past the travelers seated at the big oak tables and on up the narrow stairwell to the rooms reserved for them.

"I'm sure, Your Grace, Your Ladyship, you'll find we do all we can here, small though we are." He hurriedly climbed ahead of them, his wife following behind Moira.

The innkeeper opened the door to the front room at the top of the narrow, winding stairwell. "The best we've got—and the biggest. Will you be wanting supper? A fine mutton the wife made tonight and squab pie fresh today. Saffron cakes, anything you like."

"Mulled wine to begin with," Michael said, "we're frozen through. And chicken if you have it. Cold will do." He glanced at Moira. "Will that serve?"

"Yes," she replied.

"Fine, fine." The rotund, red-faced innkeeper bowed low again, beaming. He clasped his hands in front of him when he straightened:

"And now, my rooms?" the Duke said.

"Your—ah—" The innkeeper went blank.

Michael's expression did not change but Moira could see the line of his jaw tighten.

"Why, ah, Your Grace, the man did not say, it was—"

"Yes," Michael interrupted impatiently. "Are there other accommodations?"

"Well, ah, no, Your Grace. That is, with your servants in the last rooms we had, and this reserved for you and your, Her Ladyship—"

Michael nodded. "It's unimportant. Please see to the food for the Duchess and myself."

The little man bowed, his eyes taking in the young wife, the virile-looking Duke, his whole posture uncomprehending. As the man left Michael glanced over at the large bed, the couch by the fireplace, the table with four chairs.

"I will sleep perfectly well on the couch," Moira said into the silence.

"Out of the question," he replied.

She watched him as she took off her bonnet and gloves, her hands shaking. She laid her things on a bureau top and then unbuttoned her cloak and pelisse, the wine-colored traveling dress purplish in the candlelight. Michael stood where he had, surveying the plank floor, his thoughts very far away.

Moira turned away to warm her hands at the fire, and when she turned back he was gone, the door to the stairwell closing behind him.

She looked over toward the four-poster bed, a sound at the door turning her swiftly back toward it. "Oh, Michael, I—"

Frances stood in the doorway, her face impassive.

"His Grace said you'd be needing me to help you change for the night, Your Ladyship."

"Thank you." Moira saw the pity in the girl's eyes and for one brief instant hated her for it. Then Moira sighed and turned away, unbuttoning her cuffs.

The food was brought by the innkeeper's wife a little later, explaining that His Grace had decided to sup downstairs with the menfolk. That Her Ladyship was to go ahead and not wait up for him.

Moira thanked the woman, took a bite of the chicken, and then sat down in a great, deep chair by the fire, curling her legs up beneath her and laying her head on its wide arm, staring at the fire until she fell asleep.

Dreams engulfed her, the fire burning down inside the grate, the room quiet as outside the sounds of the inn filtered through the thick walls and doors.

A sudden chill swept through the room, opening her eyes. She focused drowsily on the fire's flames as they licked up toward the chimney still and then saw movement in the corner of her eye. When she moved her head something dark loomed in the doorway, catching her breath in her throat. The door to the hall was open, the chill coming from the open doorway. And in it a figure in a black cape loomed, its face in shadows. It was as tall as Michael. "Michael?" She found her voice and whispered, startling the figure. It moved back, closing the door as she sat up, staring at it. "Michael. . . ." she spoke his name softly. But no one answered.

In the morning Frances came to help her dress, pretending not to notice the unslept-in bed, the tired look about Moira's eyes.

"Frances?"

"Yes, Milady?"

"Do you have any knowledge of—of marital matters?"

Frances turned curious eyes toward her young mistress. "I beg your pardon? I mean—which—marital matters are you speaking of, Milady?"

Moira found it hard to speak. "The marital—duties—obligations—that make annulment out of the question."

"Annulment!" Frances stared now. "Milady!"

"Don't carry on so!" Irritation mixed with her worry now. "Do you or don't you?"

"Well, well, yes. I mean, of course."

"Why, of course?"

"I grew up in a large family, Milady. In the country." She stopped.

"Well?"

"Well, Milady?"

"Well, what *are* they?" Moira's impatience was obvious.

Frances stared at her mistress. "But you are *married*, Milady. You must know."

"Frances, we are not discussing what I know or do not know. We are discussing what *you* know."

"Well, it's, it's what happens at night, Milady, that makes annulment out of the question."

Moira looked expectantly at Frances. "Yes?"

Frances blushed and stuttered. "In—in bed, Your Ladyship."

Moira frowned then. "Yes?"

"Milady—"

"Go on, go on—"

"It's the same as with the animals, Milady—on a farm."

"In bed?"

Frances stopped. "No. I mean, you must know—I mean, did you not have, I mean, farm animals at least?"

"Frances what are you talking on about? First you speak of bed and now of farm animals!" Moira sat down, staring at the girl. "For pity's sake sit down and tell me what you're saying."

Slowly Frances did as she was bid, staring at Moira now, openly. "You haven't—" She stopped. "I mean, he hasn't—" She didn't know how to go on. "Surely, I mean, the Duke—"

"You expect me to ask my husband?"

"No," Frances spoke hastily. "No, not ask, but—but—don't you *know?*" At Moira's expression she rushed on. "What you do when you sleep together."

Moira hesitated. "Frances I need someone I can talk to who won't repeat what I say. Who doesn't gossip. Someone I can trust." She searched the maid's eyes. "Could that be you?"

96

"Oh, Milady," Frances began, "I'd never repeat one single word! I mean, Milady, there is no one here that I care one whit about except you. You've befriended me and—" Frances stopped, then. "I'd die before I said one word that could harm you."

Quick tears formed in Moira's eyes. She reached out to touch the girl's arm. "You see I have no one else to ask. And we have not—yet—slept together."

"Yes, Milady." Frances bit back her curiosity and slowly began. "Your mother never—"

"My mother died just after I was born. I lived alone with my father, with one old housekeeper who said nothing to me about marriage at all. My father and the Duke were the only ones I could ever really talk to."

"Do you—have you ever seen a boy baby?"

"Yes."

"Unclothed?"

"Yes. In the village."

"Well," Frances swallowed, "well, little boys are built differently than—than we are."

Moira blushed. "Yes."

"Well, that's for a reason." When Moira didn't speak Frances went slowly on. "Do you know how babies are born?"

"I—" Moira swallowed, still blushing. "I know how kittens are born."

"We are born in the same way," Frances said firmly.

"You mean—" Moira stopped. "You're sure?"

"Yes."

"I see. Go on."

"Your—your monthly—"

"Yes—be honest with me. Totally honest."

"Well, Milady, you see, that is, I mean the kittens and the—rest—well, there is something men do—to you—there—that, that brings the babies."

"There?" Moira's voice was faint. "But—how?"

"Oh dear." Frances was balling her hands up in her lap. "I don't know how to tell you."

"Just say it."

"Boys are built differently."

"Frances, you said that. I know."

"That's why they can't have the babies."

"Yes." Moira was a little impatient.

"Well, that—that difference, as they grow, it—grows." Moira

97

waited none too patiently. "And when they get to be men they have these powerful urges to *do* things, to a woman, with it. To make love."

"But how—" She stopped. "I mean—"

"They kiss you and things and then they put that—inside." Frances was now blushing.

"But—" Moira stared at Frances's down-turned head. "You mean—*there*? That's what love-making is?"

"Yes."

Shock filled Moira's eyes. She sat back in her chair, staring at Frances. It all sounded incredible. And yet, and yet, babies came from there. "Doesn't it—hurt?" Moira asked after a while.

"They say it—depends."

"Upon?"

Frances swallowed. "If he's big and she's smaller, well—"

Moira stared at the young maid seated across from her. She saw in her mind's eye the husband that towered over her, the husband she had never seen undressed. She blushed. "Thank you Frances, you've given me much to think about."

Frances almost sprang to her feet, glad to be released from the conversation. "Yes, Milady—can we get ready for breakfast now?"

"Yes," Moira answered absently. Her mind began to fill with the thought of his body . . . of his body standing before her. Naked. She shivered.

"Are you well, Milady?"

"What? Yes. It is cold in here, that's all. When will His Gr—my husband—be ready to leave?" She looked over at the bed then. "Where did he spend the night?" she asked.

Frances spoke slowly. "He left, Milady." Frances's lips were formed into a thin, disapproving line now.

Moira's breath stopped for a moment. "I don't understand."

"Neither do I, Your Ladyship." Frances heard her own words and then rushed on. "Master Andre is to speak to you when you're ready—"

"Yes, now. Please."

Frances left to find Andre, glad to be outside the room.

Andre knocked, opening the door as Moira called out for him to enter. "Your ladyship?"

"I understand my—husband—has been called away."

His face was expressionless. "Yes, Your Ladyship, some lands I believe, that he wished to see." Andre's voice was bland. "He did not want to disturb your rest."

98

Moira watched Andre glance toward the unused bed and then return to her face.

"And we await his return?"

"No, Your Ladyship, we travel on. As soon as you are ready."

She digested his words, trying to appear calm. "We will leave as soon as I've eaten then."

"Yes, Your Ladyship."

"Please send Frances to me and tell her I wish to wash and change."

"Yes, Your Ladyship." He bowed and left. When the door was firmly closed she let her shoulders slump forward.

Gone. She had known it, had felt the emptiness of the air around her.

Thin, wintry sunlight greeted the two coaches as they travelled on, the thin ribbon of road stretching through the brown, sodden moors. The rain had stopped, leaving the roads muddy, the mud spattering up from the wheels to coat the coach windows, obscuring the view of the black heather and the stunted broom. Of the high tors shining yellow in the morning light, their peaks crowned with granite. Great slabs of stone threw purple-stained shadows among the golden brown and gray and black.

Little white cottages nestled in rolling green hills were left far behind, the land becoming higher and harsher the farther they travelled.

Moira stared out the mud-blotched window. Misty high winds swept over the bogs and down the granite outcroppings, whistling past the moving carriages, filling her with a melancholy feeling of utter sadness. One could go mad up here on the heights, with nothing to shield you from raw, stark nature. No prettiness, no places to hide.

The sharp outlines and dark colors of a prehistoric world still lived here, man's puny efforts far away and meaningless. There was a grandeur to the tors, a grand sweep to the moors that smaller, neater, prettier things did not have.

She shivered, drawing her new fur-lined cloak more tightly around her. This place was like Michael. Untamed, wild and dangerous, the veneer of civilization as thin, as narrow as the tracks the horses now coursed down, the carriage wheels bumping over the stones and mud.

Looking out the window, her eyes seeing all before her and

nothing at all, she thought for the first time that she understood him. At least part of him. The black brow and thick dark hair, the skin the color of a gypsy's, the great, dark eyes, they belonged here. They fit this country as much as they were out of place and exotic in London. His movements turning from exquisitely precise and graceful to large and sudden were explainable here. The veneer stripped off, the reality showing through.

She looked down on the Torridge River as they crossed its stone bridge, its torrents swift as they tumbled across the plains toward distant valleys and the sea.

Bleak. She glanced at Andre snoozing across from her. The bleak look that filled Michael's eyes when his guard was down was part and parcel of this, a way of looking at life with no illusions, no expectations except harsh, uncomfortable ones. She looked down at her own hands, in her lap, clasped so tightly together her knuckles were whitened with the effort. Godless. It was that too, here, high and proud and harsh and godless. A place to go mad. A place where one could go mad and none would know.

"Your Ladyship, are you well?"

Moira looked over into Frances's concerned eyes. "Yes," she said. "Just a little tired of sitting."

"Tis no wonder, three days in a coach." Frances eyed the sleeping Andre distrustfully. "With naught but a few hours in strange beds in between."

"Frances, have you ever been to St. Maur?"

"No, Milady."

Moira looked back out. "I was born here. Where Devon and Cornwall meet. And lived near St. Maur when I was a child. But," she glanced out the window again, mesmerized by the mud-spattered desolate stretches outside, "I don't remember this. It's green in St. Maur, even in winter. Or it was. And," she stopped, "of course we travelled by sea. I've never been up here in the high moors. It's rather frightening, isn't it?"

"It's downright dangerous," Frances said flatly. "Robbers and brigands and what not. Mrs. Taft told me we'd be lucky to finish the journey in one piece, at this time of year, and that's a fact!"

The horses slowed, the first straggling cottages of the next village coming into view, granite and cob and thatched roofs with a small church in their midst, its Norman tower master of all

100

it surveyed. It sat on a hillock rising above the winding village street.

"We'll be on to Clovelly, soon enough," Andre said. He was looking out the opposite window now, stifling a yawn between his words. "And to St. Maur in the morning."

Moira almost asked about the Duke but bit off the words before they formed, unwilling to admit to either of them that Andre might know more about the Duke's intentions than did his wife.

Wife. She tasted the word, feeling its strangeness. His wife. Michael's wife. The Duke of St. Maur's wife. Her eyes misted. She looked outside, away from the others. She was none of it. She was not a wife; she was a pretense. A sham.

And they knew it.

Chapter Twelve

THEY PULLED INTO THE TINY CLOVELLY INN YARD JUST AT SUNSET. Moira stepped out and looked around her at the thickly wooded slopes that pressed close against the steep village street.

Down toward the bay and the Bristol Channel beyond, the village fell off sharply, the street stepped so that all would not go hurtling down into the waters.

Andre was at her elbow glancing down toward the bay and then at her, his eyes bright and cold. "Were you looking for something, Your Ladyship?"

"I remember Clovelly, Andre. I have been here before. But it seems so much—quieter—than I remember."

"The herring's gone. Most of the fishermen have moved away. There's only the one inn here now, and like as not it'd close too if old Hawkins had anywhere else to go."

Moira studied him for a moment. "The moors change people, don't they?"

"Your Ladyship?"

"You've lost your French accent, Andre. You sound positively English."

101

He stared at her for a moment and then, his eyes averted, he motioned toward the inn's open doorway. "I wouldn't know about that, Your Ladyship." His voice was cold. "Would you care to see your rooms?"

She followed him inside, holding her skirts up from the splashes of mud in the carriage tracks as they crossed the cobblestones and entered the creeper-covered building, the vines shading from russet to dark red to near purple against the white-washed building in the winter sunset.

The low-ceilinged front room was spanned by massive black oak beams, the walls four feet thick. A few villagers, fishermen mostly, sat at a huge refectory table, sipping beer and talking excitedly.

The innkeeper came toward them, bowing low. He showed the way up to the bedrooms, passing horse pistols and brandy kegs, passing powder flasks, daggers, and short-swords, which lined the walls up the staircase.

"Are you expecting another civil war?" Moira asked, almost smiling as the innkeeper turned toward her.

"Your Ladyship?" The innkeeper opened the door to a large, dark bedroom that looked out over a fine old cedar tree and the lych-gate that led to the churchyard next door.

"All the weaponry."

"Oh." He smiled at her, his bushy brows beetling together with the effort. "Pirates, Your Ladyship, we're always prepared."

Frances's sudden intake of breath behind her reminded Moira of the tales the maid had been filled with in London.

"Surely not pirates in these modern days, sir."

His head bobbing up and down, he spoke in an excited voice. "In these very days, Your Ladyship! The black ship was spotted not twelve hours ago!"

Moira stared at the man, her good humor plunging away. "Black ship?"

Andre was coming up the steps, carrying her small portmanteau. Her eyes followed his movement, up the stairs, toward them, as the innkeeper continued. "No need to concern yourself, Your Ladyship. You're well protected here. And there's nothing as pirates would want in Clovelly in these dark days. But it's true that they're out there."

Andre was walking into the room, lugging the case and setting it down carefully. Slowly he opened it, still listening.

"Yes, indeed," the innkeeper went on, "mind you, up in Lunnon there's none who'd know I'm sure. Since they don't as even know we exist out here. But you ask at St. Maur, and they'll all tell you of the plague we've had of pirating."

"Pirates?" Andre straightened up, his eyes devoid of expression.

"Aye, the black ship." The innkeeper's tone was hushed with the words.

"Black ship?" Andre repeated politely, his eyes glancing at Moira's as the innkeeper stood his ground.

"Black ship, black sails, black devils that man it—"

"What does it do? This—black ship?" Moira's gaze met Andre's as she spoke.

"Wicked things you'd best not be knowing about, Your Ladyship, and that's a fact. But neither women nor gold is safe on this coast when the black ship's about. Nor aught else they be wanting."

"Who are they?" Moira asked, Andre turning back to pull out her things.

"That's mine to do!" Frances whispered to him, upset, as the innkeeper answered Moira.

"Well, some say as how they're French and some say as how they're Irish, but all say they're black and bad and—and some say—" his voice lowered to a hushed reverence, "some say that even their skins be black and they be Barbary pirate's ghosts, still searching for their lost treasures as what our own old pirate lads had took from 'em in the olden days."

Moira smiled at the innkeeper. "Black-skinned men should be easy to find on the coast of Cornwall."

"Aye, ye'd think it. But have ye seen our own, up from the mines? As black as the ace of spades theeselves."

"Do you think it possible we might eat soon?" Moira interrupted the man, who would gladly have spent hours ruminating on the plight of seasiders and poor folk. Andre stood silently by as Frances unpacked the items Moira would need for the night.

"Of course, Your Ladyship, I'll be sending up right away. And for your people here?"

Moira glanced at Andre who spoke to the innkeeper. "I'll eat below, where I can hear the news."

"Ah, good!" The innkeeper bowed low.

Frances looked over at Moira.

"You don't mind," Moira asked her, "keeping me company, do you?"

"Of course not, Your Ladyship!" Frances looked scandalized at the thought.

"If you do not need me further . . ." Andre was edging toward the door.

"No," Moira said, stopping Andre in his tracks. He looked over at her, his eyes wary. "I don't. But best beware of meeting pirates. Or a black ship."

He stared at her, and then, nodding, he left the room. Frances watched him leave. "Now he is a queer one, that one is," Frances said.

Moira smiled to herself, remembering Frances's awe of Andre a week ago when she first met him. Familiarity did breed, if not contempt, at least questions. She sat down, staring out the tiny window at the patch of sea beyond the church.

"And here I've been all the time worrying about highwaymen," Frances continued, "with pirates about!"

A knock at the door brought a serving girl in, the tray she carried heavy with a great pot of tea, with saffron buns and splits, strawberry jam and clotted cream in heavy blue bowls beside the tea pot.

Frances took the tray, nodding as the girl curtsied and left. Setting the tray down on a table near the window, Frances looked back over at Moira. "Tea, Milady?"

"Emmm." Moira's thoughts were far away. "Frances, see if there's any brandy about."

Frances stopped still, her hands holding a china cup traced with pink flowers. "Brandy, ma'am?"

"Hmmmm?" Moira looked up at Frances's surprised expression. "Yes. Brandy. The brandy His Grace prefers. I'd like a small decanter sent up."

"Yes, Your Ladyship." Frances put the cup down beside Moira, still moving as if she expected to be called back, but Moira did not speak.

A few minutes later, when Frances returned, flustered from the sly look the innkeeper gave her as he had poured the liquor, Moira still sat where she had, her china cup in her hand, staring out toward the sea.

"Your—brandy—Milady," Frances said faintly.

"Emm? Oh, yes. Put it down and eat for heaven's sake, Frances, your tea will get cold."

104

Frances did as she was told, pouring her own and scooping up jam and ladling it thick on her bun.

As she ate, a tap at the door sounded.

"Come in," Moira called out, looking expectantly toward the door.

But when it opened, only the innkeeper stood there, a small tray in his hand.

"Your Ladyship." He smiled. "I thought you might also enjoy one of these." He put the tray on the table near Moira as she glanced at the bottles.

"What are they?"

"Blackberry wine and elderberry wine, Your Ladyship. More to a lady's taste than the brandy."

"Oh, my!" She laughed out loud and looked up at his concerned face. "Oh, thank you, Mr. . . . . Mr.?"

"Coomby," he said stiffly.

"Thank you, Mr. Coomby." Moira smiled at him and he relaxed a little. "I do appreciate your thoughtfulness."

He nodded, bowed, and left, Frances staring after him. After he left, after the door closed, Moira smiled wide, laughing again now, her spirits rising.

"Oh, Frances, he thinks we're secret tipplers! Imagine!" She laughed again. "He's as imaginative as I. And as wrong, I expect!"

"Milady?" Frances smiled back, but she did not understand.

Moira sighed, her smile fading. "Never mind. Just, just never judge people too soon. Or too harshly."

"No, Milady. I won't, Milady."

"Good."

The sun fell away outside, darkness enveloping the village as Frances readied Moira for bed and left her to rest, walking down the hall to her own tiny room.

The wind came up again, outside, whipping down the steep stepped village street.

Moira glanced at the small bookcase under the window and then bent to it, surprised to see a small collection of titles there.

She reached for one, picking it up and opening it wide. *Clarissa Harlowe*, by Samuel Richardson. The book was dusty and old; neglect and the damp air had sealed some of the pages together.

Moira carried it and the oil lamp over to the bedside table, glancing at the brandy decanter as she moved. What a silly gesture that had been. She hesitated and then turned to climb up into the high bed, under the three thick comforters.

She propped up the pillows and then reached for the book, opening it to the first page and beginning to read as the wind blew the cedar's branches against the side of the building.

She read on and on, the night passing away, as Clarissa was doped, was seduced by Lovelace, refusing to marry him, preferring to die . . . "that such a husband might unsettle me in all my own principles and hazard my future hopes, that he has a very immoral character to women, that, knowing this, it is a high degree of impurity to think of joining in wedlock with such a man."

Moira slammed the book shut, throwing it across the room. She stared at it where it fell, near the table and the bookcase. There were other books there. Books to put her to sleep, not to mock her with their words and bring all her fears tumbling back.

She turned out the lamp, the room now filling with moving shadows as the tree branches obscured the moon and then let its rays gleam through for moments before swallowing them up again. Over and over. She tossed and turned on the bed, tangling all the covers, pulling the pillows to her and hugging them close, closing her eyes firmly, repeating school lessons over and over in her head, willing herself to sleep. . . . The Greek alphabet, the sonnets of Shakespeare, the poems of Hannah More, anything, everything she could think of to dull her worries, to quiet her mind, until she at last fell asleep.

But sleep did not bring peace. It brought Tristan's jeering nine-year-old face, his laughter, as he said over and over, your mother's a fancypiece, my mother told me. Your mother's a whore . . . a trollop . . . your mother's . . . .

The Duke loomed up in her dream, huge and terrible in the depths of her memory, reaching out to strike his son, the sound of the crack of his hand against Tristan's cheek exploding in her ears.

And then the Duke, soaking wet aboard the ship, reaching to give her something to drink. . . . Here, drink, you must. It's only dope, my dear, my name is Lovelace, didn't you know? She screamed in the dream and then began to cry. No, I'm not like my mother, no! Your mother was impure, drink the glass down, I won't marry you, I won't! But you did, Moira, you already did. You married your own uncle, didn't you know?"

She tossed and turned in her sleep, trying physically to get away from the visions, trying to hush the voices that echoed in her dreams. I'm in bed in an inn, I'm awake, I'm awake. . . .

She turned and, in the dark, beside her bed, loomed the huge black figure she had seen nights ago, towering over her now. His hand went to her mouth to stifle the scream that began to form on her lips. Her eyes stared up in terror at a black face that had Michael's eyes. She was dreaming, she knew, she had to be dreaming. But she twisted away, frightened, and he let her move, his hand falling to her shoulder. The touch of his hand on her nightdress thrilled through her.

The apparition stared down at creamy white skin and then, its black hand moved, pulling the front of her gown loose. She stared at the hand, watching it pull her gown down, down to her waist, her breast gleaming pale in the flickery moonlight that lit the room and then fell back away. She sat perfectly still, watching the eyes that devoured the sight of her nakedness. She was acting like a wanton, she told herself, she should reach to cover herself, she should tell him to leave, she should wake up.

She wanted to do none of it. She wanted him to touch her again. "I had them bring up your brandy." She heard her own voice sounding husky and deep in her throat. "Michael. . . ." She found the words pouring out, the words she could not say to him. She was dreaming this and therefore she could tell him all the things she longed for him to know.

"I trust you," she heard herself saying to the silent figure. "I always have. Always." She stopped, unable to go on, even in her dream.

The apparition did not answer. It still stared down at her flesh with Michael's eyes, something warm and weakening coursing through her blood as she watched him stare at her nakedness. Her nipples hardened, the ache he brought to her welling up within again. And then he reached out, slowly, reaching out until he touched her, cupping the roundness of one smooth breast. She gasped at the feeling of his fingers pulling at her, she watched his great dark head lean forward toward her nipple. Her eyes closed when his mouth touched her skin, the warmth of his breath, the ache he caused, bringing her forward, closer, closer. She reached to touch his hair, felt the thick dark strands within her fingers, felt his tongue against her nipple. And then his hands, both hands now, leaning her back against the pillows, stretching over her as he had on board ship. But this time his mouth was hungrily covering her nipples, first one and

107

then the other, heat rising within her at his every touch, at the feeling of his warmth, his breath against her skin, his tongue, his teeth, his lips pulling her toward him, toward an abyss she wanted to throw herself into. She reached for him, her hands in his hair, hearing little sounds that she realized were coming from her own lips. She wanted him near, nearer, nearer. She reached for his cloak, reached to pull it away. She wanted to feel his skin against her hands, wanted to feel his heart beating against her hand, wanted—

He was gone, emptiness surrounding her, a horrible emptiness washing through her, engulfing her in disappointment. Her eyes flew open, reaching to find him, to touch the apparition, air greeting her hands, her arms. Empty air.

Her eyes wide open she stared at the room in the vague gray dawning light, the covers pulled all over the bed, her hair, her gown disheveled and the room—empty. Empty and cold around her.

The book still lay beside the bookcase, the brandy still on the table. And then her bones chilled. She stared at the table, stared at the decanter. She had not dreamed, had not, could not have dreamed. For beside the decanter stood a half-filled glass of brandy.

She stared at it in the early morning light. And then her eyes closed and she leaned back against the pillows, feeling again the touch of him. His arms were strong, his breath warm and smelling of whiskey . . . whiskey.

She sat up then. She would not have dreamed that, she would not have dreamed the smell of whiskey on his breath.

Horses clattered in the yard below, men shouting out to each other. She had not poured a glass of brandy, she knew she had not. A familiar voice sounded from outside. Startled she threw the covers off, getting up and running to the window.

She could see a great chestnut stallion when she looked out. It was being led toward the stable, a groom beside it. And then she heard his boots on the steps, his imperious knock at the door. No one knocked as he did, as if none would ever deny him entrance.

"Yes," she said, her voice still husky. The Duke of St. Maur opened the door wide, staring at her for a brief moment and then turning to close the door.

"You should at least find your robe before you invite any stranger into your room," he said.

"I knew it was you," she replied. "I heard you—downstairs."

"Oh." He turned back toward her and saw her eyes fall to the brandy decanter and the glass beside it.

When she looked up, her eyes full of questions, he waited.

"I—" She stopped.

"Yes?" His expression was quizzical, waiting for her to explain herself.

She tried to ask him, tried to form the right words and then finally shook her head.

He looked down at the decanter himself. The glass and the bottles of wine stood there too. "Spirits?" he questioned, his brow rising quizzically.

She stared up at him. Shaking her head a little, she walked to her robe, picking it up and slowly drawing it around her, for comfort. For warmth. "Michael—" she faltered.

"Yes?" He watched her carefully.

"Did you know my mother well?"

"What?" He was truly surprised. "Yes. Why?"

"Was she—ill?"

"Of course. How else to die so young?" As he spoke his voice grew harsher, memories of his own mocking his words.

"No." Moira did not hear the harshness. "I mean, was she unwell? Was she . . . mentally unwell?"

"What on earth are you talking about?"

She turned to see his eyes. "Please, please." She found herself staring up at the eyes that had filled her dream. She lost the words, stumbling over them, pleading with him. "No, I, please don't humor me. I never really knew her. Am I sane even to ask this of you?"

"Moira, what's wrong?" He took a step toward her. "She was as sane as you or I. There was nothing wrong with her mind. Why do you ask this?" He took her shoulders in his hands.

She stared up at him. "The brandy was for you."

He tightened his grip on her shoulders. "I—beg your pardon?"

Faintly, she spoke again. "I had a dream. I thought you might come back last night and then I had a dream . . . the black ship—"

"What black ship?" His hands hurt her shoulders now.

"The innkeeper. Pirates in a black ship he said—"

"And you said?" His eyes blazed at her.

"Nothing." She looked up at him, her eyes filling with tears. "Nothing."

He relaxed his grip. "I'm sorry. I didn't mean to hurt you, but I never want the black ship mentioned, do you understand?"

"I—no." Her eyes were now filled with misery as well as tears. "No, I don't."

The Duke hesitated. "Moira, having lived with your father in Brittany you are aware of my black ship. I do not want any wild-eyed fool around here to think that there's some connection between my black ship and *the* black ship that they all prattle on about. Do you see now?"

"Are you saying that they are *not* the same?" She watched his eyes guard over. "No one knows?" she asked after a moment.

"No one knows." His voice was emotionless, his eyes flat, giving away nothing.

"But there's Andre—"

"That's different," he said but he did not explain. "It is very isolated here. You are the only outsider, the only one who knows I also have a black ship."

Outsider. She stared at him. I am the only outsider. "I said nothing," she repeated finally.

"Good. Now, what is this nonsense about your mother?"

"I—nothing."

"Something must have caused the question."

"I had a bad dream."

"Bad?" His tone changed. He took one step nearer, watching her closely. "How was it bad?"

She said nothing, unable to tell him, unable to talk of it.

"And?" he prompted.

"And—I thought I was awake." She looked fearfully into his eyes, afraid of the condemnation she might find there if she told him the truth and she was wrong. If it had been only a dream. "I was confused. And I keep remembering things that were said about my mother that don't make sense. From long ago. I began to fear for my—sanity."

"Absolute nonsense," he pronounced. "Now, how soon can you be ready to leave?"

"Within the hour," she replied faintly.

He nodded, dismissing the subject. His eyes strayed back to the table on which the brandy decanter sat. And beside which the half-filled glass still sat.

"Are you—" she began, "I mean, are you planning on continuing the journey with—us?"

"Of course. None need know that I was ever gone."

110

She stared at him. "No," she replied quietly. "None need know." She watched his eyes go back to the glass.

"You must not take to secret tippling, Moira. Drink changes people."

"How changes?" she asked softly, thinking of the strong knowing hands in the darkness. She found herself looking down at his hands.

He hesitated. "It is rather like love—it makes fools of us. I would advise you to take care not to let it ensnare you."

"Does it ensnare you?" Her breath was held, her eyes large as they looked up into his. They were the color of emerald green in the morning's cold light.

He shrugged. "Men are different; some handle it better than others."

"And you?" she repeated, not daring to breathe.

He stared back into those eyes, his own darkening into blackness. "I—I—" She watched him fumble over the lone syllable, unable to go on, staring at her still. He was without words and she felt the confusion within him. She wanted to reach out toward him, feeling closer in this moment than she had ever known she could feel to another.

He broke the spell, wrenching his eyes away and in the process finding himself staring at the glass. He strode over to it, two long strides, picking it up and downing it in one gulp. Then he turned and walked to the doorway. "I'll send your abigail to you," he said in a strangled voice as he left.

She watched him close the door between them, her heart soaring. She listened to his steps recede and then turned to stare at the empty glass. "I knew it. . . ." She spoke out loud, but softly, as softly as if he were still there. "I knew . . . you do want me too. . . ."

Chapter Thirteen

THEY LEFT THE MAIN ROAD AT HARTLAND, TAKING THE COAST ROAD that led only to St. Maur, white farmhouses and cottages dotted here and there along the great expanse of the peninsula, a remote village of gray stone and slate slipping into the past, and then miles till the next one, the civilized world left far behind as they rode on down the narrow dirt road.

"What's that?" Moira asked, the windows now clean of mud, the coach glistening after the Duke spoke to the innkeeper's grooms. "That shadow?"

Andre bent his head near the window. "Buzzards flying over the coomb."

"Coomb?"

The Duke glanced outside, watching the huge birds as they sailed slowly across the quiet landscape, throwing shadows on the sunlit slopes below. "Coomb's an old name for a short valley, like that one, running up from the coast."

Moira met Andre's sidelong glance. "Andre knows his English, and his Cornish, very well indeed," she said quietly. A look of question and caution passed between the Duke and Andre as they heard her words.

"Can't help picking up local language. And dialects. I do it myself," the Duke said.

"Yes. I remember your very pure French. And then your near perfect Breton," Moira said into the silence. Frances looked up at her mistress, then kept her attention on her own lap, smoothing her skirt and saying nothing. *"Il fait up temps superbe,"* Moira said softly, enjoying Andre and the Duke's startled glances. She smiled at Frances. "I lived in Brittany for many years and learned both French and Breton. My father felt there was no excuse for living in a land, living off a land, and not learning its language. And its culture."

The Duke spoke tonelessly. "How commendable."

"There wasn't much to keep him occupied. So he spent a great deal of time teaching me a rather wide span of subjects."

The Duke angled his large frame back into the corner of his seat, across from Moira, his eyes intent. "And what all did he feel you needed to learn?"

Moira glanced out the window, listening to the bubbling cries of a group of curlews that flew up across the moors. She watched the swallows flashing in and out of ancient slate gray ruins as their coach rode on along the high cliffs, heading west. "History," she replied after a moment. "Philosophy. The classics, Latin."

"Latin!" The Duke stared at her, disbelieving. "You?"

"I." She held her ground, watching him carefully.

"Such as?" he challenged.

112

"Such as—" she hesitated only briefly. *"Vir accūsābitur."*

He stopped, staring at her for a long time. "What a strange choice," he said finally, Frances and Andre both watching them now. "The man will be accused? Why not, *vir accusabit*, the man will *accuse?*"

She tried to see past the slightly bored, slightly amused expression in his eyes, back to what he really felt. "Some science, and then the French, of course," she continued.

"My," he said. "What a lot of nonsense for a young girl's mind to absorb. He'd have been better off teaching you needlepoint and cookery."

"He could not teach me what he did not know," she replied.

The Duke turned away after a bit to stare out the window. Across from him Moira did the same, watching the stunted fir trees that slanted sideways near the edge of the cliffs, mute testimony to the winds that tore across these cliffs, whipping in from the sea, laden with salt and the bitter smells of the ocean's depths.

It was midday before the road began to track inland, through a wooded gorge, a river running fast and deep beside the road.

They crossed over a small stone bridge, the oak groves growing thicker, the ground rising slowly to the south, broken here and there by brakes of yellow gorse and thorn, while the road followed the lee of the land into a river valley blooming with autumn flowers.

"Oh!" Moira breathed the word. "It's still beautiful!"

The Duke watched her as she smiled at the suddenly green landscape, coming off the highlands, into the protected valley below.

"There's the Maur River!" Moira exclaimed, watching as the coach followed along its northern bank until they pulled up and off to the north, following the Castle Road.

She pressed her face against the window to see the old stone bridge that led across the river and to the village on Saint's Bay. "Is it all the same?" she asked, looking over at Michael now, her eyes aglow. "Is the village exactly the same?" she demanded.

He smiled, his eyes softening. "A few births, a few deaths, in ten years. But it will look the same, I imagine."

She watched the walnut trees glide past, the trees that lined the Castle Road. They passed a group of farmers' cottages that climbed toward the castle, reaching the huge stone gatehouse and going under its curved archway. Moira sat back on the

113

leather seat now, afraid to see ahead. Afraid to see up the long straight drive to the castle at the crest of the hill. She was not ready. She did not know what was expected.

And his family was here.

He watched her expression change. "You look tired."

"Yes," she answered, and then added nothing to it.

The carriage stopped, the one behind drawing near and stopping too. The Duke had the door open, the steps in place, before Robert could reach him.

"Moira." The Duke held out his hand.

She hesitated before she stood up, her eyes on the steps as she went down them slowly, gathering her courage before she looked up at the huge stone monolith before her.

It was as forbidding, as foreboding, as she remembered from her childhood. Turrets and towers rose from the wide stone building, the long avenue of trees stretching back behind the carriages, down to the gatehouse and beyond. A large stone archway encroached over the heavy oak front door. The door itself, its hinges of iron, its front studded with iron, looked as solid as a fortress's gate, as solid as a prison's gate.

Frances stood, mute, behind her mistress, staring at the huge building. "Gor, it's like—it's like the Abbey, it is," she said finally. "Or—Buckingham Palace!"

Andre had gone ahead, and the great door swung wide now as they entered, Mr. Moffatt standing just inside the great hall.

"I see you arrived safely," the Duke said.

"Yes, Your Grace. An uneventful journey." Moffatt paused. "I've done as you asked, and not called the staff together."

"Thank God; there's time enough for that tomorrow. I don't suppose, however," he said dryly, "that you had as much luck with Madame."

Moffatt's face was entirely without expression. "Madame awaits, in the North Drawing Room."

The Duke groaned and then nodded, reaching a hand out toward Moira. "We're for it now; my mother insists on seeing you. Are you ready?"

She stared around herself at the two-story Gothic entrance hall, even bigger than the one in the mansion in London. Wood carvings and stained-glass windows, wrought-iron balustrades tracing the second-floor balconies that surrounded them above, met her eyes. Two great stone staircases on either side of the hall led upward to meet the balconies. Between the two staircases a huge archway led in to the ballroom, and the great

114

windows that overlooked the inner courtyard beyond could be seen across the great expanse.

"Moira?"

"Yes." She spoke quickly now, letting him take her hand.

They walked through the entrance hall, into the North Gallery and through it, to the Long Gallery and the North Drawing Room beyond.

As they walked a brace of spaniels came barking out from a doorway near the end of the North Gallery where tall, Gothic windows filled with small panes of glass stood overlooking the gardens and sea beyond.

The spaniels came toward them, their nails chinking against the great flagged stones of the gallery floor, their happy barking echoing against the stone walls.

Michael bent down to the fat brown and white dogs that raced up to him slobbering kisses and barking with obvious enthusiasm.

"Arthur! Lancelot! How fat you've got! Who's been letting you lie idle? Good boy, good boy." He stroked their fur, scratching behind their ears, and then straightened up. He watched them sniff around Moira. "Get used to her, she'll be here for a while."

Moira bent down to let them sniff her hand. "Hello there. Which of you is Arthur?"

Michael pointed. "The one with the black eye."

"Ah, then you must be Lancelot. Pleased to meet you both." She straightened. "No Guinevere?"

"One was enough." Michael's eyes turned opaque. "Shall we get this over with?"

She heard the impatience and nodded. "Of course."

When they reached the panelled door, he took her hand again, taking a deep breath and then opening it, the dogs pattering along behind and around them as they walked inside.

Across a large room, near a huge medieval fireplace, a tall, thin woman stood near the carved stone mantel looking into a pit that would hold logs the size of small trees. She was alone.

Moira could feel Michael relax as he realized the older woman was alone. "Mother, this is Moira."

Michael's mother turned toward them, her eyes as dark as her son's. Moira hesitated. Then, after the pressure of Michael's hand squeezing hers, she spoke. "How do you do, Your Grace."

"I'm not Your Grace," the old woman said, her voice thin

with age. "Nor anyone else's. I'm his mother. You are the Duchess now."

Her voice was neither kind nor cold. Moira stared at her, seeing the severe black lines of her gown, the necklace of jet that hung from her small, bony neck. "I—but—"

"My grandfather lived to a ripe old age, outliving my father," Michael said. "My father died helping the French in their Revolution and never became Duke. Therefore Madame is— Madame." He leaned forward to kiss his mother's cool forehead.

"The confounded fool that was my husband died at thirty-one," Madame said. "In 1789. Old Henry did not see fit to die till after—" She stopped. "Until 1815," she said after a momentary pause. "So this scalawag of mine became lord of all."

Michael bowed slightly, his smile mocking. "Your words, as always, are politeness itself."

"Possibly not polite, but well chosen."

He laughed and she unbent a little, staring at Moira intently. "So, you're Edmund's girl, are you? All grown up. You look different."

"From seven to seventeen, Mother. There are bound to be changes."

"Emmm." Madame still stared at Moira. "And how'd you manage to get him to marry you?"

"I—beg your pardon?"

"Do you? No by-blows out in the carriage waiting to be brought in, are there?"

"Mother!"

"No!" Moira turned scarlet, Michael's hand holding hers more tightly. "I—it—we—"

The old woman looked up at her son towering above her. "Speaks better than that, I hope."

"You old daftie." He grinned. "You'd throw anyone into a fit of speechlessness." His smile faded. "Where are the others?"

"Waiting word to come in."

He started to object and then thought better of it.

"We'd best get it over with. We need to rest before we eat."

Madame touched a bell pull near the fireplace. Moira was intimidated as she stood under the scrolled ceiling, Madame's eyes still upon her, the dark panelling and heavy curtains oppressive in the daylight hours. Moira held onto Michael's hand more firmly, afraid he would let go.

116

And when the door opened she was grateful for his hand, grateful to hold onto something warm as Tristan walked in, his ginger hair tousled as though he'd just ridden in, his blue eyes cold above his smiling mouth. "Well, if it isn't little Moira. Or should I call you mother now?"

He walked forward, Michael stiffening. Moira glimpsed Tamaris and Mark behind Tristan, hanging back silently.

Tristan stopped inches from Moira. "And here I thought, when we were children, it was me you were after."

"That will be enough, Tristan." Michael's voice was cold.

Tristan turned toward his brother and sister. "You won't remember Moira. You were too young."

"I remember," Mark said, his eyes dark and cold.

"You were only four when she left," Tristan said.

"I remember," Mark said stubbornly, his fourteen-year-old face set and expressionless.

Tamaris hesitated and then came forward, glancing at Moira and then looking up at her father, her twelve-year-old eyes anxious and pleading. "Father—"

"Yes, Tamaris?"

"Are you home to stay, now?"

He hesitated. "For a while. Moira, this is my daughter, Tamaris. You remember Mark and Tristan."

Moira smiled at the young girl. "I remember Tamaris, too. You were the prettiest baby I ever saw."

Tamaris stared up at Moira, the kindness in Moira's eyes warming the girl's expression. "Did you really think so?"

"I did. And I do."

"How many babies have you seen?" Tristan asked.

"Tristan—" His grandmother's voice rang out. "See that tea is brought. We'll have a bite before your father and Moira go upstairs."

"Have Jemma do it." Tristan turned and strode toward the door, Mark following quickly.

"Tristan!" His father's voice stopped him as he opened it. The tone was sharp enough to cut. "Mark," he said, a little less sharply. He waited for them to turn toward him. He waited for their eyes to meet his, and then he spoke. "You will make Moira feel welcome, and you will give your grandmother the respect she deserves, and you will not leave until you have been dismissed."

Tristan looked as if he might rebel, might step on out the open door. Mark watched his older brother with hero worship

117

written plain across his face. What Tristan did, Mark would do.

Tristan reached to close the door, lounging back against it, his corduroy jacket tight across his young, broad shoulders. Mark slumped against a nearby chair.

Madame turned toward the bell pull again, the Duke handing Moira into a chair by the fire. "My children are becoming savages out here. I hope you can help teach them as well as your father taught you."

Moira caught Tamaris's sad inspection of her father. "Not all your children, Michael."

He looked down at her quizzically and then over at Tamaris. "Ah, yes, my shy one." He sat down, saying no more and the room was silent when old John opened the door.

"You rang, Madame?"

"Tea, please, and send Jemma in."

"Thank you, Madame."

"Oh, John." The Duke spoke, "Moira, this is our butler, John Ottery. John, the new Duchess."

John bowed. "Thank you, Your Grace. Your Ladyship." He bowed to Moira and then left.

"It would be easier for Moira to be introduced to the servants all at once," Madame said.

"Yes. I know. Well," the Duke added, "we'll stand 'em all up in the morning and go through it—"

Moira sat back, unsure what to add to the conversation and so said nothing. Tamaris, as the moments lagged by, drifted nearer Moira. The Duke listened to his mother's recounting of the last week's weather.

When Tamaris stood inches from the arm of Moira's chair the girl finally spoke, softly, her sad gray eyes fastened on Moira. "You're awfully young, aren't you, to be my new mother?"

Moira smiled. "I'm seventeen."

"Tristan's nineteen."

"I know."

Tamaris studied Moira's face. "Did you really think I was pretty?"

"Yes. You were. And you are." Moira reached out to touch Tamaris's hand, remembering her own questions of Solange on this very subject a few weeks before.

Tamaris drew her hand back sharply, as if where Moira touched it had burned her. Moira, startled, stared at the girl. "Tamaris, what's—"

118

The girl burst into tears, her father and grandmother looking over quickly.

"Tamaris." A soft melodious voice called from the doorway, a handsome young woman standing there.

"Ah, Jemma." Madame smiled briefly. "Yes, come in, she needs you."

"For God's sake, Tamaris," the Duke snapped, "make that noise somewhere else."

Tamaris ran to Jemma's arms, burying her face in the woman's dark dress.

"This is Jemma, the governess who attempts to teach these heathens. Moira, what on earth did you do to the girl?" Then Michael continued almost as an afterthought: "This is the new Duchess, Jemma."

Jemma smiled warmly, her curtsy brief. "How do you do, Your Ladyship?" Seeing the look on Moira's face she added: "Please don't give this a thought, Tamaris has just frightened herself, that's all. Come along now, my girl, come along, we'll have toast and tea upstairs, all right?"

"But—" Moira's words were cut off by the Duke's.

"Take the boys, too!" He stood up, his hands jamming into his pockets, his back to the room, staring out the window toward the inner courtyard as his children left with Jemma.

Tea was brought, Madame dismissing the servants. "I'll handle it, John, thank you." She looked over at Moira. "Would you prefer to pour?"

"No," Moira said faintly, "please, go ahead."

"Come along, Michael." His mother glanced up at his stiff frame. "Tea."

When he turned back toward them his anger was apparent. "There is absolutely no excuse for their behavior."

"Boys will be boys. You were no better."

"And what of the girl? She not only looks like her mother, she's inherited her—" He stopped himself, snapping the words off, staring at Moira. "What did you say to her?" he asked sharply.

"I—she asked if she was pretty. I said yes. I touched her arm." Moira's eyes flew to the old woman's. "That's all."

"I'm sure it was," Madame said. "Why are we nattering away over a child's fancies? Cream?"

"A child's fancies!" Michael stared down at his mother. "Fancies!" He turned and stalked out, slamming the door.

Moira took the cup, her hand shaking. She tried to steady it

119

and then set the cup down beside her. Visions of his gentle concern over Jean-Marc flooded before her eyes.

"Michael's letter told of the wedding but did not explain why this—sudden—marriage. Or is it?" Her shrewd dark eyes contemplated Moira. "Have you two been planning this?"

Moira bit her lip, wondering how much to say, what not to say, what he`wished her to say. "I, I think part of Michael's reasoning was that, with my father dead and I, my, being alone out there—"

"My dear girl, that explains bringing you here but not marrying you. You're not by chance—increasing—are you?"

"You mean—no!" Moira's voice took on timbre.

"All right then, why did you marry my son?"

"I told you—he—"

Madame interrupted impatiently. "I understand why he married you, or rather why you say he did. I for one do not see my son as a gentle savior of young girls. I am asking why you consented to marry him."

The words came slowly. "My father's dying wish was that I would."

The old matriarch sat back in the stiff-backed chair, relaxing the posture that had been drilled into her since childhood. "I see. Or I don't really, but it hardly matters, does it. What's done is done." She stood up, a thin, erect figure in a stiff black satin gown. "Since you obviously don't wish your tea, would you care to rest?"

"Yes, thank you." Moira stood up.

"I'll show you to your rooms."

Moira followed the old woman back to the main front staircases, pacing beside her up the shallow, wide stone steps, walking past an avenue of family portraits along the Upper West Gallery.

"These front rooms," Madame motioned toward the doors they were passing, "are Michael's. Here's your suite. As you can see, your sitting room connects with Michael's suite." Madame pointed toward a smaller doorway as they walked into a small, rose-colored sitting room. "And the rose gardens are below your windows. There's a fine view of the Channel too."

Moira gazed at the rose damask sofas facing each other across a low mahogany table, the rose marble fireplace, the creamy walls. And the door that led to Michael's room.

"It's—I've never seen anything lovelier."

"Thank you. I furnished it myself. And fought a long fight

with Lucy. She wanted to turn it into a Chinese opium den or some such frippery when she married Michael."

Moira smiled, remembering the rooms in London.

"And here are the dressing rooms and the bedroom." They walked through a small connecting hall toward the rear of the suite.

Michael strode into the sitting room and then followed them through the hall, his face a thundercloud. "She's not to have these rooms!"

His mother stared at him. Moira turned away.

"Don't be absurd!" the old woman snapped. "Where else will the new Duchess sleep? Surely not with you! It's unheard of!"

"I—no, of course not." As he spoke his voice fell lower. "Obviously that's not what I meant."

Madame in very low, very firm tones. "Now that you've lowered your voice and you are not informing the entire staff and half the county, perhaps you will tell me just what the problem is?"

He started to speak and then stopped.

"Well?" his mother prompted. "Where do you wish her to stay, and what are you prepared to have the staff thinking? As well as saying?"

He turned away. "You are, of course, right." He walked out without another word.

Madame looked over at the young woman who wore Michael's ring. "I believe your things have been brought up already," she said smoothly. "I shall have your abigail sent up to help you change for dinner."

"Thank you," Moira said. "Thank you very much."

Chapter Fourteen

DINNER WAS A SILENT AFFAIR, MARK AND TAMARIS LONG SINCE FED and to their rooms, only Tristan at the old Jacobean gate-legged table with his grandmother, his father, Jemma, and Moira.

The heavy, dark opulence of the room depressed Moira. The

heavy old silver, the thick wine-red satin drapes shrouding the tall narrow windows, the somber red Turkey rug, the chandelier thick with red Bohemia glass prisms mixed in with the crystal pendants that reflected the candle's glow down across them. All of it somehow shadowed even darker by the moody, withdrawn man at the head of the table.

The wind came up outside, the Duke glancing once toward the closed, draped windows, and then, drinking down the last of his claret, he stood up. "If you'll excuse me."

Madame nodded, glancing over at Moira now that he was gone. "Have you found all you need?"

Moira caught Tristan's insolent glance across the table. "Yes, thank you."

"My mother used to say those rooms were haunted." Tristan smiled as he spoke.

"Tristan!" His grandmother glared at him. "There's no need to go prosing on about nonsense!"

"They were the first Duke's wife's rooms too, weren't they?" he asked innocently. "Where she had crazy Louis?"

"Good grief!" Jemma laughed. "Tristan, you don't have to throw all the family secrets at poor Moira, pardon me, at Her Ladyship, at once, do you?"

"Please," Moira spoke quickly, "call me Moira. I'd feel ever so much more at home."

Jemma smiled kindly, but Tristan spoke first. "I merely mentioned it so that if she did hear noises she wouldn't think she was, you know, hearing things that weren't there. Not well. You know."

"You're making a cake of yourself!" his grandmother said sharply. "Moira's as sane as you or I and she knows it. Now come along. If you're through eating I want to talk to you, Master Tristan."

Tristan slumped back in his chair.

His grandmother rose. "Shall we?"

Moira and Jemma stood up, the old woman searching Moira's face. "It will be your place, my dear, to signify when the meal is over."

"I'm not used to such formality yet."

"I realize that living alone, out in the wilds of Brittany, with just one servant, was not the proper training for you. It will take you a bit to adjust. Why your father insisted on burying himself away out there I truly find hard to fathom."

A footman opened the door to the hall for them. "Come along, Tristan," Madame called back to the young man, waiting until he began to rise before she turned back toward Moira. "However, I do feel it will be best if you begin immediately to polish your—social skills. Christmas festivities will soon be upon us, and what with bride's visits and such, you will be forced into a situation where all eyes will be upon you. And you do now carry the St. Maur name."

"I understand," Moira replied, standing up and then stepping back as Tristan stopped inches in front of her, his smile lazy as he looked down at her, very obviously studying her lips.

Jemma touched Moira's arm. "Shall we join the Duke in the library?"

"Come *along*, Tristan." The old woman put her hand on Tristan's arm. "You can see me to my rooms."

Jemma and Moira walked slowly through the blue-slate floored halls. Tall brass sconces hung from the stone walls, throwing light across their path. Jemma, when she spoke, was hesitant, as if unsure whether she should speak at all. "Do you really wish me to call you Moira?"

"It would truly be a kindness, Jemma. You can't know how great a kindness. This is all so new, so foreign to me."

Jemma waited until they crossed the great hall, waited until they were near the library door before she spoke again, her tone still anxious. "Please, then, don't think I'm being excessively impertinent, but—"

"Yes?" Moira prompted her. "What is it?"

"There was not an, an understanding, a tendre, ever, between you and Tristan, was there?"

Moira stopped walking, turning to stare in disbelief at Jemma. "No. How could you think it?"

Jemma smiled, obviously relieved. "Please, don't credit the impulsive things the children may say. Tristan's been, well, trying to cause trouble, I think, ever since the Duke's letter arrived, informing of your marriage. He's said things to the children."

"But why?"

"I don't know. That's the reason I," Jemma faltered, "forgive me, but that's the reason I asked about you and Tristan."

It took Moira a moment to speak, her thoughts whirling around. "Jemma, I was only seven when we left Cornwall, and I've never been back, never seen Tristan, from that day to this."

123

"You never exchanged letters."

"Not even one. Nor anything else," Moira replied.

Jemma's eyes clouded. "Why would he say you had? Why would he be making up such stories? He's a little wild, but—"

"I don't know," Moira said gently, "but it can't be he's trying to hurt me, for he really doesn't know me."

Jemma opened the door to the library, letting Moira walk in first.

The Duke glanced up from his papers and then looked back down at the *Gazette*. Jemma and Moira walked forward to sit on a small dark-green patterned couch near the fire, across from where Michael sat, the spaniels by his feet.

"Moira, pour Jemma some ratafia," the Duke said. "You like to have it after dinner, I remember." He looked up at Jemma.

She smiled. "I do. Thank you, Your Grace, you are most kind to remember."

Moira stood up, looking away from the expression in his eyes when he looked at Jemma. Jemma stood too. "I can get it for both of us. You will join me, won't you?" she was asking Moira as she moved to a cabinet, showing Moira where the peach-flavoured liqueur was kept. Moira watched her, watched the fine pale hands, the dark hair that was pulled neatly into a bun at the back of Jemma's head, surprised by the heavy pain that smote at her heart. Jemma belonged here. The governess was pouring a thimbleful each of the liqueur into two tiny glasses, handing one to Moira.

Lancelot walked over to the two women, sniffing at the air inquisitively and then standing still, watching them with big sad eyes as they walked back and sat down across from the master of the house.

Arthur glanced up from his post beside the Duke's feet and then lay back, his muzzle on his front paws, watching the scene sleepily.

Moira was looking toward the shelves and shelves of books, unwilling to look at the attractive woman beside her. Jemma set her glass on a spindly rosewood table, reaching down between it and the couch, bringing out a basket of needlework.

The motion caught Moira's eye, the simple, homely gesture smoting at her heart as his look had done. They were used to this, sitting here quietly, he with his papers, she with her sewing; he with his brandy, she with her ratafia.

Moira tried to force the thought away. Jealousy was deplorable, she told herself, and could be an unwell trait if at every turn

124

she became jealous of every woman who knew him. She had no right, she told herself, no right to be jealous.

But a rebellious thought pushed up through her good intentions, telling her she had every right in the world. She loved this man. And he at least cared about her, he at least wanted her; she had seen the hunger in his eyes, had felt the hunger in his hands. The remembrance thrilled through her, suffusing her cheeks with sudden color.

"Is anything wrong?" Jemma asked quietly.

"No," Moira said. "Nothing." She thought of Genevieve sitting here, Jean-Marc beside the fireplace with the other children, and the thought hurt. Genevieve she could fight, she could try to fight at least. But how could Jean-Marc be kept from his father's side. Why should he not enjoy his father's company, feel at home in his father's house? It was no fault of his how he had come into this world.

Lancelot moved from his spot near the fire, coming near to sniff at Moira, younger and more curious than Arthur. He held his head against her knee, staring with soft, liquid eyes as she reached to pet him, the firelight flickering beyond.

A high-pitched scream wailed through the quiet house, bringing Jemma and Moira both to their feet, Lancelot barking.

"Lancelot!" The Duke's voice was stern. Lancelot turned, quiet again, to walk near the Duke's chair and nuzzle his head.

"What's—" Moira was following Jemma toward the door.

"Moira!" The Duke's voice when he called her name was very like when he had called Lancelot's; sharp, authoritative, brooking no disobedience. "Sit down."

"But something's happened. That was Tamaris, I'm sure of it!"

"Nothing's happened." He stared into the fire, letting the papers fall to the floor beside him. "Nothing at all. Tamaris is having one of her nightmares, that's all."

"Possibly I can help." Moira stood stiffly, near the door, her hands clasped tightly together, her heart pounding as she defied him. She was not used to being yelled at.

"It's not your place to help. That's Jemma's job." His eyes were on the fire, his thoughts far away. He did not turn when he heard her open the door. "It's not your concern," he added, his voice tired and dull.

Moira stopped then, at the door, stopped to look back at the man she had married. His shoulders hunched a little forward, his head thrown back against the chair, he looked too big for the easy chair, his long legs thrust out before him, his eyes now closed.

"I am your wife, Michael. For as long as I remain so, your children *are* my concern."

"How very dutiful." His eyes did not open.

Stung, she turned and left, closing the door between them.

It was not until she was climbing the stairs that she realized Lancelot had come with her, pattering down the upstairs hall, trotting on ahead.

She went past her own rooms, listening for the sounds of distress, unsure where Tamaris's rooms were. But Lancelot seemed to know and so she followed him to the children's hall, which ran across the length of the back of the castle. Turning the corner she heard the sound of crying and saw light splashing out from an open doorway.

She stopped in the doorway, looking across the pink and white room to the canopied bed on which Tamaris lay crumpled, Jemma standing over her.

Jemma looked up, surprised. "Oh, you did not need—"

Moira walked in, Tamaris turning to see her, the young girl's tear-blotched face puffy with sleep.

"Really, you do not have to—" Jemma began again.

"I realize that," Moira said. She sat down on the edge of the bed, reaching to straighten the girl's pink flannelette nightgown.

At Moira's touch Tamaris began to cry louder.

"She doesn't like to be touched," Jemma said softly.

"I've already found that out," Moira replied and then, quietly, she spoke to Tamaris. "This afternoon you frightened me, do you know that?"

Tamaris, her sobs subsiding at the quiet tone of Moira's voice, turned a little, sniffling back tears. She looked up at Moira again, staring at the green-eyed woman sitting beside her on the bed. "Are you the reason my father stays away and never comes home?"

"No," Moira said. "Truly, no."

Through her sniffles, Tamaris spoke again. "Truly?"

"Yes."

"And you were frightened this afternoon . . . of me?" Moira nodded. "Why?" Tamaris sniffled back more tears.

"I was afraid I had hurt you. And something much worse."

Tamaris watched Moira. "Worse?"

126

Moira nodded again. "Much worse. I was afraid you thought that I would—willingly—hurt you."

Tamaris didn't answer right away. She stared at Moira and then glanced over at Jemma who stood beside the bed, watching. Finally Tamaris spoke. "What do you mean?"

"Well, all of us sometimes, accidentally, hurt others. But it's a terrible thing to willfully hurt someone. On purpose. You see the difference, don't you, Tamaris?"

"I think so."

"I was afraid you thought I'd willfully hurt you. On purpose."

Tamaris watched Moira's mouth as she spoke the words. "You wouldn't?"

"Never!" Moira's voice was so firm, so strong, it startled the young girl.

"Why not?" Tamaris's eyes did not leave Moira's face. "And why did you come here?"

"I had nowhere else to go," Moira replied truthfully.

The young girl heard the words, puzzling over them, until she finally spoke again. "I believe you."

"Thank you, Tamaris. I'm glad."

"But—Tristan says you're here to take Papa away from us."

"Never!"

The young girl straightened up. "I do believe you. I want to believe you."

"You can. You wait and see, all right? I want us to be the best of friends. And look there at poor Lancelot. He's so worried about you. Would you like him to stay with you tonight?"

Tamaris slowly nodded and Moira stood up. Jemma pulled the bedding back, straightening it as the pale young girl climbed beneath the covers, letting Jemma tuck her in. Jemma reached down to kiss Tamaris gently on the forehead and then turned to reach for the lamp she'd brought in with her.

Moira waited for Jemma at the doorway, aware of the young girl's eyes on her in the darkness now. "Good night, Tamaris." When there was no answer Jemma slowly closed the door.

"Would you like some tea?" Jemma asked.

"I'd love some. Jemma, I don't understand any of this."

Jemma didn't reply. Moira followed her further down the back hall, to the south hall. "This is the children's wing," Jemma said as they walked. "That's the door to the schoolroom . . . and here's my room."

They walked inside, Jemma putting the lamp on a table near

127

the door and then walking over to the windows. She pulled the curtains wide, letting the moonlight into the small, neat bedroom.

Here there were no brocades and heavy satin, no thick Turkish rugs. Moira sat down on a narrow chair near the plain wood table, sighing. "This is the first room I've felt at home in since I left Brittany."

"Truly?" Jemma turned to stare at her, in outright surprise. Then she rang for the tea.

"My room at home was very much like this."

"Like this! But why? Forgive me, but I can't somehow credit it. With your family's wealth."

"My family?" Moira stared at her.

"You are Edmund Walsh's daughter, are you not?"

"What do you know of my father, Jemma?"

"Why—not much."

Moira saw Jemma withdraw. "Please. Tell me what you know."

A knock at the door stopped their words. As the tiny maid opened it Jemma spoke to her quickly. "Thank you, Elsie, on the table is fine." Jemma looked over at Moira. "I asked Elsie to ready a pot when I came up. You'll meet Elsie and the staff in the morning, I understand."

Moira nodded, watching Elsie's wide-eyed astonishment at finding the new Duchess in Jemma's room. She left quickly, her gossip forgotten, closing the door and hesitating a moment before going back along the hall and down the servant's hall, toward her own room.

"I'm afraid the Duke may not approve of your visiting here, in my room," Jemma began.

"My father always told me," Moira interrupted, "that you find friends where you find them. I'd like us to be friends, Jemma, I hope we can be."

"I'd like that too."

"Good. Then, please, tell me what you know."

Jemma sighed. "I hardly know where to begin."

Moira watched the other woman as she sat down on the narrow chair across from Moira's and began to pour the tea.

"I came here five years ago, when Tristan was Mark's age now, fourteen. Mark was only nine and little Tamaris seven." She handed Moira a cup of tea, a spoon laying on the saucer, cream and sugar in little china pots on the tray between them. "In those five years I doubt that the Duke has been here more

128

than a few weeks at a time three or four times a year, at most. He is not close to his children."

"He spends his time in London?" Moira asked faintly.

"I have no idea. London, travelling, whatever. In any event, he is not here, and he does not take them with him."

"Never?" Moira hesitated. "Surely he does not need to be gone so much."

Jemma's voice hardened a little. "No one *needs* to be gone for their daughter's birthday, after they've promised faithfully to stay for it." She saw Moira's expression. "Last year. It was a cruel thing to do!" She stopped, realizing to whom she was talking.

"It's all right, Jemma," Moira said quietly. "I have to know what life is like here. I don't carry tales, and I won't repeat what you say."

Jemma watched the new Duchess earnestly. "I think you could be so good for them. At least for Mark and Tamaris."

Moira smiled, but her eyes were still sad. "I'm sure you've been good for them."

Jemma looked down. "I hope so. They've been so alone."

"How did their mother die?" Moira asked, holding her breath.

Jemma stared at her. "Surely you know."

Moira watched Jemma's surprise. "No. I don't. Why should I?"

"I was trying to build up the courage to ask you. One hears so many things, but since she was your aunt and your father was there, I thought . . ." she trailed off.

"The servants?" Moira said. "Surely they know."

Jemma hesitated. "There are no servants here that were here then. Except John Ottery, the butler."

"None! But that's so—unusual. All the way out here."

"I know." Jemma stirred her tea, staring at her untouched cup. "Didn't your father or mother mention any of this?"

"My mother," Moira replied quietly, "died shortly after my birth."

"I'm sorry, I didn't know." She made a decision and looked up at Moira, staring directly at her. "I—you may have me discharged for this, but I feel I must warn you." Her voice started to fade as she realized the enormity of what she was doing, was saying. "Warn you to be careful. To be very careful."

"Please." Dread began to haunt Moira again. "What are you

telling me? People start to say things and stop. No one will say what they mean. You can't say something like that and not tell me *why.*"

"From villagers," Jemma began, "and from things the children have said, I have heard that they call your husband the Black Duke, the Black St. Maur. They say he's named after another Black St. Maur, a duke who lived a hundred years ago. That first Michael killed his older brother Henry to gain the title and drove his wife mad. His only child, Louis, went mad in middle age." She watched Moira's expression. "In 1805, at Trafalgar, your husband's older brother Henry was killed, and the Admiralty said there was reason to believe Michael, I mean, the Duke, your husband, at least accidentally, caused it." She stopped.

Moira stared at Jemma. "Go on. I must understand what you are telling me. I must know what—people—say." She had to understand, she kept telling herself, she had to know. "Go on," she said again.

"In 1815 Lucy, your husband's first wife, your—aunt—I'm told, ran away with another man, to get away from—from danger. While the Duke was gone on one of his many trips."

"He was gone so much then too?"

"They say so. At any rate, he returned, discovered her absence, and found her, then dragged her back here to the castle where he—imprisoned—her. Without telling anyone."

"Imprisoned!"

"The old dungeons are down beneath this very wing." Jemma stared at the young woman across from her. "She was found dead, and your father swore to the authorities that he and the Duke had been together, had been hunting in Devon. That they had arrived after she was found by the servants. And there were others. People they'd been with, who would vouch that the Duke had never left, that he could not have been responsible. Since your father was Lucy's own brother—it was deemed accidental."

"Accidental." Moira's voice was faint.

Jemma nodded slowly. "Yes. Somehow, they said, she must have stumbled into the dungeons and the doors had closed."

"And locked themselves?" Moira asked incredulously.

"There are large wooden beams that—that fall into place to secure the doors on the outside. Hundreds of years old. They could have fallen if the door had slammed. So they say."

130

Moira stared at the pattern of cabbage roses on Jemma's bedcovers. "And then?"

Jemma spoke softly. "The old Duke had died earlier that year. And the new Duke, your husband, dismissed all the old servants. And won't stay near the children because they, they remind him."

Moira stood up. "But he's to be pitied then. Even my own father—" She stopped.

Jemma stood too. "Yes. Even your own father said the very same thing that the Duke did," Jemma said quietly. "There are those that say your father never touched the family money because of it. They say that he inherited the entire Walsh fortune then, because of her death, and that he—never touched it. Out of—forgive me—shame." Jemma saw Moira's expression and hurried on, wanting to have it all said, all over with. "You asked me to tell you all I knew. And now you tell me you've always lived like this." She thrust her hand out, indicating the room they stood in. "And now your father is dead and you—and he—inherit it all."

"It's not like that," Moira said quickly. "People have facts mixed up. The estate was put in trust for me. And there are reasons, there are arrangements—it's not like that!"

"Good." Jemma looked truly worried. "I pray for your sake every bit of it is nonsense. But, please, do be careful."

"Careful?"

Jemma took a deep breath. "They say she, Lucy, had— accidents—before, before."

Moira's hand was on the doorknob. "Jemma, I asked you and I appreciate your, your candor. But please, now, let's stop all these stories. Don't repeat any of this again. To anyone. Things aren't like that. Truly. I can't explain, but, believe me, there is nothing to any of it. People like to talk, that's all. In a small place they have little else to occupy themselves with so they—talk. That's all." She thought of London and Lady Jersey and pushed the thought from her mind.

Jemma spoke softly "I hope you're right."

"I am. I'm sure of it. I'd best say good night."

"Yes." Jemma held the door open after Moira left, watching for a moment as Moira disappeared down the dark hallway toward the north wing.

* * *

Moira was unable to rest, her empty rooms chilling in spite of the fires in their grates. She reached for one of her new soft woolen cloaks and then closed the door to her sitting room, walking down the wide stairs. She stopped at the bottom to stare toward the hallway that led toward the library.

Resolutely she walked toward the closed door, opening it to find the room deserted, Michael gone, the fire out.

She closed the door, turning back along the North Gallery toward the tall French doors at the end. The huge building oppressed her, her steps echoing against the stone floors, the stone walls.

She opened the door, stepping out into the night air, taking in a deep breath of the fresh night air. A wall of fog obscured any view of the sea but the sound of the ocean pounding up below the cliffs drew her nearer, reminding her of Brittany and their cottage on the cliff.

Coming closer to the edge she could make out the jagged rocks that outlined the bay, the wind pushing driftwood and seaweed up the narrow beach below the cliff, the waves lapping up over the shingle and then falling back, away. The cliff descended sharply she saw as she leaned to look over the edge.

She straightened up after a moment, turning from the vista of the mist-enshrouded sea to trace a path westward, along the edge of the cliff to where it overlooked Saint's Bay, the village of St. Maur visible as a few dim specks of light across the inlet.

Her foot slipped on the wet ground. She lost her footing and then her balance as she felt the edge of the cliff giving way beneath her.

"Good grief!" A strong young voice accompanied the arms that went around her, pulling her back. "You die this soon and you'll give us all a bad name."

Her heart in her mouth, Moira turned to face Tristan. "Where—how long have—" She gulped for air.

"Have I been following you? Luckily for you since I saw you leave the house. Knowing how unfamiliar you'd be after all these years, I thought I'd better keep an eye on you."

"Thank you, but it's not necessary." She turned away, forcing his hands from where they still held her arms.

"Isn't it?" He would not let go. He reached to pull her back to face him. "We've had enough gossip about us without you adding to it. Besides, you're much better to look at than the girls around here."

132

"Tristan! I'm quite all right." She tried to move away. "I'd like to be alone."

"Not much on gratitude are you? I just saved your bloody life."

His insolent expression unnerved her. "What are you staring at?"

"You. You've surely blossomed from the chit of a girl I remember, always crying about something."

"I was not!"

"Always running to them to get them to stop me from picking on you. Really, you were such a wicked little girl. Are you still? They say he can always pick them."

"Pick—I don't know what you mean."

"Don't you know?" He started to lean closer and she wrenched away.

She stared at him, shocked.

"Yes," he smiled, "I was going to kiss you. If you'll put up with him, you'll put up with anybody."

"What are you saying! Tristan—"

"You know about her, by the way, don't you?"

The coldness that overcame her was not from the winds and the mist. "Her?"

Tristan nodded toward St. Maur. "In the village. The one at the inn. Where he spends his nights."

"I don't know what you're talking about." She tried to keep her voice steady, backing one step away from him.

"Oh yes, you do. Anyway, you'll soon see her. You won't be able to avoid it. The whole county knows about it, of course. Although I'm sure it's a bit of a shock that he'd go there this night. His first night back with a new bride." He watched her expression, seeing her blush in the dim moonlight. "But then, you'll get used to it. Just as my mother did with his lady friends then."

"Tristan, please, stop. I don't want to hear this."

He grabbed her arms again, drawing her closer. "You're even prettier when you're upset."

He leaned forward to kiss her, his lips touching hers before she could twist away, pushing against him until she finally broke free. Backing away she stared at him in horror. "I'm your father's *wife!*"

Tristan smiled. "You're not married to my father." He stared at her shocked expression. "He killed my mother, you know.

133

Your own aunt by the way. Just like he'll kill you. For the fortune he couldn't get then, my sweet cousin. That's all he wants out of you. He has expensive tastes. And his greed knows no bounds."

If he had yelled, if he had spoken loudly, it would have been less frightening. But he spoke calmly, matter-of-factly, and he terrified her. She began to run toward the house, her hands at her ears, his voice following her. "You run from me, but it's him you should be afraid of!"

She reached the French doors and stumbled inside, running along the North Gallery to the stairs and her rooms beyond. She slammed the sitting room door behind herself, leaning against it, her chest heaving. How could he know of the sham of their marriage? How could he possibly know?

"Milady?" Frances walked into the sitting room from the boudoir. "Is something wrong?"

Moira stared at her. "No," she managed to say finally. "Nothing."

Frances, disbelieving, disapproving, reached for Moira's cloak. "When you did not ring I thought I'd best come ready your things for the night."

Moira nodded, staring at the small side door across from her. The door that led into the Duke's rooms from her sitting room. It was closed.

Unsteadily Moira walked forward, sinking down onto a velvet chaise longue, staring at the folds of the rose velvet gown she'd worn to dinner. It was wilted, creased and stained along the hem by the grass and the sand of the cliffs.

She stared at it as Frances filled a tub and readied night-clothes and robes in the room beyond, keeping her own counsel about the nights her mistress spent alone.

Moira walked into the bathing room, more tired than she had realized. She sank into the steaming water gratefully, her heart sore with worry. Tristan was as she remembered. His children were estranged, all of them, and he himself distant and cold with them. A woman. Tristan was lying, had to be lying. And yet. . . . She stopped the thought, wondering if he would be back late. Her thoughts went to the village. To the woman Tristan said waited there. Her heart chilled. What if it were Genevieve? What if—what if—she stopped herself again.

"Milady?"

She looked up to see Frances watching her with worried

eyes. "You were shaking your head, Milady. Did you dislike something?"

"No." Moira shook her head yet again. "No." She put her hand out for a towel. "I am simply more tired than I knew." Frances handed a large towel to Moira, wrapping it around her as Moira stepped out of the golden-fitted tub.

Moira accepted the nightgown Frances held out to her, belting it herself, looking down. She willed the tears away. Frances felt the pain in her mistress, her own eyes becoming angry when she thought of the Duke out from the house, and her lady here alone. Again.

"He should be ashamed."

"What?"

Frances caught herself, her words having spilled out loud into the quiet air of the bedroom.

"Nothing, Milady. I was talking to myself."

Moira sat down on her bed. "You may leave. You must be tired too. It has been a long journey."

"Yes, Milady." Frances started out and then stopped in the small hallway, turning back slowly. "I'm sure he's only thinking of you, Milady."

"What?" Moira looked up distracted.

Frances hesitated. "Our—our conversation—in the inn? You remember?"

Moira nodded, struck dumb by Frances bringing it up.

"I'm sure he's trying to not—upset you. Shock you while you're settling in and all."

Moira stared into the good-hearted face across the room. Frances so plainly wanted to make her feel better. And so plainly did not believe her own words. "Have you heard gossip too?"

"No, Milady!" Frances said quickly.

Moira acknowledged her words and then lay back on the bed. "Good night, Frances."

"Good night, Milady."

Frances left Moira to her thoughts, closing the door softly.

Long hours went by, the moon traversing the sky outside her windows and still she lay awake, listening for she knew not what.

And then finally she heard his boots on the stair, his door opening and closing. She closed her tired eyes, willing him to

135

come in, willing him to tell her everything was all right, that there was no reason for the fear that was growing within her. She wanted to believe in him.

Her pillow was stained with tears, was wet beneath her cheek. She turned over, finding a dry spot on the pillow's edge, closing her eyes tight. She realized with an awful certainty that she loved this man. Still loved this man. And would. No matter what.

And that he did not know. And might not care if he did. Tears began to slide down her cheek again. If she only knew what to do, if she only knew how to get up and to go to his rooms, to please him. To make him understand.

If only she dared to try.

But this night was almost over. Her first night in the castle that was to be her home for five months. She would have five months with him and then be sent packing. A resolve began to build deep within her. He might send her packing but he would not do it unaware. He would know of her love before she went.

Somehow she would prove it.

Chapter Fifteen

IN THE MORNING MOIRA AWOKE TO THE SOUND OF MICHAEL'S VOICE booming out from his suite next door. "Andre, my coat!"

A feeling of shock thrilled down her spine, turning her toward her open bedroom door. Then voices carried from beyond her sitting room again.

"Here, Your Grace." Andre's voice could barely be heard.

"Are they ready? What time is it?"

Moira's heart calmed a little, coming awake.

"It's just gone eight, Your Grace, and the grooms have the horses ready for you to decide."

"Good. I'll be back by ten. Have 'em ready for whenever she's up after that and we'll go through the drill."

"Yes, Your Grace."

The sound of his boots rang out as he took the stone steps two at a time and then the front door slammed closed.

Moira listened still. She thought she could hear a horse trot

136

off after a moment. She closed her eyes, thinking of the plans, the desires, she'd fallen asleep with; her face turned crimson as she lay in her bed, alone in her own room.

Own room for now at least. The whole situation was a nightmare, it was intolerable. He wanted Genevieve and she wanted him. She wanted . . . something. To be close. To have him kiss her again, to feel those lips again. On her mouth, her breast—she shivered with the remembered feelings. He could not be so cold to her if he had done that. And he had, he had. Somehow maybe he was not entirely committed to Genevieve —shame rose within her, engulfing her. There was the boy to think of, and there was duty. And propriety. And—and something must be terribly wrong with her, she knew it had to be, for all she could think about were his arms, his lips, his eyes. She stopped the thoughts, trying to stuff them back from wherever they were coming from. But she could not. Her thoughts rode away down the road with Michael.

Michael. . . . His name sung within her. She was married to Michael. In name only. She was married to a man and the marriage would never be binding for he would never consummate it. The word entranced her. She now knew what it meant, what he would physically do. . . . He would consume her. . . .

She sat up, acutely conscious of her body. Of its weight, its curves, its secret places. She wanted to give them all away to him, to have him tell her what to do, show her. Respectable people, sane people, did not dwell on such things, she told herself. And yet, and yet, that little voice urged her on, they did them. Respectable people had children all the time which meant that they must—that even her father and mother must have—She stood up, reaching to ring for Frances, letting the day begin. She found her eyes closing, trying to imagine Michael's body. The thought seemed forbidden. And tantalizing. She was married to a man she did not in truth know. She wanted to know him, know him fully; know his thoughts, his feelings, his desires . . . his body . . . that tall, full, hard body.

And he was right. She was still a child. She did not even know how to do—how to make love to him. How to please him. Or even if she could.

Michael arrived back a little before ten, stiff and formal when he met her over tea and toast in the dining room.

"Are you ready?" he asked rather curtly.

She stood up, coming round to walk beside him out into the

main entrance hall, her heart thudding within her breast. He hardly glanced at her.

In the great hall, lined up and waiting in fresh uniforms and caps, were the servants. John Ottery stepped forward and solemnly led her down the line: Mrs. Daphne Norris, the housekeeper, Mr. Giles Norris, head gardener, Nan Fletcher, cook, Millie and Meg and Peg and Elsie and May, skipping Frances, and on to Tom and Harry and William and Alf, James and Roger and Robert and Jeb; footmen, coachmen, grooms, maids, scullery, laundry, and on, Andre to one end, standing by Mr. Moffatt. "You already have met Andre and, of course, our head steward, Mr. Ned Moffatt."

Both Andre and Moffatt bowed slightly, every eye including the Duke's on Moira.

She cleared her throat, trying to speak over the self-conscious tightness that shook her voice, making it waver. "Thank you very much, John. And," she turned toward the staff, "ladies and gentlemen. I trust we will get to know one another well and—" she floundered, reaching for a way out, "and Mrs. Norris, if you have a moment."

Mrs. Norris stepped forward, nodding, as John, with a glance, dismissed the others.

The Duke glanced at Moira, a little curious. Then he turned his gaze on Mrs. Norris. "Mrs. Norris, you may show the Duchess through the house now and give her the keys."

"Yes, Your Grace."

He glanced at Moira again, the same curious expression in his eyes. "I shall ride the estate with Moffatt. I won't be back for luncheon."

Moira nodded, swallowing hard, and he was gone. She watched him walking away, his back straight, his legs—she stopped the thought, turning toward the housekeeper. "The, ah—library?"

Mrs. Norris looked at the distracted countenance of the young woman before her. "If you wish, Your Ladyship, but the fire is laid in the—in your morning room."

"Oh. Thank you. If you would please, direct me, we can talk there."

"As you wish, Your Ladyship." Mrs. Norris walked forward, toward and through the North Gallery, through the Conservatory, to a small oak-panelled door off the Long Gallery. Opening the door, Mrs. Norris stepped back to let Moira pass.

Moira came forward into a small room directly under her sitting room. The morning sun brightened the room from the east and north windows, bathing the walls and furniture with pale sunbeams.

Between two large east windows a small marble-faced fireplace held a bright, warm fire, its logs crackling in the silence.

"It's lovely," Moira said, looking from the pale spring green the walls were papered with, to the darker green carpet, to the comfortable padded chairs of violet velvet, to the apple green silk cushions on the lavender couch.

The housekeeper did not reply, awaiting her employer's instructions, and after a moment, Moira motioned her to a chair.

"I want very much," Moira began, "to see the rest of the—family—rooms. And I would like to tour the kitchens and the servants' quarters also."

Mrs. Norris's astonishment was plain. "I beg your pardon, the servants' quarters?" She stared at the chit of a girl who was now mistress of Saint's Castle. Who was younger than young Master Tristan.

Moira tried to smile at the woman. "Would you care for tea, or hot chocolate, while we talk?"

"I—no, thank you, Your Ladyship. I'm sure I couldn't."

"Of course you can." Moira stood and walked to the bell-pull, determined to hold up her end of the bargain her father had exacted. "We'll have hot chocolate and some biscuits, and then we can attack this problem together. You see, Mrs. Norris, I need your help."

"My—help?" Daphne Norris had trouble believing her ears.

"Yes. You see, I'm going to be doing things quite differently than the staff is used to, I'm afraid. I'm not used to quite so much formality. And then again, I'm used to rather actively participating in household matters since we had a much smaller staff. Much smaller."

"I see," the woman said, dreading the upheaval she could see coming.

A knock on the door brought John inside.

"Yes, thank you, John. We'd like some hot chocolate and, do you think cook—Nan, wasn't it?"

"Yes, Your Ladyship."

"Do you suppose by any chance she might have any fuggan laying about?"

"Fuggan?" His eyes lit ever so slightly.

"I loved those raisin cakes. I haven't had any since we left Cornwall."

John Ottery unbent enough to almost smile. His white-haired head bowed slowly, and, with a glance at Mrs. Norris, he left.

Taking her cue from the butler, Mrs. Norris sat quietly, as if she had tea and toast with duchesses every day of the week. Or chocolate and fuggan, she corrected herself.

"Now, then," Moira began purposefully, "who decides the menus for the week?"

Christmas preparations were getting underway by these early November days as Mrs. Norris took Moira through the house, handing keys over as they walked, explaining the layout of the castle.

A large square park, called the Quadrangle, was surrounded on all four sides by the castle itself, with a carriage-way in and out at the center of the back. Above this the back, called the east wing, held the children's quarters, gun rooms and stables to each side of the carriage-way.

The south wing held the servants' rooms above, the servants' hall, pantry, and then the main dining rooms below. The front, west wing, held the Dowager Duchess's suite on the south end, over the main salons, and the Duke's suite on the north end, over the library and his study, with the great three-story entry hall dissecting the middle. The north wing held the Duchess's and the guest suites above, the North Gallery and Salon, Morning Room, Long Gallery, and Conservatory below.

The new Duchess and Mrs. Norris walked through the endless quarters and corridors, finally reaching the top floor.

"The only rooms used up here are the seamstress's here in the south wing. The rest are closed."

"Are they ever used?" Moira stared about her down the long, gloomy corridor at the top of the south stairwell.

"Over the holidays. They'll be gotten ready in the next weeks. And in the old days with house parties and all, they used to be used much more Mr. Ottery says."

Moira smiled. "This house was built for a large family."

"Yes," Mrs. Norris replied.

Movement down the stairwell caught Moira's eye. She looked down to see Tamaris hanging on the stairs, halfway down to the next floor. The little girl looked upward wistfully,

140

and Moira's heart went out to her. What must it be like to live under the burden of all these rumors about your parents. Rumors. Moira repeated the word to herself. That's all they were. People loved to gossip, always had. Always would. The fears that had cropped up when Jemma spoke, the vague niggling little doubts, now seemed silly in the bright light of day. Even the thoughts of lovemaking seemed far away and buried under the reality of the household chores.

"Hello." Moira smiled down at Tamaris.

The little girl came slowly forward. "Would you like to see the Quad?" she asked finally, shyly.

"Yes." Moira turned to Mrs. Norris. "I think I've seen enough for today. Thank you."

"Of course, Your Ladyship," Mrs. Norris replied and then left them alone.

Moira walked down to where Tamaris waited, and the two of them descended to the entrance hall below, the chain of keys now about Moira's waist chinking against each other as she moved.

"We can go through the ballroom," Tamaris said, walking forward under the great gilt archway, into the gold and crystal chandeliered ballroom. "This way." She slipped out tall doors in the French manner and stood just outside in a large, square park, totally enclosed by the walls of the castle.

A fountain gurgled near a lime tree, frost glittering in the cold November air as water fell from Pan's pipe to the stone basin beneath. Moira pulled her shawl close as they walked toward the archway that led through the back wall of the castle. Gulls driven inland by the weather wheeled and cried across the parapets that edged the roof balconies overhead, circling around the turreted corners of the building.

Moira looked up at the stone of the castle's sides, the soft winter sunlight reflected from the leaves of the lichen growing there, giving a rusty glow to the walls. Thin columns of smoke wafted out across the roof from the huge stone chimneys.

The sound of horses clattering up to the stable beyond came toward them. Tamaris, hearing it, ran forward to the archway. "It may be my father!" She disappeared beyond; Moira started after and then hesitated. She waited for a moment longer, and when Tamaris didn't appear she turned toward the inside of the house.

Tamaris's clear young voice hollered out to her. "Moira!"

141

Turning back toward the archway, Moira saw Tamaris coming toward her, Mark, Tristan, and a tall man with sandy blond hair just behind.

"Ah, our new Duchess!" Tristan was calling out: "You must meet Jack! Say hello, Mark, say good morning to our new mother." As Tristan spoke, Mark's sullen expression deepened. With a glowering look he walked past Moira and into the house, without speaking.

"You must forgive my brother," Tristan began smoothly.

"It is easy to forgive your brother," Moira interrupted pointedly. Tamaris stepped a little away from Moira's side, watching.

"Please," Moira looked up into the gentle blue eyes of the man standing beside Tristan, "I hope you'll forgive our bad manners. Won't you come inside?"

"Thank you, but no, I'm afraid I—can't." He bowed slightly. "I had not thought to meet you thus, Your Ladyship. I beg your indulgence for my unheralded approach."

"Need we be quite that formal, Mr.—?"

He bowed again. "James Lisle-Taylor, at your service, Your Ladyship. But all call me Jack."

The Duke stepped outside and then, seeing the tall blond man strode toward them, his voice loud and cold. "What is the meaning of this?" Forbidding lines were etched deep into his face.

Jack bowed. "Your servant, sir. It is my fault entirely."

"Fault? What fault do you speak of?" Moira looked from one of them to the other.

"He's my friend and I brought him here! It's my home too!" Tristan said. "You've never—"

"That will be enough!" the Duke roared at Tristan, and then his eyes fastened on Jack's. "Well?" he asked belligerently.

Moira stared at her husband. At any moment he was going to hit this man.

Jack bowed low to Moira and turned away without another word. Tristan stared at the Duke. "Is it any wonder all hate you!?" The young man turned on his heel, walking after Jack.

Moira could not take her eyes from Michael's haunted expression. "Michael, what is it?"

He roused himself, glancing at Tamaris and then turning away. "I came out to tell you a package has arrived for you." He walked back toward the open French doors.

Moira ran toward the house, reaching the doors before he did. "Michael, please!"

He stopped. "You are blocking the doorway."

"Michael—what was that about?"

Tamaris came slowly behind, stopping near them. She watched each of them in turn.

"I do not wish that—man—here."

"But *why?*"

He stared at her. "I have the right to invite, or exclude, any, in my own home. With no explanation to *anyone.*"

She looked up into his eyes. They were still cold, still haunted by something she did not understand. He towered above her, looking down from his great height at the petite young woman who blocked his path. He could have swept her aside with one hand. "I'm not demanding," she said after a moment. "I'm asking, Michael. You must have a reason for making a scene such as that. I thought you were going to hit him."

"I would have," he said. "And I do have reasons."

She watched him. "I'll take Tamaris up for her lessons." Moira stepped back into the room, holding her hand out for Tamaris. "Tammy? Would you like to go with me to find Jemma?"

The young girl moved cautiously around her father, reaching for and taking Moira's outstretched hand. The Duke watched them. As they turned away he stepped up into the doorway.

"You have no more questions?" he asked, his expression an enigma.

"No."

"No?"

She shook her head. "I believe you. You say you have reasons, and you obviously do not want to discuss them. Therefore it is either something you do not wish me to know about, or something you would be less than a gentleman repeating." She watched him. "I trust you," she added softly as he still stared at her. She could feel weakness coming to her limbs as his eyes searched her face.

"Then you're a fool," he said finally.

Tamaris's hand now clutched at Moira's.

Moira stared at him. "Am I?"

He hesitated. "Anyone who trusts without reason is a fool."

He walked on past them, walking forward toward the great main hall. As he passed by she spoke. "Then I am a fool. Or I have my own reasons."

He continued on, crossing the hall before Moira and Tamaris reached the stairwell.

Tamaris was quiet until they reached the children's wing. "Do you truly trust my papa?"

"Yes." Moira thought about her qualms, her doubts, and fears. Was it true, or was it only true that she wanted to trust him, wanted to be able to trust him? "Why?" She looked at Tamaris, hearing her talk but not hearing the words.

"Do you love my papa?"

Moira hesitated. "Why do you ask, Tamaris?"

"My mama didn't. That's why he killed her."

Moria's knees weakened with the matter-of-fact words. "Oh, Tamaris! You don't know what you're saying."

Tomaris looked up at her solemnly. "Yes, I do."

"Just because people tell you things, that's no reason to believe them, Tamaris."

"Ask Jack," Tamaris said. "He'll tell you all about it."

"Jack? You mean Mr. Lisle-Taylor? What does he know about it? What would he tell me, Tamaris?"

"He knows. I asked him." She still watched Moira. "Are you my mother now?"

"I'd like to be at least your friend. If you'll let me. No one can take your mother's place."

"Don't listen." Mark stood in his doorway. "Tammy, don't listen to her. She'll hurt you too!"

Tamaris did not even look at her brother. "Will you?"

"No. I won't."

"She will." He took a step out toward them. "She'll hurt us and she'll leave us too."

A terrible guilt smote at Moira's heart. She would leave them. She would be gone too. As their mother was. As their father truly was; he was as closed away from them as if he no longer existed either.

Moira straightened up. "Mark, I don't blame you for not trusting me. Or anyone."

"I trust Tristan!"

"Yes. I'm sorry, of course you do. But then, Mark, will you at least give me a chance?"

He stared at her, and then, his eyes sliding to the floor he turned away, back into his own room, closing the door.

Moira sighed and then found Tamaris's hand slipping into hers again.

"I'll talk to him," Tamaris said.

Moira smiled. "Thank you, Tammy."

Tamaris smiled then, her sober young face lit from within, her eyes bright and warm for the first time since Moira had met her. The young girl turned and walked away toward Mark's room, Moira watching her go.

Moira started back toward her suite and then remembered the package, ringing for Frances once she reached her sitting room.

Frances brought the package and Moira's midday meal up to the pale rose sitting room, Moira staring at the unopened package, almost afraid of what it might contain.

She waited until Frances left before reaching for it, before reaching inside to see what it contained. Then she stared at the packet of papers her father's solicitors had forwarded, their cover letter directly to the point: "Dear Lady Michael: Please find enclosed the personal papers your father left in our trust. We wish to extend our deepest condolences and remain at your disposal should you need any further—"

She put the heavy parchment down on the small cherrywood table beside the chaise longue, not bothering to read the rest of it. She reached into the pile of papers she'd unwrapped.

Letters of her mother's, letters from her father to her mother, her mother's death certificate, all lay before her. A diary her mother had kept the year before Moira was born was among them. She opened it at random, her mother's handwriting unfamiliar, the letters spiking, elongated. When she glanced down into the almost empty box, she saw a small parcel still inside, its ribbon sealed around it.

She reached for it, breaking the seal, pulling the ribbon off, opening the thin, flat packet.

Inside, a narrow household diary, plain-covered and thin, lay upon a folded sheet of paper. She glanced at the first pages of the diary, household accounts noted here and there, with notations of weather and purchases, dated 1806. Looking at it, glancing at a few pages further in, Moira realized that years had been skipped, 1812 dates appearing with cryptic notes that became longer as the pages followed one another. Then she saw a note captioned Mark. This couldn't be her mother's. Her mother was long dead by 1812. That was only thirteen years ago, she was already four by then.

She looked at the handwriting. It was different, too. This was Lucy's diary. Her aunt's diary. Michael's wife's diary.

She stopped reading, her heart pounding. She was his wife

now. She. None other. She stared down at the closed covers and saw again the folded sheet of paper. Staring at it, some part of her afraid to look further, she picked it up. She realized with a sudden clarity that, if Michael was truly guilty of any of it, she did not want to know. She did not want to doubt him. Did not want to believe any of it, true or not. Did not want to fear him, dear God, did not want to fear him. He was the only thing she had left from her childhood. If she had to fear him, if she could not rely upon him, then her father had known it. Then her father had done her harm and she could rely upon nothing.

Finally, still staring at it, she opened the folded page, reading the words that blurred before her vision: "Edmund, come quickly or it will be too late. I know now he's causing my accidents, and I found today the poison that caused the illness. Edmund, he didn't even deny it! Please don't let him do this to me, you're the only hope I have. I'm going to Jack. Michael knows about him, about Tristan, none of it matters anymore. Edmund, if you love me, if you care for your only sister at all, come at once, for he'll never let Jack's son inherit St. Maur, and he'll not let me leave. If anything happens to me or Tristan before you arrive, keep this! Help us!—Lucy."

Moira folded the paper over and over, looking at the windows from which the sun had now long faded. She looked down at the paper clutched in her fist. This was Lucy's letter. She stood up, walking to the window that overlooked the west gardens and the Bristol Channel beyond, thoughts and fears, too many thoughts and fears twisting themselves around each other.

Her father had died. Michael said at the hands of others. Michael said Jean-Marc was his own flesh and blood. She was an heiress, so they all said, and she was his wife. A wife he obviously had no intention of staying married to. He disappeared and the pirate ship appeared. He wanted none to know of his own black ship. She was the outsider, he said, the outsider who dreamed of black men with Michael's eyes.

She stopped herself, forcing herself back to Lucy's letter and Lucy dying in the dungeons, screaming probably, alone. Unheard. The children hearing stories from the servants, then the servants dismissed, but the villagers still talking.

How much did the children remember, and how much had been whispered around them? Jack. The Jack that Michael had almost hit earlier; Lucy had run to him. Or tried to. Or was it the

146

same Jack, the same one that Michael despised and would not let near?

Tristan was not Michael's son, Lucy said. And she said Michael knew. And yet he was the heir to the title, to the lands. And Tristan himself had said almost the same thing, and she had not understood. He had said that she was not married to his father. Did he then know that Jack was his father? What else had he said? Your fortune, he wants your fortune. And Jemma had hinted at the same thing. He couldn't get it through Lucy so now he'd have it all, through Moira, Edmund's and Lucy's shares.

But he wouldn't. Not if the marriage was annulled. None of them knew he had not wanted to marry her, had done it on the proviso that they would have it annulled as soon as—

She stared at the soft rose-colored furnishings around her, at the dim light now coming in the windows. Why would her father lie about his own sister's death? Had he even mentioned the letter to anyone else? Or had it lain here, all these years, buried at the bottom of a sealed box in a solicitor's office?

Why would Michael do this, do any of it? And if he knew any of it were true, why would her father let her marry a man who murdered, who pirated, who—it made no sense.

Tristan was not Michael's son, but being legally Michael's heir, he would inherit the dukedom. Would that knowledge drive a proud man to murder? Would the knowledge of his rival's existence, flaunted before him, drive him to a frenzy where anything was possible? Or could he have wanted the money all along, could all this somehow be part of some grand scheme he'd had all along? Could that be true of him? If it could be true of him, how could she think that and still love him?

How could she love a man she did not know, in the first place? She ran her fingers through her hair, loosening the pins which held it in place, letting it fall free to her shoulders.

She had loved him since she was a child, had built on what she did know, had imagined what he was truly like. But if he weren't, if she was wrong, then what? She had to find out. She had to know. October had fled, November was now slipping by. Soon it would be December. And in three months she would be of age, she would be eighteen and he would leave her. Would send her away. Jemma's warning floated up to her consciousness, her warning of things happening . . . to be careful. What nonsense.

147

A discreet tap at the door had to be repeated before she heard it and called out to enter.

Frances opened the door. "Are you feeling well, Your Ladyship? Is everything all right?"

Moira turned toward Frances. "No. No, I'm not. I think I'll retire early. Please tell Madame that I will not be down for dinner."

"Yes, Milady." Frances went to pick up the luncheon tray. "But—you didn't eat!"

"No." Moira spoke vaguely. "No. But, Frances, wait!" She saw her maid stop and turn toward her. "Have you ever seduced a man?"

"Milady!"

"Now is not the time for false modesty, Frances, I need help."

The plump little maid sat down on a chair, her eyes round with surprise. "Oh, Milady!" She was so shocked she did not realize that she had sat down uninvited in front of her mistress.

Moira was watching her with expectant eyes. "I would like to know what is—usually—done."

Frances shook her head. "I cannot tell you, Milady."

"I am a married woman, Frances. I have a right to know."

Frances almost twisted her hands. She held them firmly in her lap, her voice strangulated by her shock. "I cannot tell you because I do not know *what* to tell you, Milady!" she finally managed to say, to Moira's great disappointment.

"Oh." Moira stood up, Frances springing to her own feet beside her. "Well," Moira continued, "then we must make do with what we can imagine. Bring me up some brandy."

"Brandy?" Frances asked faintly.

"Yes. Lots of brandy. Later. Oh—and whiskey too."

"Whiskey?" Frances swallowed. "Yes, Your—Milady. Is there anything else?"

"Hmmmm?"

"A bath—or—?"

"Oh yes. No! Frances—would you prepare the shower of water for me?"

"The shower of water?" Frances could not follow Moira's thoughts.

"Yes, I think I'll try it tonight." She giggled then, a touch of hysteria gripping her racing brain. "After all, tonight is a night for courage, is it not? And with all the intrigue about us, why on

148

earth should I be afraid of a little water contraption?" She laughed then, the sound harsh. She saw Frances's expression and ran forward into her bedroom, slamming the door in between as the laughter turned to tears. Frances stared at the closed door, worried and unsure.

Chapter Sixteen

SHE AWOKE TO THE SOUND OF HIS HEAVY TREAD UPON THE STAIRS. She could imagine the polished boots as they tripped against the top step and then stood straight, Andre's voice coming through the walls, helping him to his room in the late hours.

She waited. Waited for Andre to leave. Waited for silence in the rooms beyond the small connecting door. And then she reached for the flagon of whiskey, bringing it along as she slipped open the small door, trying to see across the expanse of his sitting room.

It was pitch dark, the drapes drawn tight against the night, the fire in the grate only embers now.

She tried to quiet her breathing, walking resolutely toward the door to her bedroom, which lay open beyond, moonlight cutting a path across the wooden floor, outlining the huge bed upon which he slept.

Her heart thudded so loudly she was sure it would wake him, her stomach rising in her throat as her fear increased.

She almost turned back. The whiskey sloshed against the sides of its container as she took another step forward and then resolutely walked to the table beside the bed, carefully putting the flagon down.

Michael snored softly due to the drink that was on his breath, one arm flung out over his head. She slipped under the covers quickly, glad of the warmth, frightened nearly to death by her own actions. If he woke and threw her out, if he shamed her, telling her she was not wanted here, she would die. She knew it. If she was wrong—she shuddered at the thought and he turned in his sleep, one arm falling across her waist, pinning her where she was.

His breath smelled of the whiskey she remembered, the hard, harsh smell she remembered from the inn. Her heart swelled within her, her senses acutely aware of the man who sprawled beside her, asleep. She turned her head, his great dark brow a bare inch away. She reached to kiss it, gently, her lips soft as a raindrop against his forehead. He stirred in his sleep, her lips finding the bridge of his nose, the angle of his eyelid, bringing him half-awake with a grunt of surprise.

She stiffened with fear as he mumbled something she could not hear. And then she kissed his cheek, his eye still closed.

"Where—" His word was slurred.

"The inn . . . the inn . . ." Thinking quickly Moira spoke against the stubble of his beard.

He reached for her, grabbing her hair in one large hand and almost smothering her with a kiss at once hard and practiced. She felt his tongue invade her mouth greedily, felt the tremors that fled through her body until he jerked himself away, almost sitting up. "What the bloody hell—"

She reached for the whiskey flagon, pressing it to his lips. "Compliments of the management."

He let some of it pour down his throat before he swept it aside, sending it crashing to the floor across the room. His eyes focused now, his hands grabbing her shoulders and pulling her up. Nearer. Closer. To stare into her face. "Moira!" The word was a strangled oath.

"Now it is you who are dreaming," she told him.

His fingers dug into her shoulders. And then with a savage gesture they rent the front of her nightdress in two. She sat before him, in the middle of the bed, naked to the waist, the bed covers piled all around them. Her eyes watched his as he looked down at her, unable to disguise his reaction. "Kiss me," she whispered. "Kiss me again . . . as you did at the inn."

A strangled sound escaped his lips and then, his eyes black in the darkness, he pulled her to him, his movements fierce as he crushed her against his chest, his tongue forcing her mouth open, his hands leaving red welts where they dug into her skin. As if punishing her for making him admit his own need.

She felt the madness, the fierceness, and yet his mouth, his lips, his tongue drew her nearer. She touched her own tongue to the inner edge of his lips, feeling the tremor that ran through him when she explored his mouth, when her hands reached to his nightshirt and pulled on it. A button spilled off it and she

150

yanked at it, as he had done with hers. She heard the fabric rip as he reached his own hand to tear it open.

Dark hair matted his chest, dark hair her fingers caught themselves in, tugging on it as he reached to lay her back across the pillows.

"Moira—" he tried to speak into her hair.

She bent to his collarbone, to trail her fingers over his nipples, to reach down hesitantly to his waist, to his belly. She felt his sharp intake of breath and then was engulfed by him, his great head reaching to take her breast in his mouth, his hands on her breast, on her hips, in her hair, her body reaching up toward him, seeking the touch of him.

She lost her breath when he pulled back away, afraid he was going to leave her again. She caught at his hand. "No, no, Michael, please . . . please . . ."

His voice was as ragged as hers. "Tell me what you want."

"I want you to stay. . . . To—stay."

He felt her hands, tentative and unsure, reaching to make him feel what she felt. He saw her inexperience in every movement and somehow it increased his desire. "You don't know what you ask."

"Show me. . . ." He heard the breathlessness, the desire, in her voice, shuddering at it, still holding himself away. And then he reached for her hand, very deliberately pulling it down, placing it on his throbbing flesh.

The sound he made when she touched him made her fingers wrap around him tightly. Her hand was full of hard, throbbing flesh. His leg was beneath her arm, his thigh hardened by years of riding and sailing. Her breath caught in her throat. This was the most private part of him and she held it in her hand. Desire, new and urgent, painful, transcendent, coursed through her. She wanted him. She wanted him within her, wanted this flesh to teach her what life meant, what love was.

She reached to find his mouth, wanting to feel his tongue inside her mouth, aching to have him within her, to touch the inside of his lips, to feel the hardness of his teeth. Her hand moved ever so little. He shuddered with every movement until she learned to move back and forth along the length of him, his whole body tense, as if held in check by some savage act of failing will.

She moved her hand again, and again, pulling on his flesh, feeling the change in his body as his kiss burned fiercer. Until

151

the whole long length of him reached to fall forward, her hand pulled abruptly away from his flesh, her fingers laced within his as he covered her body with his, crushing her beneath him, her arms spread-eagled by his.

The shock of his weight made her gasp. And yet when he moved to pull away she curved up toward him, wanting the weight of him. "Moira . . . Moira . . . stop this—"

He moved to open her legs, to pull the gown completely apart, her body reacting of its own volition to his every touch. His breath was ragged and still smelling of whiskey. Words began to pour into her ear. "Stop me. Stop me now or it will be too late. . . . Stop me . . ."

"No."

"Moira . . . please . . . please . . ."

"No!" Her voice became fierce too. She reached to curl her arms around him, to pull his weight against her breast, her belly, her legs. "No, Michael . . . Michael . . . oh, Michael . . ." Her hands found his hair as he reached to enter her.

Shock, surprise, and fright welled up at the invasion as he crossed the barrier that kept them separate. Her body stiffened with the shock of it. He felt the tenseness course through her, felt the reality of her innocent shock and dragged himself back, trying to gain control of the need, slowing himself, slowing his movements, gentling his touch to respond to her surprise, to her frightened contractions.

"Oh God . . ." he was whispering into her ear, whispering her name then, over and over, feeling her relax the smallest bit, feeling her reach back toward him.

"Make love to me," she whispered.

"God help us. I can't stop. . . ." He buried his head in her hair, his face against her ear, letting her hear his whispered supplications, his uneven breath, letting her take her time until he could wait no longer.

Desire and pain washed over her in waves. He lost all reason, devouring her body, pouring out all his need, taking her, taking possession of her.

She felt the pain, but it was overlaid with so much else that she could not turn away from it. She welcomed it as it brought ecstasy along with it, flooding her body, sending waves of him through her arms, her limbs, her belly and her breast.

She clung to him as he pushed deep within her and tore all reason apart. There was nothing else alive but this moment, this

152

man within her. Her moans blended with his. Her scream when she felt all control wrested away fell into his mouth as he covered her lips. He felt his own control slip away; the convulsions that began in one carried to the other until both of them were spent, released, entwined in each other's arms.

She fell asleep to the sound of his even breathing, a warmth she had never before felt relaxing her entire body in its safe harbor, her hand now snugly encompassing him again, feeling him flaccid and content against her palm.

In the morning she woke lazily, stretching slowly, coming awake to realize she was in her own bed. She sat up, alarmed, looking at the wainscotted walls of her bedroom, shocked not to find him beside her. She stared at the door to her room, to the hallway beyond which her sitting room stood open and awaiting the morning sun.

She looked down at herself, her nightgown primly in place. *No!* She was *not* imagining—she had gone—they had made love. He could not make her think they had not! She stood up, walking to the sitting room and the small connecting door. Gathering courage she took hold of the handle. It would not open. She stared down at it. Locked . . . locked against her.

Tears began to slip out as she stood there, confused and alone.

In the servants' quarters the cook was up first this early December morning, finishing her morning bath while the household was still quiet around her. She pulled her uniform on, adjusting the skirt across her hips, and descended to her large domain below, putting on the morning tea, readying breakfast for the staff.

"Morning, Nan." The upstairs maid came into the kitchen a little later, yawning widely, her short red head flopping forward over her freckled forehead. "Is me tea ready?"

Nan nodded toward the stove, her hands coated with biscuit flour. "Do you not hear it chirping away in the kettle?"

"I hear it; don't get your dander up, Nanny."

Nan ignored the young girl's words, kneading dough and reaching for currants as Andre came into the room. "Good morning," he said.

The red-haired Elsie smiled up at him, her dimples showing. "I was just telling Nanny I was dying for me tea. I got to sleep ever so late." She waited to see if he looked at all interested but

153

she couldn't tell. Bloody foreign faces always looked so strange. But handsome.

Before Andre could reply Moffatt came in, his expression sour as he glanced at them and then sat down at the table, pulling his bowl to him.

"Good morning, Mr. Moffatt." Elsie tried to charm the lean man at the table, but the effect was lost as he mumbled something and bent to his cereal, oblivious to the conversation around him.

The bell over the doorway sounded, and they each looked up toward it.

"His Grace is up," Nan said, unnecessarily. Andre turned to pick up the silver tea tray waiting by the stove, preparing it before he carried it out with him toward the front stairs and the man waiting above.

Elsie stared after Andre, turning back to the cook and opening her mouth to speak. But when she glanced at Moffatt's back she decided against it and went to the stove instead, helping herself to a bowl of cereal and lingering over it until Moffatt stood up and stalked out, leaving the two women alone.

"Ain't it queer though around here, Nanny—"

"I don't know what you're saying."

"Oh, for fair! His Grace stalking around like a thundercloud and gone till all hours, Her Ladyship never seeing him practically, if you know what I mean . . . and her as young as me!"

"Gossip's gotten better ones than you let go. I'd be careful if I were you."

"But what do you think of all of it?" Elsie persisted.

Nan glanced up at the girl, then went back to her baking. "I don't. And if I were you, I'd keep to my own business and not worry over things that concern my betters."

"I'm sure I'm not a gossip!" Elsie drank her tea down and reached for more. Nan wiped her hands on her apron and walked past the table into the pantry as Elsie began to speak again. "But don't you wonder why he married her? That's what I'd like to know!" Elsie finished.

"That's for him to know."

"But don't you wonder?" Elsie persisted.

Nan walked back in, a great bag of potatoes in her chubby arms. She kicked the pantry door closed and stopped in front of Elsie. "No, I don't," she said flatly. "It's not what he did, it's who she *is* that concerns me. She is the Duchess and he is the

154

Duke, and I work for them and that's flat. And if you're a smart lass, you'll keep that thought close at hand. Jobs aren't so easy to come by these days, my girl."

"Bosh!" Elsie stood up, turning away from the table and leaving her bowl behind. "I'll always find a way to eat," she added.

"Just you come back here!" Nan called out. "And put your bowl by the sink. When Millie comes in there's no reason she should pick up after the likes of you!"

"Oh, bother!" Elsie spoke under her breath, coming back to get the bowl. "I'm sure," she said in a louder tone, "that it wouldn't hurt Millie to pick it up."

"It's not her place to. She knows her place, bless her, or she wouldn't work for me."

Elsie left, casting an eye toward the broad back of the cook. It wouldn't hurt her any to move a bit more either. Knows her place she does! Elsie ran quietly up the stairs, glad to be out of the stuffy, hot kitchen.

Slowing her steps, Elsie stopped before the huge oak doors at the west end of the main hall, listening quietly for a moment.

The door ajar, a glimpse of the foreign valet could be seen, crossing to the great clothes cupboard and then out of sight again. She lingered in the hallway, running her finger along the bottom edge of the first family portrait that hung near the main north stairwell and then along the bottom edge of the next and the next, testing the hangings, scuffing her shoe at a wisp of dust that blew against the coving near the Duke's door.

And then, sounds coming louder from His Lordship's suite, she slipped back toward the upstairs broom closet, slipping inside as his door opened wide, the tall, dark figure in the well-cut riding coat striding out, striding forward and down the stairs. Andre ran before him, almost reaching the front door before the footman appeared, opening it quickly just before the Duke strode past.

Andre stood in the doorway until His Grace was mounted, and then he turned back, starting up the stairs to straighten the Duke's rooms.

Within the room the young carrot-haired maid was already at work, her eyes demure and downcast when Andre entered.

"Oh!" She pretended surprise. "Forgive me, sir, I thought you gone."

"As I was," he said dryly. "Are you looking for something?"

155

"Oh, no, sir. I was just about to dust."

Andre watched her. "With no cloths?"

"Oh!" She looked down, at her hands, flustered. She blushed, and he watched her as she walked past him toward the doorway.

"What's your name?" he asked.

She smiled at him, her eyes full of mischief. "Elsie, sir."

"Elsie?"

"Yes, sir?" she asked coyly.

"Don't ever come into these rooms again." His voice went from cold to ice.

The smell of beeswax and turpentine filled the halls as Elsie was called to help Mrs. Norris an hour later, Meg and May airing the rooms on the top floor as Elsie brought up fresh bedding, fresh hangings, all of them polishing and dusting and readying the rooms for guests.

Frances, a morning tray of tea in her arms, opened the door to the Duchess's sitting room, walking inside. She knocked on the bedroom door, waiting for Moira's answer before opening it.

"Good morning, Milady."

"Good morning, Frances." Moira sat up, her eyes outlined by dark circles, her movements tired.

Frances looked at her anxiously. "Are you feeling unwell still, Milady? Maybe we should call for a doctor."

Moira did not reply. She pulled on a robe, fastening one of the frogged buttons and slipping her feet into soft satin slippers. "Has the Duke left yet?" Moira asked.

"Yes, Milady." Frances's worry showed. When Moira looked up into it she smiled a little.

"I'm all right. Truly," Moira said. She thought of his arms last night, the warmth that had encompassed her—and now the icy coldness of this morning alone. He was already away, without a word, without—

"You're sure?"

"Don't carry on so!" Moira said a bit more sharply.

"It's just—" The maid started and then trailed off.

"Yes?" Impatiently, Moira stared at the girl, hating herself for being short with Frances, knowing in her heart it was her own pain that was causing her harshness.

"I—I wouldn't want any harm to come to you, Milady." Frances hesitated and then spoke in a rush of words. "There's so many things a body hears and after our talk, I've worried that—"

"I don't want to know!" Moira interrupted. "Frances, do you understand? *I don't want to know* what they say. What any of them say!"

Frances stared at her mistress. Then, slowly, she looked down. "Yes, Milady."

"Oh, Frances, I'm not upset with you. It's just I'm so tired, that's all." She stopped.

Frances looked at Moira. "No one ever gave me a present but you. In my whole life. Nor asked me into their confidence."

"What?" Moira, lost in her own thoughts, did not follow.

"You bought me that lovely bit of velvet and seed pearls. Fit for a queen it is. I—I treasure it. And I, oh, Milady, I don't want anything to happen to you!"

"It won't." Moira reached out to touch Frances's arm. "It won't."

"It's that furriner," Frances said darkly. "Mark me, if aught's wrong, he's the wrong 'un, that Andre!" She spit out his name.

Moira stared at her. Andre. Andre of the changing accents and strange knowledge. "Has he worked for the Duke long, Frances?"

"Oh, yes, Milady. He was with him before the old Duke died, or so they say."

Andre did not like her, had not since they had first met. She had waited until he was safely away before daring to go to Michael last night, knowing instinctively he would have turned her away.

"How long—exactly—has he worked for the Duke—do you know that?"

Frances hesitated. "No, Milady. But I could find out if you like."

Moira hesitated too. "How long do you know for certain he's been here?"

"Since the old Duke died, as I said. Mr. Moffatt was talking to Mr. Ottery about it."

"I see. So Mr. Ottery and Andre are the only two from—before." She looked up into Frances's questioning eyes. "It's not important, Frances, really. I am just—curious."

Frances nodded knowingly. "Leave it to me, Milady."

Moira walked to the windows overlooking the gardens. "It's a perfect day for riding. Ask the groom to saddle a horse for me, will you? I think I'll ride to the village."

157

"Yes, Milady." Frances curtseyed and turned to leave. Then she turned back. "Milady?"

"Yes?" Moira spoke absently.

"Do you wish me to take the spirits downstairs?"

Moira turned toward the small table, seeing the decanter of brandy, the flagon of whiskey, in place. The flagon of whiskey. She walked toward it, picking it up. It was half-full. She looked over at Frances. "Was this full when you brought it, Frances?"

"Oh, yes, Milady!"

Moira smiled. "Good. Yes. You may take it."

Frances watched her mistress. "Did it—did you—I mean." She floundered to a stop. Moira turned away, staring out the window again. Moira was looking past the gardens to the sea beyond, where big fat gulls wheeled and cried out above the ocean's foaming tides.

Frances swallowed her questions, leaving Moira to her thoughts as she left with the spirits in her hand.

Chapter Seventeen

UNDER THE STAND OF CHESTNUTS AND ELMS, TO THE NORTH OF THE huge front door, a gig stood waiting, a groom holding the bay that stood between its traces, the horse's reddish-brown color catching the weak sunlight.

Moira stood beside Jeb, the stableman, her black beaver riding hat with its high crown and tricorne brim twisting back and forth in her hands. "I simply want to ride."

"The Duke left specific instructions, Your Ladyship—"

"Jeb—it is Jeb, isn't it? Yes, well, riding a horse and driving a carriage are two separate occupations, no matter how light the gig is—"

Jeb, his brow furrowed with worry, his work-worn hands thrust deep in his pockets, rocked back and forth on his feet slightly. "Your ladyship, the Duke said as how you were to drive this gig. He said being as how you're not familiar with the moors or the village, and with the old scat bals nearby—"

"What?"

"Scat—ah, old mine shafts, that is, Your Ladyship. If you're in the gig there's only so many places you can *get* to; if you're on horseback, you could get hurt."

Moira stared at the weather-worn man before her whose eyes would not meet hers. "He said that?" she asked, her tone softening.

"Yes, ma'am. I mean, Your Ladyship. He said as how it'd be my hide if anything happened to you and you was to take this out, if you went out, or else—"

She smiled then, her eyes sunny as she spoke. "Thank you, Jeb, *thank* you!"

He stared at her then, totally confused. "Your Ladyship?"

She was already moving toward the gig. "This will be fine. I wouldn't want to get you into trouble."

Relieved, Jeb still didn't understand her sudden change of heart.

She climbed up and sat down on the seat, taking the reins from the groom and trotting off, down the long, stately drive, Jeb staring after her. "Well, if that don't beat all!"

"What beats all?" Alf asked.

Jeb spat a wad of chewing tobacco out of his mouth, its wide arc arching and then landing in the gravel across from where they stood. "Nothing. Nothing at all. Saddle me up, Alf, I've got to be getting into town."

Moira waved at the gatekeeper's little girl who stood sucking her thumb by the gatehouse, her short holland smock high above her knees. Reaching the crossroads below, Moira hesitated, her heart light within her. She wanted to savor this morning.

She looked right, over the stone bridge to the road that led to St. Maur, and then left, toward the road they'd come down from Clovelly and the moors beyond.

She turned right, crossing the stone bridge and then, meaning to turn right again, toward the village, she hesitated. She did not want to share this hour alone, this hour before she would see him and he would smile at her and. . . . She smiled to herself. And whatever he wished. She made her decision and then turned left instead, on impulse following the river road until it swung up toward the high moors to the west of the river.

She climbed the high narrow road that crossed Bodmin moors farther on, the road that went all the way to Padstow. Flat-topped hills were visible to the west once she climbed out of the river valley, out of the coomb. She slowed the bay, staring at the mist-enshrouded cairns far beyond, the smell of deep moss and bitter bracken filling her nostrils.

The land was bleak up on the high reaches, the deep green of the protected coombs giving way to the black and gray and white of the windier moors, the soft breezes below changing to winds that howled free across the vast expanse of the moors, battering up against the tall cairns, ruffling across the trout streams that hastened downward from peat bogs farther inland.

She turned back, finally, edging the gig around in the narrow track, starting back toward the river and the village road far below.

Coming down the deserted lane, the bay trotting faster as he descended the steep incline, a lurch to the right was followed by the sound of splintering wood.

Moira gasped, holding the reins tightly as the gig fell sideways, toward the marsh that lay near the side of the road. The marsh was cut by bog islands, islands that looked solid but that held hidden depths, the weight of a foot causing them to sink into the slate-colored water that rippled over the marsh, churning frothy and then turning black.

The gig fell into marshy land, the horse pulled over with the sudden lurching, sinking deep into the cold, brackish water.

Moira, caught in the gig, felt the cold water rising around her. Fighting the shock of it, fighting her way free, she pulled herself toward the opening in front of the seat.

She managed to pull herself to the bench which she had been thrown from, gasping for breath, for air, as a man's voice called out to her: "Be careful! It could sink farther! Wait!"

A blue-eyed, blond-haired giant pulled her by main force up, out of the overturned carriage.

"Good grief, I hope you're all right. Are you?"

Moira looked into Jack Lisle-Taylor's kind eyes. "Yes." She was out of breath. "Thank you!" She took a great gasp of air into her lungs and then took another.

"What were you doing out here alone? What on earth happened?"

"I don't know. But the horse!" She turned away, moving to the head of the fallen animal. "He was pulled over when the carriage seat went. Do you think he's broken anything?"

Jack looked at the animal, half-covered by the cold, muddy waters, and then he looked back at Moira. "Let's unhook him and see."

160

Suiting action to words, Jack loosened the reins and the traces, then walked round to where Moira stood by the bay's head. "Let's see if he'll stand up." Jack pulled the harness, speaking now to the horse. "Come now, boy, come on. Let's see if you can make it."

Slowly the horse righted himself from his side to his belly and then, unsteadily, to his feet, still mired in the cold, brackish water.

"Come on, boy, come on." Jack stepped backward, leading the bay forward to dry ground, Moira pacing beside, her hand on the bay's neck.

"You're doing fine," she said, "you're doing fine. Oh, I think he's all right!"

Jack Lisle-Taylor stared at Moira, still holding the bay's harness. "I hope so. Do you feel all right?"

"Yes. I'm unhurt. It was just so sudden. The breath was knocked out of me for a moment, that's all."

Jack stared at her still. "You certainly have courage." He hesitated, then: "What exactly happened?"

"I don't know. There was a lurch and then a noise and then we went over sideways. It was so quick!"

"Let's see if we can right the gig," he said quietly. He walked to the bay and then directed Moira as they backed the horse nearer the overturned carriage. He got the ends of the reins out of the mud, tying them to the horse, and then, carefully, he walked around to the far side of the gig as Moira began to walk the horse slowly forward, at Jack's direction. He pushed hard on the far side, his feet slipping into the marshy land as the strain caught the bay and he stopped.

Moira prompted the bay, inching him forward, Jack pushing with all his might until the gig broke free of the water and stood upright next to the bog.

"That's far enough!" he called, "or it will go over the other way and block the road!" He grinned and Moira smiled back.

"Can't have that. Too much traffic here," she said.

"I say, must be at least one coach a fortnight. Not counting yours, of course," Jack teased her.

"Speaking of traffic, I was very lucky you were near," Moira said.

"That's strange." Jack was bending over the right wheel, the one that had given away.

"What's strange?" She walked around to see what he was looking at. "What do you see?"

161

He was kneeling beside the broken wheel, one knee of his doeskin riding pantaloons bent to the marshy ground, his handkerchief between his knee and the dampness. His fingers, encased in matching doeskin gloves, were tracing a fine line across the spoke and then the rim of the wheel. "This," he said, running his finger along the crack in the wood.

Moira bent to study it more closely. "Ah, that's what split."

"This is what split." He showed her the edge of the break. "This." He traced a finger over the inner edge. "This was cut."

"Cut!" Her surprise made her voice high-pitched. She straightened up. "Cut?"

Jack stood up, leaning to swipe at his knee with one of his gloved hands, retrieving his handkerchief from the ground. "Your Ladyship, this was no accident."

"But it—had to be. I'm here. Alone. I've ridden for over half an hour!"

The man looked down into her anxious eyes. "I'm sorry," he said, after a long pause, "I'm sorry it's true and I'm sorry it happened. And I'm sorry it was I who found you."

Moira stared at him. "Speak plainly, sir. I'm near at my wit's end as it is."

He let out a long, slow sigh, staring at his own gloves for a moment before his eyes rose to meet hers again. "Someone cut that wheel."

"But it would have dropped off coming down the castle road!"

"No." His voice when he interrupted her was quiet. "Let me finish. Someone cut that wheel, halfway through. Or more. Enough to insure that somewhere fairly distant from the castle this would happen."

"But—why?"

He ignored her question. "Who knew you were planning on coming here?" he asked.

"None! I didn't know myself. I was planning on going to the village but decided to see a little of where this road led first."

He stared at her. "That may have saved your life. Do you realize that the right hand wheel, this wheel, would have been on the river side on the St. Maur Road? You'd have been in the Maur River, gig, horse, and all."

"No!"

"Who knew you were planning on going there?"

"None, I tell you! Except—"

"Except?"

"I—I asked about the village and said one day, I'd go. But no, no more than that."

"To whom?"

She thought back over the past few days. "To Frances, my abigail. To Jemma, the—"

"I know Jemma," he said.

Something strange in his tone made her stare at him.

"Your Ladyship, you are in no condition to travel very far as you are. Might I suggest, if you wish, that you stop at my home. It's close, and if you don't feel it improper, I could find you some tea while you repair your clothing."

She looked down at herself. "Yes. Thank you. That would be most kind."

He went to unhitch the bay and bring him back to her. Moira thought then of Michael, of his reaction to this man. Of Lucy's letter.

"There you are," Jack said, handing her the reins. "May I help you up?"

"Thank you," she replied, trying to find the courage to ask those questions of this stranger, those questions that few but he could answer.

He clasped his hands to take her boot and she stepped up, into his grasp, swinging onto the horse. "Your gloves, I fear, are ruined," she said.

He straightened up, smiling a little. "In a good cause."

"Did you—know—the first Duchess?" she asked tentatively.

He stared at her. "Yes. Didn't he tell you?"

"No," she said truthfully, after a brief hesitation. "No."

He still watched her. "I see."

Then, turning, he walked to his horse and mounted, coming up alongside Moira after a moment. "If you know nothing, perhaps it's better—"

"I did not say that," Moira replied. "I've heard things. But—not from him."

Jack's pale, freckled face collapsed into worried lines. "I see."

They rode toward the edge of the village, toward his house, silently, each lost in their own thoughts.

"Here," Jack said finally, leading the way to a small gate before a stone house on the southern edge of the village.

Moira dismounted, leading the bay through the gate as Jack

led his mount ahead of her. An elderly man came from beyond the small house built of Cornish stone, taking the horses from them and leading them back toward the small stable.

"Oh!" Moira looked at the house enviously. "If only this were mine!"

Jack turned to stare at her. "This? When you have the great castle beyond?" He waved a hand and she glanced across the river, up to the rise in the cliffs where Saint's Castle stood outlined against the winter sky.

Then she looked back at the petite house with its mullioned windows and trailing ivy. "It reminds me of home," she said finally.

"Ah," Jack said, "I see." He smiled then. "May I offer you some refreshment?" He walked to the small front door and opened it wide, letting her walk on in.

Inside the comfortable front room two oriel windows looked out across the gravelled walk and the grassy plot beyond to the laburnum trees and the Maur River beyond, the castle just visible in the distance from this angle.

"I'm sorry, I have nothing for you to change into—" he said.

"Oh, no." She turned back to face him.

"But—if you'd care for a sherry to warm you after that cold plunge—"

"No, thank you. A cloth, if you have one, to wipe some of this mud off and I'll be on my way."

"You mustn't wipe it, you know. Not on that outfit. You should come near the fire, let it dry thoroughly, and then brush it off, so as to leave no stains."

Moira smiled in spite of herself. "You're quite the abigail."

He smiled back. "A man alone," his smile faded, "must of necessity learn a few things."

The tension she had felt at accompanying this man, at Michael's reaction if he should find out, was melting away. "I think I'd like that sherry, Mr. Lisle Taylor."

He looked pained. "At least, at the very least, you can call me Jack, can you not? After all, I just rescued you."

His smile was warm, his manner simple and uncomplicated. There was none of the restlessness that filled the air around Michael. She smiled then, almost shyly. "Jack, then. And thank you. I don't know what I would have done without you."

"I do." He handed her a small glass of sherry. "You would have gotten the bay to his feet, climbed onto his back and ridden home to deliver a tirade to the stableman."

She took the glass, laughing a little. "You have a rather high regard for my competence."

He watched her, his eyes belying his light tone of voice. "I've heard tell you've courage. And, then, the Duke always picks well."

She stopped, the glass halfway to her mouth. "Why do you say that?"

"Go on," he urged, "drink, it's very fine sherry, brought over for me especially. And, to answer your question, I say that for it's true."

Moira hesitated. "Tell me about Lucy."

The blond man stared at her, his eyes turning opaque. "Tell you what?"

Moira swallowed, amazed at her own daring. "What she was like. She was my father's sister, but I, I don't remember her. I must have known her. We lived here until I was almost eight, but I can't seem to place her. To remember her, from my childhood."

He hesitated, picking his words carefully. "She was— extraordinary. Intelligent, beautiful, proud . . . just, extraordinary."

Moira watched him. "You loved her."

There was a long pause. "Yes. I did."

Moira sipped at her sherry, studying the man. His expression was suffused with a sadness that was palpable. She felt as though she could almost reach out and touch it.

"What are you thinking?" he asked after a moment.

She swirled the liquor in the glass, watching it coat the sides of the crystal and then, slowly, slide away. "I was thinking about Lucy. About what really happened."

He looked down, at the glass in his own two hands, rolling it between his palms. "What really happened. She died, that's all it's safe for you to know."

"But how?" Moira persisted. "And why is it not safe to know?"

He looked up then. "The fact that you wonder what really happened means that you don't accept what was said. And that's not safe. You should let it alone."

Her face was flushed with earnestness. She leaned forward. "It is important that I do know. For her children as well as for myself. You have no idea of what's being said."

He almost smiled. "No idea?" He lifted his glass to his lips, draining it. "Don't you realize I have heard every story, every

165

variation, over the last ten years? Don't you wonder about me?" He watched her, defiant, proud, his hurt still showing in his eyes. "Don't you ask yourself why did he stay here after—after she died?"

Her eyes met his. "I thought because of Tristan."

Her words stopped him. "You know about that?" he asked softly.

"I—there are things—" She started to mention Lucy's diary, her letter, and then stopped. She had not told Michael yet. She could not first confide in this man her husband hated. Hated. She stared at the blond giant before her. She saw nothing to hate, nothing to fear.

"I see," he said, weighing his words, and then stopping. "Well, yes. Because of Tristan. Although I've tried to show him the error of staying here, staying on. He is determined to be the next Duke, determined that that—man—shall die knowing that Lucy's son, that—our son—triumphed over him. Over all. And—"

"Please, sir—" Moira stopped him, her entire body turning to stone as she listened to his words. "You are speaking of my husband."

"Your husband! Do you doubt that he—"

"Yes! I doubt it! He could not have—have—"

"Killed?" Jack's voice turned sarcastic. "So you have succumbed, too, I see."

"Succumbed?" She spoke the word slowly, quietly, staring at the man who so obviously blamed Michael for Lucy's death.

"To his—charms—shall we say. I'm told he is a prodigious lover—I see he has already succeeded in turning your head so that you cannot see the danger that lays in wait for you."

She turned away, her cheeks burning, anger, fear, questions, all welling up within her. Anger at this man for his words, fear of the truth, questions about all of it, all of it which she had yet to face Michael with. She resolved to ask him, to have it out in the open, no matter what. To end the questions, the fears, once and for all.

"I must go." She set her glass on a small side table.

Jack walked nearer. "Please, don't hate me. And know that I'm here. If you ever need anything. Will you promise me at least that?"

She saw the concern in his eyes. "Why do you care?" she asked.

"Why?" His expression softened. "You need a protector.

166

And I seem to gravitate to the role of a protector of young women."

She smiled at his wry expression. "How many young women have you protected?"

His face lost its warmth; he almost winced at the thoughts going through his head. "Not enough," he replied, faintly, in a strangled tone, "not enough."

"I must go," she said gently. "Thank you for all your kindness."

He walked beside her, opening the door for her, motioning to the old man who was now currying his horse. "Tom, bring Her Ladyship's horse 'round."

The man moved away, Moira stepping into the sunlight beside the gravelled path.

He watched her carefully. "You should not stay here at St. Maur."

She frowned. "Don't say that."

"It's true."

She shook her head. "No. No, you don't know that." Her horse was brought to her. Jack helped her up onto the bay, watching her as she looked back down at him sadly. "You should leave here, though," she said, "whether or not Tristan does. It's not good to live your life under such a—shadow."

"And you?" His eyebrows rose. "Are you not living your life under a shadow?"

"I'm married. And my duty lies here." She paused. "And my heart."

"Even if—"

"There are no ifs," she interrupted. "Good day. And I do thank you."

"Jack," he said.

She questioned him with her eyes. "I'm sorry?"

"Jack."

She smiled then, a small smile, quickly gone. "Good day, Jack."

He smiled up at her. "Remember where I am."

She nodded, turning the bay up the path. At the roadside, glancing toward the village and then down at the mud now caking on her riding-habit, she turned back toward the bridge and the road to the castle.

A horse's whinny was answered by the bay. Moira turned toward the sound. Andre rode out of the fields across from Jack's house. His eyes straight ahead, he did not look toward her. Riding fast, he headed toward the castle as she stared after him.

He was almost out of sight, as if determined to reach the castle before she did. The thought that he had followed her, had watched her with Jack, had raced back to report, filled her with a heavy unease.

Fear overtook her again; raw, unreasoning fear. She felt totally alone and completely helpless against the dangers that lurked just below the surface of their lives. Wanting to believe none of it, wanting to trust Michael, she found herself more and more assailed by doubts.

Even the castle now seemed full of darknesses barely understood as she stared up toward it. Dungeons. There were dungeons in that huge stone building. Who had been held there, had died there?

She passed the gatehouse, the small girlchild long since gone in to supper. Chestnut trees lined her way up to the top of the hill and the secrets that lay locked inside the stones of the castle. And within the hearts of the people that lived there.

She thought about confronting Michael, just coming out with it all and making them both face the truth, whatever it was. Or would he, would he just walk away and not answer?

As she neared the castle, the great wave of fear she was trying to overcome twisted her stomach within her. And she admitted to herself for the first time that she was frightened, truly frightened, of her own husband. She had given him power over her, the power of life and death he already had by the marriage vows themselves.

But she had given him more. She had given him the power of pain or pleasure. Of joy or abysmal misery. Her entire body wanted him close, she wanted to feel his arms, to touch every secret place . . . and she wanted not to fear him.

Good God in heaven, not to doubt.

Chapter Eighteen

HE WAS GONE.

Moira stared at Frances. "Gone? Gone where?"

"He didn't say, Milady."

Moira turned back to the gilt-edged mirror on her dressing table. She opened one of the japanned boxes and laid her watch carefully on the satin lining within. "When did he leave?"

"Just before you arrived, Milady."

"Just?"

Frances was nodding. "Madame was fit to be tied, telling him what with Christmas and all, and he informed her that was no concern of his. Then she said he should have a care about what people would say, and he laughed, saying that was not his concern either, and then, and then he—left."

"And Andre?"

"Gone with him." Frances looked a little curious about the question. "The Duke goes nowhere without the Frenchman, does he?"

"It seems not." Moira thought about that. "Frances, did you ever find out about Andre?"

"About Andre, Milady?"

"About how long he's worked for the Duke; I mean exactly how long?"

Frances shook her head. "None that I could ask knew, Milady, and the ones that know, I have not been able to ask yet."

"If you can, find out for me if Andre already worked for the Duke when . . . when Lucy . . . died."

"Yes, Milady." Frances, curious, but afraid to speak her questions, simply nodded. Then she moved to the blue-striped satin dinner gown she'd laid out for Moira, reaching for it as Moira stood up.

"Have the children asked for me?"

"Master Tristan was asking Lady Tamaris about what she'd told you."

169

Moira let Frances help her with the gown's gigot sleeves. "There's not much that happens in this house that someone doesn't overhear, is there?"

"No, Milady," Frances said truthfully. "I don't think there is."

"In a way, that's reassuring." Moira bit at her lower lip. "Thank you, Frances, that will be all for now. I'll be down presently to join Madame."

"She said she would be in the North Salon before dinner."

Moira acknowledged the words, and Frances let herself out of the suite, closing the door gently behind her. Adjusting her cuffs, Moira stared at her own reflection in the cheval glass across from her. Dark circles made her eyes seem tired, her color pale.

She turned toward the bedroom and walked across to the huge bed, pulling back the rose satin covers to search under the mattress for the small diary. She pulled it out, smoothing the covers and staring down at Lucy's writing as she opened the book.

Walking to a small padded armchair, she sank onto it, reaching at random and then, slowly, turning to the entries marked 1815.

And then she closed the book, hugging it close to her breast, afraid of what she might find within. She stood up, putting it back in its hidden place, smoothing the covers and walking out, toward the North Salon and her mother-in-law.

"I understand there was some problem with a carriage today." Madame greeted her with a brief smile and the question as Moira walked toward the fireplace in the North Salon.

"Accident?" Jemma looked up from her embroidery, her face concerned.

"There was no accident," Moira said after a moment.

"No?" Madame looked perplexed. "But Moffatt said there had been."

"Moffatt was wrong. There was no accident. The right wheel had been cut so as to break under the strain of the road."

"No!" Jemma's exclamation was loud in the quiet room.

Madame stared at Moira, finally turning away, toward the crackling fire. "Don't start becoming hysterical over nothing." Her voice was almost harsh.

"I was not aware of being hysterical, Madame." Moira stared

her down when the old woman turned back toward her. "I'm not easily frightened," she lied, wondering how convincing she sounded.

"Well, I am!" Jemma said. "Are you positive that the wheel had been tampered with?"

"Yes."

Madame spoke after a moment. "Many idlers in the village speak too freely. And are alarmists."

Moira stared at the old woman, knowing in that moment that Madame knew she'd seen Jack. Somehow she knew about all of it. Of that Moira was absolutely certain.

"The carriage has been brought back by now. In the morning," Moira continued calmly, "if you wish, you may inspect it yourself. Idlers and alarmists are not needed when your own two eyes show you the simple truth."

Madame was silent. Jemma took several long moments to put her embroidery away, busying herself to avoid the heavy tension in the air.

"I understand that the Duke has left," Moira said into the silence.

"Yes." Madame offered no more.

A knock at the door brought John to announce that dinner was served. The three women walked toward the far side of the castle, silent as their slippers padded against the stone flooring.

Lancelot barked from somewhere behind them, Arthur not bothering to respond. Jemma, pacing beside Moira, glanced at the black satin-clad back of the Duke's mother and then at Moira.

She caught Moira's eye and raised her own skyward, pointing toward the children's wing as she mouthed the word "later." Moira nodded slightly.

They reached the dining hall, following Madame to their chairs. Madame looked toward Moira, who sat at the head of the table now. "I think we should talk later, Moira."

"Yes. I think so too," Moira replied.

"If you'd prefer," Jemma said, "I could leave."

"Of course not!" Madame glanced at her. "Dinner is a place for light conversation. Not the discussion of—difficult, family matters. Shall we begin?" She looked back at Moira pointedly.

Moira motioned to John, realizing she had forgotten to indicate that they were ready to eat.

171

John and the footmen began to serve the first course, the women beginning to eat in silence. Slowly, random comments were made concerning the Christmas preparations, Tamaris's studies and Tristan's tardiness.

"He rode to the village, Madame," John informed Madame when asked.

"Hmmmpf! Such companions!" Madame said and then added no more.

"Companions?" Moira asked quietly.

Madame stared across the burnished table at her new daughter-in-law. "Companions!" she repeated, pointedly.

Moira said no more, watching the dressed lobster, the curried prawns, the asparagus, as they were served and removed.

The great clock in the hallway chimed nine o'clock while they lingered over dessert and coffee. Moira moved a forkful of chocolate mousse back and forth on her plate, uninterested in the food, her stomach edgy, her face sad and pensive.

Finally Madame put her fork down.

"Shall we?" Moira asked softly.

Madame stood up, a footman holding her chair for her. Jemma lingered behind.

"Come up if you can," Jemma said quietly as Madame walked out into the hallway.

Moira nodded and then followed the old woman toward the library.

The fire had been laid, the lamps turned up bright in the dark-panelled room. Madame moved past Michael's chair, sitting down nearer the fire, stretching out her hands to warm them.

"I suppose," she began as Moira closed the door, "that you've been hearing a great deal of nonsense."

"I've heard—many things."

"Well?"

Moira looked into the old woman's rather defiant gaze. "Well, what, Madame?"

"Is this why you deny my son?"

"Deny?" Her surprise stared back at the older woman. "When have I, what have I, denied your son!?"

It was Madame's turn to look perplexed. "Why does he leave so abruptly? Why does he spend every night in the village?"

"Why did he ever leave abruptly? Why did he always spend his nights in the village?"

Madame met Moira's steady gaze. And then, sighing heavily, she let her back relax, her shoulder's slumping forward in a very uncharacteristic stance.

Moira walked to her, sitting down on a small stool near the older woman. "Please, help me. I know you care about him. Please. Help us."

"Us?" The old woman's eyes searched Moira's face.

Moira hesitated. "I—I'd like to tell you about our, marriage. I thought he already had."

"He's said nothing." Madame's hurt showed through her tight-voiced reply.

"Then I shall. For I need your help. I don't know what to do."

Madame watched Moira as she explained how they had come to marry, and the agreement to annul. When she finished the old woman did not speak for long silent moments, the wind coming up outside, a dog pawing at the closed door. "Then he wishes this to be—ended—as soon as possible," Madame finally said. "You both do."

Moira swallowed. "No. At least, for my part—I—" She looked up into his mother's eyes, trying to make her understand. "I love him. I always have. I always shall."

Madame studied her. "Even now? Even with your—accident?"

"He cares about me too, I'm sure of it," Moira answered indirectly. "I do not know how much—or if it's love, but he—he comes to me."

"I don't understand," his mother said.

"Nor do I," Moira replied, walking to the door to let Lancelot in. Arthur padded regally behind. They took their places by the fire, content to be close. "I—I cannot explain, but I do know that he is not—cold—to me. And yet—and yet he will not trust, he will not admit to any feelings. He pushes me away if I try to come near." She paused. "And—there's a woman. I have come between them."

"Whom?" Madame looked up sharply to where Moira stood. "Genevieve."

Madame relaxed back. "Genevieve who?" she asked.

"You don't know her?"

"I've known several Genevieves over the years, none who were particular friends of Michael's, however."

"Who did you think I meant?" Moira asked quietly.

"I—was afraid you meant the woman. At the inn."

Moira felt her stomach churning even more within her. Over

the lump that suddenly filled her throat she spoke: "Then it's true, is it? Who is she?" Moira felt ice course through her. What a fool she was forcing herself into his bed.

"No one," Madame said. "A barmaid," she elaborated. "He's not been serious about anyone since—Lucy. Except, I thought, you."

"Tell me about Lucy." Moira stared at the old woman, trying to understand what all was happening, why he was the way he was.

"What do you want to know?"

"What she was like. And what happened to her."

"She died." Madame watched Moira and then sighed. "Pour me some sherry." She sounded very tired. As Moira moved to comply the Duke's mother began to speak. "Lucy was beautiful. Possibly too beautiful. She was unstable. It was a mistake, that marriage. But, he wanted her. Lord, how he wanted her. He was determined to marry her. And he did. Then, then she had Tristan and things began to—change."

"Change?" Moira persisted.

"He became distant. She became restless. And reckless." The old woman stopped, taking the glass Moira offered her. "I suppose you've heard the stories about that—man—Lisle-Taylor." Madame stared at her. "Why did you go to him? Did you discuss—" she trailed off.

"I didn't go to him. He found me on the road and helped me back to his house, after the gig overturned. Did Andre say I'd gone there?"

"Yes. Why do you ask?"

"I saw him. He raced back ahead of me. Do you think he spoke of it to Michael?"

"I know he did."

Moira sighed. "Then I'm sure Michael is upset with me. Tristan brought this Jack to the castle and Michael nearly hit him."

"Tristan's a fool."

Moira spoke after a moment. "Why do you say that?"

"He listens to nonsense."

"Is it?"

Madame hesitated. "Yes," she said finally.

The word itself sounded definite, and yet Moira felt that Madame was not being completely honest. She leaned down to pet Lancelot, not touching the glass of cream sherry she had poured.

"You look tired," Madame said into the silence.

"Yes. I didn't sleep. . . . And my stomach is feeling queer. I think I'll go upstairs, if you don't mind."

The old woman closed her eyes. "I don't mind. I'll be up directly myself."

"I'll say good night then."

Madame nodded, not opening her eyes until after Moira left.

Upstairs, Moira found her head filling with a dull ache. She undressed, sending Frances away and locking the doors, against she knew not what. She thought of Jemma's invitation, but her stomach tightened into a heaviness that felt vaguely ugly. She pulled the covers up around herself, laying back in the huge bed and closing her eyes, trying to relax.

She thought of the diary under her mattress and then tried to push the thought away, not wanting to deal with it, not wanting to think about any of it. She was too tired.

Fitfully she dozed, the edge of sleep coming near and then pulling away again. Later, when she did finally sleep, her dreams attacked her, forcing her face to face with the fear she was trying to ignore. In the middle of the dreams her stomach began to cramp badly. She tried to sit up, to stand up. Dizzy, her head spinning, she couldn't seem to reach the floor.

Reality mixed with her nightmares taking her into a land of half-seen devils and ugly pains inside her belly. She floundered, as though floating on the huge bed, a cold clamminess engulfing her, dulling her senses to the pain. And then nausea swept through her, leaving a hot stickiness on her skin which turned into a clammy coldness again. She was in the dungeons, her brain told her, buried alive, dying of pain, unable to cry out.

Waves of nausea and heat were followed by waves of clammy coldness, on and on, until finally she sank deeper into her dreams, hours slipping past, her body weakened by the wracking pains within.

Sounds filtered through her dreams, sounds of movement, of stealth. Using every ounce of strength she possessed she opened her eyes.

She gasped audibly. The black man stood above her again. I'm in Clovelly, her brain told her. And then the black face with Michael's eyes leaned closer. . . . I'm dreaming, she told herself, looking up into Michael's eyes. The face bent near, staring into her eyes with a look of utter confusion; pain and desire and distrust all mingled together within it. This is what he really feels, she told herself, this is what he would look like with the masks stripped away from his eyes.

Slowly it began to fade away. Desperately she fought to keep, fought not to lose, the dream. Don't go, she tried to say, tried to form the words but no sound came and he was sinking back into the shadows, dissolving into the wall itself, disappearing into darkness.

"Wait!" Finding her voice finally, she whispered the one word, startling the vision now at the edge of her sight. "Please," she added softly.

Very slowly, as if her willpower alone dragged it closer, it almost floated, coming near, coming nearer, again.

"Michael," she whispered.

"Why?" his voice asked her in the dream, the hurt still in his eyes, the face black and unknown around the familiar eyes. "Why?" The word was whispered at her again. "Why go to him?"

"Michael—" She did not know what to say. His eyes hovered above her. It came nearer, bending closer and still she stared at the lips which did not move now. Breath, hot now against her clammy skin, made her take a deep breath, transfixed, the apparition's lips so near, so very near, she could feel its breath.

A clear thought swept through her, through her dreams. She had been poisoned this night. Her eyes widened with the knowledge that the pain had a name, a reason, and then the lips above her came down against her own, forcing all thought away.

She felt hands in her hair, holding her still. She felt his weight against her, so real, so real, and pain receded. A liquid softening of her own flesh overcame her, as though she were melting into the surfaces she touched.

His mouth was against hers, tongue, teeth, lips touching, causing tremors in him that then coursed down the length of her. She reached blindly for his arms, for his hands, finding them, pulling him closer, wanting him closer, speaking his name against his lips, willing him to come back to her as he had been the night before.

She felt the ache begin in her breast and spread to her heart, to her loins, as he finally, finally, came close, his body finding hers in the darkness.

"Michael. . . . Oh, Michael. . . . I love you so." Words came pouring out of her, half-said, half-whispered, her body arching toward his, her pain forgotten in the agony of having him so close again. An exquisite agony that built within her, demanding, all doubts and fears fleeing with the touch of him. She wanted him to fill her full of himself again, to push himself so deep within her that he would never be free again. As she would never be free of the touch of him, the smell of him, the sight of him. He alone could take possession and set her free. She wanted to soar with him again, to give him anything, everything he wanted. To give him things he did not know he wanted, things no one else could give him.

His hands were hot against her body, her thin nightdress pulled away from her breast, her belly. . . . He murmured her name over and over as he bent near, agony in his voice, questions, doubts, desire, all calling out to her.

He was inside her, she was full of him, her stomach's pain stabbing back at her, stabbing through all else, overshadowing all else.

She lost consciousness, shuddering spasms from her stomach's pain making her cry out, her moans falling into the pillow that lay crushed and damp beneath her. She clutched at her stomach unawares, too weak to think, too weak to feel, her brain shutting down.

The last thought she had was of his body, of his touch, and of how much she wanted him, whether he loved her or not. Whether he had poisoned her or not. For poisoned she was, her brain told her, pain doubling her over, pushing consciousness away.

She tried to call out his name but the word would not form.

She fell finally into a deep, dreamless slumber, reality edging away, life slipping near its end.

Chapter Nineteen

DAYS FADED TOGETHER, DELIRIUM SPINNING TIME INTO VAGUE POCKets of consciousness and long stretches of floating, half-conscious, half-lost, in the inner stretches of her own mind.

Pain dropped away. She was too tired, too sleepy, to feel it, nature protecting its own.

"Moira?" A worried woman's voice spoke. Somewhere deep inside herself she tried to find the owner's name, but she could not concentrate long enough, the question slipping away too, lost in her dream-filled slumber. She floated free, dancing across the moors, feeling the wind, clear and cold; seeing Michael's eyes float with her, surrounded by that shadowy, vague, black face.

She tried to find the arms, the hands, that had held her but could not touch them, could not bring them near. And so she slept again, letting it all fade away.

The first face she saw was Jemma's. Opening her eyes in the morning light, she stared up at the governess.

"Oh, Moira, thank God!" Jemma's smile was troubled. "You gave us all such a fright!"

"Your voice—" Moira began, her voice croaking over the words. She stopped, clearing her throat, and then began again. "I heard you."

"Heard me?" Jemma questioned. "Anyway, I'm so glad to hear you. Can you eat a little of this, do you think?"

Moira stared down at the bowl of soup. It seemed an impossibly difficult thing to do. Just to lift the spoon would require too much effort. "Can't," she said finally, looking up at Jemma's concern. All her strength went into her words, into her concentration on staying awake.

"Just a little, you've no strength left. Please. Here, I'll give you a spoonful at a time, you see?" She touched the spoon to Moira's mouth. "Just a little broth. That's all. But you need it to get better."

178

"What's wrong," Moira's words were barely whispers, "with me?"

"The doctor said it must have been the fish."

"Fish?" Moira strained to remember.

Jemma nodded. "A bad piece. It poisoned you."

"Poisoned?" Moira stared at Jemma and then horror began to fill her eyes. "Poison?" she repeated, her voice a harsh whisper. "No!"

"Shhh." Jemma spooned up more broth. "Save your strength, we'll talk later. You must gain strength first. Here, one more." Jemma patiently fed Moira, bit by bit, spoon by spoon, stopping only when Moira fell asleep.

The next time she awoke Tamaris stood near the bed, watching her. Mark hovered in the doorway.

The young girl was watching Moira's eyes as they opened and then she turned toward her brother. "Go tell Jemma she's awake."

Mark disappeared, Tamaris turning back to Moira. "How do you feel?"

Moira tried to smile. "Better. Tired."

"You were very ill."

"Yes."

Tamaris studied Moira's face. "Tristan says Mommy was poisoned just like you, before she died. Are you going to run away and die too?"

"No." Moira's voice was weak. Her eyes closed. "No."

"Tamaris," Jemma said as she walked in. "What nonsense did I hear you prattling on about? Go on and play now, and don't bother Moira until she's better."

"She's not Moira to you, she's Her Ladyship, I heard Grandmother say so."

"Tamaris." Jemma's voice held a firm threat. Tamaris left, looking back from the bedroom doorway. "She won't die now," Tamaris said.

"Of course not!" Jemma snapped, and then, turning to smile at Moira, she spoke more softly. "Children should be seen and not heard. Especially these children. How are you feeling?"

Moira nodded a little. "What day is it?"

"Tuesday."

"Tuesday! I've slept since Sunday!?"

Jemma smiled. "More. This is Tuesday the twentieth. You've been in bed over a week."

"A week!" Moira thought about that. "It's almost Christmas, then."

"Yes. And guests will be arriving by Thursday."

"I should be up!" Moira tried to sit and then fell back.

"Oh no you don't. Not until you can keep some real food down. Frances?"

Moira turned on her pillow, seeing Frances now in the doorway.

"Frances," Jemma continued, "if you'll bring up some porridge and cream for our patient, we'll begin to fatten her up. She's determined to rise."

"Yes, ma'am." Frances smiled at Moira. "I'm ever so happy you're better, Milady."

"Thank you." Moira watched Frances leave. "And you, Jemma, thank you."

"That's unnecessary. Frances and I have both been glad to help."

"Every time I woke you were here."

Jemma's face clouded for a moment. "Nothing more will happen to you."

Moira watched her. "You think, you think—"

"I think nothing. But I warned you to be careful. And Frances and I both decided that until you could watch out for yourself, we would do so."

"Thank you," Moira said again, softly. "Is he home? Michael—" she added.

"No. No, he hasn't been back."

"He left—that day—" Moira was trying to sort out dreams from reality, "didn't he? He and Andre?"

"Yes, that afternoon. Before dinner." A shadow crossed Jemma's face. "Don't you remember?"

"So many dreams. Can't tell which are real and which—"

Jemma nodded. "You were delirious. But it's all over. And only Frances and I heard you."

"Heard?"

Jemma hesitated. "You kept calling out for His Grace. You're truly in love with him, aren't you?"

Moira closed her eyes, not answering.

Frances brought the porridge. Tristan walked in a moment later, just behind her. "I saw food coming, so I assumed you were awake," Tristan said. "And I assumed you were better. May I come in?"

"I don't think—" Jemma began.

"Yes," Moira said quietly. "Yes."

Tristan walked nearer the bed. "Good grief, you're an absolute wreck!"

Frances glowered at him, but Jemma laughed. "I'm sure you'll do wonders of good for her with pretty speeches such as that!"

Tristan stared at the thin-faced young woman who lay in the huge bed, her skin drawn, her eyes sunken in deep purple circles. "A friend of yours is very worried about you. He asked if he could call."

Moira stared up at Tristan, not answering.

"Who?" Jemma asked, and then, realizing, she just stared at Tristan. "You can't mean Jack!"

"Why not?" Tristan challenged.

"He's—the Duke won't allow it."

"The 'Duke' is not here. And these are rather special circumstances. I would say at this point it's up to Moira. Wouldn't you?"

Jemma looked down.

"Well?" Tristan asked Moira. "Do you want to see him or not?"

She watched Tristan's face. "If you wish, and if it won't cause trouble—"

"Haven't you noticed how trouble comes to this house no matter what we do?" Tristan turned and left, Frances glowering at his back now.

"Come now," Jemma said as Frances sat down near Moira. "Let Frances give you the porridge. You don't want to be abed for the whole of Christmas. You'll miss all the fun."

"And all the pirates," Frances added darkly.

"Pirates?" There was sudden strength to Moira's voice. "What pirates?"

"It's nothing," Jemma said. "Not to be concerned about. The village is full of stories about the Ghost Ship."

"Ghost?"

"The Black Ship full of the ghosts of Barbary pirates, or some such nonsense. You know how superstitious these people can be. Some poor old man thought he saw it, and now for over a week, there've been tales of it being sighted up and down the coast. If you ask me, too many villagers drink too freely."

"Drink! Sighted! They looted Squire Dalmouth's down near Padstow. Took the women, stole the gold—"

181

"Oh, stuff!" Jemma said loudly. "I'll believe it when I see it here."

"Don't say that!" Frances crossed herself. "Don't say that!"

Moira ate a few more mouthfuls and then lay back. "Please, thank you both, but I'd like to be alone for a bit." She smiled at them tiredly.

"I don't know if you should."

"Just for a bit," Moira repeated, watching them glance at each other. Then Frances stood up.

"Do you wish the door closed?" she asked.

"Please."

Frances nodded, moving toward the door as Jemma walked through it. "But I'll be right here in the sitting room if you need me!" Frances added.

Moira nodded, and then a thought occurred to her. "Frances?"

Frances looked back at the young Duchess. "Yes, Milady?"

"How did you get in?"

"Beg pardon, Milady?"

"When you found me."

Frances turned toward Jemma, who was already in the sitting room. Jemma, hearing the question, came back toward the doorway. "I found you," Jemma answered. "Or rather, Frances came in to help you dress a week ago Monday and when she couldn't rouse you came to me. I was just going down to breakfast. I saw you had a fever and called for Madame. She sent for the doctor."

"But, wasn't my door locked?"

"Locked?" Jemma looked puzzled and then looked at Frances.

Frances shook her head. "No, Milady, it was not locked."

Jemma shook her head. "No, Milady, it was not locked."

Jemma watched Moira's confusion. "Did you dream that you locked it?"

"It's not important," Moira said faintly.

They left, closing the door carefully. Moira stared up at the ornate ceiling for long, silent moments. Then she turned, slowly sitting up, and tried to stand up alone, beside the bed.

Her knees gave way, and she sank to the floor, taking deep breaths before slowly reaching for the hidden diary. Gaining it, withdrawing it from its hiding place, she reached up and thrust it under her pillow.

Then, slowly, she raised herself up, to her knees, to her feet, leaning against the bed, pulling herself back beneath the covers.

For long moments she lay still, listening for sounds outside, regaining her breath. When all was quiet, except the occasional call of a curlew outside her windows, when her breath became more even again, she turned away from the door.

Pulling the diary from beneath her pillow, shielding it from view with her back, she opened it, beginning, slowly, to read.

The first entries were as she remembered, short household notes, dates and amounts, people entertained, what was served.

And then, the break of years, as if the writer had grown tired of keeping accounts, or begun to feel it was unnecessary amid all this wealth.

The diary began again, three years before Lucy died, cryptic notes of Tristan's health, of Mark's cutting his teeth, of colds and flu and first steps, first words; 1811 slipped by without a word about Michael written on its pages.

The entries for 1812 began the same way, but then in a sentence here and there, a few words changed the feeling of the passages: gone again; he didn't arrive back; left. They began to tell a tale of frustration that slowly began to build, the entries longer, more and more diatribes, less information, more worries and fears spilling out in longer and longer notations as 1812 became 1813, then 1814, 1815.

". . . Today he won't speak to me at all. I should never have told him about Tristan, Jack was right. Now he doubts Mark, I see it in his eyes."

". . . We arrived back from London today. I told him I felt ill, could not remember about Mark. He wouldn't even discuss it. Now the doctor says I'll have another . . . trapped."

". . . What can I do, he's gone again, ill all the time now. Wrote Jack to come, can't go on like this."

". . . He hates me . . . laughed when I told him another baby. He doesn't think it his, I can see it."

". . . Jack's arrived back, thank God, I have someone to talk to. Told him all, all . . . he says leave. But how, he'll never let me go. And the children."

". . . Ill, worse this time than the others . . . found the tunnel . . . my God, he's wicked, what can I do, too ill to think."

183

". . . Won't let me out of his sight. Andre saw Jack leave last night, I know it, can see it in his eyes. If he hurts Jack I'll kill him. Kill us all, what does it matter?"

". . . Watching every move, he has them all watching now. Ever since the baby was born. Poor girlchild, child of my illness, she's not well . . . sick again."

". . . Poison! Wrote Edmund, for God's sake help us, followed him in tunnel . . . found weapons, he saw me. Must get away. *Must get away.* But they watch all the time now. Can't leave my poor babies, what can I do, no word from Edmund. Watch all food now, only eat fruit, things I fix. Things from other's plates. Won't kill me, have to get away. Have to save children from this . . . poor babies, my poor babies. What will happen to them without me?"

". . . He's leaving! Now's my chance. They think me ill again. Pretend I've eaten the poison, tonight, tonight! He says Edmund's coming . . . too late . . . I'll be gone. They'll not get my money . . . They're in it together! I see it all now. That's why Edmund said nothing about Anne and Michael. Her child looks no more like Edmund than Tristan does Michael!"

Moira stared at the page. Her eyes went back over the individual letters, rereading them. They must be recombined. They could not be saying, could not mean what they seemed to mean, what they spelled out.

She closed the book, staring at its cover. Plain, stark horror crept like ice through her veins. It was not true. Could not possibly be true. Her father could not possibly have connived at anyone's death. . . . He could not have.

She remembered the voyage from Cornwall to Brittany all those years ago. Happy times. They were happy then . . . Tunnel. What tunnel was she talking about? What on earth could she have meant?

The sound of a man's heavier tread outside and then a knock at her sitting room door came through the closed bedroom door. And then a knock at her bedroom door, Frances opening it. "Milady, Mr. Lisle-Taylor is here."

Moira turned toward the doorway, the diary out of sight. "Have him come in."

Jack walked in past Frances, stopping near the bed. "My God, what have they done to you! You must leave here at once!"

She smiled weakly. "A little difficult at the moment."

184

He looked around for a chair and then brought one near the bed. "How are you feeling?"

"Fine."

"Fine! You almost died!"

"No."

"Yes. Ask the doctor," Jack replied.

"He—told you?"

"We're old friends. The doctor and I. That's how I found out about you."

"Oh. Not—Tristan?"

"No. Moira, forgive me, may I call you Moira?"

She nodded.

"Then, Moira, you must do one thing immediately. If you do no other." He looked into her eyes, his worry evident. "Please, you must make out a will in *anyone's* favor. *Anyone's* favor—just not his. Then you'll be safe."

"Safe?" she repeated the word.

"Safe. He wants the Walsh fortune. Moira, I *know*. I—went through this with Lucy. Please, he'll have no reason to harm you if there's no gain to be had."

"What—" Madame's voice rang out from the doorway. "What is this man doing in my house!?"

Jack still stared at Moira. "Please, protect yourself." He stood up.

"Get out. *Get out!* How *dare* you enter this house!" The old woman's voice shook with fury.

Jack turned and left as the old woman turned her fury on Frances. "You're discharged!"

"No!" Moira spoke with as much strength as she could muster. "No!" she repeated. "She did not invite him and she does not know who he is. She is not at fault and she is in *my* employ."

The old woman's hands shook. "You invited him?"

"Yes."

"No," Tristan drawled from the doorway. "Very generous of you, dear Moira, more than I expected of you. I invited him, Grandmother." He faced the old woman, lounging against the doorframe, his eyes slightly bemused.

"You!" Madame spit the word out.

"I," he said softly.

"Please, Madame, Tristan—" Jemma walked in, drawn by the loud voices. "This is not the time for anger. Moira's not strong—"

185

"Madame—" Moira stared at her mother-in-law, "did Michael kill Lucy?"

There was a sudden blank silence in the room, as if all held even their breath for long, slow moments.

Madame stared at the young, frail-looking woman on the bed.

"Answer her!" Tristan's voice rose loud. "Answer her!" he screamed, his voice turning hysterical as he repeated the words over and over. "Answer her, answer her, answer her—" He looked demented as he stood there, chanting at Madame.

"Shut up!" Madame spat the words at him. Then, without so much as a glance at Frances or Jemma she glared at Moira. "What if he did?" Tristan's voice faded away behind her. "What if he did! She was unfaithful, she flaunted her unfaithfulness, she bore another man's child and was proud of it, was proud of it. *Proud of it!* She was *insane!* She tried to kill her own children! Look at Tamaris, look at what her mother did to her! Would you let a monster such as that survive? If my son killed her, then she deserved to die!" Her voice faltering finally, her eyes filling with tears, she brushed past them all, leaving utter silence in her wake.

Tristan folded against the door and then, blindly, stumbled out, past a horror-stricken Frances, a shocked Jemma.

Finally Jemma turned and left the room. Frances still stared at the young Duchess.

"Milady, we should leave here, truly. Now. Before he comes back. I *knew* there was danger. Please—"

"No."

"But—"

"No, Frances; please send for a solicitor."

"A solicitor, Milady?" Frances's worry showed.

"Yes. I wish to draw up a will."

"Oh!" Frances's eyes filled. Then she turned and left too, Moira alone now in the silent room.

She reached slowly for the diary and then just held it in her hands, until Frances returned.

Chapter Twenty

THE HOUSE WAS FILLED WITH CONVERSATION AND ACTIVITY THE afternoon Moira slowly descended the stairs a few days later. Eunice and Pomfret had already arrived from London.

"Ah, Moira!" Eunice walked toward her, across the Conservatory. "Come sit. You *do* look like death itself!" Her voice lowered. "My dear, we've got to get you plumped up. . . . Mother!" Eunice called out to Madame, who stood near the windows. "I was just telling Moira we must ring for cakes and ale to plump her up!"

Eunice, her arm linked with Moira's, walked with the younger woman to the chairs near the windows. "That bad-boy husband of yours is not back yet. Now where did he go, fess up."

Moira sat down carefully, her eyes meeting Madame's anxious gaze. "Eunice," Moira said finally, "you know your brother. Why do you think he took a flying trip?"

Madame stared at Moira, her eyes softening as Moira finished.

"Some land dealings I'll wager," Eunice replied.

"Pomfret!" Moira smiled at him. "How are you?"

"Capital! But you—we hear your food didn't agree—"

Moira nodded. "Isn't it terrible?"

Eunice sat on the arm of Moira's chair. "Of course we immediately thought you were increasing already—"

"Eunice!" Madame interrupted. "Where are your manners?"

"Oh, I say!" Pomfret interjected.

Moira smiled. "So soon?"

Eunice watched her new sister-in-law carefully. "It's happened before." Eunice watched even more carefully. "And you're not saying you're not."

Moira thought about all the things Michael had told her of London gossips in general and Eunice in particular. "Eunice," she smiled gently, "I promise you, you'll be the first to know when I am. All right?"

Eunice smiled, looking over at Madame. Then, standing, she

187

walked nearer. "Mother, she is as bad as Michael; you can't get a straight answer out of them. You are the only help I have."

Madame's voice was quiet, her eyes softer when they rested on Moira. "Eunice, curiosity is an unattractive trait."

Pomfret stood up, yawning pointedly, touching the back of his hand to his mouth. "I say, we're to the village for the fair, what? And you, my dear," he stared at Moira directly, "you're to go with, or to relax here?"

"I think I'll be here, to hear all about it, when you return."

"We'd best change then, Pommy." Eunice stood up. "How soon do we leave?"

Pomfret looked indulgently at his wife. "Soon as you're together, love. Come along." He stood beside her now, nodding to Moira, kissing Madame's hand. "We'll be down presently, Madame."

John Ottery stood at the far end of the Conservatory. "Excuse me, Your Ladyship—"

Moira turned toward him. "Yes?"

"A Genevieve Durlac and son have arrived. They say they are your guests."

Moira turned quickly toward him not wanting Eunice to see her shock. "Yes, send them in, please." Her voice was steady, her face calm when she turned back around.

Eunice hesitated at the doorway, holding Pomfret's arm, turning back toward Moira. "Friends from Brittany, Moira?"

"Paris, actually," Moira said, turning back to see Madame's expression.

Madame remembered the name Genevieve. Moira smiled a little, still seated when Genevieve and Jean-Marc walked in behind John Ottery.

"Ah, Genevieve. Jean-Marc!" Moira opened her arms and Jean-Marc ran to her, hugging her lustily.

"Moira!" he yelled happily. "Where's Monsieur?"

Genevieve walked in more slowly, her stance sedate, almost regal. When she saw Moira closely she stopped.

"But what's wrong?"

Moira stood up, Jean still near her. She reached out to Genevieve. "I don't look that badly! And it's just indigestion." She glanced toward Eunice. "Have you met Eunice, Michael's sister?"

"No—but you!"

"It *is* indigestion. Though Eunice is determined it's an addition to the family, no matter what I say. And already!"

188

Moira's words were light, but her eyes, shielded from Eunice, pleaded with Genevieve.

"Ah." Genevieve smiled slowly. "Well," she hugged Moira and then glanced at Eunice, "how do you do?"

Eunice nodded, indicating her husband. "Pomfret, my husband."

Genevieve smiled at him.

Eunice walked away, and Pomfret followed her down the hall.

As Genevieve sat down, Madame stared at Moira. "Genevieve?" she asked Moira, Genevieve responding, "Yes, Madame?"

Moira nodded to Michael's mother. "I'm sorry. May I present Michael's mother, Genevieve Durlac and her son, Jean-Marc."

Madame was looking closely at Jean-Marc as Genevieve spoke. "Oh!" She looked as though she would say more and then did not. She sat back, Jean-Marc coming near to lean against the arm of her chair. "How do you do, Madame."

Moira looked down at her own hands. They looked frail, not like her hands at all.

"John." Moira glanced toward the butler. "If you will show our—guests—to the Red Suite."

He bowed. "Your Ladyship."

Genevieve and Jean-Marc stood, walking with John to the hallway and on upstairs as Madame watched Moira.

After the room was quiet, after all were gone, Madame spoke. "This is the woman you referred to?"

"Yes."

"And the boy?"

"He said Jean-Marc was his—own—flesh and blood." The words were difficult for Moira.

"And why was she invited here? What trouble is this?"

"I don't know. I did not invite them."

"But she told John—"

"I know. And I shall ask her. But I didn't think I should go into it with everyone here."

"No. No, of course not. You still care about my son," Madame said slowly.

"Yes. I do."

"I thank you. For my family's sake. And for my son's sake." She stood up, walking slowly across the long room and then, slowly, she turned back toward the young woman. "Moira?"

"Madame?"

The old woman's eyes swam with tears. "I am proud to have you as my son's wife. And he is a fool if he does not see what he has."

Moira felt the tears welling up in her own eyes. "Thank you." She looked down, trying to stop the tears, telling herself that her weakened condition was causing the feelings of helplessness, of hopelessness, that welled up within her.

Genevieve and Jean-Marc were here. He must have invited them. But Genevieve had said they were Moira's guests. Moira stood up, going over the words spoken, determined to find out once and for all where she stood.

Walking up the stairs, Moira hesitated near the guest suite, across the hall from her own, and then seeing Frances within, motioned to her. "Frances, would you please ask Madame Durlac to come to my rooms?"

"Madame Durlac?" She stared at her mistress.

"She's in the guest suite."

Frances, curious, nodded and left.

Moira sat down in a soft chair near the fireplace in her sitting room, staring at the figures in the Oriental carpet beneath her feet.

Genevieve walked in a moment later, Frances behind her. "Moira?"

Moira looked up. "Genevieve," she began and then, once the name was out, Moira realized that Frances knew. Her expression changing, Moira could see that she remembered the name. And the day in Hyde Park.

Genevieve sat down. Moira told Frances to bring tea and then turned back toward Genevieve. "I—was not expecting you."

"He did not mention?" Genevieve asked.

"No. It seems we meet again, as we did before."

"Oh." Genevieve looked at the younger woman earnestly. "Then I must thank you for being so kind as to take us in, yet again. I understand he is not here."

"I assumed he would wish me to take you, and Jean-Marc, in." Moira hesitated. "Genevieve, what is between you and—my husband?"

"Your—?"

"Yes." Moira watched her intently.

"I—has he said nothing?"

"He has said nothing," Moira confirmed.

190

"Then, I must ask that you—ask—your husband."

Moira stared at the woman and then nodded. "Yes, of course. I shall."

Genevieve stood up. "I am grateful to you." She started toward the door and then hesitated. "I—would like to congratulate you. Both of you."

Moira realized she meant for a baby, that she had misunderstood downstairs. She started to speak and then didn't, Genevieve closing the door.

Moira leaned back and closed her eyes, weariness washing over her. Frances found her so when she returned with the tea. The maid's eyes were reproachful. Setting the silver tray on the table, she picked up a cup and began to pour. "I'm sure it's none of my business, but I can hardly credit that woman coming here." Frances put a cup beside Moira. "What nerve!"

"It makes no sense," Moira said finally.

"It certainly doesn't, and I'd say much stronger than that, Milady."

If he truly wished her harm, Moira reasoned, if he really were trying to be rid of her and keep the inheritance, too, then it was the worst folly to bring Genevieve and the boy into it. He could not do any of this, she told herself, he would not.

Unless it was a war of nerves that he was waging. Unless he thought that the presence of the boy would make anyone think it innocent. She kept going over all she knew, somehow feeling that she had all the keys to the puzzle and that if she could only put them together she'd know what was really going on, what all of it meant, what really had happened long ago. And just three weeks past. But the only answers that made sense, that fit what all had been said, were answers she did not want to believe.

"Milady? Is there anything else I can get you?"

"No, thank you. You may go."

"Go?"

Moira was absently stirring her tea. She looked up as Frances spoke again.

"But, Milady, I've been sleeping here, in the sitting room, since, since—You've not been alone," she finished, "since then."

The honest concern in the girl's eyes touched Moira. She smiled up at Frances. "What would I have done without you?"

"Oh, Milady." Frances didn't know how to reply to the unexpected praise.

"Ever since I arrived in London, you've been not only a help, you've been a friend. Even a teacher," Moira added, a small smile reaching her lips again. "And I thank you. For everything."

"Oh, Milady! I think you're the most, the best, you deserve so much better! I—" Stumbling for the right words Frances's passionate speech trailed off.

"There is no need for you to stay here now. I'm not in danger."

"I just feel better being near. Just in case."

Moira put her cup on its saucer, standing up with it and walking toward the bedroom. "You do as you wish." She stopped by the door to the small hall. "And you know I appreciate your concern. But, if you're uncomfortable, go on to your own room, I'll be fine later. I'm going to lie down until the others get back from the village."

Moira closed the door and looked at the walls of her bedroom. Slowly she walked from the doorway to the east windows, from the windows to the bed, to the north windows, to the wall that led back to her door. That wall had the bathroom beyond it. She turned toward the south wall, the wall that bordered the main hall. The north wall was an outside wall, looking out onto the gardens and the sea. The east wall was half an outside wall. The windows and the fireplace between them looked out toward the moors. The balance of the east wall bordered the upper part of the chapel.

Chapel. Priest's holes. She stared at it, at the wall, and then, slowly, walked toward it, touching inch by inch from the edge of the window that looked east, along the castle wall, pressing, trying to find a secret doorway, an explanation for the locked doors being open. For locked they had been. She clearly remembered locking the outer door.

She found nothing. The reality of another key, of someone in the household unlocking that door, could not be gotten around. Unless they came in from the Duke's sitting room, through the small connecting door.

"Milady! Milady!" Frances was pounding on her door. The sound of a pistol shot echoed as Frances opened the door. "Robbers!"

Moira stared at Frances as she stood in the doorway, shaking visibly.

"Lock the sitting room door!"

Frances ran back to the sitting room, locking the door to the hall beyond and then running back to the bedroom, Moira locking the bedroom door behind her.

"Help me with the sheets," Moira said. "We've got to get out the windows. We've got to go for help!"

Frances moved quickly to pull bedding off the bed, Lucy's diary falling to the floor unseen. The sounds of men's boots and oaths filtered through the walls as the two women pulled sheets together, tying them quickly, reaching for blankets, for covers, the pounding on the sitting room door loud.

"The door to the Duke's Suite!" Moira stared toward the bedroom door.

"It was locked," Frances said.

"From which side?" Moira stared at Frances, thinking of the small connecting door from the Duke's sitting room to hers. Then the sounds grew louder, someone was hacking at the hall door.

A sound behind Moira turned her and then Frances toward the east wall. Frances stifled a scream, her hands at her mouth, as the east wall opened, a huge, black man standing in the opening.

He stepped forward as Moira stared first at him and then the wall. "I tried to find that. How—"

He pulled her to him, pulling Frances, too, toward the opening as fists began to pound on the bedroom door. Pushing them into the darkness of the open hole behind the wall he stepped inside, pressing a lever and closing the wall, just as the fists and feet of the men outside burst through the bedroom door.

Voices filtered through the wall, into the total darkness behind as a voice said quite distinctly on the other side: "The sheets! The window! Quickly!"

The sounds of boots racing out was the last sound Moira heard as she was pushed forward, into the darkness. Frances gasped beside her and Moira found her hand, taking it in her own and squeezing it. "It'll be all right."

"No talk!" The man they could not see spoke with a thick accent.

The darkness had narrow sides that Moira scraped against as she stumbled forward, a long, narrow corridor of some kind was what they were in. But no cobwebs. No cobwebs.

They stopped finally, at a wall which closed off the narrow walkway. Frances was crying quietly, her hand still held by Moira's. "Shhh," Moira said, "we'll be all right."

193

"But—but—"

"No talk!" The harsh, deep voice spoke in a whisper that carried authority.

Frances, shaking badly, found Moira's arm around her, steadying her without words.

And then there was a pale light, and the wall ahead opened into a narrow circular stairwell. They moved forward, the huge black man closing the wall behind them before going forward.

His cutlass slung carelessly through his belt was a potent threat. He looked as though he'd use it in a moment, with no regrets.

He pressed on an area of wall down the narrow spiral stairs, the wall swinging open. Moira realized she was in one of the four turret towers. The east tower, it had to be. Then they were descending into a long narrow tunnel, the dank smell of damp earth permeating the length of it.

As she felt the man's broad hand on her back, as she kept hold of Frances's hand, the thought of this being the tunnel that Lucy had spoken of hit her hard. And then she thought of the diary itself. The diary that now lay in that room, open on the bed or fallen to the floor as they pulled out the bedding. Open for all to see.

She realized that it could hang Michael. That it could even now lie in the hands of his enemies, whoever they were.

Moira squeezed Frances's hand hard, then let it go, pressing herself back against the dark wall, holding her breath as she heard Frances, sniffling, continue on ahead. Then, one step at a time, afraid every step that their captor would know, that a light would come from somewhere and he would see her fleeing back down the dark tunnel, she ran silently back, toward the stairwell, toward the narrow corridor and her own room.

Cautiously she stopped, finding the wall to the corridor, pressing it, cursing it silently. Remembering how she could not find the lever that opened the panel in her own room, she searched in the darkness for the lever that would control this opening. She hardly breathed, afraid every moment that she would be pulled back.

Finally she saw the wall begin to move. It opened slowly, the dim light from the turret stairwell visible now. She closed it behind her. For some reason she wasn't sure of, she did not fear the man who had taken them this way. She wanted to keep the route safe from the intruders, whoever they were. From the other intruders she corrected herself, ruefully, as she ran up the stairs to the next floor and pressed the stone walling, trying to retrace their steps exactly, trying to remember what she'd seen the man do in the dim light. She'd counted down the steps when he had pushed them forward, now she counted back up them.

She pressed and pushed, and the unyielding stone wall did not move. She stared at it intently, seeing a smaller stone square and pressing it, the wall slowly opening. Halfway open, afraid to wait for it, she ducked inside, racing quickly down what she knew was a long, straight, dark hallway.

To the blank wall at the end which meant that she'd found the wall to her room. She groped around in the darkness, trying to find a lever. There were no sounds from the other side of the wall, but she was curious. She stayed quiet, touching all along the wall, her eyes useless in the darkness.

A niche in the wall, a touch of her fingers, and the wall began to open. She stayed close against it as it opened, looking out into her bedroom.

Her jewelry case was thrown to the floor, its contents spilled out onto the carpet, chairs overturned nearby. The bedding was still all over the floor, dragged toward the north windows. And, under the bed, in plain view, was the narrow volume of Lucy's writings.

Moira cautiously stepped into the room. Not until she walked toward the bed, not until she reached under it for the book, did she hear the sounds of people in the next room.

Crouched over, under cover of the huge bed, she moved toward the open wall, the diary in her hand. Once near the wall she slipped behind it, pressing the panel she'd found, holding her breath until the panel slowly closed.

Halfway down the dark secret passage she heard noises. Cautiously she neared the turret stairwell.

Sounds of boots and men's voices filtered through the stones of the walling, running down, beyond, as Moira hesitantly opened the wall, slipping out and running lightly down the steps, around the curve of the stairwell, counting the steps to the next level. She pressed the wall, pushing through it and on down into the pitch blackness beyond.

A hand suddenly gripped her shoulder in the blackness. She gasped, then, quietly, she moved forward. "I came back by myself. I had to get something," she said quite steadily, surprising herself.

There was no answer from the unseen man. They moved

quickly down the pitch-black tunnel, on and on, the smell of the damp earth stronger, the feeling of walking deeper and deeper into the earth oppressing Moira.

They did not catch up with Frances, they did not speak, as the man, his hand on her arm, walked fast, almost pulling her along with him.

Out of breath, she stumbled against a crate of some kind, nearly falling, and when he reached to prevent her fall, she grabbed the diary close. His arms around her for a brief moment, he made sure she was upright, and then they plunged on again.

Finally they reached what seemed to be a dead-end. Moira stood still, realizing that she was trembling. A cloak was thrown around her shoulders and fastened, the unseen man standing close, his hands still on her shoulders, his fingers gripping her tightly.

Her breath caught in her throat, fear clutching at her now, the man leaning close and then abruptly pulling back away, a moment of total stillness between them before he moved away. "Who are you?" she whispered into the darkness.

Then a blindfold fell across her eyes, her hands tied a moment later. She gasped, struggling against the bindings as a coded knock brought cold salt air swirling around her.

A man spoke and then another, their voices urgent, the words a language she did not understand. She stumbled and almost fell, the diary slipping out of her grasp. She tried to catch it, heard a startled exclamation beside her and then felt herself being lifted. "No, give it to me!" She twisted around, trying to grab for it with her bound hands, her arms flailing out against the man who carried her. "I'll scream, I'll—" Her voice rising she took a deep breath and then felt the rocking of a boat beneath her. She lost the scream, realizing that the wind and the sea mist and the rocking boat meant they were far from the castle. None could hear her.

She tried to push against the side of the rocking boat, tried to loosen her blindfold, but someone straightened her up, the blindfold still in place.

She was lifted aboard a ship a little while later, carried through corridors, deposited in a cabin, and left alone. Or alone she thought until she heard Frances beside her, untying her blindfold, releasing her hands.

"Oh, Milady, what's happened?!"

"Nothing!" Moira, angry at herself, threw the cloth and the

196

rope they'd bound her with across the dark cabin. "I tried to remedy a mistake and stupidly let it slip away again!"

Frances did not understand. "Let what slip away? What mistake, Milady?"

Moira shook her head impatiently, standing up and walking to the small-paned window that looked out on a tiny section of the deck. She strained to see out it as Frances came near.

"My stomach won't stay put!" Frances wailed, "I don't know if it's me fears or the horrid lurching under me feet!" Feeling more ill by the minute, she forgot protocol, all her thoughts concerned with her rising stomach.

The narrow view Moira could see once she pushed the curtain aside showed only a portion of the decking and a wall of fog. She twisted to see upward and then stopped, her indrawn breath expelled slowly. A portion of a huge black sail was visible.

Frances was hanging onto the drawn curtain, watching Moira's expression change. "What is it?" she whispered. "Oh, what's wrong now? What did you see?"

Moira looked around the small cabin, lit only by the erratic light from outside as the fog covered up the last of the sun.

"We're on the pirate ship, it would seem."

As Frances moaned, Moira patted her shoulder and turned her toward a narrow bed to one side of the cabin.

"We run from them and to them, it would seem." Moira helped Frances sit down. "Here, lie down on the bed and stop fighting it. It's rather like riding a horse."

Frances whimpered as she lay back. "I can't ride a horse, neither. Oh, Milady, what's to become of us?"

"I don't know, but there's no need for melodrama. We're bound to be more valuable to them alive and well, so stop worrying and try to rest."

"Rest!"

"Yes, rest. I'll be right here, in this chair." And suiting action to words Moira sat down.

"Aren't you—don't you feel unwell?" Frances spoke low, her words caught between deep breaths, trying to keep from gagging.

"No. Now don't try to talk so." Moira stood up, walking to the door to test the handle. Locked.

She paced back and then threw herself into the chair, her teeth knawing at the knuckle she thrust between them.

All thought muddled by the last hour, she tried to analyze the

197

situation, the danger they might be in, but only kept coming back to the reality of being locked in this dark cabin, with none to know that they were here, none to rescue them. She realized then that she'd trusted because the man who had grabbed them was like the man in her dreams. Because he knew about the secret passage, and Lucy's tunnel.

How foolish she had been began to be plain as she listened to Frances's moans.

Chapter Twenty-one

SOUNDS OF MOVEMENT OUTSIDE THE CABIN STIFFENED MOIRA'S posture. She sat rigid in the wooden chair as the cabin door opened. A huge black man loomed in the half-light. Walking forward, he leaned down over the bed where Frances slept fitfully now. Moira stood up quickly, looking toward the door.

"What are you doing?" she asked, her eyes glancing from the open door to the bed.

Not answering, he leaned down to pick up the sleeping Frances as another black man blocked the doorway. Frances woke, her upset stomach forgotten as she stared at the man who was lifting her out of the bunk. She screamed, Moira racing to pull at the huge man's arms.

"Let her alone! Don't you dare!" She switched from French to English to Breton, trying to make the pirate understand. He ignored her in all three languages, carrying the screaming Frances out. He did not even seem to feel Moira pulling on his arm, swearing at him to let her maid go.

The other man, still standing at the doorway, now stepped inside, reaching for Moira and pinioning her arms as the first man left, Frances's screams for help echoing back toward the cabin.

Moira's arms held fast, she flailed at her captor with her feet. "If you think you'll harm one hair on her head. . . . Let me go! How *dare* you hold me!" She swung her foot hard, hitting his shin. "You bloody fool, let me go! By God, I'll see you hanged!"

"Hardly likely." Andre stood in the doorway, calm and cold.

"You!" She stopped, frozen by the sight of him.

Andre walked inside, motioning to the man who now released her. Moira rubbed her arms where he'd held her tight, seeing the black that had rubbed off on her.

"Lampblack!" Moira stared at Andre. "I see you don't bother with it!" Her eyes went to the open doorway.

"I wouldn't," Andre said and she saw the pistol in his hand. The man closed the cabin door. She could hear the bolt thrown and no steps echoing away. He stood just outside, waiting.

"Well?" she demanded, crossing her arms and staring at him defiantly. She gripped her own arms tightly so that he would not see her shaking hands.

"Your maid will not be harmed. I merely wished to speak to you alone."

"There were easier ways! And there is nothing to be said." She spat the words at him. "Where is the Duke? What have you done to him?"

"Nothing—yet." Andre slipped a hand into a breast pocket, bringing out a document. "If you'll read this, much will be explained."

She stared at him contemptuously. "Nothing you have, nothing you can say, interests me." Her words were defiant. "I see you've now lost your 'French' accent altogether."

Andre flamed a lamp into a strong blaze, turning the wick back to burn brightly and then holding out the papers toward her. "I am not, as you have guessed, French. I am an agent of His Majesty, King George IV." He paused. "And you had better read this."

"If you think I'd believe one word—"

He motioned toward the papers.

She stared at him and then grabbed them from him, as if to touch what he touched was repugnant to her. She looked down at the papers and then, slowly, sat down, in the narrow wooden chair, rereading the documents as he spoke.

"I think you can see that they are official credentials."

"But—" She looked up at him, her confusion evident. "But what is this ship? What are those men?"

"Pirates. And worse. In the employ of your husband. My life is now in your hands."

She stared at him. "My husband is not a pirate!"

"He is. And worse. I've been assigned to bring him to justice and have been able to prove none of his crimes, until now."

Her eyes widened. "Why—now?"

199

Andre smiled. "Thanks to you, Your Ladyship. This is what you went back for, isn't it? A bargaining tool?" He reached into the pouch which was slung over his shoulder and brought forth a slim, small, plain-covered diary. Lucy's diary. When Moira saw it her heart stopped.

"That's mine. Please return it immediately." She reached for it but he held it up, away.

"I'm sorry. It is state's evidence."

"No! It's—there's nothing there that is proof of anything!"

"There is everything including motive. You of all people should realize that."

"I!" She stared at him. "Why do you say that?"

"Hasn't he been determined to do away with you too?"

"No!"

Andre smiled, a small, cold movement of lips and teeth. "No?" His tone was full of mockery. "Come now, you were even driven to make out a will—"

She couldn't take her eyes from his. "How do you know that?"

"It's my business to know everything that goes on in that household."

"A spy! And Michael trusts you! Have you no shame? No sense of honor?"

"Do you deny you made out a will?"

She smiled then, as cold a smile as his own. "Of course not. But could you not, with all your—subterfuge, acquire a copy?" She watched him stare at her now. "No," she said softly. "You could not. For if you had you'd know that I left everything I have, everything I ever will have, to Michael."

Andre stared at her in disbelief. "That's ridiculous."

"But true."

"There's no need, he'd inherit in any event." Andre's voice had lost some of its assurance.

"But I wished to tell the world and all that not only legally, under the law, but by my own desire, he should have all that's mine."

Andre stared at her. "Why?"

Her face showed her contempt as well as her defiance. "That's none of your business."

Andre still hesitated. "And if he's working against the government?"

"He isn't."

"If I prove to you he is?"

200

"Then he has good reason."

"What?" Andre demanded.

She stopped. "I don't know anything of what you say. But he's done nothing wrong. That I *am* sure of, nothing!" As she said the words she realized that they were true. As she'd always known when he was near, as she'd always cared, she knew the man she'd loved since childhood could not be what they said.

What any of them said.

"If you try to use that diary," she told him, "I'll deny it! You can't even know that's Lucy's handwriting!" She stared toward the door. If these were Michael's men aboard ship, if he'd been honest when he told her this was Michael's ship, she could scream and they might come.

"But you can," Andre said. "There must be other things with her handwriting on them in your father's papers, if nowhere else."

"And if I say it is not?"

"You'd be lying to government agents." Andre stared at her. "Why would you protect a man who wishes you dead?"

"He doesn't."

"You're a fool if you can't see it!"

"And you're a fool if you can know him and think him capable of such acts!"

"Who then?"

Her eyes clouded over, a great sigh escaping her lips. "I don't know . . . I don't know."

"Do you admit it could be him?"

"He hasn't even been near when—"

"How convenient. Neither was he when his first wife died. Also conveniently."

She stood up, pacing back and forth as she spoke, nearing the bolted door with each step. "I do not wish to hear it, I do not wish to hear it." She reached the door and then she screamed for help, screaming as Andre came at her, screaming as the door was unbolted and opened.

Michael stood in the doorway. One thought welled up within her. "Be careful! Michael, he has a gun!" She was shouting at her husband now but Andre did not make a move toward the Duke. She stared at Andre, realizing he had let her go, had let her scream, had not even drawn his weapon at the intrusion.

She stared at the man who was her husband, whose bed she had climbed into that night weeks ago . . . and whom she had not seen since.

"Wouldn't it be more comfortable in my cabin?" Michael spoke coolly, as though nothing had ever happened between them. His eyes were opaque as he stepped back and walked out of view. Moira stared after him, seeing Andre walk to the doorway and hesitate. He stood, just outside, waiting for her to follow.

Silently, finally, she did follow them out, walking down the familiar corridor. She passed the main cabin.

"This is the Black Saint!" She was inside the oak-panelled captain's cabin, Michael turning toward her. He held a cut crystal decanter in his hand, studying her from across the cabin. "Yes. You were taken to the first mate's cabin, which you had not seen before."

"But—" She stopped, staring at him as he poured a glass and handed it to Andre. "Michael, I tell you, be careful! This man is a government agent!"

"I told you," Michael said to Andre.

Grudgingly, Andre nodded. "All right. But I had to make sure."

"Make sure of what?" Moira asked into the silence. "Who are you? You are a government agent, those papers were real!"

"Yes. They are," Andre said.

Michael motioned her to a chair. "He is a government agent."

"But—" She looked from one to the other and then walked forward, sitting down in the chair he indicated. "He said—"

"Andre, you may leave us. It's time Moira knew what has been happening."

Andre finished his drink in one gulp, Michael's eyes never leaving Moira's face. "I'll go see to the maid. And the others," Andre was saying.

"Others?" Moira asked.

Michael hesitated for only a moment. "Genevieve and Jean-Marc."

"Oh." Her voice was small. She looked down at her own hands in her lap.

"Would you care for a drink?" he asked her, pouring before she replied. "It may be strong for you . . . but I seem to remember you fancy—whiskey?"

She looked up then, her eyes full of questions. He reached out a glass toward her and she took it, her hand shaking. But she did not taste it.

Michael stood at the fireplace, one hand on the mantel, one foot on the hearth. He did not look at Moira, he watched the flames shooting up within the stone-lined pit that kept the fire well below the grate, out of danger of being swept loose with the ship's movements.

He began to speak as she watched him. "My family still has many relatives in France. And friends. We came from there."

"I know," she said into the silence which followed his words.

"Yes. Well, my father died fighting the Revolution and, afterward, after Napoleon was in power, many had to flee. Your father and I—helped them."

"That's why we moved to Brittany?"

He nodded. "He said there was nothing to keep him in Cornwall. Too many reminders of Anne, your mother."

She stared at him, remembering Tristan's words. And the diary. "Did you—and my mother—" She floundered, unable to bring the words out.

He turned back then, staring at her. "I read it," he said. "Lucy's diary. I read all of it."

Moira watched him.

After a long pause he walked nearer her, staring down at her. "Would you like to go out on deck?"

"Yes." She stood up.

The moon played games behind the cloud banks. Michael paced beside Moira as they circled the deck, walking toward the stern. She shivered and he roused himself from his thoughts, seeing her discomfort. "I didn't think . . . here." He untied his cloak, putting it around her shoulders. His hands lingered for a moment but when she bent her head to touch her cheek against the back of his hand he withdrew it, thrusting both his hands into his pockets now.

"You'll be cold," Moira said quietly.

"No. Moira, there was never anything between your mother and me. No matter what Lucy said. Or imagined."

Relief swept through her, buckling her knees. As she stumbled he caught her, his hands strong and warm. "Are you all right?" His concern filled his voice. "Are you still unwell?"

"No, I mean, yes, I'm fine," she said weakly. "Oh, Michael." She stared at him with large trusting eyes.

He stared at her. "Did you think me guilty?"

"I—I couldn't know," she replied simply.

"And—of the rest? You defended me with Andre."

"You heard?"

"Every word." He stared at her, his eyes full of pain. "You were ill when I—that last night—you were in pain, weren't you?"

"Not while you held me," she said softly, fear, hope, worry, all striving for place within her.

"That was unpardonable."

"You couldn't know. . . ."

"I should have known, should have seen, you were unwell. I was not thinking of much," his tone took on harshness, his anger at himself apparent, "except my own desires. Which are unpardonable, in our—circumstance." He spoke stiffly now. "I shall never expect you to forgive me for so taking advantage—for not keeping my word regarding our—arrangement."

"I came to you," Moira said softly, touching his arm.

He pulled away, his whole bearing stiff and erect. "After my unforgivable excursions into your rooms. I can only say in my defense that drink lowers the morals—the. . . . None need know. Ever. You should not be forced to suffer for my lack of—of sense."

Moira looked down toward the waters that lapped up against the black ship's sides, the sounds of the ship quiet around them. Her heart was breaking within her. "Is that all any of it meant to you? You felt—nothing?"

"I assure you that there is nothing to hold you here."

Her voice was a bare whisper. "I see."

He hesitated. "And your will—that should be changed, of course."

She looked up then, tears glimmering in her eyes. "You heard?" Her voice was barely audible.

His eyes searched hers. "Why? If you thought me guilty, if you didn't—know—as you said, then why did you make out that will?"

She was tired. "I didn't think you guilty. But if you had been it would not have mattered."

"Not matter?" He reached to turn her toward him, reaching to see her face in the moonlight.

"No." Her voice was listless now. Genevieve was here. Genevieve had won. She had nothing to give him that he wanted. Nothing.

"But why would it not matter?"

"Why did you come to me at the inn that night?" She stared up at him. "You have no answer to give me . . . nor do I have one to explain my actions to you . . . You would not understand if I tried. Just let it be. I am shamed enough."

He stiffened at her words. "Yes. I see." He forced himself to go on. "Moira, Lucy was locked in that dungeon. That part is true of what they all say. And it could not have been an accident. I've tried it a hundred times since. There's a catch on the bar that has to be pulled back from the outside. But it was not me." He tried to see her eyes. "You know my—faults—but I do not want you to think that of me. I—it was not of my doing."

"I know."

"You know?" He swallowed, affected by her simple trust in his words, in he himself. More affected than he wanted to show. More affected by her mere physical presence than he wanted her to see. He fought with himself for control. "Lucy sent the diary and the letter to your father to create more trouble."

"She was unwell," Moira said softly.

He took a deep breath. "Soon after we married she told me of her—liaison—with Lisle-Taylor. And of—the child. Which she already carried." His voice hardened. "She thought it a great joke. Later, later her mind began to go. I thought it just meanness, but it was more." He stopped. "My shame is that she would convince me that she loved me. She would come to me—"

Silence settled around them. "As I did," Moira said quietly.

"Oh no, no!" He turned toward her, taking her arms within his. "No, don't think that—it was—different. So different."

Moira stared up into his haunted eyes. "But you didn't send her away." She started to add, as you do me, and then could not speak the words.

He watched the green eyes clouding over. "No," he whispered the word. "No. I didn't send her away. Until she attacked Tamaris."

"Attacked?"

"I never touched her after that. Never. Look at Tamaris's wrists closely. That's why she cries out in her nightmares, why she cried out when you touched them. She was two . . . when Lucy tried to kill her . . . she said the baby cried too much." His voice was matter of fact; he tried to sound calm, detached.

"Oh . . . no. . . ." Moira's horrified words were as soft as the night breezes.

"I hired people. Never left her alone as the diary says. Never let her out of their, or my, sight, after that. She wrote

205

Lisle-Taylor and your father, judging by her diary. Lisle believed her. What happened that last night—I—I don't know."

Moira hesitated. "Could Jack know?"

Michael's eyes were hollowed with pain as he forced himself to talk about it, to answer her. "I don't know. But why? He had no reason."

"That we know of."

"That we know of," he repeated. "Moira, I vowed, I *vowed,* I'd never love again, never again. Never care. I—it's too deep, Moira. I can't change that. I don't even want to change that."

"I see," she said finally.

"Do you?" He turned toward her. "Do you?"

She took a deep breath. "And Genevieve?"

"Genevieve is my cousin Henri's wife."

Moira watched his face as he spoke, feeling her knees weaken again. She grabbed hold of the rail so that he wouldn't see. Her brain reeled with his words. His cousin's wife. His cousin Henri's wife. His nephew! Jean-Marc was his flesh and blood *nephew.*

Michael continued to speak. "Henri is in line of succession for the French throne. After we rid France of the megalomaniac Napoleon, instead of getting better, things have been, if anything, worse. Charles X has been systematically following his predecessors and ridding himself of any who could lay claim to his throne. He plotted against his own brother, his nephews and cousins die mysteriously." He paused. "Since King Charles himself plotted to gain his throne, it's not remarkable that he doesn't trust any of his relatives. In any event, Henri and Jean-Marc were ordered to be held."

"Held?" she asked quietly, trying to take it all in, her heart soaring again within her. . . . It was not Genevieve, Jean-Marc was not his. . . . It was the past that kept them apart, not another love. The *past,* only the *past.* . . .

"Under arrest, for all intents and purposes," he said. "But fortunately Henri had friends who heard of the order and helped them escape. They had to go separately. Genevieve and Jean-Marc reached your cottage. Henri was already gone when your father and I reached the inn. But Charles's agents were still waiting." He stopped. "Somehow they knew. Or hoped. And so they were there to stop us when we arrived. Your father was hurt."

"I know."

206

He looked out across the water. "There was no way to avoid it. Believe me, if there had been—"

"I believe you." Moira touched his arm.

"I brought Genevieve and Jean-Marc to London with us. And posted men to try to find out what had happened to Henri. Genevieve was beside herself with worry that he had perished too. As your father did." He cleared his throat. "Word came after we left London that he had survived and later, he reached some—friends."

"So you left to find him while we traveled on to Clovelly," Moira said.

"Yes. And have him transported here. When he was I sent for Genevieve and Jean-Marc."

"To meet you both at St. Maur today."

"Yes. Henri's here now. And so are they."

"But why didn't you just tell me!? Why didn't you trust me?"

He hesitated. "It was dangerous for you to know. If anything happened."

She watched him. "And you didn't trust me."

He looked her in the eye. "I could take no risks with their lives. No unnecessary risks when so much was already at stake. And someone may have told the authorities in France of our activities. They were waiting for us."

"You couldn't think that I—" She stopped. "But I did not know where, or whom—" She stopped, speaking again slowly after a pause. "Andre's charade just now was to show I was not to be trusted." When Michael did not deny it. "And the robbers?"

He smiled then, a fleeting smile, quickly gone. "Ah, yes, the robbers. They cover well for us, for our real activities. We, Andre and I, have been trying to track down French spies who are here trying to find out Henri's whereabouts. Among other things. The pirate ship is an easy means to explain the black ship that unloads its human cargo in remote places. That attacks certain people, certain places, and takes documents as well as women and jewels. The women are released unharmed. But I fear their sensibilities are crushed to admit it, so they make up the most lurid tales. The jewels pay for many Frenchmen's new lives." He stopped, looking far out to sea and then: "Andre told me of your accident. And when we got back today, he sent word of your illness."

"Word?"

"Genevieve."

"Oh," Moira said.

"She was quite concerned about you. Seemed to think you most desperately ill and—in the family way."

Moira looked away. "I know. I let her think it. I even said as much to her. I thought if people knew it was poisoning they would think, they'd assume—"

"They'd blame me," he finished for her. "You weren't sure yourself, were you?"

She took a long time to answer. "No," she said finally, in a quiet voice. "No, I wasn't. Not entirely."

The Duke was leaning against the rail again, his back to it now, his hands stuffed deep into his pockets. "And yet you still made a will in my favor." When she said nothing, he continued. "Why?" There was no answer. "Why, Moira?" he asked again. "Please. I must know. I must understand *why*."

She did not meet his gaze. "I thought if it was you, if you wanted it all so badly, that, that you should have it."

"I told you once before. Only fools trust."

"Then I'm a fool. I told you so then." She looked up. "And so was my father, for he trusted you too, did he not?"

"You would let me have it all. All you have. Because your father trusted me? Is that the reason you come to me in the night too? You bring yourself, your fortune—and if I wanted even more?"

She misunderstood his words. "If you wanted more, if you wanted my life, then, yes. You could have it."

He stared at her.

"But not because of my father," she said.

"Why then?" His voice was low, his eyes black, unreadable.

"Don't you know? Michael, I love you. Surely you know that." When he did not respond she rushed on. "I've loved you since I was a child. If I don't know you, if I'm wrong about you, then I know nothing, no one." She tried to see within his eyes, tried to make out what he was feeling. "I don't want to be sent away, Michael. In March. I, I want to stay." Her heart was pounding within her breast, her heart in her eyes.

"Why?" he whispered.

"Do you remember the story I told Jean-Marc?"

"No."

"In the church, the day of the funeral. About the princess who—"

He looked away, out over the rolling waters. "Yes, I know. She was another fool who trusted the wrong man."

"Or woman?" She watched him spin around to search her eyes then. "Were you hurt so very badly?" she asked him. "So badly that the whole rest of our lives need suffer?"

His eyes turned even darker, the intensity of his gaze hurtful. "I have nothing to give," he said in a very definite, flat tone.

She took a breath, afraid to push him farther. "What happens now?" she asked him finally. "I—those robbers. . . ."

"They were an excuse," he answered finally, "to get you out of harm's way. You and your maid will make the trip to Ireland with us so that you'll be safe."

"Ireland! But what of your mother?"

"I shall get word to her somehow. You had to be gotten away. When Genevieve told me of your illness I realized that you had been ill—gravely ill—when I—" He stopped, his voice harsh when he continued. "I realized what I had done." He went on more briskly, "I went to check the gig today. The wheel had been cut. It was no accident. Therefore your illness could not be an accident either. You could not be left unprotected."

"Why not? If you do not care what happens to me?"

"I never said that!"

"Michael, then tell me you do care! What *are* you saying!?"

"I am responsible for you."

She stared up at him, hurt. "Responsible."

"Yes." He watched her eyes cloud with hurt again, hating the pain he saw in them. "I've told you. Plainly. I have nothing to give you."

"You already have given me what I need."

He grimaced. "You'll find, my girl, that that's not enough to build a life on."

"I don't mean your body." He stared at her, her forthright words continuing. "I love your body; surely you don't need to look so shocked about that, you know that already. But that is only part of it. You have given me trust. In small measures. At times. I treasure that, for I know what it means to you to give trust to anyone, no matter how little or how fleetingly. And you have given me your pain and your needs—yes, you have, and that is what I *do* need. That is what I want from you."

He grabbed her close, finding his arms unwilling to let her go. "Do you know what you're saying?"

"Yes."

"You do not even know if I am guilty or what has caused all this; who is to blame or who tried to kill you! I am the best suspect! The best excuse for a culprit! You *know* that!"

"Yes, you are! So help me find out who is behind it, for it *wasn't* you!"

"Oh—" He buried his face in her hair before the words could come tumbling out, before he told her of his need, his love. He could not bring the words forth.

A discreet cough brought Michael's head up to see Old Tom standing nearby. "Begging your pardon, Your Grace, but you said as how you wanted to know when the tide changed."

"Yes." Michael tried to sound calm, standing straight now.

Old Tom winked at Moira and then left them there, alone.

"Who do you think is causing all this?" she asked Michael when they were alone.

"I don't know. Andre thought you were causing it all to lay the blame at my feet. To sabotage the resistance."

"Me?" She stared at him. "And did he think I connived at my own father's death? Did *you?*"

"No. Never." He still held her arms in his hands. "No." He spoke more softly. "Never."

"But you let him have his chance to prove you wrong. To prove me false. Tonight."

"I let him have his chance," Michael agreed. "I could not ask him to take you on trust. And I was bringing you on board with Henri, when you knew so much about us already."

"I'm surprised Andre let you," she said bitterly.

"It is my ship," Michael replied quietly.

She stared out across the water. "And now?"

"And now the tide is changing and we make sail for Ireland."

"Where are we?"

"It's called Saint's Cove. Or rather the cave you came down the tunnel to is on Saint's Cove. It's half under water at high tide. We're anchored just off the cove."

"And no one knows?"

"The land for twenty miles in that direction," he pointed east, "and thirty in that," he pointed south, "is mine. The castle grounds lie to the west and here, north, is the Channel."

"Lucy knew of the tunnel."

"Yes. I didn't know that. In spite of what she says in the diary, I never found her there, or even knew she had found it."

"Do you think she really believed you to be a pirate?"

"I don't know." Pain closed down within him. "I don't know what she thought. Or felt. But I'll tell you one thing." He stared at Moira now, his eyes still sad. "She never trusted me." He paused. "As you seem to do so easily. Unquestioning as to whether I'm fair or foul, no matter what I may have done." His eyes hardened. "And I'll tell you something else. I could have killed her. I don't know why I didn't. And if I'd found her with, with that—I would have. *I would have* and never regretted the consequences." He pulled away as he spoke.

She reached out to touch his arm. "I'm glad you didn't."

He stared into her concern. "Why do you believe me?"

"Because you have no reason to lie to me. I could be killed and thrown overboard and none the wiser. Pirates would be blamed. You have everything of mine in any event. There is no reason to lie to me."

"But I still might be," he said, watching her.

"No."

"No?"

She took her hand, slowly, from his arm. "No. I would know if you were. I'm sure of that now. I think I may know you better than you know yourself."

He was quiet then. She stared down at the sea. Feelings of shyness engulfed her as he stood there so near her. His physical presence towered over her, the reality of his strength, of his body, so close to hers; the reality of her new knowledge washed through her, her breath almost stopping as they stood now, quietly, side by side.

A black-faced man came toward them across the deck. "Your Grace, Madame Durlac said to come quickly."

Michael straightened. "What's wrong?"

"The gentleman."

Michael started after the sailor, Moira behind him. They descended to the fore cabin and walked inside, the sailor standing guard outside.

Inside the fore cabin, Andre stood near the bed, Genevieve seated on it, putting wet cloths on the forehead of a thin, dark-haired man.

Michael walked forward, Moira behind him. "What is it?" Michael was asking.

Henri opened his eyes, his smile weak. "I'm afraid I misjudged a small wound."

211

Genevieve looked up at Michael, her eyes filled with worry. "There is a saber wound in his side! Look!"

"Henri!" Michael stared at the wound and then the man. "You said nothing!"

"A scratch," he said faintly.

Moira watched the man whose coloring, whose features, were so like Michael's. Henri was much thinner, much shorter, but his hair, his eyes, his nose, were the same.

"It's no scratch!" Genevieve looked up at Michael, pleading. "We must go back. Feel how feverish he is! He'll never stand the Channel crossing. Oh, Michael, to come so far, to be so near! You can't let me lose him now!"

"He's burning up," Moira said quietly, feeling the man's brow. "He's very weak."

"We must go!" Henri spoke through gritted teeth, not opening his eyes. "There is no other way."

"There's one," Michael said. He looked across the bed at Moira. "The room over the chapel. Beyond your room."

She thought of that long dark corridor the huge "black" man had propelled them through. A room was hidden there somewhere, in that darkness. "We'd have to carry him to it. Can we make the cave in time?"

"If we hurry. The tide's changing. It's possible."

"Then we'd best try," she said.

Genevieve looked from one of them to the other. "What are you saying?"

Moira smiled at the other woman. "That there is a way and that we must use it. Quickly." Moira looked up at Michael. "Genevieve and Jean-Marc can stay with Henri. Andre can find a doctor and bring him, there must be one who can be trusted."

Michael nodded. "There is. I can reach Goreston and have him return here to help."

"And," Moira continued, "Frances and I can 'escape' and return. That way I'll be in my room and can get messages to you. And food. Whatever."

"And be back in danger again! We still don't know who—"

Moira smiled gently. "We'll find out if I'm back."

"But the maid—"

"I can vouch for her silence. And we've got to find out who it is who's doing all this. The answer to that will be the answer to Lucy's death, too, don't you see?"

Michael stared at her. "So you're just to walk back in and let them try to kill you?"

"Kill her!" Genevieve looked from one of them to the other. "What are you saying?"

Moira shook her head, still answering Michael. "I'll be cautious. You'll be near. Michael, it will never end until we know who it is."

He stared at her, realizing she was right. "Then I'll arrive back, too. Andre, ready the boat."

Moira spoke to Genevieve. "Where is Jean-Marc?"

"In the next cabin—asleep."

"I'll see to him. You stay with your husband."

Genevieve grabbed Moira's hand as she crossed near, kissing it and looking up at her with eyes full of shiny tears. "How kind you've been! And your father dead because of us."

"Don't think that," Moira said quietly. "He had done this before. For others. It could have happened before. Or would have another time. I accept that now, and you must believe it, for it's true. He wanted to do what he did."

"We've interrupted your new marriage."

Moira smiled sadly, looking over at Michael and then back at Genevieve. "We did that ourselves."

"You must accept our thanks."

"Shhh." Moira released Genevieve's hand, turning to leave.

Michael followed her out. "I must thank you too," he said softly. "I can't thank you enough. For everything."

"Everything?"

"Genevieve. Jean-Marc. Even Tamaris and Mark. And Madame and the staff. You've played your part well."

"Yes." Her heart skipped a beat as she spoke. "You can."

"I beg your pardon?"

"You can thank me. Enough."

He watched her. "How?" he asked finally.

There was a fraction of a moment that went by before she built up the courage to answer him. "Don't make me come to you."

He stared at her still. "What?"

"Don't—go to the inn—each night. Stay. With me." She waited for his reaction.

He simply stared at her still. And in his gaze she found the hunger she'd seen in the darkness. "You—you can still have it all. No one need know . . . It is not too late," he told her.

"You still wish me to leave?" She stared up at him, her heart breaking.

"I gave my word. You have seen me at my worst. I—I don't

213

want to be the cause of your losing the chance to—to live your own life with a husband your own age. To have what you should have."

"Your Grace?" Mr. Talbot's voice came toward them. "The passenger is calling for you."

And still Moira searched his eyes. "Tell me you do not want me to stay."

He stared down at the eyes he had learned to love. "I do not want you to stay."

She pulled away then, turning back toward the cabins. "I'd best see to Jean-Marc," she said, her voice breaking along with her heart.

He watched her go. After she was safely gone he whispered the rest. "I want you to have so much more than I can give you."

The moon was high overhead as the ship rode the swells near shore.

Chapter Twenty-two

AN HOUR LATER MOIRA HELPED FRANCES ACROSS THE MOON-swept lawns, her arm around Frances's waist.

"I don't know, Milady. I just don't understand—"

"You don't have to," Moira cut in. "Just think of one thing. That more lives than just ours depend upon your silence."

"But what do I say?" Frances wailed softly.

"You say that we got away from our captors. And when they ask more, you may cry."

"Oh, thank you, Milady!" Frances sounded relieved.

The castle loomed before them. They crossed beneath the chestnuts and elms near the front of the house, walking in the front door, the first footman coming forward and then stepping back as if he'd seen a ghost. "Your Ladyship!"

Moira smiled. "Yes, back from the dead. Where's Madame?"

He stood stiffly. "In her rooms, Your Ladyship."

"Thank you." Moira helped Frances across the entrance hall. "Can you walk up or do you need help?"

214

"I can manage, Milady."

Moira smiled at her. "You go on to my rooms and lie down. I'll wake you after I've seen Madame."

Frances tried to smile and then just nodded. "Thank you, Milady."

Moira patted her arm. "Go on, I'll be there presently." She watched Frances mount the north stairs, and then Moira herself started up the south stairs toward the dowager's suite.

Knocking at Madame's door, Moira took a deep breath before walking in.

"Moira?" Madame's voice was low. She stood up, walking forward. "Oh, my dear!"

Moira took the older woman's hands. "I'm here, I'm fine."

"But how? And the others?"

Moira started to speak and then stopped. "Have you had no word?"

"None! The robbers came and you were gone and we didn't know what had happened!"

Moira wanted to tell her, wanted to tell her all of it, and then did not, afraid of why the message had not reached her, of what had gone wrong. "Frances and I got away, but I don't know about the others," she said finally.

Madame watched her closely. "Do you feel all right? Have they hurt you?"

"No, we got away and then we hid. There's nothing to worry about with us." Moira decided to stick to the story she would tell all else. "But we were worried about what had happened to everyone else here."

"Oh, Moira." The old woman's eyes filled with tears. She leaned forward, holding Moira close. "Tristan's gone. And your friend and her little son."

Moira almost told the old woman the truth. And then she realized Tristan was missing too. She said nothing, trusting Michael to make it right when he arrived.

"The authorities are already on the trail."

"What?" Moira moved back a little, to see Madame's eyes. "How could they be so soon?"

"They came to the house. They arrived and we knew nothing to tell them, except that you were all hostages—"

"They came here!" Cold fear swept through Moira. "Without your calling, without being asked? They couldn't have just come! Who told them?"

The old woman shook her head. "None here. Oh, I'm so glad you're all right. If only Michael had been here! I didn't know what to do."

"It's all right now." Moira tried to calm herself as well as the old woman. "Tell me about the others. Was anyone hurt?"

"No, miracle of miracles, no. Jeb was hit, but it's only a bump. Eunice and Pomfret had gone to the village and didn't even know until they came back."

"And Tamaris and Mark?"

"They heard, but hid in the Heir's Tower. You know, off Tristan's rooms? They're fine, but they didn't want to go to bed without knowing about you."

Moira smiled, tired lines etching themselves around her eyes. "I'll see them in the morning. I'm sure they're asleep by now. The others will be all right. Don't worry so. If I can escape, then so can they."

Madame sighed. "It's just that Tristan has such a temper. I'm afraid he'll get them upset with him and, and—"

"I'm sure he's all right. I'd better see to Frances, she's still quite upset."

Madame released Moira and then stood, stiff and erect, before her. "Yes. And you. You should have rest, after all you've been through—to have to go through this too!"

"I'm fine. Truly. I am much, much better. We shall talk in the morning if you like."

Moira turned to go, Madame calling out after her. "Moira!" She turned back. "Yes?"

"Be careful!" The old woman's worried eyes stared at her. "I shall be. I promise."

As Moira left and started across the hall Jemma called to her from the doorway to the children's wing. "Thank God, you're back! Are you all right? What happened? Where have you been?"

"I'm fine. Frances and I got away. I must see to her now, but we can talk in the morning."

Jemma stared at Moira doubtfully. "Got away? I mean, of course. In the morning then."

Moira crossed the main stairwell and walked to her rooms. Frances was in front of the fireplace, a poker firmly in her hands. "Oh, Milady!"

"What is it?" Moira closed the door to the hall. "What's happened?"

"Nothing, Milady, nothing more I mean. I just don't want to be alone, I'm so afraid. And I keep hearing things!"

Moira sighed. "Frances, don't frighten *me* so! Possibly I should have come back alone and left you safely there, aboard ship."

"Oh no, Milady!" Frances tried to pull herself together, pushing her disheveled hair back from her forehead, staring earnestly at Moira. "You mustn't be alone till we find out." She stopped, seeing Moira's finger to her lips. Frances nodded, speaking more softly. "Besides, I couldn't have taken five more minutes of that rolling back and forth, forth and back." Frances stopped, looking rueful as she remembered the pitch and toss of the sea. "Just saying it makes my stomach start to quake again."

"I don't think you were made for the adventurous life, Frances."

"No, Milady, that I'm not!"

"Lie down now. Get some rest so you may be of help tomorrow."

Frances obeyed, Moira picking up the lamp Frances had lit and walking on into her bedroom. She stared around at the disordered mess, remembering the locked door of the night of her poisoning. She'd not asked Michael why he'd unlocked it. She put the lamp on the table nearest the bed, slowly unbuttoning her robe, thinking of what he'd said aboard ship.

She had so wanted him that it had never been real to her that mayhap he would not want her. The cold reality of that possibility smote at her. He had said he did not want her to stay. He had no reason to say that now unless it was the simple truth.

She stared across the room toward her own reflection in the pier glass, backlit by the lamp behind her. She was no blonde and blue-eyed lovely such as Genevieve, nor did she have the glorious beauty she'd seen in the portraits of Lucy. Their coloring was similar but she had none of the easy grace, the haughty aristocracy of those ladies. She thought of the woman at the inn. She had not dared to ask about her. She wondered what he would have said if she had. For she must be there. Madame knew about her, it was not only Tristan.

She climbed into the bed, turning toward the east wall, staring across the darkness at it. Behind it Michael would be helping Henri to safety. At least she had his trust finally, if not his love.

Her eyes closed, her thoughts fading into dreams of Michael holding her close. Later, much later, the moon crept far to the west. Sounds of muffled stealth brought Moira awake, her heart pounding; the sounds reverberated in her ears as she calmed herself, realizing that this was not danger. She wondered why the rest did not hear, why the house did not come awake with the noises?

And then she thought of the empty chapel and armory below these rooms, both two stories high. Only the secret room next to hers. Only her own room was near enough to hear the sounds of that corridor, of that room hidden by the walls and ceilings.

Lucy's sounds in the night. Moira listened to them, almost the sound of mice in attics, but louder, heavier. And murmured voices.

Had she thought herself mad and then become so in truth, Moira wondered, shuddering. She thought of Tamaris, Tamaris who still cried if any touched her wrists, who still had nightmares that brought her awake screaming in the night. The children deathly afraid of their own mother, the father unable, unwilling, to face them, trying to help, trying to rescue others since he could not help, could not rescue, his own.

The sound of bootsteps came nearer. If she'd been asleep, if she'd been unaware of what lay beyond that wall, she would never have heard the boots that came near, nearer, and stopped.

Moira held her breath, listening for the wall to open, waiting for Michael to step through, for she knew he stood there still and silent, on the other side of the panelling.

The wall remained smooth, unmoving. Moira watched it, her breath bated. No sound of steps retreating. No sound at all. She pictured him, standing there, staring at the wall.

How long she waited she didn't know. She thought about calling out to him, thought about opening the panel. But she did none of it. It was his decision to make. And so she waited.

If he came through the panel, if he opened it and stepped inside, she would run to him and throw her arms around him and tell him that she loved him.

She waited.

And then, finally, she heard him turn, heard him move back, away. Tears splashed down now as she turned her head away from the wall, burying her head in the pillows, crying alone.

Chapter Twenty-three

MORNING BROUGHT FRANCES IN WITH HOT TEA AND BISCUITS, HER face wreathed in smiles as she went about the business of readying Moira's bath, seeing to her clothes, chattering on as she worked.

"They think me a regular heroine out of a book, they do. Can you imagine! And Jeb saying as how I'm much too delicate looking for him ever to have expected such bravery. But that as I was ever so pretty that lucky it was we got away or he knew as what all would have happened! And how we must have been so frightened and all."

Moira heard little, watching listlessly as Frances prattled on in the boudoir after the bath was taken, after the soft, blue gauzy morning gown was fastened into place.

Moira sat at her dressing table, watching Frances work with her hair, pinning it into an artless cascade of curls, threading a baby blue ribbon through the curls.

A knock at the sitting room door was answered, and Tamaris stood in the boudoir doorway after a moment. She smiled shyly at Moira. "We heard you'd escaped, but I wanted to see for myself."

Moira stood up, curls and ribbons half-completed, to come to Tamaris, to lean down and hug her tightly. "Oh, I'm so glad to see you! I wanted to tell you last night that we were all right, that I was sure the others would be too, but you were asleep when we arrived."

Tamaris clung to Moira. "I don't want anything to happen to you," she said fiercely, holding onto Moira still.

Moira tried to reassure the girl, then, slowly, she disentangled her, looking at the pale young face before her. "And where's Mark?"

Tamaris nodded toward the hallway. Moira walked, with one arm around Tamaris, toward the outer hall.

Standing there, hanging back, was Mark. He stared up at Moira mutely, and then he stood up straighter, coming away from where he leaned against the wall. He now looked at her eye to eye, his expression unreadable.

"Thank you for worrying, Mark," Moira said softly and then she walked nearer. Tamaris stood a little aside as Moira reached out to hug Mark. He hesitated and then stepped a little closer, letting her hold him. "They'll be all right," Moira was saying, "I'm sure of it."

"They say you escaped. And got Frances out, too, that you walked all the way back."

Moira looked into his eyes, trying to see what he was feeling. He glanced at Tamaris and then back at Moira.

"That was brave for a lady. And I guess it means you wanted to come back here, doesn't it?" he asked.

She looked from him to his sister. "Of course I did!"

"I told you so!" Tamaris said.

"Children." Madame's voice carried toward them as she walked down the north hall, coming nearer. "Children, let Moira finish getting dressed." She shooed them both away and then followed Moira back into her sitting room. "My dear, Michael's just arriving back, isn't that wonderful? Now everything will be all right."

"Yes. Everything." Moira hesitated. "Have you told him of all that's happened?"

They walked back into her boudoir.

"He'd heard already, but he wants to see you, to find out precisely."

Moira sat down at the dressing table, Frances hurrying to finish threading the ribbons through the piles of curls. Madame stood watching. She looked as if she might speak, and then, glancing at Frances, she waited until Moira stood up, until they walked out into the hallway, alone.

"Moira, I don't know how to say this, but, you must speak to Michael. The children, Tamaris in particular, have grown terribly fond of you. More so by the day. I could see their worry and concern for you through all this. Even Mark is coming round slowly. These children are becoming too attached to you. If you plan, if Michael still plans, as you said, to annul your marriage, well, if this continues and they grow even fonder of you, and then you leave, it will be too terrible a blow to them. After, after all they've been through. It would be cruel."

Moira bit at her lip, her eyes meeting Madame's. "You're right of course. I will speak to him about it. About all of it."

Madame watched her. "Is it still—not—your wish? To annul?"

"I will do what Michael wants," Moira said softly.

"I see." Madame reached out and patted Moira's arm. "You love my son—I know. And he is a fool if he forces you away." She saw moistness sparkling in Moira's eyes but did not mention it. "We'd best not keep him waiting. This might be just the thing to snap him out of his complacency. I'm sure he's beside himself with worry."

But when they reached his study, when he turned from Jemma who already stood there, he betrayed no anxiety. Andre stood, impassive, behind the Duke's desk, sorting papers into order.

Moira realized that to the two women who did not know the truth of the situation, Michael must seem terribly unconcerned.

"Well," he said as she walked forward, Madame still beside her.

"Well!" Madame spoke crisply. "Is that all you have to say!?"

"I have much to say," he replied. "Alone," he added.

Madame glanced over at Jemma. "Did you require something, Jemma?"

"What? Oh, no, I was just telling His Grace how tragic it all was. And of Tristan. And was just about to tell him of Moira's guests who were abducted and did not escape."

"Guests?" His brow rose as he studied Moira's face.

"Yes," she replied evenly. "Genevieve and her son had just arrived for a visit; you remember them. I introduced you—"

Madame looked from Moira to her son and then glanced at Jemma.

"Ah, the widow," Michael said. "Yes, of course." He spoke to his mother. "What are the authorities doing to find them?"

"I don't know, they spoke to the staff. Jemma, what did they say?"

She shook her head. "They were asking questions. They volunteered nothing."

"I'm glad you thought to call for them quickly," the Duke said to his mother. "It may help. But I don't know how you got them here so promptly."

"I didn't send for them."

"You didn't?"

"I did," Jemma interrupted. "I ran to the stable and rode into St. Maur for help."

221

Michael stared at her. "But there's no government official in the village."

"I was looking for men, to come back and fight. But luckily when I got to the inn two government men were there. Because of all the reports of the pirate ship. They said they'd chase it, they'd check every inch of coastline till they found it."

"Did they say how they hoped to proceed?"

"Only that," Jemma replied.

Madame was staring at the governess. "You mean you took it upon yourself, without informing me, to—"

"There wasn't time!" Jemma interrupted, her voice rising. "I ran for my life! And yours! We all could have been murdered, or worse." As she spoke her voice became louder and more defiant. "And with all that's been happening to Moira I thought of nothing but getting help!"

"Of course," Michael said into the silence that followed Jemma's words. Moira could see Madame was not used to having her employees raise their voices to her. "Now," Michael added, "I'd like to talk to Moira."

Madame shook her head, turning away. "I must say I at least can understand Jemma's outburst. You two are certainly calm when you speak of it all." She stopped by the doorway. "Michael, you are my son, but I do not understand you." She walked out the door. Jemma hesitated and then followed her.

Michael glanced over at Andre as he spoke to Moira. "Shall we walk a bit?"

She let him lead the way to the hall and the north gardens just outside. Once outside the sun felt warmer than it had these past weeks, and she turned to see the garden's winter blooms beginning to give way to the first awakening of bergamot and lavender. "Look at the flowers, Michael." He did as she asked, then looked back at her quizzically. "Don't you see, it looks as if it were spring instead of winter!"

"Not here."

"In Brittany none of this would be blooming for two more months."

"Winter is mild here, in our coomb, don't you remember? Even the lime tree in the Quad grows here. That's why my ancestors built here."

"But buds are forming on the rose bushes and it's not even quite Christmas yet."

"And there's a Cornish island that has palm trees."

She stared at him. "I don't believe it!"

"You should. It's true. Some mad explorer brought them back from the South Seas."

She looked across the bracken and the golden broom that trailed away beyond them as they walked toward the sea edge of the cliff. "I was in bed for so many days it seems as though I'd slept through winter."

"If you go up on the moors, you'll see winter aplenty. And wait a little longer and you'll see the transformation in truth here. If the days continue as mild as they've been." He paused. "It's not wise to speak of any of this other in the house."

"I know. Frances always seems to know what everyone in the house has said and done."

"Aye, they all do." He took her elbow on a rough bit of the steep path that led down to the narrow beach and then they were alone on the shingle, Moira kicking at the small, water-worn stones and pebbles that lay in loose sheets beneath their feet.

"We always seem to end up by the sea."

He did not answer. No other people were in view from the west curve of the beach to the base of the cliff to the east. She looked up along the cliffs that towered above them now.

"None can hear us even if they're up there listening," he said, following the direction of her gaze.

"I wasn't thinking about that. I was thinking of them, of Henri and Genevieve and Jean-Marc. Hidden up there."

Michael paced beside her. "Henri's terribly feverish. That wound has not been attended to at all."

"Have you a doctor for him?"

"Yes. He arrived last night—late."

She said nothing for a moment, thinking back to the boot-steps in the middle of the night. "Then this doctor knows now, about the tunnel and all."

"He's helped before. And with your father," Michael added.

"One of your troops?"

Michael shrugged. "He can be trusted."

"Michael, what about Tristan? Where can he be?"

He turned to watch the whitecaps foaming up toward the bottom of the cliff that plunged sheer-faced into the water back behind them. "I don't know what he's up to. He's so rebellious, so full of hate. I fear he has too much of his mother in him."

A faint shout carried on the wind toward them. Looking up,

John Ottery could be seen at the top of the path that climbed from the narrow beach to the cliffs above. He was waving his hands, cupping them to his mouth.

"What?" Michael shouted back, but the sound was lost in the sea winds. "We'd best go up."

They started upward, the Duke behind Moira.

"So sorry, Your Ladyship, Your Grace," John was still out of breath when they reached his side. "But I was afraid of that path, and you're wanted at the castle. Customs officers." He was still trying to catch his breath from the long walk.

"Customs?" The Duke's face was expressionless.

"Yes. To see Her Ladyship and her maid about their escape. They want word of the pirate's last known whereabouts they say."

"Frances!" Moira's horror-stricken voice carried its meaning to Michael. She began to walk more swiftly forward.

"She fainted dead away." John was pushing hard to keep up with the two of them, his old legs stiff as they covered the uneven ground toward the gardens and the doors beyond.

"Fainted?" Michael asked. "Why?"

"She said she couldn't be asked to remember such things. When they told her it was King's business they were on she cried out for the Duchess and fainted dead away. Couldn't raise her for naught. When I left they'd let her be carried to her room."

Michael's amused eyes met Moira's concerned ones. "It seems she's overwrought."

"As well she should be," John said loyally, reaching the door a fraction ahead of them to open it wide. "After all the poor gel's been through."

"Yes, John, you're quite right," Moira said, walking inside. "It would make anyone's nerves give way."

"I just say you're to be admired, Your Ladyship; all the staff says as how you saved her life. And calm as can be about it all."

Moira cleared her throat. "We do what we can, John. And it would be improper for the Duchess of St. Maur to break down and parade her emotions before the whole county."

"Oh, quite, Your Ladyship! Still, it's admirable, as how you can do it."

She glanced at Michael, who was trying to look innocent as his eyes gleamed with humor at her discomfort over the undue praise. "I have the Duke's help," she said through almost gritted teeth.

224

"Ah yes. Now." The Duke sighed. "But how you managed alone with those terrible brigands, black they were too, you said?"

"Black as coal tar!" John said.

"What an appropriate choice of words," Moira said dryly, glancing at the Duke.

"And nary a word out of 'em! I told the officers as much."

"They must have been wicked." Michael shook his head dolefully from side to side.

"I'm beginning to see their merit," Moira said with considerable asperity in a voice barely above a whisper. "If you don't stop, I shall scream."

"Can't." Michael's voice was low too, John pacing ahead to open the door to the main salon. "Wouldn't befit the Duchess of St. Maur."

"I'll 'Duchess St. Maur' you, you're enjoying this!" She hissed the words so that John wouldn't hear.

He shrugged, grinning for a moment and then controlling his face into proper lines as John opened the salon door, looking back toward them now. They walked inside as the butler announced them and withdrew.

Two uniformed men stood near the two-story front windows, looking ill at ease as they turned toward the man and woman who approached them.

The Duke stopped in front of them, Moira just behind and a little to the side. "I understand you wish to speak to the Duchess, but you must understand that she's been ill and now has had to endure this outrage."

"Yes, Your Grace, Your Ladyship. Lieutenant Harold Dunsforth, at your service." He bowed slightly, as he spoke, his hand on the hilt of his sword. "And Sergeant Dilke." The lieutenant bowed toward Moira then.

The sergeant bowed slightly toward the Duke and then the Duchess.

"Would you care for refreshment?" the Duke asked. "I would. I hope you'll join me." He walked to the bell pull and rang it. "Please. Sit."

Moira was moving to a silk damask couch, sitting on its pale yellow cushions as they moved to chairs nearby, standing stiffly until the Duke walked near.

He threw himself onto the couch beside Moira, stretching his long legs out and then, casually, putting one leg across the other, looking toward the men with a slightly bored expression.

Moira showed more tension, sitting erect and pale, staring straight ahead as the two government men sat down across from the couch.

Michael reached for Moira's hand. "This has, of course, been quite trying for the Duchess. I hope you can keep the interview as brief as possible."

"Certainly, Your Grace," the lieutenant answered, interrupted by John who appeared at the door.

"Brandy," Michael said and John nodded, withdrawing.

After John left the lieutenant turned his attention toward Moira, smiling. "Your Ladyship, we are interested in ascertaining in which direction the pirates sailed—"

"Pirates!" she exclaimed.

"Why—yes." The lieutenant was startled, both he and the sergeant sitting forward now, their eyes intent. "Do you mean you didn't know they were pirates?"

Michael's hand stiffened a little. She could feel him willing himself to relax.

"Gentlemen, I'm at a loss," Moira said. "I thought they were highwaymen."

"Highwaymen!" They both stared at her, Michael eyeing the line her dress made, from throat to waist.

"Since they took us by coach," she continued, "and took us inland I had no idea! In London we hear so many stories of your highwaymen, out here . . . that I naturally thought—"

"You didn't go to sea?" The sergeant finally spoke, something in his voice making Moira look at him more carefully. His voice did not fit his position.

"Nowhere near. How could we possibly escape from a ship?"

"We thought possibly you swam." His tone was respectful and yet not. The Duke looked as if ready to drop off to sleep, his hooded eyes studying the sergeant, unnoticed. Moira realized this sergeant was used to command. And that he did not believe her. And that his expression was the same when he looked at the Duke. He knew. Or he thought he knew. Something.

"Don't be absurd!" she replied. "Do you think my maid could manage anything as difficult as that!?" Moira spoke sharply. "And kindly be more civil or we shall end this interview at once."

They all stared at her now.

"I assure you, Your Ladyship," the sergeant began, Moira cutting him off.

"Now then," she said, turning her attention to the lieutenant. "You are the lieutenant, are you not? You *are* in charge here?" He nodded slightly. "In any event, lieutenant," Moira said, ignoring the sergeant, "my maid and I were blindfolded in my rooms. We were taken at gunpoint, along with my jewels, across I don't know what ground, but we made it to a road, or track, and were put in some kind of enclosed coach. My maid was hysterical and one of the men hit her, to quiet her." Moira found as she embroidered the story that more details were occurring to her. "Which helped somewhat. They did not speak at all, to us, and we'd probably be dead or worse, right this minute if they hadn't had trouble with their horses."

"Horses?" the lieutenant asked politely.

Moira nodded. "Yes. I know not what, being unfamiliar with horses, and, as I say, they wouldn't speak in front of us. And we were bound and blindfolded. But I could hear low voices from near the horses when we stopped. And then the carriage was rocking back and forth something fierce."

"Possibly they got caught," Michael drawled. "In a rut, don't you know?" he explained to the two men.

"Possibly. But I stumbled out and dragged poor Frances down with me. My blindfold moved slightly, and I saw, with one eye, mind you, some large rocks and began crawling toward them, very slowly. Frances kept hold of my skirt, crawling too. The coach was between us and the two men."

"Two," the lieutenant said quickly.

John appeared with the brandy tray and they were silent until he set it beside the Duke and poured for them all, distributing the glasses. When he withdrew Moira spoke again.

"Yes, two. I could see their legs on the other side of the carriage, up near the horses."

"No more than their legs?" the sergeant asked in his almost snide tone.

Moira ignored him. "They wore dark pantaloons, if that's any help."

"They certainly don't sound like sailors of any sort, pirate or not," the lieutenant said. "They'd have worn wide nankeens for one thing. And headed for the sea."

"Definitely pantaloons. Dark," she added. "Surely you've heard all this from my maid?"

"We were unable to question her. She fainted."

Moira sighed. "Poor Frances. She did then too. I don't know how I got her back, I assure you."

227

"You were, ah, at the rocks?" The lieutenant brought her back to her narrative.

"Oh, yes. Well it was dark by then, as I'm sure you realize. And it was very dark last night. I got us to the rocks and my ropes were so loosened I could wiggle my hands out of them. They hadn't bound my feet or we'd still be there I fear. I threw off my blindfold, then got Frances's off, and we got behind the rocks and then began to run, while they worked on the carriage. I forgot to loosen her hands till later, poor dear. But we got away."

"How fortunate," the sergeant said dryly, the lieutenant giving him a dissatisfied look.

"Actually they did not seem to bother to try to find us." Moira spoke still to the lieutenant, ignoring the sergeant and his comments. She stared into the lieutenant's earnest eyes. He was prepared to believe her. "I suppose since they had my jewels and whatever else we weren't important enough to them to bother about."

"We understood there were more than two," the sergeant said.

"Obviously there were only the two with the Duchess," the lieutenant answered for her. She ignored the other man still. "They must have split up," the lieutenant said as he looked back at Moira.

"It sounded like an *army* as they pounded on my door," Moira said truthfully, "but two were all we saw before they blindfolded us. And two were all there were with us on the road. Or at least, when they stopped the carriage, there were only two."

"Of course," the lieutenant said. "You did not know where you were then?"

"Unfortunately, I've just arrived, and my maid is from London also. We wandered, forever it seemed, until a road looked at all familiar, and we followed it and, of course, eventually arrived."

"And you, sir, were not at home?" the lieutenant asked.

"No," the Duke replied. "I returned this morning, having heard on the Padstow Road a garbled report. I thought my lands ransacked, my wife and family dead."

"How convenient that the prisoners—escaped," the sergeant said.

"Convenient!" Moira sat straight up, fury showing in her words and her eyes. "How *dare* you! Sergeant, I would *hope* that the King's own men would have better information. My best friend and her young son were also kidnapped, as well as the Duke's oldest son! *And have yet to be found!* Meanwhile you sit here prattling away and asking stupid questions! Do you mean to tell me that not *only* have you not apprehended these highwaymen, but that you have been chasing some fancied *pirates* while right here and now this all has happened, our people are still God knows where and you are not even *aware* that they are missing, let alone the extent of these crimes!?" She turned toward the lieutenant. "This is unforgivable, unconscionable! Not only am I subjected to this impertinent man's questions, but you are not even *looking for our people?* You waste all your time on some nonsense about pirates, or whatever excited villagers say, and true crime goes unheeded? What have you been doing since last night? A member of this household reported this crime—to *whom* did she speak? She said it was an official!"

The lieutenant glanced at the sergeant. The sergeant nodded slightly. "There are three people still missing?" the lieutenant asked the sergeant, obviously upset. He stared at the other man. "Well?"

"Word has gone out—"

"Enough!" the lieutenant interrupted, turning toward the Duke. "Your Grace, I am ashamed to have caused you any further distress. I had no idea your son, and guests, were still missing. My companion has not informed me of all the particulars."

"When I was in the service," Michael drawled quietly, "a junior officer could have been dismissed for such omissions when reporting to his superiors."

The lieutenant stood up. "Apologies are in order. This man is not my sergeant."

"*Lieutenant* Dunsforth!" the sergeant interrupted. "This is King's business!"

The lieutenant held his ground, his bearing stiff and formal. "Nevertheless, the Duke is entitled to an explanation at this point. Mr. Dilke here is from London, special assignment, in regard to pirate attacks, which he assumed," the lieutenant glared at Dilke, "*prematurely,* this was. He is operating secretly, and we must ask your silence on the matter."

"Of course," Michael said, Moira staring at the man's angry eyes. He was not pleased. "I'm sorry we cannot be of more help on that head, sir," Michael said to Dilke.

229

Dilke stared at the Duke. "You have never been at home when the pirates, or whoever, attacked, have you, Your Grace?"

"They have never attacked my home, sir. At least not yet, it would seem. But if you mean, when there have been sightings and rumors in the vicinity, we seem to hear them all the time."

"A few weeks ago, Michael," Moira interrupted, "we heard of that Squire what's his name's fate. That was the closest they've been, isn't it?"

"Oh, yes. I left upon word of the trouble, to see if I could help."

"And what luck for you," Dilke continued, "the highwaymen came last night when you were absent."

"Surely you know that it's not luck, Sergeant, or whatever your rank is, that I am seldom far behind these sightings."

"Not luck?" Dilke stared at the Duke.

"No. And what is your rank?"

"It's *Mr.* Dilke, sir," Dilke responded stiffly.

There was a momentary pause, Michael staring hard at the man. "From London, are you?" His words were almost a challenge. The lieutenant looked from Michael to Dilke.

"Yes!"

"Special assignment regards the pirate reports?" Michael's brow rose slightly.

Dilke shot a murderous look at the lieutenant. "Yes, since it's already been said, yes!"

"Strange," Michael drawled, staring at him. "Strange that I don't know you then." Michael glanced at the lieutenant. "If you contact the Foreign Office in London, Lord Castlereagh or George Canning, they'll tell you what the government wishes said about why I'm never far behind these 'pirate' sightings."

"Yes sir, of course, sir." The lieutenant was visibly impressed. "And are there pirates hereabouts, sir? We hear so many stories and half of them conflicting."

Michael let a moment pass, still studying Dilke, who began to look a little uncomfortable. "So do we, Lieutenant." Michael tore his eyes from Dilke after a moment, looking more kindly at the lieutenant, speaking man to man. "Whether there are pirates or not, there is *someone* perpetrating the stories, and the government has reason to suspect that French spies are behind it all."

"The Devil you say! Fomenting more of their bloody revolutions!" the lieutenant exclaimed and then, almost blushing, he bowed low to the Duchess. "Begging your pardon, Your Ladyship."

"I'm as shocked as you!" the Duchess replied, turning toward her husband. "Is what you do dangerous, Michael?"

He covered her hand with his. "It's not for you to know about, or worry about, my dear."

"But how brave of you! How very brave!" Moira stared earnestly into his eyes, getting a little of her own back, her mouth twitching slightly.

His eyes held glints of humor, realizing what she was doing. She stared at him still, knowing that in that serious face with its straight planes a stranger would not see the humor that lay hidden in those eyes. She wondered how much of it she herself had missed in the weeks gone past. And Genevieve was his cousin's wife! The thought intruded and she pushed it back, her heart light for the first time in all these weeks. His heart was not with Genevieve!

The lieutenant was apologizing again, ready to leave. Moira stood up as Michael did, Michael giving another, pointed, quizzical, look over at Dilke, which the lieutenant saw.

"I shall report to London myself," the lieutenant said, "and we shall get to the bottom of it. I sincerely hope that we can find your—"

The door to the salon burst open, Tristan, begrimed and obviously fatigued, striding into the room, staring at Moira.

"How'd you get away!?"

Michael stared at Tristan. "And you?"

"What?" He looked at Michael. "They didn't catch me. I rode after the robbers."

Moira stared at Tristan as the lieutenant swung toward the young man. "Rode?" the officer repeated.

"Yes. I got to the stable and waited. Three of them went out and down the drive, to their horses and away. I followed them across the moors—lost them just this side of Clovelly."

"Clovelly!" Dilke said loudly, surprised.

Tristan stared at the man who had spoken and then the officer beside him. "Who are these people?"

"King's men," Michael said. "Trying to locate you and the others."

"But," Tristan turned to stare at Michael, "who would dare attack the castle like that? Who were they?"

"I think I know who sent them," the Duke said.

"What?" Dilke stared at him.

"Sir, if you have any information at all—" the lieutenant began, stopping as Michael raised his hand.

"The topic we were discussing," Michael said, "precludes me from saying more. Suffice it to say, if you check with London as I suggested, gentlemen," Michael stared at Dilke pointedly, "as *I* intend to, concerning Mr. Dilke here, I'm sure all will be explained."

"But—how—" Tristan looked at Moira and trailed off as she came near.

"I'm so glad you're all right!" Moira said. "We thought they had you too!"

"But I was told on the road you'd been kidnapped!"

"As I was, but I got away, up that same road!"

"So there were at least five," the lieutenant said. "Excuse me, sir," he said to Tristan, "but did the men you followed have a woman and boy with them?"

"No. Why?"

"My friends, Genevieve and Jean-Marc," Moira answered.

"Kidnapped too!" He stared at her and she nodded after a moment.

"I'll see you out," Michael said to the men and then looked over toward Moira. "Coming?"

She turned toward him and, seeing his outstretched hand, came toward it, Tristan pacing behind.

They reached the main hall, watching the King's men leave, Moira suddenly weak, her body wilting from the strain. Michael caught her, holding her against his side as she stared at Tristan still.

"Thank God you're safe."

Tristan stared at the two of them. "You were worried?"

"Of course we were worried!" Michael's voice rang out, the two footmen near the great oak doors staring straight ahead, as if the room were empty.

Tristan turned toward the south stairs, starting up them. "I'm filthy, I must change."

Michael turned toward the nearest footman. "Inform Madame that Tristan is home and well."

As the man sped away, Michael helped Moira toward the stairs. "Can you make it?"

"Yes." Her voice was tremulous. As they started upward she

whispered to him, her hand on his shoulder. "I'm sorry, I don't know what's come over me."

"I do," he said. "The strain's beginning to tell. You've been ill, and now all this."

"Michael, I thought it was all over when Tristan appeared. How did he know what to say, how could he—"

"Shhh."

They reached her rooms, Michael helping her inside. Frances lay collapsed across the couch.

"All right, my girl," Michael told her, "they've gone."

One eye opened cautiously, and then Frances sat up, speaking quietly. "Oh, Your Grace, Your Ladyship! I didn't know what to do, what to say!"

"You were splendid," Moira said.

"Truly?" Frances's eyes glowed.

"Truly."

"Yes," Michael added, "and brilliant besides."

"Oh, Your Grace!" She almost simpered with her pleasure. "Milady, what's wrong?"

She sprang to her feet as Moira began to lean more heavily against the Duke.

"Frances, could you bring up an invalid's tray? Porridge, whatever sits lightly when one's ill?" Michael asked pointedly and she nodded, withdrawing.

"I'm not hungry."

"It's not for you," he said. "It's for Henri."

"Oh!" Moira tried to rise as he sat her down on the bed. "Genevieve and Jean-Marc—"

"They're fine. We'll get things for them, too. Just rest a moment." He paused. "When the maid comes back I'll take it to him."

"And the household will think you're dutifully staying by my distraught side."

"Are you?" he asked. "Distraught?" he added.

She shook her head. "I'm all right. But Michael, what Tristan said—"

Michael tried to smile, but now, his eyes full of concern for her, he found it more difficult. "Not luck, my dear. Planning." He watched her. "Didn't you wonder why you were secreted out through there when the others were pounding on the citadel from without?" He waved toward her wall.

"Yes. I thought then that it was—others—who were out

233

there. And your men rescuing us . . . Michael!" she exclaimed, staring at him now. "That's why you didn't want me in these rooms! Isn't it? So I wouldn't hear, wouldn't question—so none would know."

He did smile then. "The men out front were decoys. Genevieve and Jean-Marc were gotten out through the east turret, to the tunnel, as you were. I wanted no harm to come to any of you. The men the servants saw *were* dressed as highwaymen, my little fabricator." He paused, seeing her eyes widen. "And they took off by horse, as Tristan said. Not, unfortunately, across the lawns to a coach." She looked down at the silken covers on her bed. "At any rate, they were to head inland, head east and decoy any followers."

She looked up at him again. "You should have told me! I could have ruined all!"

"I was just about to on the beach. But we were interrupted by John, remember?"

"But I could have said *anything!*"

"True," he replied, after a moment. "But I knew you'd do nothing to endanger my men."

"Or your ship," she added softly. "Or the Black Saint." He smiled then and she spoke slowly. "Do you realize what you are doing?"

"I beg your pardon?"

"You are trusting me," she said softly.

They watched each other, Michael staring at her soft, full lips, Moira watching him lean ever so slightly toward her. She did not move, did not want to break the spell.

He forced his eyes away finally, staring into hers, trying to find answers to all his questions, all his doubts. And fears.

"It could never work," he said finally.

"What could never work?" she asked him softly.

"Our—" He stopped, his eyes clouding over. "Anything."

"What will happen when they query London about you?"

"Hmmmm? Oh, that's true enough."

She stared at him. "You are working for the Foreign Secretary?"

"I've been known to, in my time. You are very inquisitive."

"May I ask one more question?"

"Yes."

"Why did you unlock my door the night I was poisoned?"

"I don't know, I thought—" he started and then stopped,

thinking of her body rising up toward him, of her arms. . . . She watched him now. He shook his head. "This is not proper," he said.

"Will you come to me this night?" she asked softly, reaching out to touch him as Frances came back in with the tray. Michael turned away, Frances eyeing him cautiously as Moira spoke to his back. "Michael, will you?"

He stopped in the doorway, staring at her. "You may leave," he told Frances, his eyes never leaving Moira's.

Frances put the tray down, looking from one of them to the other and then still hesitated. "Milady?"

"You heard His Grace, Frances." Moira did not take her eyes from his.

Frances shut the hall door behind herself as she left, the sound loud in the silence. Michael reached for the tray and started for the hidden panel. He touched the wall and it pulled back, sliding open at his touch. And then he started through it.

"Michael," Moira called out, "you did not answer."

He paused only briefly. "You said only one more question." And he was gone, the wall closing between them.

Chapter Twenty-four

LATER, AS THEY FINISHED DINNER, THE FAMILY SAT AROUND THE huge table in the dining room, Eunice going over events with Moira for the tenth time.

"We can't possibly celebrate the holidays with Moira's friends abducted," Madame was informing Michael. "It would be totally inappropriate."

"The children," Michael replied, "must have their celebration. And the servants. It's too much to ask them to give it up. Moira understands, I'm sure. Moira," Michael called out to her at the opposite end of the table, "I was talking to Mother about the holidays, about not depriving the children of Christmas."

"I can do without it very nicely," Tristan said from Michael's right.

"I quite agree with Michael." Moira glanced over at Madame.

"I'll tell the staff so there shall be no misunderstanding. And you, Eunice, and Pomfret," she included them each in her gaze, "we can't have you going away without Twelfth Night and all!"

Michael almost smiled, returning to his food as his mother watched his reaction. "You care about the girl," she said quietly.

"What?" He looked up into his mother's observant eyes. "Of course."

Madame shook her head a little impatiently. "Those are just words." She held his gaze. "She would be good for you, if you'd let her be."

He drained his burgundy, a footman drawing near to refill it. Michael spoke softly after the man retreated again. "Let her be?"

"Forsake these other—alliances," Madame said, "stay home at night and give the girl a chance at your affections."

"A chance? To what?" His eyes were amused, but beneath the amusement lurked something else she couldn't read.

"To be your wife in truth!" Madame's voice was low, but fierce.

Pomfret glanced toward her and then Michael, his eyes signalling caution before he looked across at Eunice who was engaged in conversation with Moira. Tristan sat morosely eating his food beside Eunice.

"I beg your pardon?" Michael's calm, almost flippant manner irritated his mother, and she spoke plainly.

"You should be begging hers. You've made her a laughing-stock. Gone your first night home! To that—that—'woman' at the inn. Gone every night thereafter! What do you suppose the servants and the villagers are saying? Do you think your bit-o-muslin says nothing!? She lords it over all, telling them of how she's preferred to the Duchess."

"She does not!" he exclaimed, becoming quiet as the others looked toward him.

"Ask any who'll tell you the truth. How do you suppose I know about all of it?" his mother asked in a low voice.

He stared at her, the reality, the truth of what she said, staring him in the face. He looked down the table at Moira as she sat patiently enduring Eunice's never-ending questions. "Eunice!" he called out, waiting until his sister looked up toward him. "Let my wife alone!"

Eunice stared at him. "What?"

He cut through her beginning words. "I've heard nothing but your incessant prattle and gossip and questions. Talk to someone else or shut up. Let Moira alone. You've asked the same questions ten times over! Give over! What do you hope to gain?"

Eunice stared at her brother and then at her husband. "Pomfret!"

Pomfret saluted her with his wineglass, draining it and holding it up to be refilled. "My dear Eunice, he's right you know. You've not stopped for over an hour. After all, this isn't London you know."

"Well, I never!" she exclaimed.

"That's the point. You never quit," Michael said.

"Please—" Moira interrupted them, her voice calm and quiet. "We're all a trifle on edge. Can't we be a bit more understanding of each other?"

"Here, here," Tristan said into the silence that followed Moira's words.

Michael glanced at him. "You could have been killed trying to track those robbers alone. Don't do that again without getting help to go with you."

"Again? Do you expect them back?"

"You never know."

Tristan stared at Michael. "Wouldn't it simplify everything for you if I was? Killed, I mean?"

Eunice stared at the boy. "What on earth do you mean?"

Michael reached across the table for Tristan's arm. "Have I *ever* said that? *Ever*?"

Tristan stared at the Duke, twisting his arm away. "You don't have to."

"You know I've never said it, or wished it, nor aught else to hurt you. Tristan, there's no need for this—battle—between us."

"No?" Tristan replied. "Do you really think not? What about my mother?"

"That's not between you and me."

"No?" Tristan looked defiant and unconvinced.

"Shall we?" Moira said quietly, ending the impasse. She stood up at the opposite end of the table, Eunice and Madame, Pomfret and Michael following suit. Tristan came slowly to his feet as the others left the dining room, walking toward the library.

Jemma joined them as they crossed the great hall. Moira waited for Jemma to come down the last two steps. "Is everything all right?" Moira asked.

Jemma nodded. "Tamaris had one of her nightmares, that's all. With all that's gone on, it's to be expected."

"You should have called me."

"And taken you away from your dinner?" Jemma asked.

"You were taken from yours," Moira pointed out as they walked behind the others, toward the library. Eunice looked back, as if ready to ask Moira about Tristan's outburst, but she saw Jemma and stopped.

"In any event, it wasn't necessary for us both to be there." Jemma flashed a brilliant smile at Eunice, who nodded a little and turned back to her husband. "And she's fine now," Jemma added, "just fine."

They walked into the library, Eunice and Pomfret near the fire, Madame seated in a chair to one side. Michael sat down in his comfortable old chair, Arthur and Lancelot coming to him.

Lancelot went up on his hind paws to gain more affection, leaning his front paws against Michael's thigh. Moira walked with Jemma toward the couch they'd shared before, Jemma reaching down for her sewing.

Michael glanced over and before Moira sat down called out to her. She came toward him, the dogs turning to search her hands for tidbits, their noses nuzzling close. "Sit, please," Michael said, indicating a chair nearby.

She glanced at it over the ottoman in front of his chair and then, deciding, she sank down onto the ottoman. Her arms around her knees, she looked up into his eyes. "Yes?"

"Am I supposed to say something?" he asked her, that curious, humorous glint reappearing in his eyes.

"You called me over. I thought—"

"Yes?" he prompted when she stopped.

"I thought you wished something."

"I do."

She looked up at him intently. "Yes?" she asked again.

"I wish the pleasure of your company."

"Oh." She swallowed. "I see."

"Do you?" He watched her.

"I'm not sure." She looked down, pensive, and then turned toward the fire beside them. "I imagine this has to do with, with what I asked."

He reached over the arm of his chair to give the fire a prod

238

with the poker and then, laying it back, he watched her slip from the ottoman to the floor beside it, in front of the fireplace. He stared down at her, her auburn hair burnished by the fireglow, her expression an enigma as she stared at the leaping flames.

Swinging his long legs around, he moved to sit on the floor beside her, the dogs pushed from their favorite spots now, lying nearby and staring at the humans in front of the fireplace. The others in the room stared at the two of them too. Moira looked up into Michael's eyes.

He watched the logs crackle and splinter as they flamed up. "Do you think we can pull it all off?" he asked softly.

"Which?" she asked back.

With his eyes shielded from the other's view, he raised them toward her room. "Them," he said softly.

"We have to." Impulsively she covered his hand with her own and then, realizing it, she started to withdraw it. But before she could move he was tracing patterns across the back of her hand with his own free one. He turned her hand after a moment, holding it within his as he began to trace light patterns across the palm of her hand, her wrist, her forearm.

"I hope so," he said, but she kept losing his words in the feel of his hand tracing lightly across her skin. Her eyes closed and she leaned back against the ottoman, hearing him speak of the Christmas traditions that would be played out these next days, the festivities, the food.

Behind them, abruptly, Jemma stood up, one of her balls of yarn falling from her grasp.

"Are you quite all right, Jemma?" Madame asked her.

"Quite!" Jemma reached to stuff the yarn into her workbag, Moira and Michael both glancing round in time to see Jemma stride out, closing the door firmly behind herself.

"Now what," Eunice began, "was that all about?"

"None of your business, I'll warrant, my dear," Pomfret replied.

"I suppose it's not my business about Tristan's ugly accusations either!" Eunice said to her mother.

"Tristan is a very trying chi—, young man," Madame amended, glancing over at the younger woman who was now her son's wife. "He is still upset over his mother's death, as is only fitting. And as to Jemma, I have no idea. We were simply discussing the children's education."

"How odd. And just when Michael and Moira were so cozy."

Eunice looked over at her brother. "Michael, you'd not given the girl any false hopes, had you?"

"Eunice! Of course he hadn't!" Madame interrupted as Michael stiffened.

Moira, feeling his reaction, reached to press his hands with both of hers. He stared at her, answering Eunice slowly. "Sweet Eunice, no. I'm not a fool, no matter what you may think of my morals." He turned back to stare at the fire, lost in his own thoughts.

"I should talk to her," Moira said. "I'm sure it's worry over me. I told her we'd talk and we've not gotten the chance."

"She was upset by us. If it was on your account then it's because she suspects me of—suspects me. I can't have servants in my employ who are not loyal."

"She is loyal. I'm sure of it. And she's not a servant, she's an employee."

"At this juncture, I fail to see the difference. However if you wish to go to her, do so."

"It's just that she nursed me through it all. Michael, I would be less than grateful if I didn't at least try."

He nodded, acknowledging her words, and after a moment Moira stood up, looking back down at him and then walking on out, after Jemma.

After another moment, Michael stood too. "If you'll excuse me," he said stiffly to the others, and then left.

Madame watched him follow Moira out.

"Goodness, can't the lovebirds wait till it's a proper time for bed? Any old excuse and they're off," Eunice said.

"Eunice, my pet," Pomfret took her hand, "what about a bit of cards before we turn in?"

Madame stood up as Pomfret finished speaking. "Excuse me, I'll be back presently." She walked to the door and then called out to Michael who was almost to the front door.

He stopped, turning toward his mother, not speaking. His face was set.

Madame stopped just in front of him. "Where are you going?"

"Out." His eyes were cold, his answer direct.

"Why?" she asked him just as directly.

He glanced up the stairwell and then looked back at his mother. "Because fate stepped in and gave me a chance to think."

"Think? About what?"

240

"Think about the fact that she has doubts too. And that she should have—that I can never be what she needs. I'm too old for her, my lifestyle is—inappropriate for what she should have. I—I don't wish to discuss it!" He opened the door and strode outside, a footman racing toward him. "A horse!" Michael said to the surprised footman.

Madame walked forward, to stand in the doorway, staring after her unhappy son. "And if she doubts?" His mother's voice carried to where he stood. He turned around to see her, amazed that she would speak so in front of the servants. "If she does, do you blame her?" his mother asked. "What reason have you given her not to doubt?"

He stared back at his mother. "There is nothing I can do."

"There is. Stop blaming yourself for Lucy and Henry! Stop forcing others away—Moira, your own *children!*" Madame spoke more quietly now. "Start thinking more about Moira and less about yourself!"

"It is Moira I *am* thinking of!"

"Is it?" And with that Madame turned her back on her son. She went back inside, into the hall, crossing it to rejoin Eunice and Pomfret, dreading every step.

Chapter Twenty-five

UPSTAIRS MOIRA KNOCKED ON JEMMA'S DOOR, WAITING TO HEAR Jemma cross to it. When Jemma opened it the two women stood facing each other.

"Yes?" Jemma asked.

"May I come in?"

"Of course." Jemma stepped back.

"Jemma, what is it?" Moira stood just inside the room. "I thought that we were friends."

"So did I," Jemma said bitterly.

Moira hesitated. "And are we not?"

"You'll let him get away with it!" Jemma lost all caution. "I could see it in your eyes tonight. For a few tiny crumbs of his attention you'll let him get away with all of it!"

Moira stared at Jemma. "All of what?"

"What? Lucy and your 'accident' and your poisoning and God knows what all else!"

The bitterness in Jemma's voice was deep, her eyes strained with an aversion that was almost hatred. Moira stared at her, shocked. "Jemma, why do you care so?"

"Because he's ruined Jack's life!" Jemma's voice rose.

"How Jemma?" Moira asked quietly, after a moment to absorb what she had just heard. "How?"

"How? You can ask that?" Jemma laughed, the sound nearly hysterical. "He's obsessed with Lucy, with her death, that's how! He vowed vengeance then and he's never stopped hating, never stopped planning—"

"Planning? Planning what?"

"How to catch the great Duke at one of his games! Oh, don't think Jack doesn't know! The Duke of St. Maur plays a great many games. And sooner or later one of the victims will be he himself!"

Moira tried to take Jemma's hand but Jemma pulled back, away. "Jemma, why do you care so much what he's done to Lucy or Jack, or me?"

"Why? Because I love him!" Jemma was near hysteria. Moira stepped forward, staring at the governess.

"You love him?"

"I've loved him since I first met him! I knew then the Duke had done something wicked to him! I could tell by how he spoke. But he'd say nothing. The gentleman that he is, he wouldn't tell me about it, about any of it, for the longest time."

"Jack," Moira said faintly. "It's Jack you love?"

"I told you I did! Now, dismiss me! Go on, go on!"

Moira turned slowly away, walking toward the door. Before she closed it behind herself she looked back. "I'll not dismiss you, Jemma. But if you feel you can't work for us. . . ."

"Us!" Jemma spat out the word. "Can't you see you're in danger? Or do you want the man to get away with your death, too?"

"Michael's killed no one, Jemma."

"And who did then?"

"I don't know. But it wasn't Michael."

Jemma stared at her. "He's convinced you he's innocent, hasn't he? Somehow he's convinced you. Then who *is* causing all this? Or do you think they really *are* accidents?"

Moira bit her lip. "They are not accidents. My gig was tampered with, my food was poisoned. Lucy was locked within—within. And I do not know by whom. Or why. But, someone has done all of it."

"*Someone!*" Jemma said derisively.

"Yes." Moira stared at the governess and then quietly walked on outside, closing the door to Jemma's room. Moira hesitated and then walked on toward the main staircase and down, toward the library.

But when she opened the door to the library only Madame looked up at her. He was not there.

"Moira, I need to talk to you before you go up." Madame stood, walking toward her daughter-in-law.

"And—Michael?" Moira asked hesitantly.

"He—he went out." Madame tried to soften the blow.

Moira looked down. "I see." Her heart turned to lead within her.

"Walk me to my rooms, will you?" Madame asked.

"Of course." Moira swallowed the hurt that welled up at the words. Simple words. He had gone out. In the end someone else, maybe anyone else, was to be chosen over the girl he had been forced to marry. "You wanted to talk to me?"

"Don't take it to heart, my child. Men are seldom logical in their affections. He will come home."

"I cannot insist he love me simply because I love him."

"But you can! And I believe he does. Moira, I think that is the problem. He is afraid to care. He is trying to insulate himself against his own emotions."

"And me."

"And you. Oh, Andre was asking for you. I'm not sure why."

Moira stopped in her tracks. "Oh, I'd best look for him before—I mean—"

"Go on, go on, child." Madame patted her hand. "I can find my own way."

But Moira accompanied the older woman, walking slowly up the steps beside her as the dowager's hand grasped the railing firmly, pulling herself up step by step.

Once Madame was safely in her own rooms, Moira turned toward the north wing, reaching her own rooms and closing the sitting room door behind. She glanced around, calling out for Frances, and then, receiving no answer, locked the hall door, looking quickly into the boudoir, the bath, and then her bedroom, finding no one.

She looked for the key to the wall panel, picking up a lamp as she pressed the panel. Nothing happened. She walked to the fireplace, staring at it and then at the window between the fireplace and the inside wall. She pressed around the window frame and then felt movement, gasping as the panel began to slide open.

She pushed at it, slipping inside and then thinking of the unlocked bedroom door. She ran back to lock it, its lock still useless, hacked away and not yet fixed.

She glanced back toward the sitting room and then went through the panelling, closing it behind her so none could follow. At least she knew where to find the lever on this side of the wall.

She raised the wick of her lamp, throwing brighter light ahead of her, down the narrow corridor, until she saw a tiny door. Opening it slowly, the inside loomed dark ahead of her. "Genevieve?" she called out softly, only to hear, "Shhh," and breath expelled in relief as she stepped inside.

Another lamp was lit, the two together showing the outlines of the man on the bed, emaciated and gray. Genevieve stood near the bed, Jean-Marc asleep on a pallet on the floor. Andre stepped out from the shadows behind the door, looking apologetic.

"I didn't know it was you," he said quietly, lowering the club she saw he'd held, ready to use against an intruder.

"How is he?" Moira whispered.

"The doctor gave him something to help him sleep. He's resting. More than that," Genevieve shrugged helplessly, "I don't know."

Moira turned toward Andre. "You sent for me?"

"I—thought—the Duke was with you."

"No." She hesitated only for a moment. "I was with Jemma."

"Jemma."

"She's overwrought."

Andre hesitated. "If you have a moment, Your Ladyship."

She nodded. "Do you know how to reach me, if you need help?" she asked Genevieve.

"Yes. Andre showed me."

"Good. I'll be there through the night. And I'll check with you first thing in the morning. Is there anything else you need now?"

Genevieve smiled ruefully. "Besides a miracle—nothing."

Moira smiled. "Mayhap that will come too." She walked out,

Andre closing the door and following Moira back to the end of the dark corridor.

"You closed it?" he asked.

"Just in case," she replied.

"Then, just in case," he whispered, stopping her before she pressed the panel. He leaned against the wall, listening. She doused the lamp to a flickering glow, pressing finally when he motioned toward her and followed him, slowly, out into her bedroom.

She raised her lamp a little, the glow from it brighter again, casting light across the shadowy room. "I locked the sitting room doors," she said. "None should be in here."

Andre checked the locked doors, walking back toward her after a moment, to where she now stood, near the windows. His voice was low. "I'll be brief. Friends have sent word that there will be a search of the castle."

"Search?" she interrupted.

"Customs. Someone is pushing to find the Duke guilty of something, anything. We think it to be French spies."

"Counterspies?" she asked softly.

"Madame, your husband has been responsible for hundreds of people's lives, personally. Their whereabouts, their very lives, rest upon his shoulders. He alone knows a thousand details, a thousand secrets of the whereabouts, the names, the plans of these people who were rescued from the guillotine because he alone, among many, cared. And *dared.* He has served his own government well in matters that can never be acknowledged. More than that I cannot, I will not, tell you. But mark my words, there are those who want him discredited. Or dead. I must speak to him immediately. He does not know of the plans to search here. And we must get Henri out of here before someone finds him. The ship *must* be gone from the cove or all will be lost!"

"Then you must go to the village," Moira said tiredly.

"I've been to the village. To the inn," he added. "He's not there, has not been seen."

"But—" She stopped. "Are you quite certain?"

He nodded. She could see the worry in his eyes.

"You care about him, don't you?"

"I am on official orders," he said stiffly. "His safety is paramount to my superior's plans."

"But you do care about him," she said again.

245

He started to speak and then, slowly, his eyes watching hers, he nodded. "Yes," he added finally. "I do."

She smiled a little. A very little. "As I do. If he's not in the village, would he have gone anywhere else without telling you? Any meetings, or—anything?"

Andre shook his head. "Never."

Moira began to fear in that moment. "Then," her voice cracked, "then, he may be in danger. Caught—or hiding."

"Caught by whom, for what?" Andre asked.

She shook her head. "I don't know."

"Hiding—he might have seen something, gone to investigate."

"When are they to search the castle?" Moira asked.

"I don't know." Andre was worried and it showed. "It could be as early as morning. They'd never dare come during the night without proof."

"And," she searched his eyes, "is there any proof to be had?"

"No," he answered. "Except, possibly—"

She waited.

"Possibly, if they captured one of the men," he continued.

"Surely they'd not talk!"

"Not in the ordinary way of things, no, Milady."

Moira tried to think clearly. "So we are faced with a dilemma." She thought for a moment. "Can the ship be sailed without Michael?"

"Your Ladyship?" He turned to stare at her.

"The ship was sailed here, while we came by coach. I assume it's been to Ireland before?"

He nodded, dubious.

"Well, does Mr. Talbot know the Channel water, know the course, the Irish coast?"

"I—yes, I'm sure he does. He's sailed it enough."

"Enough," she interrupted, "to do it without Michael at the helm?"

"I don't know."

"Find out."

"I beg your pardon?"

"Find out. If he can then we must take no chances. Henri, his family, and the doctor must sail at once. Without the doctor, Henri has no chance of surviving the voyage. But here he'll have no chance at all if he's found. They must sail at high tide. Before the castle can be searched."

"But the Duke—"

"The Duke is either choosing to be silent or forced to be. In either case we cannot jeopardize Henri. It would be the worst thing we could do for Michael. If he chooses to be silent, then he has a reason, and if we're wrong he'll stop us. If he's forced to be silent then we shall have to find him. Find out who—and why—he's being kept away."

"It's not the government," Andre said with authority. "If it were, I'd know."

"You'd better talk to Talbot and get the doctor and the rest ready. They can't be found here no matter what else! I'll find out if anyone else is missing and meet you here. In—an hour?"

He nodded, going back to her bedroom and through the hidden hallway as Moira unlocked her sitting room door. She slipped out into the main hall, her heart pounding. The thought of Michael's being in danger, of something happening to him, froze all other thoughts within her.

She went down the main stairs. Andre descended through the tunnel to the cove, now half-filled with water, and the dinghy moored there, rowing out to the ship.

Chapter Twenty-six

AN HOUR LATER, MOIRA FACED ANDRE, STARING AT HIM AS HE SPOKE. "The ship can deliver the—cargo—without the Duke," he said. "The doctor says, if there is no choice, that possibly the patient can withstand the voyage. He will go with the patient, to give all the help he can. None have seen the Duke," he added finally, his face etched with worried lines.

"Nor can I find him here," Moira said. "First we must see to the safety of our guests. How sure are you that the castle is under suspicion, that it will be searched?"

"As sure as I'm standing here. Oh, they'll use the excuse of the robbery, to find any information to help return the people reported kidnapped. But in reality they'll search for old priest's hidden chambers, anywhere ammunition and booty could be hidden. Anything that can help them find enough to hang him."

247

"But why? And who? You both say he's working for the government. Surely they'll stand up for him."

"No."

"But why?"

Andre paused. "There are political factions, Milady, you'd not understand."

"Try me," she said. "My father taught me about the ways in which this world is governed."

He began slowly, sure that she'd not be able to make head nor tail of it all. "There is government support here for the relief of the French aristocracy—strong support. But, of necessity, silent support. Some merely wish to be humane to people unjustly persecuted; some wish to insure that constitutional monarchy will prevail, there as well as here. I am to assist the Duke in his attempts to bring French leaders who are in danger to safety. But the support is at once financial and sub rosa. Because there are factions who do not wish there to be any risk of our government becoming more embroiled in the French situation." He stopped for breath.

"Go on," Moira told him.

"Those who wish to maintain the status quo are against any help to any Frenchmen. And then there are others, deadlier, who wish to abolish *all* aristocrats, French and *English*. These last are playing a deadly game of hide and seek. They want the Duke dead, as well as their own monarchy—and ours—ended. They're fanatics and they have the law on their side. *All* the laws, French and English. It *is* the official policy of England not to interfere in France's affairs. It *is* against official laws to transport enemies of the French state. And, at the very least, they wish to prove some manner of piracy against the Duke, even if they have to invent it. Which they are perfectly capable of doing. Any part of any of this is deadly for the Duke. And his government could not come to his aid, could not admit to be secretly supporting what they are publicly denouncing."

"Oh, Andre." Moira stared at him. "They'd let him die!"

Andre nodded.

"Were you there—when my father—"

"Yes. He died fighting to insure Henri got away."

"Then Michael's willing to die for Henri's life, too. What can we do?"

"There must be no evidence, no reason, to hold him, much less try him. For if they get their hands on him, they'll not wait for official sentence."

248

Moira stared at Andre. "We must get Henri and Genevieve and Jean-Marc away. To the ship. And the ship away, out of danger. Can you handle that?"

"Yes, but what of him? He may need me here."

"His first wish is for them to survive. Andre, only you can give him that."

He stared at her.

"I shall find him," she continued. "No matter what it takes. In the morning, if naught's been heard, I *shall* find him. And there will be no evidence here against him."

Andre, unwillingly, nodded. "You are more sensible than I, Milady."

"No. But we each need the other to get through this. Can you get them out tonight?"

"Yes," he replied.

Her thoughts went back to the inn, where Michael spent his nights. "I shall wait until morning and then begin a search. And, if necessary, call in the authorities. You must be gone by then."

"And all sign of us."

"Yes. I wish you godspeed back. We'll need you. *He'll* need you. Now get some rest and get them out of here."

Andre almost smiled. "I'll get them out and *then* I'll rest."

Moira reached out, impulsively hugging him. "Godspeed."

He was almost shy with her now. He turned to leave, and Moira watched him until he was gone, until the door was closed.

And then, wondering what had happened to Frances, she began to undress, pulling the bell pull before walking on into the boudoir and closets beyond, slowly changing for the night.

She was unpinning her hair when a hesitant knock at the door brought Meg into the room after Moira called out to her.

"Oh." Moira looked up. "Where's Frances?"

"I don't know, Your Ladyship. After dinner she went for a turn around the grounds and I've not seen her since."

Alarmed, Moira stared at the plain-faced maid. "Have you told anyone?"

"Well, no, that is—" Meg trailed off, obviously uncomfortable with some knowledge she didn't wish to impart.

"Meg, this could be serious. Very serious."

"Well, it's just that, as she was with Jeb, and as Jeb's not been around either, it, well, I figured as how—"

"I see." Moira hesitated. "Thank you, Meg, you may go."

Dropping a swift curtsy Meg left hurriedly, glad to be out of it, picturing in her mind's eye the trouble poor Frances would soon be in.

Moira finished unpinning her hair, her thoughts lost in a maze of worry and fear. Michael was probably at the inn, with the woman, no matter what Andre thought. Frances and Jeb were probably dallying on the grounds somewhere. But what if they weren't. . . .

What if they weren't. Who would dare interfere with Michael? She stopped the thought, remembering Dilke's attitude earlier. And if Frances had been waylaid by the unprincipled, hard-hearted Dilke, what would he not threaten, what would he not do, to be able to accuse Michael?

Walking to her bedroom, Moira tried to sort out all the strings that pulled together to make the warp and woof of her worry, her fear. But it all tangled into the confusion a cat would make with a ball of yarn.

A sound turned her in her tracks. A slow thump against her sitting room door brought her back to stare at it. Slowly, she opened the door. Lancelot stared at her, his eyes dark and shiny, his tail wagging confidently back and forth.

"Lancelot! You gave me a fright!" She stared at him. "Oh, all right, come in, come on, I could use some company too." She stared down at him. "I thought your master would be here tonight. Did you think so too?"

She closed the door, Lancelot pattering behind, into her bedroom. "Where's Arthur?" Lancelot stared up at her, his gaze solemn, his tail wagging slowly still, forth and back. "You like me at least, don't you?" She reached to pet him as she sat down on the bed.

Sounds from beyond the wall brought a low growl from Lancelot as she was dimming the lamp. And then, at her soft command, he stopped his growling, jumping up on the bed instead and nuzzling close. "Oh, Lancelot!" She reached to pet him. "He's all right. He's just got to be. And we must stay here to make sure none get by us this night. Get to—to anywhere they shouldn't."

She closed her eyes, willing herself to sleep, the dog making himself comfortable beside her. But sleep would not come, and it was hours before she finally fell into a troubled slumber, dawn slowly beginning to lighten the eastern sky out beyond the windows.

* * *

Morning arrived full-blown later and with it John Ottery knocking ceremoniously at her sitting-room door. Moira awakened slowly, answering the knock, her eyes still filled with sleep.

"Yes?" She looked out at the correct visage of John Ottery.

"Your Ladyship." He proffered a sealed envelope. "This has just been delivered. It is marked urgent and so I thought—"

She took it quickly, looking up at him. "Yes, thank you, by all means." She tore it open quickly, quickly reading it as John walked away.

But it was not from Michael. It read: Your Ladyship, if you'll meet me at the village churchyard at noon, I will have the news you are waiting for. Jack.

Moira stared at the piece of paper, rereading and rereading the few words until she had them memorized. She crumpled the note, letting it drop to the floor as she went toward the boudoir to dress for the day.

Lancelot padded after her, lying down to watch her, his head on his paws.

Frances still had not come up. When Moira went down to breakfast, trailing Lancelot behind, the footmen were fidgeting at their posts, ready for the festivities that were beginning this Christmas Eve.

Moira ate her breakfast alone, finishing her toast and tea, unable to eat any of the dish after dish that was laid out on the sideboard in the dining room after the footman informed her the Duke had not returned.

She finished her tea, telling John she would ride into the village early. When she mounted the chestnut, the children, Madame, Eunice, and Pomfret were still abed.

The stableman who helped her was not Jeb. "Have you seen Jeb this morning?" she asked the young red-haired man. His face was closed away. "No, Your Ladyship." He looked away and then turned away, Moira watching him walk back toward the stable.

The chestnut mare reminded her of her own chestnut, in Brittany. She realized she had not ridden since the day of the accident, had spent weeks so enclosed with rumors and fears and questions that she had seen nothing yet of this land.

It seemed years past instead of a few weeks ago when she had left the cottage on the cliff behind, when this had all begun.

She mounted the horse, standing on the mounting block and settling herself into the saddle before riding away, down the long, long drive, turning toward the Maur River at its end and heading toward the village of St. Maur across the river and on down toward the sea.

As she neared the village she slowed the horse, watching the villagers as they set up the morning's wares in the booths of the Christmas Fair. She rode slowly past the first of the thatched-roof cottages, toward the church and the churchyard beyond, seeing the surreptitious glances, hearing snatches of the whispered comments.

Moira felt on display, realizing that these people had been waiting weeks now to meet her, to see her, to be able to say, I've seen her, she's good, she's not, she's pretty, she's not—whatever they decided upon a glance, a look in passing, the words of a servant: she's kind, she's haughty.

Moira realized that these people were curious, were bound to be, about a new Duchess, a new wife for the man, for the family, that had carved this land out of wilderness long ago, putting down roots, creating jobs and food and safety for the people who came to work for them, to work their lands, to set up the village and settle down.

The inn was straight ahead of her now, just before the turn that sent the road out along the edge of the bay, the cliffs rising higher and higher beyond, a wind shelter that eased the weather for the village, for the lands that nestled in the lee of the cliffs along the western edge of the bay.

Moira rode down the narrow cobbled street of St. Maur village, seeing the sign that proclaimed the Saint's Inn in front of a low white-washed building. Near it, across the road, thrust out into the water, was a long, narrow dock that moored fishing boats were tied to, the herring gone from the waters, the men scrabbling out incomes from their narrow plots of land.

She brought the horse to a stop, climbing down and tethering the mare to a narrow iron ring that was set into the wall along the inn's front side.

Moira walked into the low-ceilinged front room hearing the silence that fell as she walked forward. Her boots sounded loud against the stone flooring in the silence.

"Excuse me." She looked the innkeeper straight in the eye as he stood behind the tavern's bar. "I'm looking for a friend of my husband's."

The bald innkeeper stared at her, his mouth almost dropping open. "Ah, Your Ladyship, I—" Words failed him. He glanced at the other people, the men who stood at the bar. None would look up from their pints of bitters to meet his gaze or hers. Finally he nodded toward a small side room.

Through its timbered doorway, across the front room from the tavern bar, a few long trestle tables filled the next room.

And at one of them, near the far wall, sat two men and a woman. Moira glanced toward them, then away. Jack sat there. And he sat with the man called Dilke. Moira glanced back. The woman was dark-haired, her features aquiline, not at all the rosy-cheeked barmaid Moira had expected.

"I've forgotten her name." Moira looked the innkeeper in the eye, her heart thudding against her ribcage.

He hesitated, worrying if the Duke would approve of his telling the Duchess anything at all about his light-of-love.

"Her name, please!" Moira's tone was imperious.

"Norma."

"Norma, yes, I remember," Moira fibbed. She looked out toward the front door and then back toward the small group in the pub. "I don't wish to disturb her. When Norma is through with those men, please ask her to meet me in the churchyard next door. But not in front of those men—understood?"

"Yes, Your Ladyship."

She nodded and then as she turned toward the doorway she turned back once more. "Don't forget."

"I won't, Your Ladyship." He stared at her. "The churchyard and not with the others about."

Moira nodded and left, the man staring after her, shaking his head. One of the men glanced after Moira. "If I had one at home like her, I'd not go traipsing off leaving her to spend her nights alone."

The middle-aged innkeeper scratched his bald pate. "And Her Ladyship coming here to talk to his doxie! The ways of the nobility are strange indeed, Alf."

Outside Moira started across the cobblestones, leading her horse toward the church. The hamlet of St. Maur was enclosed on all sides save toward Saint's Bay by great wooded hills. White-washed cottages with tall chimneys stretched down the narrow street, laburnum and white clematis crowded close around, while Saint's Inn was half lost in towering fuchsias and creepers.

She tied the chestnut to a railing at the edge of the innyard, walking through the nearby lych gate into the small cemetery. A flight of stone steps led around the side of the little church. She glanced at the weathered tombstones, with their plain stone faces and plainer names carved thereon. On one she saw a legend that stopped her. She read its face with a faint smile. "James and Prudence Rowe: He first departed, she for one day tried to live without him, liked it not, and dy'd."

The sun splashed down on young grass that crowded up in small green tufts around the base of the stone markers. The mild winter of Cornwall's villages and sheltered coves passed easily toward spring. Christmas in Cornwall.

The side door leading into the centuries-old stone church was made of oak and well weathered. Moira pushed it open, the ancient, mossy smell of the cemetery yard filling the inside of the building, too. Lichen covered the wall outside, ivy tendrils creeping across the windows, dimming the morning sunlight to narrow strips of gold that fell across the quiet pews.

A great wooden screen divided the nave and the chancel, its cornices elaborate and beautiful, the altar beyond it made of deeply carved wood, too.

Moira turned toward a magnificent alabaster tomb in the south aisle. Louis III, 1789. She realized she was looking at a marble effigy of Michael's father. It topped the rich, canopied tomb, lying on one side of a great marble bed.

Staring at it she realized the other side, the empty side, was waiting for Madame's effigy. She shivered then, wondering what Madame felt when she stared at this tomb. Did she never come, always using the castle's chapel, or did she come here occasionally and ignore it, looking elsewhere.

The air seemed damp and cold inside the old church now.

"Gruesome, is it not?"

Moira turned toward the rich, female voice. The woman in the main aisle, looking quietly at Moira, smiled.

"Norma?"

"Yes." She smiled slightly. "But I think you must know that. And, before we speak, may I ask if your husband knows you are here?"

Moira's hesitation was brief. "He does not. He cannot for he has not been home since yesterday evening."

"Not—" Norma digested Moira's words. "And," she watched Moira's face closely, "you asked that my—companions—not know you wished to talk?"

Without a word Moira pulled Jack's note from her reticule, handing it over to Norma to read. Once Norma had she looked

254

up at Moira. "We must not stay here. He could come at any moment. Come with me."

"He said not until noon—"

"But he might wish to satisfy himself that none else are about."

Moira followed the woman past the tomb of Henry III and his wife, Maud, across from Louis's tomb, and out the far side-door, stepping out into a gravelled path lined with tall dark cypress trees intermixed with ancient oaks.

"Cypress!" Moira exclaimed, surprised.

Norma glanced back at her, motioning for Moira to follow her up toward the cobbled street, toward the crowds milling already around the booths of the fair.

"Louis, your husband's father, imported them from Italy on a whim. They pleased him."

"I saw his effigy," Moira said unnecessarily.

Norma glanced at the new Duchess. "Not very impressive once you've seen Michael, is he? Excuse me, Monsieur le Duc—"

Moira watched the other woman. "You are French then."

"Ah, yes. Didn't you know? Come along?"

"Where are we going?"

"To disappear among the crowd. We can talk in the open more safely than in seclusion. That is, if you don't mind being seen with me."

Norma watched Moira glance toward the bay lapping up at the end of the street, cob-walled, thatched-roof cottages and clusters of people becoming thicker, open casement windows looking out on either side of the narrow street. "Of course not," Moira replied.

Ahead of them peddler's stalls were arranged in front of the houses, people from the surrounding countryside milling about; the stalls were filled with long silken laces and rows of pins, with amber bracelets shining in the sunlight as a girl held them up toward the sky. Silver spoons, golden rings, pasties wafting the smell of their hot, baked crusts and mutton and chicken fillings out toward the crowds.

Jesters in fancy costumes walked about in the crowd, and off to one side a puppet show was set up, children already entranced before it, their thumbs in their mouths, their hands held by transfixed mothers who watched the show with as much delight as their offspring.

255

A group of young men threw for prizes near a mountebank who called to all to come near and see for themselves the pills and ague spells, the love potions and youth remedies.

Tumblers performed near a rope-swing where an adventurous lass allowed herself to be hurtled ever higher, her squeals more of pleasure than of fear.

Moira walked on through the crowd of women in their mobcaps, men in their dark, shapeless jackets, Norma pacing beside her.

"Your Ladyship—"

"Please, call me Moira."

Norma stopped walking for a moment, then spoke as she glanced around them. "You truly mean that. Why do you trust me at all?"

Moira chose her words carefully. "My husband trusts you."

"How do you know that?"

"He has spent much time with you."

"Yes."

"For years."

"Yes again."

"He would not do that with someone he did not trust."

Norma turned her attention back to the younger, prettier woman. "You truly care for him."

"Is that so strange?" Moira waiting for her to answer. "Don't you?"

"He's my best customer."

"Surely more than that. You must care about him," Moira persisted. "You know him well."

Norma hesitated. "He is in danger."

"More every minute," Moira replied. "But—who? And why?"

Norma moved closer to a group of morris dancers in Robin Hood costumes who were dancing wildly to the accompaniment of pipes.

"The man who sat with me, the small one—"

"Dilke," Moira interjected.

"You know him?" Norma stared at her.

"He came to question us before Michael left yesterday."

Norma spoke quietly. "Your husband often leaves without warning."

"Not without Andre."

"Without—" Norma's voice rose and she fought to control it before she continued. A man and his three children jostled past

256

them, glancing at them and then staring as he looked at Moira's face and costume.

Norma took Moira's arm. "I was wrong. You stand out too much here, too many will recognize you. Others will at least know you're a nob and out here alone—"

"A nob?"

Norma smiled faintly. "Nobility."

"Oh." She stopped. "Oh, my."

Norma moved toward a small cottage, and Moira followed her into a kitchen which took up half the building. An old woman glanced up from a seat at a rough-hewn table where she sat rolling out dough.

"And?" The old woman's question was in French, her curious eyes following Moira as Norma spoke.

"It's a moment of quiet out back we need, if you're willing."

The old woman shrugged, then went back to her pies, the peat smoke creeping up from the fireplace to hover in the corners of the ceiling, stinging Moira's eyes.

"This way." Norma walked toward the back of the cottage, Moira following slowly.

Moira looked back as they walked out into the narrow plot of ground behind the cottage. The old woman did not look up from her work.

"Who is she?" Moira asked.

"She was my servant—in a life long past," Norma answered, Moira's eyes widening. "Moira, do you speak French?"

"Yes."

"Good, then let's. I am not what I seem. But I am the 'contact.' Do you understand? There's nothing between your husband and I."

"But—all those nights—for years." Moira stared at her.

"A good cover, n'cest pas? He has slept in my rooms on nights he's drunk too much. He tried to forget you know. His brother, his wife, now your father—all of it. And in those rooms he can be nameless. He is only another man there, not a Duke, not a spy, not a hero, not a father with obligations he doesn't know how to discharge. Nothing but a nameless man who feels all of the guilt and none of the pride of what he's done."

"You love him too," Moira said quietly.

"I worship him. But not the way you mean. Oh, believe me, I tried to make him care. Years ago. I'm not saying that we never—that we haven't—"

"I understand," Moira interrupted quickly.

257

Norma watched her. "My father, my brother, my maid," she pointed toward the old woman in the kitchen beyond, "and I myself are all alive because of him. Only because of him. I fell a little in love with him. Who wouldn't? But he never loved me. And his time here is spent drinking and forgetting. And making the alibi so that when strangers pass through he is here to see them. So that none thinks it strange if he engages in drunken frolics with them. So that none are the wiser about what he is truly doing, or which nights he slips away unseen, and returns by dawn."

"But he's gone! He's disappeared!" Moira broke in, her worry overflowing. "And Andre does not know to where, nor do any. It was assumed he was coming here—"

"No, he did not." Norma's voice hardened. "And Jack sent you that note."

"Yes," Moira replied.

"Jack came in to see me with a government agent."

"Dilke," Moira supplied. "I saw him."

"Yes, you said you knew him. They are trying to find evidence against Michael—the Duke. They wanted to know what I knew of his companions."

"And?"

Norma smiled but her eyes remained cold with the memory. "I told them a long story full of how he'd promised me many things and never done them, one of them to set me up in my own establishment. They became weary of my complaints against him, and forgive me, against you."

Moira spoke after a moment. "Then we shouldn't be seen together."

"You're right. This was a mistake." Norma stared off across the fish shed just past where they stood, staring past the nets that were spread out nearby, an old lobster pot lying broken, tumbled to its side. The bay lapped up beyond, across the shingle of the beach.

"There's something else," Moira said. "My maid, Frances, is missing, and I think the stableman Jeb as well."

Norma spoke quickly. "Jeb? I saw him with that Dilke earlier."

"Oh no." Moira's composure left her. She sat down on an upturned barrel, her shirts falling wide around her. "Oh, Norma, if Dilke's gotten hold of Frances, if he's threatening her, she's not strong—and she knows things she shouldn't."

"And Jack is either a part of it, or honestly trying to warn you."

"Honestly? Sitting with Dilke?"

"He could be staying here, to find out what Dilke knows. Or he could be a spy."

"A spy?" Moira shook her head. "No, I don't believe that. I believe he could harm Michael; he hates Michael. But not a spy. I just don't believe he could be that. I've talked to him, and he seemed truly worried about my safety and—"

Norma watched Moira closely as she digested the information. "You may trust too easily."

"Or too quickly?" Moira asked gently and then went on. "I do not trust him, at any rate. But I have no where else to turn at the moment and he did send that note."

Norma nodded, a small smile coming to her lips. "Too quickly, as in trusting me? That too, possibly, but you can. Trust me, I mean."

"And you think not of Jack?"

"I'm not sure of him. I just don't know."

"Then I must find out. It's nearly noon. I'm going to keep that meeting with him."

"And I?" Norma asked. "What can I do?"

"I so hoped that Michael was safe, or that you knew what had happened, where he'd gone. Now, you're the only one who will know where *I* am if—if anything should happen to me."

Norma reached out to touch Moira's arm. "I can do more. I can go where you can't. I can make sure of your maid."

"Frances."

"Frances. And if you're not home within, what? An hour? Two? I can bring help to the church."

Moira nodded. "I'd best hurry. I don't want him to think I'm not coming." She turned away and then just stood still for a moment before she turned back to face Norma. "Thank you. For Michael as well as for myself."

"Be careful. He wouldn't want harm to come to you."

Moira stared at the woman. "Why do you say that?"

Norma smiled then. "When he drinks too much, he rambles. Didn't you know?"

"That he rambles?" Moira asked quietly.

"That he cares," Norma replied gently.

Moira looked down, shaking her head. "No. I—he doesn't let me near."

259

"He's frightened of you."

"Of me!" Moira stared at the other woman, watching Norma closely as she walked nearer across the cottages's small sea-yard.

"Didn't you know that either?" Norma asked. "He's frightened of caring again, for anyone. His brother and his wife both died. And he's been blamed for the deaths of both. Maybe by now he even thinks it's true, that somehow he did harm them."

"How?"

"By caring for them."

"He can't really think that," Moira said. "And he can't have done any of those things they accuse him of."

"I know," Norma said quietly.

Moira left then, walking back inside and through the small cottage, past the old woman who still rolled out pastry shells. The woman now resembled Solange in Moira's eyes, and she smiled at her with a warmth that was lost before. "Thank you," Moira said.

The woman did not reply. Moira walked out into the festive street, past the crowds, the booths, walking up the gently inclining cobbled street, into the churchyard, through the lych gate, as the chapel bell tolled twelve.

Chapter Twenty-seven

MOIRA GLANCED AROUND THE DESERTED CHURCHYARD AND THEN started toward the church itself. Walking inside she looked down the empty aisle, starting for the nave, when a voice called her name low. She turned toward the sound and saw Jack coming out from behind Henry's tomb.

"You startled me," she said.

"Sorry. I didn't want to chance anyone else finding us here."

"Why?"

He watched her. "You must realize by now the depth of the intrigue surrounding your husband."

"What is happening?" She watched him carefully.

His eyes, blue and calm, turned warm when he looked at her. "Moira, you are in danger. Do you know that now?"

"Yes."

He stepped forward, reaching to take her hands and then letting his own fall back to his sides before he touched her. "I met a man who is going to search the castle."

It took Moira a moment to speak. "Why?"

"He has proof your husband is a criminal."

"Proof?" she asked faintly.

Jack nodded. "So he says."

"You said you had the news I was waiting for."

"I know where the Duke is being held."

"Held! Why? Where!?"

Jack stared into her concerned eyes. "You look very concerned about a man who wishes you evil."

"Jack, please believe me, he's done nothing wrong."

"You seem so sure of that."

"I am positive of that."

Jack turned away. "Come with me then."

"Where?"

"I must stop at my house and then we'll go to him."

"Why should we stop? Every moment we wait could be—"

"Moira," he interrupted, calling her by name again, "I need to have a weapon with me." He opened the church door for her, and slowly she followed him through the lych gate and past the inn, to where his gig stood waiting.

Moira glanced toward the chestnut and then let him remain tethered, climbing up into the gig with Jack's help.

"Why are you willing to help at all?" she asked when they were seated.

"I'm not helping him. I'm doing this for you. Only for you." It was a short drive to his cottage on the edge of the village, and they spoke no more until Jack stepped out and looked back up at her, holding out his arm. "Will you come in? I can offer you some sherry again, to fortify your courage for the events ahead."

"I don't need it. Please, we must hurry!"

"Yes. Of course. I'll be back presently." Moira sat on the bench of the small gig, her entire body tensed against the visions that kept crowding into her mind of what might be happening to Michael. She knew not to trust Jack. But she had no other avenue down which to search. On her guard, she waited.

Jack was back presently, a pistol visible in his waistband. "We can't just walk in. That could be dangerous."

"Yes." Her posture still tense, her hands turning her reticule back and forth in her hands, she waited impatiently for him to step up. "How did you find where he was? Who is holding him?"

Jack turned the gig around, coming out onto the road and turning away from the village, heading toward the bridge. "I talked to a man from London," he said as they started toward the Castle Road.

Moira sat quietly until they turned onto it, the chestnut trees sliding by them. "But why would he tell you, this London man? And where are we going? This is the road to the castle!"

"Didn't you know of its secret chambers?"

"You mean he's being held here!" She turned to stone as she sat beside him. If someone was holding him here, if the London man Dilke was holding him here, had Henri gotten away? How long had they been there? She could feel every bone in her body stiffen, her blood going cold. "Secret—chambers?" If they knew of secret chambers, did they know of the room, of the tunnel.

"That pile of stones," he looked up toward the huge stone building ahead of them, "has many deadly secrets." He hesitated. "I don't know how he's managed to convince you that he's innocent, but he's not, you know."

"How—how can you know that?" she asked, stalling for time, trying to find a way to help, to get Michael away from whoever was holding him. "Where are they holding him? Who is it? How many are there?" Her questions came tumbling out.

Jack's voice turned hard. "I *know* that because since he killed Lucy and got away with it I've tracked and traced his every movement."

"His—every movement?" she repeated, trying to sound calm.

Jack did not answer her question. "He killed his own brother to gain his dukedom." Jack's voice filled with derision. "And they wouldn't prosecute him because of his position, his name, his family—"

"His brother died in battle! It was not his doing!"

Jack laughed, the sound short and sharp. Driving off the castle road, around the side past the servants' wing, he spoke again. "That was their excuse, you mean. Do you know he couldn't even be buried in the chapel?"

"I beg your pardon?"

"You were looking at the tombs. Henry, the oldest brother. He's got a plain marker near the door we walked out; he can't have a marble effigy inside, for he was never Duke."

"But neither was Louis, Michael's father; his effigy is there and he was never Duke."

He didn't answer. "And Lucy, poor Lucy," Jack went on. "He drove her mad you know."

"How?" she asked quietly, watching the pain on the man's face.

He shook his head. "I don't know. If I knew, I'd probably have killed him with my bare hands."

He stopped the gig near the stables behind the castle, stepping down and then coming round to help Moira down. A stable boy came toward them.

"Your Ladyship." The boy touched his forelock, pulling on it self-consciously. Jack handed him the reins of the gig.

Jack ignored the boy, single-mindedly going forward. "This way," Jack told Moira. "To the secret tower."

She stared at him. "The secret tower?" She saw him striding off in the wrong direction. He was walking to the southeast turret, not the northeast.

He turned back toward her, waiting for her to catch up.

"I don't understand," she began.

"In a moment you will. I want to show you what the authorities are after."

"But Michael—"

"I'm taking you to him."

"But—where is he?"

"Follow me."

She stopped in her tracks. "Where?"

"Come along, or he'll be dead before you see him again."

She stared at Jack, and then the words pushed her toward the doorway that led to the stairwell. She saw the stableboy in the outside doorway. "Have you seen Jeb yet?" she called out, turning Jack back toward the boy.

"No, ma'am. I mean, Your Ladyship." He stopped, one foot inside the carriagehouse, the other still in the graveled drive beyond.

"Hurry!" Jack said.

"Yes," she said to him, then turned back toward the boy. "Tell John Ottery to meet me in the morning room in twenty minutes."

The boy nodded and left, Moira turning and following Jack, hoping she'd forestalled any danger. Jack moved to the stairwell at the far end.

"Where is this? Where is he?" she asked.

"It's called the Heir's Tower up above. Tristan's rooms are up above," Jack said, stepping into the dark, circular stairwell.

She followed him, seeing much the same sight as in the opposite tower, looking at the large-hewn stones of the walls, worrying if John Ottery would understand to look for her if she didn't meet him. First Michael, then Frances and Jeb, then Moira herself. Someone would have to realize that something was amiss. But would they realize in time?

And in that moment she realized she truly feared Jack. She felt the anger in him, the nervousness, as he motioned her forward, ahead of him, down the stairs, the pistol's butt gleaming in the dull, dim light.

"The old dungeons," Jack said, pushing her a little forward as they reached bottom. "You remember, where Lucy died?"

"Why are you bringing me here?"

His pistol was now in his hand. "Don't yell or you'll not live to regret it. Or see him."

"What have you done with him!? What have you done with Michael!?" Her voice rasped over the words.

"Michael, Michael, can't you say anything but his godforsaken name? I'm giving him a chance to find out what he put Lucy through!"

"He didn't!"

Jack laughed. "Let him tell you!" He shoved her forward, a small window high up the stone wall throwing a dim light across their path as they left the steps, crossing a narrow, bare corridor, passing cells. "You see these?" Jack asked. "These are where the lords of the manor used to jail miscreants, as judge and jury." He pushed her forward. "Now, I'm judge and jury!"

"Jack, please, think of yourself. Of Tristan! You don't want this on your conscience."

"I am thinking of myself! And *Tristan!* His mother's death will not go unavenged! Your husband may have paid off, or threatened off, the authorities, but not me, not *me!* It's taken years to get this chance, ten long years!" Jack threw the bolt on the huge wooden plank that cross-barred a narrow door deep in the bowels of the castle. His gun was in his hand.

264

It was totally dark inside the cavern beyond the door Jack now opened. She could see nothing. And then, her eyes adjusting to the gloom, she saw a crumpled mass. "Michael!" she whispered, turning in the same moment to shove Jack, to grab for the pistol.

But he was stronger. Thrown off balance he still held the gun and he clipped her skull with the butt of it, watching her fold to her knees. He shoved her forward, stumbling over to close the door. To bolt it closed leaving the room in total darkness. "Can you hear me, Your Grace?" Jack's voice carried through the door. "I hope so, for now you'll end as you let her end, wasting away, unseen, unheard. . . . But you'll have your loving wife with you so that you can watch her die too."

Moira forced herself nearer the door, holding the side of her throbbing head. "Jack, you can't do this. This is murder!"

"Murder! Of course it's murder! And when Dilke comes, which won't be soon, I'll see he's delayed long enough, never fear. He will find the criminal dead of his own plots! There'll be no more deaths!" His voice was fading farther away.

She heard a door clang shut somewhere beyond, a door she'd not seen in the darkness.

"Michael? Michael, can you speak?" She crawled near him, the ground damp and musty, the sound of the small scurrying things all around them in the darkness. She reached the huddled mass, reaching out slowly, terrified that he was dead already, terrified of the thousand and one possibilities that she didn't want to face.

She felt a cloth and followed it behind his head, to where it was knotted. "Oh, Michael, please, please be all right," she whispered over and over as she unbound the cloth in the darkness.

He took a great ragged gasp of air.

"Michael?"

"Yes." His voice was hoarse.

"Oh, thank God." She reached to feel along his arms toward his hands. "I thought you dead."

"Where's he gone?" Michael spoke slowly, getting his breath, letting her unbind his hands.

"I don't know."

"Do any know we're here?"

"Possibly—a stableboy. And John should look for me soon. As should—Norma."

"Norma!"

"I went to find you. Dilke is going to search the castle, thank God now, at least he'll find us."

"But Henri!"

"Andre took all of them to the ship during the night. They're on their way to Ireland, the doctor with them."

"At whose order?"

"I thought—I mean, Andre said they'd probably search and that he didn't know where you were—to ask what you wished done, so I said leave. Before anyone came."

There was a lull in the words. She finally loosened the ropes on his hands enough for him to release them from their bindings.

"When Jack brought me up the road," Moira said into the silence, "I was afraid that Dilke had you here, that somehow he'd caught Andre and you and—everyone. But it's only Jack who's here."

"You went to Norma?" Michael asked after another moment of silence.

"I thought, even though Andre said not, that possibly you might have seen, or talked, to her."

"And?" He was working swiftly with the bindings on his feet.

"And we talked. She knows I was going to see Jack, to meet him, for he sent a letter saying he knew where you were."

The blackness that surrounded them was unrelieved by even a ray of light. In the dark she could not see what he was thinking, what expressions crossed his face. The large bolted door shut them away from the small bit of light outside this cavern. She heard him swearing at the bindings on his ankles, pulling at them.

"Let me help." She reached downward, toward his legs, feeling him stiffen as her hand touched his thigh. She moved down his leg, feeling her way, down his calf, to his ankle and the rope that bound it to his other ankle. His hands were fumbling beside hers in the dark.

She touched his hands with hers. "My hands are smaller," she said.

He released his grip on the bindings, and then, feeling her hands at his ankles, he reached to grab them, holding them tight for a long moment, wordless, before releasing them.

He slowly sat back, leaning back to rest his weight on his palms as she worked. "You're sure you can manage that?" he asked.

"Faster than you were."

"Remind me to tell John this floor hasn't been swept in generations by the feel of it."

She had loosened the ropes a little, still working on them. Now his ankle bones did not chafe each other. "How did he do this to you?" she asked as she worked at them.

"I was riding—" He hesitated. She could hear him breathing in the dark. "Not to the inn, Moira." She said nothing. "Moira? Did you hear me?"

"Yes."

"It's true. I thought of it. I thought of many things. But I did none of them. I just wanted time to think after all we'd—talked about. So I took off across the moors. He shot me from behind."

"Shot!!" Moira's hands stopped. "Where—my God—"

"Shhh. Keep working. I've got to be able to at least stand when he comes back."

"Do you think he'll come back?"

"He has to. Hate is driving him. He has to hear me crack, or see me dead."

"Where—are you hurt?"

"My side. It's just grazed. But it knocked me off the horse and gave him a chance to try out his pistol butt on my head."

"He's good at that," she said bitterly.

"He hit you? I couldn't see!" Anger filled him as he felt the ankle bindings loosen. "By God, I'll teach him!" She got the ropes all the way off, letting them fall to the side.

"Michael, he gave me sherry the day I got sick. It must have been poisoned."

"What?" Michael's voice lowered, suspicion creeping over the single word.

"It's a long story," she said.

Michael's voice was almost harsh. "Suppose you begin it."

She sighed. "You're ready to think the worst, aren't you?"

"Weren't you? When Jemma spoke?"

"No." Moira sat very still.

"No?"

"Michael, Jack's the one who found me on the road when the wheel broke. He helped me to his place. And gave me sherry to steady my nerves. He's the one who showed me that the wheel had been cut."

"How convenient that he was there."

Another thought came to Moira, overshadowing the rest.

267

"He planned all of it. I don't know how he could get to the gig, but he must have done all of it and then waited for me on the road, and followed when I went in the other direction. He would have killed me then and there and had you blamed for it. And when that didn't work he gave me poison." She hesitated. "Thinking to have you blamed again. But how did he get you in here last night, without someone hearing?"

"I don't know. This wound didn't allow me the benefit of staying conscious."

"Oh, Michael." She reached to find his hands again, the small scurrying sounds around them lost to her ears. "How did he dare come here? Someone could have seen."

"Jeb *should* have seen!"

"Jeb's gone."

"What?"

"Jeb and Frances—they've been missing, too."

"Frances!"

One thought after another tumbled out; maybe Jeb was hurt, maybe Frances was with him, or if Dilke had them Frances might be so frightened she'd tell all. . . .

Moira shivered. "And Jack was with Dilke and Norma today," she said out loud.

"Dilke and Norma?" There was a long pause. "She must be on to something."

"Michael?" Her voice was low.

"Yes?"

"I'm so frightened." He reached to pull her nearer, groaning a little as she touched his side. She pulled away quickly. "Did I hurt you?"

He pulled her back. "No. And anyone with sense would be frightened right now. I'm frightened myself."

They were silent for long minutes, the stone wall and the stone floor hard against their backs, their legs. She lay against him, her head on his shoulder, a strange feeling of peace coloring her fears. She felt him shiver. "Are you cold?" she asked.

"No."

"Is it painful?"

"My side? I've had worse. No, it's—" The words came slowly, as if he were forcing them out. "It's being here." He hesitated. "Where she died."

Moira felt him shudder, the feeling of oppression worse in the dark silence. "It'll be all right, they'll find us."

"Why did he bring you?" Michael's voice rose with anger. "Why in God's name should he hurt you, he'd already got me! I don't want to be responsible for your death too!"

"Too? You're not, Michael, you're not!"

"No? If you weren't married to me, if she hadn't been, if my brother had not tried to save me when I was hit, if your father had not tried to help my cousins—" He stopped, sounds outside filtering through the thick door. Moira held her breath, waiting, and then heard Jack's voice.

"How do you like it, Your Grace? Have you had your fill yet?"

"Please," Moira said loudly, "please let us out. He's hurt, he must have a doctor!"

"He'll have a doctor all right. He'll have the same one he let poor Lucy have!"

"Taylor!" Michael spoke harshly. "Let her out. I'll tell you what you want."

Moira turned to Michael in the dark. "What do you mean?" she whispered. "You can't trust him."

"Let her out," Michael repeated. "Let her away."

"And then what?" The voice was nearer, muffled by the wood.

"Then I'll tell you what you want to hear."

"You'll confess," Jack said.

The words came hard. "I'll—confess."

"Michael!" Moira's voice was horror-stricken. "What are you saying!"

"Let her out," Michael repeated. "You've nothing against her. You've no reason to keep her."

"Have I not? And just what will happen when I do? She'll run for help and you'll get away with more crimes. You'll deny it all and she'll believe you, she'll think you're doing it for her and love you more. No, I'd rather see just what will happen to you when I let you watch her die. When you go through the nightmare that's kept me awake all these years."

"Jack?" There was another voice outside: "I don't like being down here. Jack, why'd you bring me down here?" Tristan's voice came nearer.

"Tristan! Tristan! Help, help us!" Moira shouted.

"What—what was that?" Tristan's voice was nearer. It sounded strained, unnatural.

"Tristan!"

"Where's Jeb?" Jack said out beyond the door.

269

"Oh, God," Tristan's voice was strangled. "What *is that* sound? What have you done?"

"Where's Jeb?" Jack's voice rose again, harsher, more strident.

There was a pause before Tristan answered, his voice choked, his words stuttered. "He's taken that man, that lieutenant, to Clovelly, as you said."

"Good. They won't be back for hours."

"What are you doing!? What's going on!?" Tristan almost screaming the words as Jack began to unbolt the door. *"Don't open that door!"*

"Tristan!" Moira was still shouting, trying to get him to hear, to answer.

Moira felt Michael's hands press hard into her arms. "Shhh," he warned her. "Help me up," he whispered.

She got to her knees and then to her feet, reaching to help Michael as the door began to swing slowly open, the sound of Tristan's pleading voice outside, saying "Stop it. Stop it. Don't open that door. Don't open it."

A dim shaft of light hit the front of the cell, the back wall still in total darkness around them. Jack stood in the doorway, Tristan just visible beyond, their eyes not accustomed yet to the blackness inside the cavern.

Michael leaned close to her ear. "When I go for him, run. Run as fast as you can. Do you understand?"

"Well," Jack said. "You wanted out. Now I want you to tell my son how you killed his mother."

Michael moved forward unsteadily, unseen. He was nearer Jack now. "Yes, but how do I know you'll let her leave?"

Jack turned toward the sound of Michael's voice, still unable to see, his hand holding the pistol. "You don't."

Michael edged nearer. Moira feeling her way along the opposite wall in the darkness, edged nearer the open doorway too.

"Tristan," Michael called out, "you're going to let him do this?"

"Do . . ." Tristan's eyes were large, his pupils dilated as he stood in the dim room beyond, staring into the black pit of the dungeon. His voice was unsteady, was at an unnaturally high pitch. "What is happening, who is that in there now? Why is anyone in there again? Please—"

Michael lunged for Jack, yelling at Moira to go. Moira pushed past them as Jack struggled to get the gun into position to shoot. Seeing the pistol aimed at Michael, Moira grabbed for it, wrenching it out of Jack's hand as, off balance, Jack fell backward, Michael on top of him, half in, half out of the dungeon.

Moira stared at Tristan who was edging away along the dimly lit corridor. "No," he said, staring at her. "No, you can't, you can't come out of there. You can't be. . . ." His voice was close to a whisper.

"Tristan, what is it? What's wrong with you?" she asked.

Michael rolled off Jack, his breath heaving from the effort and the pain in his side. "Moira!"

Jack was getting to his feet, Moira turning to see him approach her. Jack was coming toward her from one side; Tristan stood on the other side.

"Tristan," Jack called out, "get the gun from her."

Tristan moved farther away, not closer, stumbling over his own feet, his eyes glazed as he still stared back at Moira, his eyes never leaving her face. "Let me alone, let me alone. Get away from me. . . ." he said over and over, as if reciting a litany.

"Tristan!" Jack yelled again. "Tristan! What's wrong with you?"

"No, no." Tristan's words were mumbled, muffled by his arm which was now over his mouth as he stared at Moira, horrified.

"Moira!" Michael shouted the warning, trying desperately to get to his feet, using the wall for support, as Jack lunged for the gun. She wrenched it around, pulling the trigger as he grabbed for it. The sound was loud in the narrow stone chamber, reverberating around them. Jack slowly slipped to the floor.

Michael was to his feet, moving along the wall toward where Jack had fallen, a strange whimpering sound beginning low in Tristan's throat and then building louder. Michael took the gun from Moira as Tristan babbled. "There's another bullet," Michael warned Jack.

"No, no, no, no," Tristan babbled repeatedly. "No, don't hurt me. . . . Don't hurt me again!"

Moira, feeling faint, used the wall to hold herself erect, walking toward Tristan.

"Tristan, please, what is it? I couldn't help it, he would have—"

"No! Stay away from me!" He was pressed into the corner, against the stone slabs that lined the corridor. "Please," he

271

whimpered, "you're dead. You can't hurt me now. Go away. I killed you. You're dead. You can't come back to hurt us anymore."

Moira stared at him in horror. "Dead?"

"Dead! Dead, I shut you in there. You've got to be dead. It's all over. . . . No more knives, no more . . ." he whimpered.

Michael, the gun in his hand, straightened up slowly, bracing himself with his hand on the wall, staring toward Tristan.

"Moira—" Michael's voice was strangled. "Go find help."

"But you're hurt and—"

"Go!" Michael was using all the strength he could muster to remain erect. "Now!"

She moved slowly past Tristan as he cowered in the corner and then raced up the stairs, screaming as loud as she could. The young stableboy came running and then, behind him, John Ottery turned away from Norma who was gesturing wildly at him.

"Get help!" Moira said almost incoherently to the stableboy who reached her first. "Get men! And a gun!"

Norma heard her. "Bring men and guns from the house!" She yelled at the boy. Moira had already turned back toward the turret, racing for the stairs, John and Norma behind.

"He's hurt," Moira said, over her shoulder, heading back down the dungeon steps, feeling her way in the dimness as the light from above faded away.

Michael was propped against the far wall of the long stone passage that led to the dungeons. In the dim light from the one tiny window high on the stone wall she could now see the dark splotches that had seeped out all over the left side of his shirt.

He was pressing his hand against it, staunching the flow of blood, his right hand barely holding the gun on Jack who now sat, holding his arm and staring at Tristan, an expression of horror distorting his features.

Moira moved to Michael's side, throwing herself down beside him on the stones. Norma and John, just behind, stopped where they were, looking toward Tristan who was flattened against the opposite wall in an unnatural position, his eyes large, words babbling from his mouth as he stared toward the open dungeon door.

"No, Mama, don't hit me with it, don't hurt me. No, not this time. . . . It's a knife!" His voice rose high and clear as a small child's. "Don't do it! No, go away, go away, you go away. Don't

272

hurt the baby! You hurt Tammy with it. Don't hurt me with that knife!"

Tears were filling Michael's eyes, falling down his cheeks unheeded. He bent his head, shaking it a little, the mystery solved. Moira took his right arm, took the gun from his right hand gently.

"Oh God, what have I done?" Jack's voice trembled.

Norma walked toward him as the sound of men's feet came down the stairwell.

"What *have* you done?" Her voice was cold. "Where's the girl and the stableman? What's to happen to the Duke? Where's Dilke?"

"Oh God." Jack stared over at Tristan, his voice, his eyes, full of horror. "I thought it was St. Maur. That's why I did all of it. That's why—and it was Tristan. Oh God, it was my own son."

Tristan's moans had fallen to a whimper. Jemma raced into the passageway behind two footmen, one of them carrying a gun.

"Jack!" she screamed, oblivious of the others, seeing only the bleeding from Jack's arm. She raced toward him, dropping to the floor beside him. "What have you done to him?" She looked up at the others, hatred filling her eyes. "What have you done?"

"Ask him," Norma said. "Ask your precious Jack who brought all this down upon us."

Jemma stared at each of them in turn and then saw the gun in Moira's hand. "You!" She started to stand, but Jack's hand went out, stopping her.

"No."

"Oh, Jack," Jemma's eyes filled, "what have they done to you?"

"Tristan—it was Tristan, all along . . . all these years." His voice still disbelieved his own words.

"Tristan?" She looked toward Tristan and then stared, transfixed, at the boy. The whites of his eyes were unnaturally full now, his gaze thrown back, up toward the ceiling, his mouth slack. A tiny edge of spittle creased one side of his lips, trickling to his jaw.

"We must get him to bed. He should never have been brought here, it's unbalanced him completely." Michael's voice was thin, used up by pain and shock and loss of blood. "We must get the boy to bed."

"Yes." Moira turned to the footmen. "Bring him along."

"Up the stairs, his room is above." Michael could get out no more.

"You must lie down yourself." Moira motioned to John and then handed the gun to Norma.

"Bring them—" Michael began.

"Yes," Norma replied. "Yes, I'll bring them."

"Now." Michael forced the word out, forced himself to try to stand, John holding the Duke's left arm, pulling it around his own shoulders as Moira did the same on Michael's right.

"Yes. Get Jack up," Norma said to Jemma. *"Now."*

"He's hurt!"

"His arm is grazed. Get him *up!*"

Jemma moved, helping Jack to his feet and then Norma motioned them forward, past Michael. They followed the footmen, who were half-carrying, half-dragging, the crying Tristan. Norma motioned them on up the steps. "If you think I won't use this you're both fools," Norma said as they moved. "The man you tried to kill saved my life as well as that of everyone in my family. I'd sooner see you dead right now than in prison. *Both* of you!"

John and Moira, on each side of Michael, moved slowly forward, Moira's arm around his waist. She could feel the sticky wetness that soaked through his shirt, staining through to her dress.

"I can't," he said as they started up the steps.

"Oh, Michael, please. Just this one more." Moira's voice was soft, coaxing. "Just this one. We'll rest here a moment. You see? Now one more. Just one. Here we go."

On and on, slower and slower, they circled up the ancient stairwell, old John breathing heavily from Michael's bulk which was now becoming dead weight against him.

Moira felt her shoulders aching, wrenching with pain from Michael's weight, from the strain of it all. She ignored it, concentrating on her own words. "One more. Ah, that's it. Just one more—"

"It's not just—one—more!" Michael managed to get out as they stumbled under his weight. John and Moira forced themselves and Michael up another step and another, until the two footmen came back down toward them, Norma calling out from above. "Let them help, he should be carried. Moira, let them help!"

Moira unwillingly let go of Michael's arm, grabbing his hand

274

back as the two young men took over from John, holding Michael's bleeding body higher, carrying him with John's help.

She held Michael's hand firmly in hers, talking to him the whole way up until they reached the upper floor and went on toward his suite.

His eyes were closed now, his breath barely audible. The stains on his face from the dirt of the dungeons, from his own tears over Tristan, were visible now in the brighter light of the upstairs hall.

Norma pushed Jack and Jemma forward, behind the others, as John Ottery pushed himself to move faster, past them all when they reached the upstairs hall. "I'll send for a doctor."

Moira nodded, half-hearing him. He went on ahead. She still held Michael's hand, the footmen turning the corner, crossing the upstairs gallery, the great entry hall and two stone staircases beside them now as they moved across the upper gallery, John Ottery disappearing below.

They reached the Duke's Suite, Moira opening the door. The thought that she'd never been in these rooms before fled through the back of her mind as they walked across his sitting room to his great front corner bedroom beyond.

Chapter Twenty-eight

THE ROOMS LOOKED LIKE HIS ROOMS IN LONDON, LIKE HIS CABIN aboard ship: oak-panelled walls, dark-red carpet, burnished brass and silver. They fit him, Moira thought incongruously as they laid him on the bed and she walked near to pull away the shirt, to see the wound, to see what must be done.

"Get me a sharp knife and clean cloths, hot water and some broth—quickly!" Her voice rang out, and the one footman fled as the other stood back watching, near Norma who held the gun on Jack and Jemma still, just inside the bedroom doorway.

Jack sank to a chair, holding his arm. "The gun's not necessary." He sounded defeated.

Jemma knelt beside him, reaching to pull his sleeve away from the wound that creased his arm just below the shoulder.

"It's not?" Norma asked, staring at him.

"I give you my word," he said tiredly.

"What about hers?" Norma asked as Moira spoke too.

"Don't listen to him! He has no word, he shot Michael in the back!"

"Let him be! He's been through enough!" Jemma said loudly.

"He!" Moira turned on Jemma, her eyes blazing. *"He?* Has he been hounded for years by scurrilous rumors? Has he lived in the shadow of being unjustly blamed for the deaths of those he loved, blamed by people who never would speak it to his face? Has he had a wife betray him and the man she betrayed him with hounding his every step ever after? And *you,* what all have you done to find the truth? You've never heard Michael say a word against any, *any,* not even—" her eyes found Jack, her anger burning within them. He looked away. "Not even *you!"*

"He's hurt!" Jemma cried out.

"Good! Good that he feels a little pain! Look how much he's caused!" Moira shot back. "He tried to murder Michael!" Hysteria caught the edge of her voice, and she fought it back down, pushing it away. There was no time for it now. No time for anything but Michael. "As well as me," Moira finished, turning back toward Michael.

The footman arrived with the things she'd asked for as Jemma asked Jack what Moira meant. Moira began to cut away the shirt, staring at the ugly wound in his side. Tears filled her eyes, the fear that clutched at her breath hardly letting her breathe.

She reached for the basin of hot water and a cloth, and then methodically she began to clean the wound, watching his now bared chest as it rose and fell with his labored breath.

"It will be all right," she said, over and over to him. "The doctor will be here shortly and all will be well. Never fear, it's all over, it's all over now."

"The authorities," Jack said slowly. "Dilke."

Norma turned on him, taking a step closer. "What about them? And what about the Duchess's maid and the stable-man?"

"She's—" Jemma began and stopped.

"Norma!" Moira called out, never looking away from Michael's wounded side as she worked to clean it. "Jeb's gone to Clovelly for Jack, but we must find Frances!"

276

Norma raised the gun and aimed it straight at Jemma. "Speak."

"You wouldn't—" Jemma began and then stopped, seeing the hatred in the other woman's eyes. "It would be murder!"

"I would already be dead, if not for him," Norma said softly. "Do you think I'd care if they hung me for killing you?" She spoke very softly, a space between each word. "It would be well worth it, for what you've done to him."

Jemma stared at her. "Frances is in my room," she said at last.

Norma looked up at the footman who stood, gaping still at the scene. He turned and ran toward the hall beyond. "And Dilke?" Norma turned back toward Jack.

"He's to come here—question Frances—and—search."

"For?"

"Whatever he can find."

"When?" Norma spoke harshly.

Jack answered, his words coming slowly. "I sent Jeb to Dilke this morning. Told him some of his—the Duke's—accomplices were waiting in Clovelly, waiting to talk. I've given him many tips, thanks to Jeb. And Jemma. And . . . and Tristan. I wanted time with the Duke before I—before I killed him."

"Killed him!" Jemma stared at Jack. "You weren't going to kill him! You were turning him over to the government, to be tried for treason, you told me so! All the places, all the people, Tristan and I found out about and told you about—"

"You fool," Norma said softly to Jemma. "You silly little fool."

"Traitor," Moira said.

"I'm no traitor!" Jemma said hotly. *"He's* the traitor! Tell them, Jack, tell them how the government wants him, tell about all his crimes, the laws he's broken. *Tell them!"* Her voice rose as she stared at the man she'd loved since first she'd met him.

He looked down at the floor, his arm throbbing, his reason for living gone.

"He used you," Norma told her. "He cultivated you so that you'd do his dirty work for him, and you believed it all. You'd have been accomplice to murder for a man who cares nothing about you!"

"That's not true! None of it's true! You weren't going to kill them," Jemma said slowly. "It wasn't you who—" horror began to fill her eyes, "it wasn't *you* poisoning her and making that accident happen. Tell them. . . . Tell *me!"*

"You don't understand," Jack said, looking up at her as her voice stopped. "I thought he'd killed Lucy. I thought he'd gotten away with it, like he's gotten away with all the other high-handed things he's done. Because he's one of *them*, because he's above the law, beyond it! I wanted to make him crawl! I wanted them to try him for her death, since they wouldn't listen about Lucy. But even more I wanted him to suffer, I wanted to *see* him suffer, to see the woman he loved die right before his eyes. . . ."

"You were going to kill her." Jemma stared at him. "Tell me you weren't really going to—"

"Yes," he said finally, looking over at Moira who still bent over Michael. And then at Norma. "Yes, I was. When the gig didn't kill her, when the poison failed, I was going to shoot her and then him and say I'd found them, had killed him for killing her. Dilke would want to believe it. No one would have been surprised after all the—"

"After all the rumors you've kept alive for all these years," Norma said into the sudden silence. "It's you who's kept people talking and questioning and gossiping!"

"I've waited to get my revenge. So long. . . . So very long. I wanted him to die knowing my son, *my son*, was now *Duke*, had it all. . . . Was one of *them!*" His voice began to choke over the words. "Had all of it. . . . And, instead, it's he who wins again. . . ."

"Wins!" Norma spat out the word.

Jack looked up at her. "She wouldn't leave him. Lucy. She tormented him. And me. But she wouldn't leave him. My only hope was Tristan, my only reason for living to make sure he inherited—"

"Not your *only* reason." Moira's voice was stone cold. "You wanted to harm Michael, to hurt him, to kill him!"

"Not my—only—reason," Jack agreed slowly. "No. And now, now it's all gone."

"Not quite," Moira said. "You've gained your big victory, you've hurt him all right. . . . You've hurt him mortally."

"But now there's no reason," Jack said. "Don't you see how much worse it all really is? Now," he added faintly, "now there's no reason. He didn't do it. He didn't kill her." There were long pauses between his words. "A nine-year-old boy. A frightened, panicked child killed her. . . . My own son—" he broke off, his voice choking with tears. "Killed her and forced

278

the memory away until—until *I* made him face it all today. . . .
I've sent my own son mad."

Jemma still knelt beside him, her brain registering random
words as the enormity of it all sank in. "Then you did just use
me. You never cared, would never have cared, for me."

"Oh, Milady!" Frances called out to Moira, racing toward her.
But when she saw Jemma she stopped. "Her!"

"It's all right." Norma waved the gun, Frances moving back
as she saw it. "The saints preserve us! Who are you and what's
happening now!?"

"It's all right, Frances. She's a friend," Moira said.

Frances skirted around the others, coming close to Moira.
Looking down at the wound in Michael's side she stifled a small
scream. "What have they done to him!?"

"Are you all right?" Moira looked up at her as she tried to
bandage the wound, pressing it against his side tightly, trying to
stop the blood that still seeped slowly out.

"Yes, and it was *them*. I heard them talking, it wasn't His
Grace at all—"

"I know—" Moira interrupted, "but how did they get you?"

"I was walking with Jeb, and he turned on me! I thought he
meant to kiss me, but, well, you know, and he hit me instead!"

Norma spoke to Jack. "Are there more in this? More than
Jemma, Tristan, Jeb and you?"

He shook his head. "No."

"What all do you know? What all do you think you know,
about the Duke's—travels?"

Jack answered slowly. "He's been followed to Brittany. The
ship, that blasted ship no one can ever find. Some London
contacts told us he owned a black ship, had it in London."

"My father," Moira said suddenly. "You caused my father's
death—by giving word ahead of when he was coming, where
he was going—"

"I had no idea that—"

"You didn't *care*. You were so blinded with hatred that it just
didn't matter who else got hurt along the way. Innocent or
guilty!"

He said nothing, his shoulders caving in.

The sound of heavy boots outside brought Moira around,
staring fearfully at the open door. Andre walked through it.

"Andre!" Moira stared at him. "What's wrong? Why are you
here?"

He strode into the room toward her, glancing at the others, his eyes widening when he saw Michael. Then he stared at her hard, his gaze warning her not to speak. "All is well, with me," he said. "I sent them on ahead, but had a little trouble getting back." He said no more, turning to study Michael's side, to feel his forehead. "I see you found Frances. And the Duke."

"Tied and gagged I was!"

"In Jemma's room," Moira told him. "That man—Dilke is on his way from Clovelly. He's coming here to search for—for God knows what—with Jeb."

"Jeb!"

"Jemma and Jeb—they've been finding out what they could. And Tristan. And telling Jack."

Andre looked over at the sandy-haired man, his eyes narrowing into slits. "And I'll just wager who he's been passing the information on to."

"They traced you to Brittany. They've got people in London who are paid to tell all they hear—or see." Moira spoke quietly and swiftly. "They're trying to prove the ship exists, they've known about it because of London."

Andre stared at Jack and Jemma. "Why are they coming here?"

"I told them of the stairwell," Jack said weakly.

"Stairwell!" Andre spoke harshly.

"To the dungeons." It was Moira now who warned Andre.

"Moira, what is going—" Madame came through the sitting room, slowing to a stop as she neared the bedroom door, taking in Michael on the bed, Norma with the gun, Jemma kneeling beside Jack.

"Stay back!" Moira called out, stopping the old woman just as her eyes took in the wound in Michael's side.

"Oh no." Madame's voice turned frail, coming toward her son. "What have you done?" she asked him.

"He's done *nothing!*" Moira said. "It's *him!*"

Madame stared over at Jack. "You—" She breathed the word, her voice lost. "And you?" She stared at Jemma now, watching as Jemma slowly lowered her eyes.

Eunice's voice could be heard downstairs, near the stairwell, Pomfret's voice below her, saying something back.

"Close the hall door!" Moira hissed. Andre moved first, racing to it, closing it and then locking it as the two outside climbed the stairs and went on to their own rooms.

"We were in the village," Madame said, "at the fair," she added unnecessarily. "It was Prize Day and since Moira was still in seclusion because of her friends' disappearance I had to award the best dancers. The best archers." Her voice fell away. "The day before Christmas," she added slowly. "John said you'd gone to the village early. We looked for you, the children looked all over. We thought you'd changed your mind and were to give out the prizes. But we—couldn't—find—you." She sank to a hard-backed chair beside the bed.

Andre came nearer, trying to help with Michael.

"What has happened, Moira?" Madame looked up at her daughter-in-law, her eyes frightened, her voice as unsteady as her hands now when she reached to touch Michael and then let her hand drop back to her lap. "What is all this?"

A knock at the outer door brought Andre to it. Coming back, a rotund little man walked in beside him. "The doctor from the village."

Moira moved to let the doctor near. His eyes widening, he glanced toward the others and then saw Norma. He stared at her, at the gun, glancing back at Moira quickly and then down at Michael.

"Oh my." He began to undo Moira's bandages. She wiped Michael's brow with a warm cloth, gently washing away the dirt and the tear stains from his cheeks. "What's all this about?" the doctor asked.

"Are you a doctor or not?" Andre challenged.

"Yes, of course—"

"Then *doctor*. And leave the rest to others."

The doctor saw the challenge in Andre's eyes. He turned and saw Moira looking at him even more intently. Quietly, he leaned down to the wound and began to swab the darkened blood away, probing the wound with his fingers. "The bullet is still inside," he said, reaching for his bag.

Moira sighed as she watched the man bend to his task and then she looked over at Madame. "You'd best see to Eunice and Pomfret. Keep them away, please, or all London will soon know of this."

Madame stood up slowly, letting Andre help her to the sitting room and then the hall beyond, locking the door after her.

When Andre returned he stared at Jack. Then he stared at the footman who still stood nearby. "Can you lock him up below? In one of the cells?"

"No!" Jemma stood up quickly.

The footman nodded, and Andre motioned toward Jack. Jemma took a step forward, and Norma waved the gun at her. "Don't try my patience. Or you'll not be around to worry about him. Or aught else."

Jemma stopped in her tracks. "Jack!"

He looked back at her. "It's all right. I deserve it. It doesn't even matter."

"I love you!"

He shook his head as they led him toward the outside door. "Don't say that. I love no one. Not since—then."

Jemma stared at Norma. "I'm going with him."

Norma hesitated. "Andre?"

Andre shrugged. "If she wants to be put in the same cell, fine. It's one less to worry about right now."

Norma motioned with the pistol and led Jemma out as Moira stared at what the doctor was doing. "How can I help?" she asked.

"By letting me work!" the doctor hissed at her.

Andre reached for Moira's shoulders, pulling her back, away. She tried to twist out of his grasp but he held her more tightly. "I'll hurt you, if you insist. But I assume you don't want to worry him," Andre said.

"He can't hear!" she wailed.

"How do you *know?*" Andre said, quieting her, leading her out to the sitting room as the doctor worked on Michael, Frances stoically helping Andre with Moira.

"Oh God." Moira bent to sit on a narrow wooden chair near the north windows.

"Milady, you *must* hold up. For him."

"But he—"

"*He* needs you."

She swallowed, looking up slowly to face Andre. "What shall I do?"

"When the vultures come, they can't see this mess, or all will be lost."

"Why? Someone attacked the Duke and that's that!"

"Tristan?" He stared at her. "Jemma? What of what they'll say? As well as Jack."

She looked down. "What can we do?"

Andre let out a long, low sigh. "I wish I knew."

Sounds of shouting came from outside. Moira stared at Andre. "What—"

Andre made a quick decision. "Go—see. I'll stay here with him—in case."

"But—" She stood up and then, seeing the pistol in his belt, the knife in his hand now, she walked toward the door. "Lock it behind me. Take him to the room, beyond mine—just in case."

Andre nodded. Moira walked out into the hall where the dogs were barking, Eunice and Pomfret coming down the stair well toward her.

"Moira!" Eunice stared at Moira's dust- and blood-stained gown, her disheveled hair. "What on earth is happening?"

"Robbers again, hide in your room!" Moira said, thinking quickly.

"Robbers! Again? My God." Eunice's mouth made a perfect "O" as Pomfret dragged her back up toward their rooms above.

"Lock yourselves in!" Moira said to Pomfret. "I'll let you know when it's safe!" Moira ran toward the gallery and across to the children's wing and Tristan's rooms beyond, heading for the southeast turret.

At Tristan's door Moira stared at the empty bed and then ran across the room, on down the turret stairwell and across the open carriage house, out to the graveled path beyond.

She could see Jack and the footman who'd held him racing across the lawns, heading toward the long stretch of land that led to the cove. Jack pulled out, farther ahead.

Moira ran back up the turret, to the floor above and down the back hallway, past Tamaris's room, to the other turret. As she started down it, Tamaris came out of her room, starting toward Moira.

Racing down to the lower level, Moira pressed the stone panel, racing on ahead as Tamaris came running behind, slipping through the opening, following down the long, dark, dank tunnel.

Moira was far ahead, Tamaris coming slowly and then more and more quickly.

Moira fled down the tunnel, knowing it was the fastest way to the cove, trying to head Jack off. He mustn't escape. Nor Tristan. They'd tell Dilke and all would be lost.

Moira stumbled, breathless, down and down through the black tunnel and then to the end, pounding against the wall, finding the panel by sheer luck. It slid open slowly, and she stepped out into the cave and then through it, into the sunlight.

Tamaris followed her, coming toward the daylight as Moira stopped, seeing Tristan at the top of the cliff above, the cliff that surrounded the cove. Jack came into view a moment later.

Their voices were loud, the wind carrying some of the fury away, but the words falling toward her.

"Let me alone! You'll never get me!"

"Son—listen to me!"

"Listen! I've listened long enough! I don't want to hear it! I didn't do it, he did it! He did it! Or you did! I know you did! It wasn't me!"

"Tristan!" Jack's voice was wrenched out of him, trying to make Tristan listen.

"You must have! Or he did. Someone did. Not me. I couldn't kill my own—my—I couldn't! I didn't! How dare anyone say I did—"

"Tristan, please—"

"Don't you dare! You're not my father! I'm the heir to St. Maur! I don't know you, I don't even *know* you!"

"Tristan." Jack was walking closer, trying to sound calm. "Son—please—"

"Stay away from me! You're trying to make me do things! Bad things! You're crazy, *crazy!*"

Tristan lunged for Jack, grabbing at his throat. Along the edge of the cliff high above they struggled.

Tamaris edged out of the cave, coming up behind Moira slowly. "No—" She started to move and Moira turned quickly, seeing the child.

"Tammy! No!" Moira reached for the girl as she screamed her brother's name out.

"Tristan! Don't!"

Tristan, locked in the fight with Jack, turned toward the sound of the scream and tripped, near the edge, sending both of them over the edge of the cliff, plunging down toward the narrow stream, toward the hard rocks, far below.

Moira pulled Tamaris back, holding her close and pulling her into the mouth of the cave, shielding her from view as the footmen above leaned over to see Jack and Tristan dashed against the rocks at the edge of the stream. Moira could hear Jemma screaming above. Holding Tamaris close, Moira's voice was fierce as she spoke into the child's ear. *"No!* You've been through enough! What they do is no concern of yours!"

"Tammy! Tammy!" Mark's voice was carrying toward Moira as he stumbled down the tunnel. Dully she remembered she'd not closed the tower panel, that she'd left all of it open in her headlong flight.

Mark appeared at the end of the tunnel, seeing Moira holding his sister. Tamaris was shaking hard, her teeth chattering.

"Mark." Moira's voice cracked. "Help me. Your father's been hurt. Tammy's not well, help me get her back."

He hesitated and then came forward, helping Moira pull Tamaris back into the tunnel, up toward the house. Moira stopped, closing the doorway, leaving a wall of stone behind them in the empty cave. The tunnel was black with the cave shut off from it.

"Moira?" Mark's voice whispered toward her.

"Yes?"

"What's happening? What is this place? What was all the yelling?"

"Your father's been hurt. People are coming to search the castle. Mark, there's no time to explain right now but *no* one else must know of this tunnel."

"I see." His young voice suddenly sounded firm, adult. "And Tammy?"

"Can you keep her close while I see to your father?"

"Yes. What's wrong with him?"

She hesitated. "He's been shot."

Mark was silent for a moment. "Will he be all right?"

"I hope so. But his only hope is if you help. Can you keep Tammy quiet and with you? They mustn't know, when the people come to search, they mustn't know about this tunnel."

Mark nodded in the darkness and then quietly spoke. "Has my father done the things they say?"

"No. He's only done things you can be proud of."

Across the darkness, she could feel Mark nodding. "No one will find out. Not from us."

"Oh, Mark, you'll be saving your father's life!"

They reached the turret stairwell, Moira helping Mark get Tammy up the stairs after she closed off the tunnel.

Then, with them safely toward the children's wing, she walked back alone toward the Duke's Suite, praying silently.

Frances met her as she knocked and waited by the hall door. "Milady?"

Moira nodded, weary. "Andre?"

"Here." Andre stood in the bedroom doorway. "The same here. What was it?"

"Tristan—ran. Jack, got away, ran after him. They fought and, oh, Andre—" She shuddered. "They fell off the cliff, onto the rocks in the stream by the cove."

Andre stared at her. "You're sure?"

"I—saw. I got Tamaris and Mark away, but they know of the tunnel now." Moira sank to a chair. "I'm so tired." She heard Frances asking questions, heard Andre's quiet voice, and then she heard nothing more, sinking into oblivion.

Chapter Twenty-nine

THE SUN HAD FALLEN BEYOND THE MOORS, THE SOFT TWILIGHT hours lighting the sky out beyond Moira's windows as Frances called softly to her. "Milady? Milady?"

She felt her arm being gently shaken. She opened her eyes. "What happened?" Moira asked slowly.

"You fainted, Milady. Master Andre says to wake you. He says to tell you they're here."

Moira sat up, the sudden movement making her head swim. "How is he? Where is he?"

"Andre?" Frances looked perplexed.

"Michael!" Moira's patience snapped. "What on earth is wrong with you!?"

"Oh!" Frances stared at her. "What's wrong? People dying all over the grounds, people getting shot and fainting dead away and lord knows what all and me being trussed up like the Christmas turkey itself. How can you ask what's wrong with me? What's wrong with *you?*"

Moira stared at the overwrought Frances. By a force of will power she controlled herself, speaking again. "Frances, would you please bring Andre here? I must know of the Duke."

"I will!" Frances snapped as Moira lay back against the pillows, flouncing out of the room in a huff, muttering to herself about the ungratefulness of some people.

Moira closed her eyes. If she could keep Frances angry she wouldn't be frightened, wouldn't say the wrong thing to those men. Those men . . .

Andre arrived in her room, walking more slowly when he saw her still abed. "Are you unwell?" he asked.

"I'm fine!" Her voice came out strong and sure. Gingerly this time, she sat up. "What's happened?"

"You passed out—"

"And then?"

"I've told all that the Duke was hurt in the struggle over Tristan." Andre hesitated. "Tristan's and Taylor's bodies have been recovered."

"Dead."

He nodded.

His words began to register in her mind. "All, you've told all—they're here!?" She began to panic and he stepped forward.

"You must seem calm! I've made them wait to see you first. Before him."

"You've not told me about him." She was afraid to ask, afraid of the answer.

"He's asleep, the doctor is still with him."

She stared at the man who was so close to Michael. "Is it really Andrew?" she asked after a moment.

"Is what—" He stopped, looking a little embarrassed. "Oh, my name. My accent's not *that* bad."

"No. It isn't. You fooled me for quite a while."

"Until?" he asked.

She smiled then. "Until Cornwall. And your familiarity with things Celtic." She spoke of Andre, of small things, of anything to calm herself before meeting those men again.

He grinned. "Aye, it's me failin'." He slipped into English with no trace of any accent except that bred of the tors of Cornwall. "And Andrew it tis."

She took a deep breath. "Where are our visitors?"

"They," he said, as if touching rotted cheese, "are being regaled with how the robbers came. By your sister-in-law."

"Oh my Lord."

"The very words Dilke himself is saying, I'm sure. At least to himself."

"I must go down," she said faintly.

Andre hesitated. "Are you sure you're well enough?"

"I have to be. Did you—move—Michael?"

"No, he's in his own bed, with the doctor attending to the—wounds of battle."

A new thought occurred. "What about the doctor?"

"The doctor knows they shot the Duke and then got away, after we captured them, and then they killed the Duke's son as well. He's told them so already."

"They've seen the doctor?"

"Yes. I had him come down to them. And I told them they could not search the house or *move* from the main salon until either you or Michael, excuse me, the Duke, gave the word. Your Ladyship," he added.

"Oh, for God's sake, don't go formal on me now!" Moira stared at him. "Titles! Lord! If we get through all this—" She stopped, taking a deep breath.

"I sent the doctor to them, to keep them—occupied a little longer—while you rested," he added after a moment.

She started toward the door, stopping to look back at him. "They do not know of Tristan being—Jack's son?"

"No. He'd hardly have told of that, would he, when he wanted the lad to inherit St. Maur?"

"No," she answered slowly. "No, I suppose not. Jemma?"

Andre grinned again. "Well, I'll be bound, it seems she was in love with Jack and just ran away in all the melee."

"Ran?" She stared at Michael's closest friend.

"Aye, that's what all say. Course, there's always the possibili-ty that she's bound and gagged, like Frances was. Sort of tit for tat, as you might say, only in a safer place. Which is why I'd rather like to keep them from looking over the castle too closely. That and them coming on the children."

She spoke faintly. "I'd best go down."

As she started away Andre was following her, speaking softly. "Course the Duchess herself fell into a rare faint," he said as they walked down the upper hall, "when she found that Jack Lisle-Taylor, who'd been here, in St. Maur for years, was the one who was robbing the countryside and the castle as well."

She took a deep breath. "I see," she said.

He smiled a little. "I figured the least he could do was make up to the Duke now what he's cost him all these years in rumors and grief."

She went on down the stairs. "I'll be brief. I want to see Michael," she said as she descended.

He watched her and then rounded back around the upper gallery, walking into the Duke's Suite beyond.

* * *

288

Downstairs, Moira walked slowly toward the main salon, hearing Eunice's voice as she crossed the hall. "I can't imagine what the government thinks it's doing. Why, we're being literally *besieged* here! We'll have to dig up the moat and *refill* it. Mr. Whatever-your-name is, I assure you we expect better, ah! Moira! Dear heart, how *are* you?"

Moira walked in, toward the yellow damask couch from which Dilke now rose. She glanced at Pomfret, who smiled and then seeing the two men who stood behind him, near the fireplace and Madame, her face became cold, her manner aloof.

Madame looked shrunken from worry in her black satin gown. She stared up at Moira. "Is he—" Madame asked faintly.

"Would I be down here if all was not as it was?" Moira walked to the older woman, reaching to touch her cheek. "He is as well as can be expected." She turned to Dilke. "Sergeant, where is your friend?"

"I—beg your pardon?"

"The lieutenant, wasn't it?"

Dilke hesitated. "He is on other government business."

"I see. Well, I appreciate your promptness."

Dilke stared at her. "Promptness?"

Moira turned to stare at him hard. "You certainly have not forgotten this time! As you did the last! The particulars of the case?"

"No," he said stiffly. "We have not."

"Good," she said mildly. "Then, may I hope you have word of our friends?"

"Friends?" He eyed her suspiciously.

"Who were kidnapped!" she snapped, glancing at the other men now. She continued to Eunice, "This is the same man who came before when Frances and I barely made it back with our lives and he seems to have forgotten what he was called here to do!"

"I beg your pardon, but—" Dilke began.

"As well you should!" she interrupted. "Because of your lax handling of this affair my stepson is dead. *Dead!* And my husband lies above."

"We were not aware—" he began again.

"Obviously!" she snapped.

"Not aware!" Eunice broke in, "Sergeant Whatever-your-name-is." She stared at the man as if he had the plague. "I, for one, am returning to London post-haste with a complete, *complete,* report of your incompetence and the utter ineptness of your men!" She glanced pointedly over at the two men behind Pomfret. "I've been here less than a week and have had to escape with my life *twice!* What kind of authority do you pretend to possess? Who is your superior?"

Dilke stared at the great girth of the woman.

"Eunice," Moira said into the hush, "don't bedevil the poor man. However—" she stared Dilke straight in the eye, "perhaps you can tell me, just who this man's accomplices were?"

"I—cannot—"

"Well," she said impatiently, "who has he been seen with!?"

Dilke stayed silent.

Moira stared at him. "Why are you here if you did not know, were not aware, that we had sent for help again?"

He hesitated and then, slowly, pulled out a slip of paper. "We received this from Mr. Lisle-Taylor."

She took it, glancing at it briefly and then handing it to Eunice. "Would you look at this?" She turned to Dilke. "In the first place that says Clovelly, *not* St. Maur! In the second place, it seems you are ready to traipse over the countryside at the word of criminals but we can get no protection at all!"

"Your own stableman vouched for its accuracy!" He spoke quickly. "He said the Duke's a smuggler!"

"Our—?" She looked totally confused.

"Jeb Hinsley," Dilke supplied smugly.

"But Jeb does not work for us."

"I beg your pardon!" Dilke barked the words at her.

"Keep a civil tongue in your head, Sergeant, or you'll live to regret it," Eunice put in before Moira spoke.

"Jeb Hinsley is in Mr. Taylor's employ and has been since we caught him stealing and fired him."

Dilke stared at her. "Working for Lisle-Taylor."

"Whatever his name is."

"Can you verify this?" he asked.

"Oh, I say!" Pomfret finally spoke. "This is rather much, don't you know? First off, she's the Duchess of St. Maur and should be spoken to as such. Your Ladyship, Your Grace, some such, out of the likes of you chaps." Pomfret glanced back at the two now uncomfortable men who stood silently behind him. Then Pomfret returned his attention to Dilke. "And now you're doubting her word!? What kind of gentleman are you!?"

290

"A government servant," Dilke replied, his stance erect.

"That's hardly an excuse for bad manners, what?" Pomfret stared him down.

"You won't be a government servant for much longer, I'll warrant," Eunice said quietly, clearly, and very, very distinctly. "And neither will these others. If you don't *all* have a care."

Moira stood up, walking to the bell pull and praying silently as she rang it. Smiling into Madame's worried eyes, Moira walked near to lean forward and kiss her forehead gently. "Never fear, it won't be long now," she said softly.

A movement high up the wall caught Moira's eye as she straightened. She realized that someone was watching from the widow's walk, the edge of the upper gallery that faced into the main salon on one side and the ballroom on the other. The widow's walk had high windows, called peeps in the days when pregnant women and new widows were not allowed to join in the general festivities. In those days they hovered upstairs, overhead, looking down from their unseen niches.

"Yes, Your Ladyship?" John Ottery, correct and forbidding in his butler's uniform, stood in the doorway, drawing her attention back to the job at hand.

"John, these—gentlemen—are from the government and wish to know—"

"I'll ask!" Dilke interrupted her, earning John's distaste.

"Of course," she said quietly, staring at John with unaccustomed directness.

He saw the look and then bowed, slightly, to Dilke.

"Your name?"

"Ottery, sir, John Ottery."

"Very well, then, Ottery, the Duchess states that Jeb Hinsley has left the Duke's employ."

"Yes, sir," John replied.

"Yes? When?"

John hesitated. "I'm not sure, sir."

"You must have some idea of when."

"Yes, sir. I do."

"Well, man, out with it!"

John's face was impassive, only his eyes showing the dislike Dilke was engendering within him. "Some time, past, sir. Quite some time past."

"She says it was soon after she arrived!"

"She, sir?" John asked innocently.

291

Dilke's arm swept out toward Moira. "Her!"

John's voice took on a haughty reserve. "Are you presuming to speak of the *Duchess* in those terms?" He left the sir off very deliberately and Dilke noticed.

"Well, Jeb says differently!" Dilke said. "What do you think of that?"

"I think he probably would rather not admit that he was let go."

"Why was he let go?"

"Cheating," John said promptly. And ambiguously.

"We told you he'd stolen!" Eunice said immediately.

"That will be all," Dilke said, dismissing the man, his frustration evident.

One of the two men with Dilke motioned toward him. Dilke glanced back and realized the butler had not left. "I said—"

John spoke over Dilke's words, looking directly at Moira as if the little government man did not exist.

"Is there anything else, Your Ladyship?"

"No, John, thank you." Moira smiled at him and he turned, walking slowly out, completely ignoring the three men.

One of the men was speaking low to Dilke. The sergeant moved his head impatiently.

"If my sister-in-law tells you a domestic is no longer employed, just what is your problem?" Eunice demanded, staring Dilke down when he turned around.

"We've heard stories," he said ominously.

"Oh my, yes! So have we!" Moira said. "And *all* put about by this man Taylor, this friend of yours."

"Wait!" One of the men spoke and then questioned Dilke. "Is that true? Was this man a friend of yours?"

"No!"

"And you know, I'm to blame for some of them myself," Moira said.

"You!" Dilke turned toward her then.

She nodded, praying his knowledge was as superficial as Jack had let on. "You know, Michael's been visiting me in Brittany for years."

"Brittany!" He stared at her.

"Years!" Eunice looked shocked. "At—your age?"

"Yes," she said to both of them. "That's why we tried so hard to let none know."

"You're from London," Dilke said.

292

"Just before we came here, we stayed in London for a few days, but I'm from Brittany."

"Lady Jersey can vouch for that!" Eunice said. "You do know who Lady Jersey is, don't you?" She looked down her nose at the fat little man.

"Yes," he said through his teeth.

"I was just talking to her before we left, about the romantic elopement and all of these two," Eunice said placidly.

Moira was staring at Eunice, glad of the help, nonplussed by her words.

"We've tried our best," Moira said after a moment, "our level best, to keep his trips to Brittany secret. Even, I'm afraid, from dear Madame." Moira sank to a hassock beside the old woman. She was no longer able to stand without shaking. "You do forgive us, don't you?"

The old woman stared at her, as did Eunice and Pomfret. Then, when she spoke, the old woman smiled. "A son has fewer secrets than he thinks from his mother."

"Oh!" Moira smiled back at her, reaching to kiss her cheek. "Well, it doesn't matter, for we're married now and that's that!"

"Oh, I do say!" Pomfret said, quite squeamish about the direction the conversation was taking.

"Of course, we knew," Eunice said slyly. She looked at Dilke. "But what has any of this to do with finding this man's accomplices, and the woman and child they still hold?"

"Eunice," Moira spoke quietly, "I think this Dilke here may be one of the accomplices. What is the name of your friend in the government?"

"Lord Liverpool, the Prime Minister," Eunice said over Dilke's objections to Moira's words. When he looked at the two men he had brought with him he began to look ill.

"It's not true!" he said to the men. "It's ridiculous!"

"You certainly have helped the culprits at every turn. Much more than the victims," the taller man said, his face creased into worried lines. "That wild goose chase to Clovelly proved nothing, and was at this Taylor's insistence, I might add. Where are these missing people? What have you done to find them, or protect these people?"

Moira studied Dilke. "I think we'd better ask as to your letters from the government. What your exact position is, in all of this. Neither Lord Castlereagh nor Mr. Canning has informed the Duke of your presence here. We have people dead, people missing, and wounded, and you prattle on about a disgruntled ex-employee."

Dilke pulled himself together. "It is not necessary to bring them or Lord Liverpool into this matter."

"I think it is," Moira said quietly.

Dilke motioned to the men. "If we may offer our condolences at your losses, and the Duke's—ill health—"

"Ill health!" Moira exploded. "He's been shot! He is wounded and all because of your ineptness! And still you do nothing! Nothing!" she said louder, as Dilke turned toward the other two men who were bowing toward her.

"Your Ladyship," the taller man said, "we will trouble you no further on this head. And we shall see that the local authorities do their duty in helping you."

"I should hope so!"

They left the room, their boots echoing back down the hall. When all was silent, Moira leaned against Madame's chair, breathing heavily.

Eunice held Pomfret's hand now, squeezing it fondly, as John appeared in the doorway. "The gentlemen have gone, Your Ladyship."

Moira nodded gratefully. "Thank you, John. For everything."

"What about me?" Eunice asked as John left smiling. "I deserve some credit for *my* play-acting, too, don't I?"

"Eunice!" Pomfret exclaimed.

"Well, I do!" she said.

Moira stared at her, as did Madame. "What do you mean?" Moira asked finally.

Eunice smiled. "Jeb was very much here and bustling to and fro yesterday morning. Let alone when we got here. And we talked of his disappearance all the way to the fair, Mother, don't you remember?"

"Pardon me," John said from the doorway, "but he *had* left the Duke's employ some time past it would seem. And he's been cheating on us, that's for sure," John added, a proprietary tone to his voice.

Moira smiled at him and then at Eunice. "You're a devil, John Ottery," she said, looking back at him. "But a Cornish one, and I don't know what any of us would do without you!"

He bowed a little, smiling broadly and trying to cover it. When he straightened again his expression was as controlled as ever. "If you wish anything else?"

Moira shook her head. "We'll ring."

He left as Eunice looked over at Pomfret. "Well, why are you so disapproving, my pet?" she asked.

"There's no need to shout about good deeds," he said, earning a dirty look from his wife and a smile from Moira. "Especially when they are one's *own* good deeds."

Moira stood up. "I must get back to Michael."

Eunice stood up as Moira walked toward the door. "Do you think he'll be all right?"

"He has to be," Moira said and then left.

She closed the door, leaving them to their own conversations. She walked slowly toward the north stairs, fatigue and fear taking their toll.

"Was it all right?" Mark asked when she reached the gallery, stepping out from behind a statue of King Henry VIII.

She smiled. "Was that you—up at the peep?"

"You saw me?" He sounded disappointed.

"Only I—none other," she replied. "And I was looking up or I would not have either."

He brightened then.

"How's Tammy?" she asked.

"Better. She cried a long time. Now she's sleeping."

"Did you hear—about—?"

"Yes. About Tristan." Mark spoke quietly. "He's dead, isn't he?"

"Yes."

"Trying to stop the robbers," Mark added.

"He was very brave," Moira said finally.

"I know." He stared at her. "Take care of my father."

"Oh, Mark, I'll try—I promise that!" She reached forward, pulling him to her, hugging him. "You've been a great help."

"I have to be," he said solemnly. "I'm heir now."

"You're more than that."

"I am?"

"Yes. You're his son, and he loves you dearly."

Mark stared at her, tears slowly forming in his eyes.

"And," she continued, "as soon as he's well, there's going to be a ban on any more tears in this house! Understood?"

"Understood." He still watched her.

"Agreed?" she asked.

"Agreed," he said back slowly. "Moira?"

"Yes?"

"Will you stay with us? Or are you going to leave us?"

She bit her lip. "I want to stay."

He reached out and hugged her then, pulling quickly back. "We want you to stay too."

Her eyes filled with tears, unbidden, unwanted, tears. She watched him turn away and walk back toward Tammy's room before she turned and went across the gallery to Michael's suite.

Chapter Thirty

THE SITTING ROOM DOOR WAS OPENED, WHEN MOIRA KNOCKED, BY Andre. Norma sat by the bed, in the other room, getting up when Moira walked in.

Norma spoke softly. "I was told to keep out of sight." She glanced ruefully at Andre. "So I decided to be of use and spell the doctor." She nodded toward a large chair where the doctor now rested, his eyes closed. "He was up delivering a baby all night, he said. Now this."

Moira smiled. "They're gone now. But you're welcome to stay if you wish."

Norma shook her head. "No. I should get back. And—if I stay, I may end up a little in love with him again."

"He might want you here when he wakes."

Norma shook her head again. "He'll want none but you." She searched Moira's eyes. "You are wonderful not to be jealous."

"Oh, Norma." Moira thought back over the past weeks. "I've been jealous of you and everyone else, *everyone*." She thought about her own words. "You know, I do believe I've actually grown up."

"You've been through enough." Norma reached to squeeze Moira's hand. "Take care of him."

As Norma started out the bedroom doorway Moira spoke again. "We will come to see you, to thank you, as soon as he is well."

"We?" Norma turned back toward the younger woman.

"If you'll allow us. I know he'll want to."

"No wonder he loves you." She walked on out.

Loves me, Moira thought, loves—me. She turned toward the stricken man on the bed. His eyes closed, his breathing shallow, he looked pale, his gypsy-look gone. He looked like a boy, pale, frail, in need of succor.

She walked nearer, glancing at the doctor and then sitting down beside Michael's bed, on the hard-backed chair Madame had sat on so much earlier.

Moira reached for his hand, taking it in hers and holding it close. "Can you hear me? Norma says you love me. You've never said that to me. . . ." She saw the doctor stir, his eyes opening to glance at her before he closed them again. "I hope it's true," she whispered, watching his breast heave with the effort of simply breathing. "Oh, Michael, you have to get well. We all need you so much."

Andre stood in the doorway. She looked up finally and saw him. "Can you come?" he asked.

She let Michael's hand rest back on the covers, walking slowly out to where Andre was pacing back and forth. "We've got to do something about the governess."

"What?"

"She wants to talk to you."

Moira looked over at Lancelot and Arthur who lay near the sitting room fireplace, staring up at her soberly. "They look as if they know he's ill." Andre said nothing and after a moment Moira spoke again. "Where is she?"

"I'll take you to her," he said.

Moira followed Andre back down to the dungeons, to a cell along the corridor near where Tristan had flattened himself, hours before, against the wall. She stumbled, and Andre reached out to help her. "What is it?" he asked.

"Nothing." She shook her head. "I stumbled, that's all."

He helped her down the last step, holding her arm as they walked to the cell. Unlocking it, Andre motioned Moira back and walked in first. Then he motioned to her to come forward, on into the cell, holding a lamp high.

Hesitantly Moira stepped forward.

Jemma sat, bound and gagged, in a corner of the dimly lit cell. Moira walked forward, toward the woman in the bindings.

"I'm here," she said, looking down at Jemma.

Andre reached around Moira to loosen Jemma's gag.

"Moira." Jemma stared up at her through the dim light. "I didn't know." She tried to read Moira's expression. "I didn't realize."

Moira said nothing.

Jemma began again, slowly. "Please, what are you going to do with me?"

"You don't even ask about him," Moira said.

"Jack's dead." Jemma looked down. "How—is—he?" she asked finally.

"I don't know."

"I'm sorry."

"Are you?" Moira asked softly.

"You *must* believe that! I didn't know Jack wanted to kill anyone! I thought he was going to turn him over to the authorities for what he'd done to you and Lucy and—and the smuggling."

"You mean what you thought he'd done. So they could kill him. It's all the same, isn't it? He'd have been dead in any event."

Jemma said nothing.

"What is it you want?" Moira asked.

Jemma stared at the dusty stone flooring. "I want to go away."

"Where?"

"I don't care—anywhere. Anywhere. I can't stay here!"

Moira turned away. "No, you cannot." She walked out, Andre beside her.

After he locked the cell, after they had climbed the turret stairs, Andre spoke. "Canada, I think."

Moira sighed, her shoulders slumping. "Whatever you think best."

"Moira." They were walking down the south hall now.

She turned toward him. "You've never called me by my name before."

"You saved us all. In the salon. Thank you."

"I had help."

Andre looked down. "If there's ever—anything—I can do. . . ."

"Help me get him well."

"He'll get well. He has to."

She almost smiled. "I said that a little while ago myself."

They reached the upper gallery, John Ottery, looking up toward them from the floor below. "Your Ladyship?"

She looked down, stopping at the head of the great stairwell. "Yes?"

"The staff was wondering about Christmas dinner tomorrow —and all."

298

It took a minute for the words to register. "Tomorrow is Christmas," she said, as if she'd just realized it. "My Lord, it's still Christmas Eve. Of course. And?"

"Well, with—all . . ."

"The children should have Christmas and the staff—and what about all the Twelfth Night festivities?"

"All arrangements are made."

"Then go on with them. I—I may not attend all, all the festivities but I hope you'll explain to the others; that they'll understand. And some things will be done quietly, because of Tristan."

"Of course." He nodded to Andre and left the hall, heading back toward the kitchens to inform Nan and the others.

"That was generous of you," Andre said.

"Generous? I want no mourning around me. I don't want to have all tiptoe around waiting for him to die. He's not going to die. He's not!" she said fiercely.

And, with that, she walked on ahead, back to Michael's side, back to watch the doctor as he attended her husband.

The carolers did not come in the morning. The villagers, knowing of the tragedies, stayed away out of respect. The staff served Christmas dinner for the children, for Eunice and Pomfret and the Madame, the Duchess eating in the Duke's sitting room, within earshot if he needed anything. Andre hovered about, the doctor gone now, the vigil now beginning in earnest.

"Your Ladyship," Frances knocked at the door, "letters from the solicitors for you."

Moira waved her away. "Later. Put them in the morning room." Frances nodded, turning away.

"How is Madame?" Moira asked.

Frances looked back. "She doesn't look well. And—the Duke, Milady? We're all praying for him."

"Thank you, Frances. Please, thank everyone. He's—I don't know. He seems the same. He's—not conscious—yet."

Frances left, more worried than she wanted the Duchess to see.

The children came in later, tiptoeing near the bed and then leaving quietly, Tamaris kissing Moira good night, telling of Jemma's departure.

Moira listened as if it were news to her.

"Who's to teach us now?" Tamaris asked.

"I will, if you like. As soon as your father's well."

"I'd like that," Tamaris said. Mark stared at Moira solemnly. And then he leaned forward to kiss her cheek. "Good night," he mumbled, self-consciously.

"Good night," she replied, and they left with Frances. Andre tended to the fire.

"Will you sleep here again, Milady?" he asked.

"Yes. Andre, Andrew, what will you do now? When he's better he can't continue—"

Andre watched her. "Not for a long time. If ever. I don't know. I hadn't thought about it. I hadn't thought past getting him better."

"I know," she said softly. "But we must plan. Planning makes it real. Deciding what we'll do when he's well makes it real that he will be well. Do you understand?"

He didn't answer right away. "I know what the two of you should do." At her look he continued. "You should take the ship far away and just idle away your days for a while. With no worries. No cares."

"The children have never been aboard her, have they?"

"No."

"They should get to know the *Black Saint*. It means so much to him."

"But—hard to explain the ship—after all the stories."

"That's easy." She smiled tiredly. "I wanted a black ship, since there'd been so many stories about one. So we bought one. And we can sail her right up to Saint's Bay, in front of all."

He shook his head. "I don't know."

"I do." She stared at the fire, thinking of Michael getting well and all of them traveling to the South Seas she'd always wanted to see, on board the *Black Saint*. Showing the children the world. And letting them get to know their father. "No more secrets, Andrew. No more secrets."

The fire crackled on in the fireplace, Moira staring at it as the hours ticked slowly by.

Chapter Thirty-one

JANUARY TURNED INTO A PERFECT CORNISH FEBRUARY, THE DAYS warm and quiet, spring truly arriving.

Moira walked into the morning room, and the faint smell of magnolias from the tree near the rose gardens just outside the open casement windows came in with the breeze.

She glanced down at the small pile of correspondence on her desk, sitting down after a moment to see to it. She conscientiously pulled the great leather housekeeping book out of the drawer and then opened the tray of creamy ivory notepaper, the St. Maur crest rich and impressive on the heavy plain bond.

Bowls of spring roses stood on the petite mantel of the narrow marble fireplace, tall silver candlesticks on either side.

"Moira!" Tamaris opened the door. "Can you come? We've got everything ready."

"Oh, I've got so much to go through, all this mail's been neglected for weeks—"

"Bring it with you!"

Moira saw Tamaris's expectant expression and gave in, standing up, picking up the mail and a heavy silver letter opener. "Where are we going?"

"Near the summer house, come along!"

"Yes, Tammy," Moira said meekly, following the young girl out through the Conservatory and across the lawns. A bluejay was scolding them and the rabbits alike as they crossed toward the small summer house and the picnic chairs and baskets that had been set out near an old stone wall that edged the stand of apricot and peach trees. The wall was covered with lichen, tiny flowers peeping out white here and there along it.

Madame looked up from her chair. Mark nearby was pouring lemonade, his riding breeches stained from the grass he was sitting on. "Mark," Madame began to reprimand him, but Lancelot and Arthur's mad barking as they saw Moira approach stopped her.

The dogs raced forward to be petted by Moira and back then to where they sat near Michael's chair, Lancelot barking every once in a while as he chased after a bluejay that dipped low above them. Arthur looked on in mature bliss, lying at Michael's feet, every once in a while joining in the chorus of barking and then lapsing back asleep, at his master's feet.

Lancelot chased blue butterflies and rabbits, jumping over the mossed rocks that lined the tiny spring stream near the edge of the nearby bracken.

Moira sat down, next to Michael, on a great Henry Holland chaise longue that matched the ones Michael and Madame were occupying, drinking in the peaceful conversation, the sun-soaked warmth of the lawns.

"What have you brought with you, Moira?" Madame asked.

"All the mail I've neglected for weeks now."

"Tsk, tsk," Michael said, opening one eye. "What's all this?"

"Don't know yet." She leafed through the envelopes with her name on them. "A letter from Solange." She looked up. "Did Andre see to selling the house in Brittany?"

"Yes. He should be back soon."

"Oh, and a letter from Jean-Marc!" She glanced down it swiftly. "I'll read it later, but they've reached America by now. He wrote just before they boarded ship."

She laid it on her lap, picking up another one, the fruit over the nearby wall glowing like gold when she glanced up. The warm, soft air smelled of sunshine and the sweet juices of the apricots and peaches ripening nearby.

"Eunice and Pomfret want us to come to London when you're well."

"Not bloody likely," Michael said.

She glanced at the last envelope. "Oh, I forgot, those solicitors sent this the day—" She stopped the sentence, refusing to think back on that gloomy Christmas, the terrible ordeal of Tristan's burial in the tiny cemetery yard next to the village church.

She skimmed down the covering letter, two folded documents with it. "They say there's an offer on our old estate, on Walsh Abbey, and that they cleared out the last of Father's papers from the house in Brittany."

"You don't want to sell your family home, do you?" Madame looked shocked.

Moira glanced at Michael. "Will you look this over later?" She handed him the offer, Madame watching the two of them.

"Yes." He took it, seeing his mother's inquisitive expression.

"Moira may have need of the Abbey. Or she may prefer to live in London when she's able."

Moira was looking at the first folded page enclosed beneath the offer from the solicitors. "Here," Moira said to Michael. "This is the will I made out when you were gone."

He stared at her. "That should be revoked now."

"Why?"

"Other arrangements will be necessary, obviously, sooner or later," he finished stiffly.

Madame looked out across the lawns, toward the coppice where Tamaris and Mark now raced with Lancelot. Arthur stood up after a bit, walking ponderously toward the children. Michael was reading the will as Arthur sat down near the play, watching Tamaris and Mark and Lancelot career around the coppice, thick with mountain ask and hazelnuts, jumping over brier that grew out from tumbles of mossed rocks. Then Arthur slowly stood up, coming back to Michael, settling down again, too warm and lazy to bother about chasing after them, their whoops and hollers carrying back on the warm, drowsy breeze.

Madame stared at the children and then looked away, closing her eyes, contented.

Moira was reading the other folded note that had been in the envelope. "Oh, Michael!"

"What? What's wrong?"

She shook her head. "Nothing. Listen. 'Dearest daughter, if you are reading this it means something has happened to me and you are going through my papers.'" She looked up. "This was there, with them, all this time." She looked back down. "'Please contact Michael, he will handle all the necessary arrangements for you and make sure that you are protected no matter what the legal situation. You will find that a very large inheritance is yours, if he can help fight for it—your grandfather's will left the estate in such straits that I hope you never have cause to read this. I want you protected. But, dear heart, if something has happened, and you are reading this, know that I love you still and that you must rely upon Michael. He will help with everything and insure that you are all right. There are papers in safekeeping with my solicitors in London, Johnson, Brownsberry and Cooper—papers belonging to your Aunt Lucy. Burn them. They were put in storage with all the other things from the Abbey when we left for Brittany. I've never been back to London, and I've not trusted any others to get them for me. They are there, with everything else, in your name. All will be sent to you upon word of my death. Moira, do not read them and do not show them to Michael. They will only bring him more grief than he has already been through. And to no purpose. Your aunt was unwell. Very unwell. That is why I did not let you near her. She died just before we left Cornwall, with a knife in her hands; a knife she'd just attacked the children with, God forgive her. And one she'd have used again. She did not know what she was saying or doing. When Michael and I returned from grouse shooting she had somehow done away with herself. Please burn those papers as I would have done myself if I could have gotten to them in time. Make sure no harm comes to Michael through them, or it will be on my head for not destroying them sooner. We've done work over the years that needed to be done, and I'm not sorry if it has ended like this. I love you, you know that. But I feel you'll be safe, that Michael will insure it no matter what. And, dear child, on the day you have to read this, know that I have gone to your mother. It will not be an unhappy thing for me. . . . All I wanted was to live to see you reach your majority so that you were safe. I love you. Father.'"

Tears gleamed in Moira's eyes. She stared at her husband. "Oh, Michael, what a lot of grief could have been avoided if I'd gone through his things before we left."

"There was no time."

She swallowed hard. "I know." She handed him the letter. He was silent for a long time after he read it.

Tamaris ran toward them now, flinging a ball back at Mark, her brown and white gingham dress billowing out around her, her white stockings gleaming against the green grass, her black shoes losing their polish in the depths of the bracken and the gorse.

Michael looked up at them, beyond the coppice, to where the ground began to rise slowly toward the moor, the purple heather in the distance broken here and there by yellow gorse and thorn.

"Mark," he called out after a bit as they ran closer. "Call Alf and Tom, will you? I want to go in for a while."

Moira sat up straighter, swinging her legs from the chaise longue to the grass. "Are you feeling unwell?" she asked anxiously.

"No. I just want to rest inside a while."

She stood up. "I'll come."

"No."

She stopped where she was, staring at him. "No?"

He shook his head, the footmen coming toward them from the back of the castle, Mark racing ahead of them back across the wide lawns.

"I'm not ill any longer."

"But you can't walk yet. You're still weak—"

"No." He stared at her, his expression an enigma. "I would rather be alone."

She swallowed hard. "I see."

The two footmen stood beside him now, helping him to his feet, bracing him between them. He looked over at her. "It's soon time to speak of what is to happen now."

She stared at him, fear making her heart beat wildly. "Now?"

He tried to read her eyes. "You have been the greatest help, the best of nurses, but I no longer need the care. Or the pity."

"Pity." She stared at the proud man before her.

"I don't want to presume upon your kindness forever. Possibly you may want to remove to Walsh Abbey for the next few weeks until your birthday."

She didn't reply, the children losing their laughter, their faces going solemn as they heard the end of the conversation. Finally Moira looked over at him again: "I will never presume to force myself upon you again. If you wish me gone, then go I shall."

Madame stared up at her son as he was helped away, across the lawns. "Of all the stubborn, foolish—*men!*" She stood up, staring at Moira. "And you, why don't *you* say something about how you feel!?"

"I've tried." Moira shook her head a little. "He knows how I feel, Madame. It doesn't seem to matter."

Tamaris came close to stand beside Moira. "Are you all right? What were you talking about?"

"Nothing, Tammy, everything's all right."

Mark watched her sad face. "Moira, you're not going to leave us, are you?"

Moira bit her lip. "I don't want to, Mark."

Madame was walking toward the covered entry to the quadrangle, far across the lawns.

"We'd better have the chairs taken in," Moira said, sitting down on one of them and staring at the sunlit sky.

Mark pulled Tamaris's arm. "Come on," he said, walking away, his sister behind him, asking questions.

"Where are you going, Mark?"

"To talk to Father!"

She said nothing, hard put to keep up as they raced now across the grounds.

Inside Madame was walking up the stairs, rounding the top of the stairs and heading toward the door to Michael's sitting room as the footmen walked out, just ready to close the door.

"One moment!" she said imperiously, walking inside, past them. She closed the door behind herself, turning to stare at her son who stood now, near the fireplace, alone.

"You can walk again!" she said, watching him turn around toward her.

Michael shrugged. "Yes. Not much stamina yet. But my legs'll carry me. We just tried them out on the stairs."

"What are you going to do about Moira?"

"I beg your pardon?"

"You should be begging hers!"

He stared at her. "I—"

"Don't interrupt me!" she snapped. "I don't want to hear any claptrap about duty or pity or whatnot. You know as well as you're standing there that she's in love with you."

"I—"

"Be quiet! I'm not finished yet!" She glared at her son. "If you're too proud to admit you care, or too stubborn, or too *frightened* to let someone close to you, then I wash my hands of you. I'll move to London with the children and you can rot out here alone!"

Michael stared at his mother, who turned away now, opening the door to see Mark and Tamaris hesitating outside. She held the doorknob, glancing out at the children and then back at him. "And taking her away from these children! You'll never be happy if you do this, if you send her away—never!"

"Send her—" Michael began.

"Yes, send her! She told me about the terms of your arrangement and don't look like such a thundercloud! She had to! You were gone and things were happening here!"

"Away?" Tamaris stood now by the open door, Mark just behind. "Oh, Father, you can't!" She turned and ran down the hall.

"Excuse me," Mark said to his grandmother, stepping inside and closing the door in her face. "Father—" Mark looked his father square in the eye. "We must talk. Man to man."

Michael stared at the boy. "Yes?"

"I have never asked a thing of you."

306

Michael sat down then. "No. No, you haven't."

Mark hesitated. "We haven't—seen much—of each other."

Michael looked down, not wanting to meet his son's eyes. "No, Mark, we have not."

"Ever since Moira came things have been different here. She likes us. Tammy's happier. Even with all this—all the trouble— things are better than they ever have been."

"Mark, we have to think about what's best for Moira."

"Isn't it best for her to have what she wants? She wants to stay."

There was a silence. "Possibly we just want to think that's what's best for her. . . . Possibly she would find out in time that it was not what she wanted."

"Tell her you want her to stay!" Mark challenged him.

"I—"

"Tell her." Mark challenged again. "If you can fight armies and pirates and government agents, you can tell one girl that you love her."

Michael looked up at the challenge in his son's eyes. "Yes, you're right," Michael said softly. "You'd think so."

Mark was silent, unsure of what else to say. Finally he turned to leave. With his hand on the doorknob he spoke again: "If she goes, I'll go too."

"Where?" Michael asked the boy.

"I don't know. But if you don't want her to stay, if you won't let her stay, then I don't want to stay either."

"Mark!" Michael stood up. "It's not that simple! Maybe she deserves more than we can ever give her! Have you thought of that?"

Mark stared at his father. "That's just an excuse because you're afraid to tell her."

"She's half my age, she's nearer your age than mine!"

"What's that got to do with anything?"

Michael stared at his son. Mark opened the door and walked out, toward the children's wing and his sister, leaving Michael to sit back, alone, staring at the fire.

Moira could not face supper, could not face the heavy air of unease she knew would surround them all. She pulled out the diary, Lucy's diary that Michael had handed her back, and the letter. She stared down at them and then walked to the fireplace in her bedroom, feeding them into the fire. She watched the papers slowly curl into black ash.

307

"There, Papa," she whispered to the flames. "Can you see?" She stood up, walking to the windows that looked down upon the moonlit rose gardens, looking out toward the sea that edged the cliff far beyond, thinking of the first days she'd spent here.

A few months . . . a lifetime ago. She thought of the inn and of the fevered dreams she'd had. And of the night she had spent in his bed. Her gaze drifted toward the east wall, remembering all the fears, all the hopes, that had propelled her through these last weeks, last months.

She sat down on the windowseat for a long time, dozing off as she listened to the surf pound up at the cliff's edge far beyond, far below.

The fire flickered low, her head heavy on her arms, her legs cramped from being curled up on the seat too long. Frances woke her when she came to stir the fire, to put another log on. Even though the days were turning mild, the nights were still chill.

She allowed Frances to help her get ready for bed and then dismissed her, walking over to the fireplace herself and moving the poker to stir up the embers.

The window she'd left open was letting in cold sea breezes, damp and sticky, making her shiver as she prodded the fire. She walked back toward the window, closing it and then laying down on the huge, ornate bed.

Which would not be hers much longer. Her last thoughts were of what she would do alone. Without him. And of what her life would be. . . . Rich. Divorced. Annulled. Whatever he called it. The words spun around in her tired brain, and she hugged the pillow close, her tears spilling. Too many tears these last months. She'd never care again. Not about anyone. It hurt too much.

She slipped into a troubled slumber, tossing and turning with the visions her dreams brought her.

Something woke her later, something not quite heard, but then, remembered. She kept her eyes tightly closed, afraid to look, afraid she was wrong. Afraid she had dreamed the sound of bootsteps on the other side of the east wall, standing there now.

She held her breath. And then the panel opened, the footsteps coming closer across the floor, softened by the thick Turkish rug.

When the sound stopped she opened her eyes to find

Michael staring down at her. No black paint. Just his face and his eyes and something very frightened in his eyes.

"I—there are so many more suitable—suitable—husbands for you. Nearer your age. Their whole lives ahead of them. As yours is."

"None that I want."

He stared at her. "None that you've met, you barely know any others. You deserve the best."

"I'm in love with the best."

His breath caught. "Moira—"

"Do you want to give me away to someone? To have me go to someone else? Kiss someone else?" Her heart was racing with her brazenness.

He made a sound deep in his throat and reached down to pull the bedcovers away, to scoop her up in his arms.

"Michael!" As he lifted her she clung to his neck. "You're not well, you barely can walk yet—"

He was proving her false, carrying her effortlessly toward her hallway, toward her sitting room beyond.

"You'll hurt yourself. Michael, where are you taking me?" Her arms were around his neck, the scent of him strong in her nostrils. He smelled of fresh air and soap and leathers; his hair so near her cheek she reached to bury her face in it.

He faltered as her lips touched his ear and then had the door between their suites open, carrying her across his own sitting room.

"Michael, what are you doing?"

"Taking you where you belong," he told her, kicking his bedroom door open to find a sleepy-eyed Andre jumping up from a seat near the fireplace. Andre rubbed his eyes when he saw what the Duke carried.

"Andrew, you're in the way. . . . Leave us." Michael reached out and deposited Moira on the huge bed as Andrew beat a hasty retreat, closing the door behind himself.

"I love you." The words came slowly, cautiously, and then more and more urgently, more and more loudly, as he joined her on the huge expanse of bed, bringing her into his arms. "I love your courage and your honesty and your trust and your humor and your kindness and your lovemaking and your body and your your—Moira, I love you so much. . . . I love you, love you . . . love you." He buried his face in the curve of her shoulder, feeling her arms strong around him, hearing her words, the endearments that fell like honey into his ear as he held her close. "God help us, I love you and that may be a curse, my sweetheart, all that I care about die."

"Michael," she told him softly. "My sweet fool," she laughed gently, "all *everyone* cares about die. That's nature. Michael, tell me you love me again. Please, I need to hear it, I love you so much, I've loved you so much for so long. . . . Tell me . . . *Tell me!*"

And he did.

With tongue and hands and lips and body and soul.

For the rest of their lives.

If you
enjoyed the
passion and adventure
of this book...

then you're sure to enjoy the Tapestry Home Subscription Service℠!

You'll receive two new Tapestry™ romance novels each month, as soon as they are published, delivered right to your door.

Examine your books for 15 days, free...

Return the coupon below, and we'll send you two Tapestry romances to examine for 15 days, free. If you're as thrilled with your books as we think you will be, just pay the enclosed invoice. Then every month, you'll receive two intriguing Tapestry love stories—and you'll never pay any postage, handling, or packing costs. If not delighted, simply return the books and owe nothing. There is no minimum number of books to buy, and you may cancel at any time.

Return the coupon today... and soon you'll enjoy all the love, passion and adventure of times gone by!

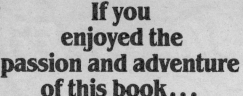

HISTORICAL *Tapestry* ROMANCES

Tapestry Home Subscription Service, Dept. RPSR 12
120 Brighton Road, Box 5020, Clifton, N.J. 07015

Yes, I'd like to receive 2 exciting Tapestry historical romances each month as soon as they are published. The books are mine to examine for 15 days, free. If I decide to keep the books, I will pay only $2.50 each, a total of $5.00. If not delighted, I can return them and owe nothing. There is never a charge for this convenient home delivery—no postage, handling, or any other hidden charges. **I understand there is no minimum number of books I must buy, and that I can cancel this arrangement at any time.**

☐ Mrs. ☐ Miss ☐ Ms. ☐ Mr.

Name	(please print)

Address	Apt. #

City	State	Zip
( )		
Area Code Telephone Number		

Signature (if under 18, parent or guardian must sign)

This offer, limited to one per household, expires September 30, 1984. Terms and prices subject to change. Your enrollment is subject to acceptance by Simon & Schuster Enterprises.

Tapestry™ is a trademark of Simon & Schuster, Inc.

Tapestry
HISTORICAL ROMANCES

Breathtaking New Tales

of love and adventure set against history's most exciting time and places. Featuring two novels by the finest authors in the field of romantic fiction—every month.

Next Month From Tapestry Romances

BOUND BY HONOR
by Helen Tucker
IRISH ROSE
by Jacqueline Marten